Dear Reader:

The novels you've enjoyed over the past years by such authors as Kathleen Woodiwiss, Rosemary Rogers, Johanna Lindsey, Laurie McBain, and Shirlee Busbee are accountable to one thing above all others: Avon has never tried to force authors into any particular mold. Rather, Avon is a publisher that encourages individual talent and is always on the lookout for writers who will deliver *real* books, not packaged formulas.

In 1982, we started a program to help readers pick out authors of exceptional promise. Called "The Avon Romance," the books were distinguished by a ribbon motif in the upper left-hand corner of the cover. Although the titles were by new authors, they were quickly discovered and became known as "the ribbon books."

Now "The Avon Romance" is a regular feature on the Avon list. Each month, you will find historical novels with many different settings, each one by an author who is special. You will not find predictable characters, predictable plots, and predictable endings. The only predictable thing about "The Avon Romance" will be the superior quality that Avon has always delivered in the field of romance!

Sincerely,

WALTER MEADE
President & Publisher

Other Avon Books by
Katherine Myers

DARK SOLDIER
WINTER FLAME

RIBBONS OF SILVER

KATHERINE MYERS

AVON

PUBLISHERS OF BARD, CAMELOT, DISCUS AND FLARE BOOKS

AVON BOOKS
A division of
The Hearst Corporation
1790 Broadway
New York, New York 10019

First Avon Printing, April 1985

AVON TRADEMARK REG. U.S. PAT. OFF. AND IN OTHER COUNTRIES, MARCA REGISTRADA, HECHO EN U.S.A.

Printed in the U.S.A.

WFH 10 9 8 7 6 5 4 3 2 1

TO KELLY
The inspiration for all
my leading men

ACKNOWLEDGMENT:
Special thanks to Martha Sipe for
all her assistance with proofing
and for the encouragement.

RIBBONS OF SILVER

Rogue!
'Tis your careless way
That plagues me.
You tread on caution,
Gamble with fate
And wear away my fortress
With your tender assault.

Reckless,
Wild,
Carefree of consequence,
You toss your life to chance.
And I?
Thrown into your hands.

You possess my name and title,
Bought by silver coin,
While ribbons of that same hue
Bind my heart.
'Tis my woe
I cannot escape
The latter part.

Chapter I

AFTERNOON SUNLIGHT fell through the hall windows and spilled across the oak floor, turning the wood from brown to dark gold. In the empty room, lighter squares marked the places where furniture had stood for years.

Kenna M'ren walked into the entry room, her hollow footsteps echoing what she was feeling inside. Where was the corner table with bowed legs and intricate scrollwork, the antique porcelain vase that had sat atop it filled with pussy willows in spring or wild flowers in summer? It was the same throughout the house; the furniture of her childhood, the ancient Scottish portraits of ancestors, even the thick loom carpets: gone. Old friends, all, they had gone on the auction block the day before, carried away by this collector or that local buyer, and it had been like watching comrades at the executioner's block.

Empty now, a mere shell of its former self, Moldarn House still managed to hold its dignity, and Kenna tried to do the same. She would let no misting of tears mar her departure; after all, she had known this day was coming for a long time now. Financial difficulties had first shown themselves in the dismissing of extra staff while she and her brother Braic had been away at school.

Papa had been a generous man to any in need, for his heart was too soft when a friend was in trouble and asked for help. Generous, too, at the gaming tables and with wild investments. There had been little return from that! she thought unhappily.

Perhaps if Cedric M'ren had had the watchful eye of a wife to guide him, things might have turned out differently. But her mother had been taken from them when Kenna was only eight, and Cedric had not remarried. She and her twin brother had grown up under their father's love, and their housekeeper Nessie's care. She had been stern; indeed she still was, at seventy-one.

Kenna looked out the windows at the stark Scottish hillsides. Rugged in early spring, before the heather bloomed, they were still beautiful to her. She stiffened her back. One last farewell to Moldarn and she would be gone. Her homestead, hewn of stone and oak by her ancestors, was one of the finest manors in Auchinleck. But when she and Braic had come home from school, they had discerned changes. Their father worried over the books, the ledgers a mystery to him. There were fewer servants, and sections of the sheep's grazing land had been sold. More and more, as they grew older, they found the land slipping away, the numbers of sheep being cut back, bought up by eager neighbors. But Papa, with his dreams for success with this invention or that scheme, was blind to the destruction of Moldarn.

Eventually, the only servants remaining were the cook and the faithful Nessie. So when she and Braic came home to stay, they started to help out, for there had been no gardener, no stablemaster or chambermaids. And despite the efforts of brother and sister to be discreet, their poverty was obvious to neighbors and friends. The irony of it was that the M'rens were the local ancient thane, Cedric having borne the title of earl.

Just six months ago, the Earl of Moldarn had passed away in quiet slumber at the age of sixty-seven. Poor Braic had struggled with the books and in the fields, but there had been too many expenses and too few sheep left for Moldarn to survive. Rather than let it all be taken for taxes, they auctioned off their family things and put the house up for sale. Nessie had left, weeping bitterly at separation from her "bairns" as she took the stage to Galloway to live with her widowed sister. The sales had procured enough to give Nessie a comfortable settlement, and the M'rens enough to start again.

Kenna turned instinctively to the mirror, but it too was gone, a stained square on the papered wall where it had hung for years. No beveled glass reflected the fair face, saddened in this moment of farewell, nor the eyes, gray as stormclouds, sheltered beneath dark lashes. Despite the absence of the mirror, she smoothed back her auburn tresses, but despite the liberal use of pins, tendrils still escaped, for it was thick and meant to fall in a heavy mass of waves down her back. She sighed and then turned, hearing the sound of steps on gravel.

Kenna went to the door and looked out, expecting to see Braic coming up the walk. Cursing under her breath, she pulled back into the shadowed comfort of the entry hall. She had planned to escape without seeing Glen Kinross.

Her heart beat a rapid warning and she stood as coolly as she could, preparing for his approach.

The Kinross clan was large, with many cousins and family members living in Auchinleck. But Glen had been the one cousin to steal her heart. It had been a tender heart, too, she recalled, when they had first noticed each other four years ago.

Bold and brash, Glen had that winning bravado that had stripped away her shyness. The girlish love for her brother's friend still plagued her, she could admit now. But he was another woman's husband she reminded herself. And that had been a hurt she would never forgive. His attentions, so warmly appealing, had been cut off as abruptly as sunlight by a cloud. After that, he and SueAnn McDuff had had a brief but wild courtship, followed by marriage. Memory still held a sting of reproach.

"Kenna!" Glen said, stepping through the doorway to stand smiling at her from across the hall. She chided herself for the thudding in her breast and stared back at him with all the cool reserve she could summon. Had she forgotten how handsome he was, with that square jawline and those Scottish features? His hair curled golden about his head, and straight eyebrows with sharp corners sheltered deep eyes. Yet it was the roguish smile that threatened her.

Slowly he walked toward her. "I did not want you to be going away without a good-bye. And from the looks of things, you'd be doing just that!"

"I have said all my farewells," she answered.

He lifted a brow, looking at her with a steady

stare. "Do not be running away from Auchinleck, Kenna."

"Is that what you deem it?"

"It is."

"Then what would you have Braic and me do, live in an empty house until it sells?"

"There are those who would take you in until the time that you could settle yourselves."

She looked at him in surprise. "What are you saying, then?" She disdained to use the name that came so easily to her lips.

"Stay for a while, two months at the least." He stepped near, slipping his hands about her waist. "I'd forgotten how beautiful you are, lassie," he said, bending near.

She looked down, lest he try to press his mouth to hers. "Do you forget that you are a married man now? Still nearly a bridegroom, and yet you come to court so freely with me? Take your hands away, Glen Kinross."

He laughed softly, but did not remove his hands. "Not until I hear from your lips that you will not stay, that you want to leave Auchinleck."

She looked up at him, her gray gaze unwavering. "I will not stay."

"Will you say you have no desire for my touch?"

"None."

"You disdain it?"

"I do."

"You dislike me?"

"No," she said slowly. "The truth is, I hate you." Her words were so soft, so carefree, that he was taken aback for a moment. Then he laughed, the golden sound echoing through the empty house.

"Then I am encouraged, Kenna. For your hate can only be born of love." He bent his head, as swift as the attacking plunge of a hawk, to prey upon her lips. She was pulled to him, captive of his strength as his mouth ravished her own. She struggled helplessly in his grasp until she managed to wrench herself free, stepping backward. Her resolve was shaken for the moment, but she folded her hands together, staring at him in cold appraisal.

"Coo! You are a mixture of ice and fire! What have I given up?" He shook his head. "You were meant for passion, girl."

She smiled slowly, the first smile he had seen today. Softly she said, "Perhaps you are right. But you will never know for sure, will you?"

His own smile vanished. "You should be mine."

"You made that decision."

"Not I! I tried to tell you before, it was the clan's doing!" He took a step forward and she took one back, refusing to let herself be pulled into his arms again. "Ah, Kenna! You did not want to be my bride anywise. A woman like yourself is meant to be a mistress."

"Do not insult me, sir."

"It was meant as a song of praise. Come stay with me, I've money now to buy you a place in Duncairn, not ten miles away. We could have pleasure, you and I! We were meant to share it."

Good enough for mistress, not for wife. The hurt of his words made her stand haughtily before him.

"Need I jog your memory? SueAnn is your bride, or do you forget her so easily?"

"What do you care about her?"

"She was my friend, before your affection for her

separated her from me. And now she is your wife."
She stared at him with ice in her eyes. "Can you not
be loyal to her, at least? Go home to Holmhead."

"The marriage vow means naught to me now!"

"Ah! There we differ. I shall be loyal to mine."

He looked at her, confusion in his features.
"Yours?"

"I forgot, you do not know. I was wed three days
ago."

"I've no stomach for games, Kenna."

Slowly she lifted up her hand until a beam of sunlight glinted off the golden ring on her finger. "It is
no jest."

His face grew angry, his cheeks reddening. "You
accepted an offer from Angus Stuart! Fool! He is
nearly an old man!"

"You do not know my husband. He is a Mr.
Fauvereau, an American businessman."

"But how did you meet him? You had no chance to
see anyone here!"

"I have not met him yet. Braic and I are leaving
for the ship to take us to him."

His anger baffled his wit. "Then how in the name
of saints can you be wed? You make no sense."

"By proxy. Braic stood in for him, you see, so that I
might become Mrs. Fauvereau months before I arrive."

"Proxy!" He snorted in derision.

"Aye, Glen. Legally wedded by our local justice."

"But why? In time you could have had any man
you wanted!" His anger consumed him.

Any but you, she thought, but said nothing of that.
"With Moldarn gone, there's no reason for me to
stay. America might appeal to me."

"America! 'Tis a land of barbarians and rough-cuts, I've heard. They were torn by a civil war not long ago, and the land is full of unrest which speaks of danger. You'll not be safe there, Kenna. I beg you not to go. We can have this proxy thing annulled. It is said that the land is full of savage Indians; is that what appeals to you?"

She shrugged. "You need not worry about me. I shall be safe enough under Mr. Fauvereau's protection."

"Why you accepted this marriage is beyond me. Who is this man Fauvereau?" he demanded.

"I told you. A wealthy American businessman who wants a wife of title."

"You married him for money!" he said, astounded.

She looked at him with no hint of a smile. "Did you do less?"

Silence fell between them, and for the first time he looked away. She lowered her voice, reining in the emotions she felt.

"You paid no attention to SueAnn, not even a kind word. And then you gave your affections to her in such a torrent that she was swept away. Your marriage was as swift as propriety allowed; will you deny it was for her bountiful dowry that you wed?"

"Do not vex me, Kenna!"

"Then do not belittle me for doing that which you have done."

"It was my family's decision," he said wretchedly. "And, yes, it was because of her wealth! But those kinds of decisions are made every day by clans. What you have done is to sell yourself to this foreigner who only wants a wife with a title."

8

"Much worse than selling myself as your mistress? No, I do not think so!"

"It is a mistake you've made," he stated, his golden countenance still darkened by anger.

"You can say that, after your own marriage decision? We are at the parting of our ways, Glen. You'd best go home to your wife."

"I'll go. But I'll tell you ere I leave that someday I'll have you, lassie. And no one, or thing, shall stop my taking you." His voice chilled her, though the tone was soft enough.

A shadow moved across the threshold, and they looked up to see Braic coming in. Her twin brother was as different from her as a sibling could be. His sand-colored locks were in contrast to the brightness of her auburn ones, his dark brown eyes opposite to the steel of hers. He was broad of shoulder with a square jaw and strong hands; she tall and slender, with a grace becoming to watch. Braic had his father's carefree manner, while his sister was the more quiet of the two, her somber ways making her appear the more mature. But now Braic was sobered, stern to a degree she had seldom seen.

"Glen. Why are you here?"

"I came to say good-bye. I haven't seen you or Kenna since . . ." His voice halted.

"Your wedding banns were posted," Braic supplied.

They were all uncomfortable, and Glen tried a smile. "I did not want you to go away thinking us enemies."

"Are the trunks all aboard the wagon?" Kenna asked, lest Braic say harsh words.

"Aye, and it is time to be going."

They all stepped out and Braic locked the front doors. He then lifted his sister aboard the wagon, trying his best not to show his hurt. He loved Glen. They had been close friends, and it had disappointed Braic very much when he had married into the McDuff family. Braic had always teased that one day his best friend and sister would wed. It had been more than a jest to him, though. The last six months had been difficult for Kenna's brother, and she tried to soften his pain. She looked down at Glen Kinross.

"Thank you for coming to see us off," she said with some kindness, but only for her brother's sake. Glen took her hand in his for a moment, but she pulled it away.

Braic snapped the reins, and the horse and dray, borrowed from their kind neighbor Angus Stuart, moved on. The large Clydesdale clopped down the road and up the slight knoll. There, Braic stopped the horse, and both he and Kenna turned for one last look at Moldarn.

It stood with solemn dignity, windows staring blankly back at them. Sunlight glanced off the stones, and yet it seemed to possess a forlorn air. Glen Kinross still stood by the front steps, watching them go. Braic pulled out his kerchief and wiped his eyes as he snapped the reins and urged the horse to move again. He turned his back on his home.

Kenna pulled her eyes from Moldarn and the man she had loved. She forced her gaze to the road that ribboned away before them.

There must be no looking back.

Chapter II

KENNA STOOD on the board walkway outside a brick-faced building and, for the tenth time, glanced at the double doors with their frosted panes and etched designs. But it was the squat black printing at the corner of the glass that caught her eyes: GENTLEMEN ONLY. The double standard chafed at her as much as the starched collar of her traveling jacket. Somewhere, on the other side of that set of doors, was Braic, who was seeking out her husband.

They had arrived at the San Francisco harbor this very day, and there had been no Mr. Fauvereau to meet them. But he had been listed as residing at the Palace Hotel, so they had engaged a cab with a driver to take them there. After passing through the confusion at the wharf, they had traveled into a city that sprawled over hills like a long serpent. She had feared that Glen's predictions of America might be true, yet when they arrived she found it was not barbaric. But, then, neither was it civilized. She had been in the teeming streets of both London and Glasgow, and neither had possessed this vitality.

There was a recklessness in the air. The roaring

winds off the Pacific exhilarated her. The city itself was constructed of new pine over charred frames that spoke of continual building and growing.

They had traveled down steep roads that plunged, leveled off, then plunged away again. The ride had taken her breath away, though Braic claimed he enjoyed it. They traveled down rows of streets lined with flat-faced wooden buildings that sported tawdry advertising announcements. The people they passed had open faces. The men, most of whom wore handlebar moustaches, often were escorting neatly dressed women in elegant hats or lace shawls. But it seemed to be the young men, who eagerly sought their fortunes in this city of gold, who were the source of the electric excitement that was so contagious.

She and Braic had arrived at the Palace Hotel and found that although Mr. Fauvereau was registered, he was not in his room. The helpful clerk informed them that he had mentioned going to the Gentlemen's Club, only a few doors down the block. They had left the impressive hotel with its tiers of balconied rooms, and sought the club.

Braic had told her to wait outside, as instructed by the sign, and he would see Mr. Fauvereau out. So here she stood, waiting, as the afternoon grew old. Since the dinner hour had come, the streets were nearly empty, except for an occasional passing wagon or carriage.

What am I doing here? she said suddenly to herself as her sense of dread mounted. The long voyage had been tedious, even though the clipper had moved as fast as any ship could. And although she had longed for freedom from the ship, she had dreaded the coming of this moment. How many times had she questioned the signing of those papers since the deed had been done? During dark and restless nights aboard the clipper, she had dreamed of the faceless stranger, she had wed by proxy. Often, in fear, she would imagine his features, but they were always shadowed by the dream. On other nights, the unknown face would take a form like Glen's, yet she was afraid of this, also. She never told Braic of her misgivings, for once the action was taken she had been bound, and there was no sense in fruitless regrets.

She remembered the first time her father had broached the subject. She had actually laughed at the strange proposal. Her father's cousin, a practicing lawyer in America, had written to him more than a year ago. There was an affluent businessman, who was interested in wedding a lady of title. And Fergus McDoo, aware of his cousin's financial difficulties, had written on behalf of the American.

Kenna had thought it a jest, yet when the laughter faded she sensed a sober tone in her father's voice. She had loved Glen, during the last summer, and had no intention of considering the proposal seriously. Her father had mentioned it a few more times, but in this one thing she was adamant. So it was not until after his death, when she and Braic were sorting through his papers, that she was aghast to learn it was not at an end after all. There was much correspondence with McDoo, which had been passed on to Mr. Fauvereau. Through these letters, they learned that the American had loaned Cedric M'ren several large sums of money. Kenna, appalled at her father's indiscretion, had immediately written to him, explaining her father's death and their difficulties. She promised to repay the money as soon as possible.

His reply had left her even more upset. He stated that the money was not his immediate concern, but her father had led him to believe that she would comply with the proposal. He urged her to reconsider, offering to arrange a letter of credit for their needs. Should she agree, they must follow certain conditions. For the sake of time, the marriage must be performed by proxy, the papers being enclosed. And she must arrive no later than June fifteenth. He had closed with his condolences for her father's death, almost as if it had been an afterthought. There had been no word of assurance, no kindness that might encourage her to hope for an acceptable marriage. She had read over the letter until the creases wore it apart, studying the strong yet neat handwriting, hoping for a clue to the man. She had discerned nothing.

Then Glen had suddenly married SueAnn, leaving her with the ache of rejection. At this point, the threatening letter became a contract of hope. There was a way to escape both their financial and their emotional pains. It was a refuge which she took with no more thought. Even Braic had been eager for the new excitement of America. She had written back, a letter as curtly vague as his own, enclosing the marriage license now that the form was completed, with her signature, Braic's, and the judge's.

But since that time, she had given much thought to it all. Had she sold herself and her title? But had not her father already done that by borrowing on a promise he could not keep? More than money, there had been honor to think of. Since the M'rens had been thanes in Scotland, honor had been their most important ideal. Kenna felt she must uphold her family's honor. There was no other way to settle the debt. Yet one other thought plagued her. What of that dark intimacy between husband and wife? She knew nothing of the act which frightened milder maids who already knew their betrothed. Kenna was not a little daunted at the idea of sharing her bed with a stranger.

Two men galloped by on horseback, and she stepped back into the recessed overhang, brushing the road dust from her brown skirt. What was taking Braic so long? Certainly Mr. Fauvereau had not changed his mind.

The man named Grey walked down the street toward the Gentlemen's Club, slowing his stride a bit as he caught sight of a young woman before its doors. She was turned away from him so that he could perceive only a slight curve of cheek and jawline. But her hair, auburn in color, caught gold from the fire of setting sun. She wore a dark brown traveling suit, a skirt and short jacket over a soft white shirt. He knew from her attire that she did not belong in front of the building she stood before.

"May I assist you?" he asked languidly, and Kenna turned around to see a man looking at her. She had heard no one approach, so deep in thought had she been, and a blush spread up her cheeks, tinging them coral.

She was thoroughly taken aback by the man's presence and his looks. He bore no bright locks on his brow like the men she had known. His were black, darkest ebony above a tanned face. His brows and lashes were of that same black hue, protecting eyes of indigo. The blue contrasted with his dark countenance.

"May I assist you?" he repeated. The words were kind enough, she thought, yet there was something in the voice which suggested more.

"What makes you think I need assistance?" she countered. He studied the face. It was a perfect oval with fine features, a soft mouth, more inviting than she knew, and eyes as gray as his own name.

"A woman isn't usually here, this time of day, without an escort." His voice was cool, sliding across her. He did not appear to be a rough fortune hunter, for he wore a dark business suit with a smartly tailored vest over an immaculately white shirt.

"I am not without an escort," she replied. "Mine is in there." She nodded at the double doors.

He raised a dark brow in surprise. "In there? It appears he does not take his duty seriously. Perhaps I could offer my services instead."

"Thank you, no," she said primly, and he noticed the softness of her body despite her rigid stance and the straight cut of her suit.

"Do I detect a slight accent?"

She looked at him with the granite stare he was coming to like. "That depends on which map you stand on. It is your voice that seems foreign."

He smiled, flashing white teeth at her. Nessie would have called him a devil's offspring, she thought. "True. Then, as the foreigner, might I ask for a kindly welcome?" He leaned closer and her heart began to thud. Was there danger from this dark man? She looked down at the filigree of gold on her finger that by rights should mean protection.

16

Kenna was not sure if the ring her husband had sent would be enough to ward off this stranger.

She stepped back and he wondered if this woman, who stood so sure of herself before him, could truly be unaware of the reason he approached her? Her grace and assured demeanor spoke of experience.

"You'd best be about your business," she warned. "My escort will be back in a moment."

"He is a foolish man to leave such a fair woman unprotected. Perhaps I'd best wait until he returns to do his job properly."

She felt a tingling irritation at this black rogue. Let him be on his way so that she might return to worrying about her future. She lifted her chin a bit to look him straight in those dark blue eyes. Tall for a woman, she was only half a head shorter than he.

"I doubt that my husband would approve," she said softly.

He raised his eyebrows in disappointed surprise. "You are married?"

"I am."

"And your husband is in there?"

"Aye, and he'll be coming through those doors any minute, so you'd best be gone." And what would her husband do when he came out to meet her? Once again the worry began.

"Let me give my condolences," he said and she looked at him in surprise. "It is a loss for all but your husband. Good day, Mrs. . . ."

"Fauvereau," she supplied.

He stopped and looked at her in bewilderment. "You are . . . his wife?"

"I see you've heard of my husband," she said a bit worriedly.

"Yes, I have," he said, but still his eyes sought out her hand and the orb of gold on her ring finger.

"Then you know he would not want any man to annoy me," she said, daring to draw protection from what she had read in his letter.

"No," he said slowly. "He would not want any man to touch his woman."

"Good day, sir."

He nodded. "Mrs. Fauvereau."

He opened the double doors, stepping through them and disappearing from view. As he went, her worries returned doublefold. Perhaps she should not have been so rash as to presume on her husband's name. Where on heaven and earth was Braic?

A few minutes later, just as she was ready to ignore the black printing on the door window and step inside, it opened and her brother stepped out, greeting her with his carefree grin.

"You do not need to be standing out here anymore, sister. He'll see us now."

"What took so long?" she said with exasperation. "Was there some problem?"

"No, he was busy, I guess. I had to wait for him. Come on in, Kenna." He opened the door, and she stepped into the cool interior, glancing around. Tied-back velvet drapes of light blue hung on either side of an entryway leading to a room filled with comfortable leather chairs where men sat conversing in low voices; the smell of pipe smoke wafted through the room, but she was quickly led down a hallway papered in a blue and white print. Mumbled voices and soft piano music could be heard, and the distant sound of a woman's laugh.

Kenna's face flushed as the import of the sound

registered. Suddenly the reputation of the Gentlemen's Club appeared doubtful. Was that the reason the stranger had shown surprise that she waited outside? She groaned inwardly. He had shown considerable surprise that Mr. Fauvereau was her husband. Did he bear some reputation as a formidable man? His letter seemed to speak of power, and all the men of power she had known had not been desirable. She envisioned her husband as a scowling, obese being, glowering at her with mingled disgust and desire. What folly had she wrought by signing the marriage certificate?

She was dragging her feet, dreading the moment of their meeting. Her mouth felt dry, her palms moist. "Braic," she managed, "have you met him?"

"No. They only told me he would see us."

"Oh."

"Kenna, if it isn't to your liking, we can have it annulled. I won't be having you go with a man you cannot stand."

"A bargain is a bargain."

"I know how you feel about honor. And I also know how you've been worrying yourself sick over this whole thing. You cannot hide something like that from me, girl."

She stopped and looked at him gratefully. He put his arm around her, giving her a gently comforting squeeze. "As I said, if he isn't to your liking, I'll end the marriage before it begins. That's been my plan all along."

Her tension eased a bit as they reached a door at the end of the hall. Braic knocked. A muffled voice bade entry, and he pushed the door back, letting Kenna step in first.

"You must be Lady M'ren," a wickedly soft voice said as the man approached her. "I am Grey Fauvereau."

Kenna stiffened as if she were carved from marble. She stared into eyes as blue as a late summer's sky. Grey turned to Braic. "And you must be Lord M'ren." He extended his hand and they shook, her brother studying the frame and form of her husband. "I'm sorry about the mix-up. I was told that the clipper wouldn't be arriving until tomorrow. I had no idea that it would dock a day early, though I am pleased, since it is much to my benefit."

Braic smiled. "No problem. The clerk at the Palace Hotel said you had come here, so we sought you out. But then there was trouble in locating you."

"I went out to drop off some papers at my lawyer's office two blocks down. I just got back." His eyes rested on Kenna. Embarrassment made her glance away. "Forgive me, I'm not a very good host. Please sit down; I've ordered some refreshments."

He pulled out a chair for Kenna, and she sat down, primly folding her hands in her lap. She lowered her eyes, staring at the golden ring that bound her to this man.

"Tell me, Lord M'ren, how was your sea voyage?"

"Please, my name is Braic; the title is foreign to me."

There was a rap at the door, and a young woman dressed in dark blue silk brought in a tray of refreshments. Her attire was nothing like what the serving maids in Britain wore, making Kenna's suspicions of the place mount. Braic was recounting their course of travels as the girl left, and Kenna sipped the cool drink and glanced around at the plush furnishings of the room to keep from staring at the dark man who talked so freely with her brother. No, he was nothing like she had imagined, not in her wildest dreams! Unbidden, the dark thoughts came to her of that secret happening between husband and wife. She glanced up at him, only to find his eyes staring steadily at her. Inwardly she moaned. The traitorous heightening of color made Grey smile as he listened to Braic's colorful description of their arrival.

There was another knock at the door, and the girl entered again. Kenna caught the coy smile she slyly sent to Grey. She set down a tray of three plates filled with potatoes, meat, and three vegetables.

"Refreshments?" Braic questioned.

Grey smiled and shrugged. "I took the liberty of ordering dinner, since it is growing late. I hope you haven't already eaten?" Braic assured him they had not, as the girl put down a basket of rolls before leaving. Her brother ate heartily, but Kenna could hardly force down a bite of potato.

"Lady M'ren," Grey said softly, "I hope you will not be upset if we begin to travel tomorrow."

She looked at him in surprise. "Sir?"

"I know that you must have been anxious to arrive and be off the ship, and now I must ask you to board one again. It is imperative that I return home."

"I assumed from your letter that San Francisco was your home, since it was the only destination you spoke of."

"No, I had to come here for business reasons. And I've stayed too long as it is."

"Where is your home, then?" Braic asked.

"It's in the Idaho Territories, a bustling little town called Silver City."

Kenna had never heard of it. Perhaps that would be a reason to be let out of this contract. He had said nothing about going off into the wilderness! But did she want out of this marriage? She did not know. The only thing she was certain of was that Grey Fauvereau was a threat to her as no aging or obese businessman could be.

"I hope that there are opportunities there for a willing worker," Braic said. "I'd hoped to find a fortune in San Francisco to go along with my title."

Grey laughed softly, a devilish sound. "Silver City makes 'Cisco look like a pantywaist."

"That wild, eh?"

"That promising."

Braic nodded with anticipation. "That's what I came to America for."

The meal, which seemed to last a tediously long time to Kenna, finally ended, and Grey drew out several colorful bills, tossing them casually onto the table. "Let's go back to the Palace. I've reserved rooms there for several days, just in case you came early."

When they reached the street, it was dark outside, an inky blackness dispelled by jewels of lights in windows and on lamp posts. Despite the warmth of the day, the air had grown chill.

"Then we'll be leaving tomorrow?" Braic asked.

"At the earliest. You could have left your things to be transferred to the *Northern Clipper;* I was planning on it, had I caught you. We'll be traveling up the Oregon coast to the mouth of the Columbia."

They reached the Palace Hotel, and he stopped in the lobby to get a set of keys from the clerk. Then he guided them toward the spiral stairwell and they climbed upward. Kenna panicked. Was she simply to say good-night to her brother and retire with this threatening American? How could he expect her presence on this first night? She could feel his eyes boring into her back, as she had felt them on her all night long. From the moment of their initial encounter, she had sensed the reckless passion of this man. It was quite possible that Mr. Grey Fauvereau expected his wife to begin her role within two hours of meeting her. Reaching the third floor, they walked down a narrow hallway until Grey stopped at a door and unlocked it. He pushed it open and turned to her.

"This is your room, Lady M'ren. I hope everything is suitable."

She glanced inside the lovely furnished room, which also contained her trunk and baggage. She looked up at him. "Thank you, Mr. Fauvereau. This will be fine."

She stepped inside and shut the door, leaning against it lest he change his mind. She stayed there until the thudding in her chest stilled. Then she glanced around to see a room tastefully done in green and white, with a comfortable bed, side table, and two chairs with dark green brocade seats. She opened a bag and pulled out her nightgown, changing into the comfort of the gown and hanging up her traveling suit. She was too tired to do anything else. Besides, they would be leaving in the morning. She spent the next few minutes brushing her hair.

There was a knock at the door, and her heart began to hammer. She stood frozen for a moment as the knock was repeated.

She stepped near the door. "Who is it?"

"Who else?" Braic's familiar voice replied.

With a sigh of relief, she hastily opened the door. He smiled at her. "Are you all right?"

She nodded.

"Just thought I'd check. My room's across the hall, and Grey's is next to it. If you need anything, I'm there."

"Thank you, brother."

His smile broadened. "Why such a dour face, Kenna? He cannot be as bad as all that." Her silence prompted him on. "I think he's most affable, and received us kindly. I will admit I had fears about that! You will confess he was most kind?"

She sighed in acquiescence. "Aye, most kind." She tried to shut the door, but he stopped her.

"And most handsome! I was afraid he might be a doddering old fool or some young thimblebrain. But instead he is a man's man."

She said nothing, but looked at him steadily. "You do agree he is handsome, don't you, sister?"

"Yes, Braic, he's a handsome man. Now will you go to bed?"

He grinned at her in the boyish way that was so winning. "I'm going. Good night."

He left, whistling to himself, obviously pleased. He knew Kenna better than she knew herself.

She shut the door and bolted it, extinguishing the lights and climbing between the cool sheets. Tiredness swept away her worries, and she drifted off almost immediately.

Grey climbed into his own bed, hearing Braic in the hall and then a door closing. He lay on his back, staring up into the blackness, his hands beneath his head.

Kenna M'ren was nothing like he had imagined. When he had sought her title, he had given little thought to the woman. He had needed her title for great monetary gains, using every pressure he could think of, including the indebtedness. He had assumed, as was probable, that Lady M'ren was an aging spinster who would be so willing to gain a husband and free herself from debt that she would rejoice in a proxy marriage, even if it entailed traveling across an ocean. He had never thought about what he would do with this titled wife once he acquired her. Somehow he had thought to separate title from wife and keep the former. But now she was here, asleep in a room across the hall from him, and she was absolutely everything he had not expected.

He was amazed to realize that his wife, a very real woman of flesh, was quite beautiful. He recalled her fair features and creamy skin. Her granite eyes, long and etched by thick lashes, held a challenge that belied her primness. And despite the way her glorious hair had been demurely swept back, it only made him want to unpin it and entwine his fingers in it.

He cursed himself for reserving separate rooms. He had given little thought to the future of his newly acquired wife, who, in his mind, was to be little more than another possession. But the vision of a future with Kenna was pleasurable.

He smiled into the darkness, deciding that he must be careful with this woman, for she was not like the forward women of 'Cisco. Perhaps the separate rooms would be best for tonight; there was always tomorrow or next week.

For the first time in his adult life, the idea of marriage appealed to Grey Fauvereau.

* * *

Faintest morning light filtered in through the window of Kenna's bedroom. She heard the distant sound of wagon wheels and the bray of a mule as the morning's first traffic started on its way.

She lay in that limp state between slumber and awareness, when there was a light rap on her door. Her eyes opened, and she stared around the dim room as the knock was repeated a little more loudly. She threw off the covers, sliding her feet to the cool floor as she moved to the door. What did Braic want at this early hour? She slid the bolt back and opened the door.

A small gasp escaped her. Grey stood at her door, fully dressed.

His eyes drank her in: the mass of tangled hair that hid a glint of tarnished copper; her gown, a soft white thing which did little to conceal the softer curves of womanhood. He smiled slowly, his voice low.

"Good morning."

Kenna stepped behind the door, looking around its edge, her hair hanging down her side. "What is it?"

"I'm sorry to wake you, but we must be leaving for the *Northern Clipper* early. If you can be dressed and packed in a quarter of an hour, we can catch some breakfast."

"I'll try, Mr. Fauvereau," she said curtly. He stopped her from shutting the door.

"My name is Grey."

She said nothing, yesterday's humiliation still raw in her memory.

"I realize that we did not get off to the best start yesterday. We were ill-fated. Do you hold a grudge?"

She raised an eyebrow. "A grudge? That my husband accosts me on the street with improper advances?"

"I offered assistance."

"Oh, you offered more than that," she said in a low voice.

"I was attracted to you, even though I had no idea who you were. If anything, that should speak for me."

"Indeed. Right along with your playing me for a fool, leading me on without being gentleman enough to acknowledge your true identity!" she said, now wide awake with anger.

"And what would you have had me do?" he said, his voice taking on a mocking tone as he swept off his hat and bowed low. "Begging your pardon, madam, but I *am* Mr. Fauvereau, your husband. Pleased to make your acquaintance, Lady M'ren!"

She groaned. "Certainly one so forward did not have his courage fail him? Yet rather than speak up, you let my brother drag me into a place of doubtful reputation to first meet my husband!"

"Well, yes," he said uncomfortably. "But as I said, I did not think you would arrive until today. This morning was the posted time of arrival. But then, I forgot how sensitive you genteel nobility are."

This remark further fueled her anger. "And I did not know what barbarians Americans truly are."

He scowled at her, his face growing stormy. "Oh, yes," he said, laughing softly, a low, threatening sound with no joy in it. "You have yet to learn of us barbarians."

Kenna felt a tingling of fear, yet she stood her

27

ground. "This open doorway is no place for an argument."

"You are right," he said, stepping in and slamming the door behind him. "This is much more private."

"How dare you come into my room!" she cried in outrage.

"How dare I?" He looked at her in mock surprise. "I am your husband, Mrs. Fauvereau."

She felt a chill sweep around her like a sudden draft, and she was quite aware that the soft white material of her gown was little protection from his burning stare. Yet she stood her ground, showing no fear. She clasped her hands together lest they tremble.

"Yes," she said slowly. "I am your wife. But we are still strangers, and the title is not comfortable to me. There will be no easiness starting into this marriage, I can see, yet if you wish to get along with me at all you had best show regard for me as a lady."

Grey looked at the beautiful woman before him with the tangled hair falling like burnished silk down her back, her mouth, no doubt softly sweet in sleep, held in tight check. "Oh, I assure you, Kenna, I have nothing but the highest regard for you as a woman."

Somehow he had managed to twist her words; she felt her anger rise anew. "Then will you leave so I may get ready?"

He nodded. "Yes, I'll do that. But not until I get what I came for."

"And what is that?" she asked, thinking in vain of legal documents or the like. She saw the slow smile spread across his tanned features, and her eyes widened. The way he looked at her, the blue fire in his eyes, he could not possibly want . . .

He stepped toward her, grabbing her arms tightly and pulling her to him. Kenna stifled an outcry as his mouth came down over hers, conquering it in passionate possession. His arms encircled her, drawing her to his manly strength. The nightgown was little protection from that iron embrace. There was such domination in the caress that she felt her very limbs weaken. Finally, he let her go, and she stepped back, gasping for breath. He nodded as if well pleased.

"I never did get to kiss the bride," he said casually. Then he pulled a pocket watch from his vest, springing it open and checking the time. "Make it ten minutes, will you?"

He turned and strode out the door, shutting it behind him. Kenna threw herself across her bed and screamed into her pillow. Then she picked it up and threw it across the room.

Deciding that the brute might return and haul her with him even if she were half dressed, she ran to her trunk, hastily drawing out fresh undergarments, skirt, and blouse. She did a hasty toilette using the bowl of cool water, then, donning fresh underclothes, she pulled on a white blouse with muttonleg sleeves that ended in a long narrow cuff, the bodice sporting rows of tiny pleats. She quickly did the buttons and tucked it into a long skirt of dark blue, fastening the narrow waist before pulling on the silk stockings and applying the buttonhook to the rows of black shoe buttons. Then she sat down before the mirror, running a brush through her heavily tangled hair. Her fingers deftly wound the mass into a soft curve at the nape of her neck and tied it in place with dark blue ribbons.

Her ears picked up the low voices of the two men outside her door as she threw things into the trunk and valise. At the expected knock, she caught up a shawl of softest plaid and pulled it about her as she opened the door.

Without another word, she went with them down the stairs and into the large dining hall. At this early hour, it was nearly empty, and Grey drew out her chair. She sat down, ignoring him. He was well aware of her icy disregard, and he smiled to himself. This woman was going to be a challenge to tame.

A young man came and gave them menus which Kenna studied intently. She would not so much as give this rogue the time of day.

"Your food is foreign to us," Braic said. "Perhaps you would order for us."

Grey agreed, and as the waiter returned, he said, "We'll share a large plate of fried potatoes. Do you want your eggs fried, Lady M'ren?"

"Poached, Mr. Fauvereau."

"Toast, Lady M'ren?"

"Bread, Mr. Fauvereau."

"We'll have ham, applesauce, and coffee," he concluded.

"Tea," Kenna interjected.

"And do you want a spoon with your tea, Lady M'ren?" he asked with mock politeness.

She lifted the dove-colored eyes to his. "I'd prefer a fork, thank you, Mr. Fauvereau."

The waiter stared at them in bewilderment before snatching up their menus and hurrying off to the

RIBBONS OF SILVER

kitchen. Braic leaned back in his chair, studying the two whose eyes were locked in combat.

"My, my! It seems that you have both quite taken to the role of wife and husband with hardly a day gone by," he said in amusement.

Grey broke his gaze away to glance at his new brother-in-law. "Your sister is angry with me because of our first meeting."

"You hardly said more than a few words," he said, baffled.

"We met before. She was on the street when I was returning from my lawyer's office. I chanced to offer my services."

"He was overly forward," Kenna said.

"I offered my protection."

"It appeared that the one I needed protection from was the one who offered."

"You should be flattered." Grey shrugged. "It isn't every young woman that I'm drawn to."

"Only the pretty ones," Braic supplied.

"That's true. I knew nothing of her title."

"But it is that which you married me for, sir; need I remind you?"

"Kenna," Braic chastised. "You should be happy that your husband finds you pleasing. It will make for a better marriage."

"You have a wise brother."

Her words were cut short by the arrival of the food. As requested, her tea came with an extra fork. Under Grey's watchful eye, she stirred her tea with it before putting it down and sipping the hot drink.

They had barely begun to eat when Grey signaled to a man who had just entered the dining room. Portly and short, he had a bulbous nose and a red fringe around a bald head. Upon seeing them, he grinned and strode toward their table and was invited to join them.

"Well," Grey said. "Do you recognize your cousin Fergus McDoo?"

Braic and Kenna looked at him in surprise. "You are Fergus McDoo?" Braic asked him.

"Aye," the man said, pulling up a chair. "And you must be Cedric's offspring. Let me give my condolences on your father's passing. Cedric was a good man." His brogue was thicker than theirs, for they had been schooled in England as well as at the finest schools in Scotland.

Braic shook his hand, smiling his friendly greeting. Grey offered the lawyer some of the potatoes, scooping them onto an extra plate. "Fergus," he said. "Why did you not tell me that Lady M'ren was such a beauty?"

Fergus laughed. "I dinna know! I've not seen her since she was just a wee one. But her mother was fair, so I thought she might be."

Grey smiled. "I thought, since she came from your family, that the resemblance would be to you. I feared I would have to put blinders on her before leading her through town."

Fergus and Braic roared their laughter, though Kenna could find no humor in the comment. "And how are these newlyweds getting along?" the lawyer asked.

"Not too well," Braic interjected, before either could answer. "It appears that they are at odds already." He took a mouthful of ham as Kenna glared at him.

"Sounds like married life to me," Fergus said,

32

copying his younger cousin. "Though I thought you would be glad to have a titled wife who is fair also."

"Indeed I am!" Grey said. "But it appears that Lady M'ren finds fault with the groom."

Kenna ignored the statement, and Fergus raised his thick brows in surprise. "Indeed, lass? From what I have seen, women are most pleased with Fauvereau. He is wealthy and handsome; just what more could you be wanting?"

"Not to be pawed at and drooled over," she blurted.

Fergus and Braic looked at each other before bursting into laughter. "What else is a wife for?" Braic said.

"Braic! Do you take his side?"

"Aye. Too long you have fought off the advances of suitors, sister. You need to remember that this man is your husband." His voice softened in understanding as he turned to Grey. "Had my sister come to know you, it should be different. But suddenly she finds herself thrust into a stranger's care. A little kindness will win her over, and a touch of patience, too. I've loved her my whole life, and I know she has a tender heart."

Grey leaned back in his chair, studying Kenna. "Good counsel, brother," he said softly.

Braic smiled at his sister. "He's not a bad sort, Kenna. And you did admit last night that he was affable and handsome."

Kenna looked at him in exasperation and Grey sat up in his chair. "Mr. Fauvereau is not interested in my opinions."

"His name is Grey. He'll never be a husband until you call him by his given name." He looked at his brother-in-law. "And my sister's name is Kenna. Please use it. The only title she needs now is Mrs."

"Agreed," Grey said. He looked at her with his blue eyes. "Kenna?"

She met his gaze. "Grey?"

Fergus chuckled softly, pulling the napkin from his chin and opening his pocket watch. "I hate to cut a good meal short, but we'd best be leaving. I'll be traveling with you back to Silver City."

Kenna was glad of this, feeling at ease with this cousin she barely knew. Unfortunately, she could not say the same about the man who helped her from her chair and handed her her shawl. Seldom had she met a person who left her so ill-at-ease and uncertain of herself. After leaving several bills at the table, Grey led them from the dining hall to where their carriage waited. Kenna saw that her trunks and other luggage had already been loaded. Grey helped her inside, his hands like steel bands about her waist as he lifted her up. She sat primly in the corner as the three men entered, Grey taking his place next to her. The coachman snapped the reins and the horses stepped high, pulling the carriage quickly down the sloping streets. Fergus carried the conversation and she felt at ease listening to his familiar brogue.

"Do you think you'll be making it back to Silver City in time?" he asked Grey.

"I think so," her husband answered in the unusual drawl she had heard so frequently since landing in America. "Braic and Kenna have arrived a day early, and if all goes well we can be there in record time."

"Is there some reason you must be back by a deadline?" Braic asked.

Grey gave a sharp nod. "The fate of my business depends on it. I must explain it to you when we have a chance to sit down with some ale. It's quite involved. Here we are," he said as the carriage pulled onto the dock, jerking to a halt.

They alighted, and Kenna saw the *Northern Clipper*. Much smaller than the ship which had brought them to America, and more travel-worn, it also looked fleeter. It rocked on the green-gray sea, moving restlessly beneath it. The wharf was already busy at this early hour as she watched their things hauled aboard the clipper. She watched the dizzying dive of a gull, feeling that the movement represented her very existence. She had fought back the surging of homesickness which was not all that different from the fear and nausea of seasickness. She had worn a brave facade upon her arrival in this wild seafront town, and felt the thinness of her courage when she met Grey Fauvereau. Now she was to be whisked away to some unsettled territory. She locked her knees, bracing herself against the dizziness she felt. Would there be savage Indians, as Glen had predicted? She could not ask for fear that Grey would see through the veil of her bravery.

"Kenna." She heard her brother's voice. "We must go aboard now." She glanced at him, and he read her apprehension. She looked away in shame that such weakness was showing. He slipped his arm about her. "You need not fear the journey, or the man," he said softly. "I think that fate has smiled on us. Grey is a good man that I feel sure you can come to care for. And as to the journey, I am glad of it. Here in America, you judge a man for the work he does, not for how genteel he is, or how poor." A note of bitterness crept into his voice. He had not put the past behind him either. He needed her confidence to bolster him as much as she needed his.

She smiled up at him, smoothing the lapel of his coat. "With you by me, I've no fear of the journey." Her assurance was a bond between them.

They went aboard the clipper, and she stood at the deck rail as the ropes were released, the wind whipping tendrils of her hair free from their pins. Braic and Grey had thrown off their jackets and were pulling rope with the men to hoist the sails. They applied brawn to the task and she watched the muscles working beneath the fine fabric of Grey's shirt. There was a sensuousness to the movement, like that of a galloping stallion, as he pulled along with the others until the dingy canvas caught the wind and cracked into a stiff billow. Kenna grabbed the rail as the ship vaulted into the waves like a dolphin into the sea.

Grey caught up his jacket and came to stand beside her. "We are on our way. We should reach the mouth of the Columbia in four days, if I've calculated right." He leaned on the rail and turned to look at her. "I know that this must all seem the most improper way to begin a marriage. We have hardly had any time to get to know each other."

He leaned a bit closer, and she wondered why such a kindly statement loomed so threatening. "It is hard for me to think of myself as a bride."

"That is because the groom is still a stranger. But I assure you, I plan on taking time to get to know you, Mrs. Fauvereau. There will be little else to do on this ship."

His words brought a sting of embarrassment and a

betraying blush to her cool expression. This dark stranger could not possibly speak of knowing her in the biblical sense? She glanced up into his blue eyes, their iciness at odds with his slow smile. She grasped the railing tighter.

Braic came up to them. "Your things are stowed below now. You'll be in the women's room."

She looked at him questioningly. "This clipper is small, I'm afraid. We will be staying with the crew, and you will be sharing a small room with two sister missionaries. I'd best help Cousin Fergus take his things down."

She watched him go, then turned her gaze to the diminishing shoreline. Grey steadied her with his hand at her waist as a sudden surge made Kenna falter. He was standing very near, his breath stirring her hair. "I am sorry that we had to travel so soon."

She casually moved away, turning to look at him with the steel sheathed beneath her lashes. "No apology needed," she said softly. "The accommodations are fine."

He laughed. "You need not bother with fencing words. I do not mind that you are unwilling to play the part of blushing bride. I prefer . . . another sort of bride." She looked at him in surprise, but he continued. "You are a mystery to me, Kenna M'ren. I cannot understand why you accepted an offer from a stranger to be wed by proxy, to travel across the ocean to a land and a man you knew nothing of."

"You set the terms."

"I did. But I did not believe that someone like yourself would be the one to accept them."

"You know nothing of me," she stated flatly, her anger beginning to kindle.

"I know you are beautiful, well bred, and have a fine mind."

"Had I possessed the last two qualities but been a homely lass, should you have cared? You would have tossed me off as if I were common."

"You are not, so we will never know. But you intrigue me and I mean to figure you out." He reached up and fingered a wisp of auburn hair. "And I will, Kenna. I will come to know all of you." He looked at her so steadily that she felt he saw right through to her chemise.

"Black devil!" she said under her breath as he turned and went to speak to the clipper's captain. There would be no peace with him following her trail like the hound after the fox.

For two days they traveled with a stiff wind in their sails, moving along a coastline thick with fir and pine, and fog winding around the entrails of the thrusting rocks. It was rugged, harsh in its savage landscape, and beautiful. Kenna enjoyed the time on deck, even managing to make polite conversation with Grey. He could be quite affable. Other times he was impossible. The two sisters, who planned on setting up a Christian missionary school in Seattle, were quite friendly, and the most polite people she had met since her arrival in America.

On the third day, they moved into fog that slowed their travel, and Grey was in continual conference with the captain, frequently urging him to take a risk, as they were losing time. But the captain was a levelheaded man, not to be bullied into risking his ship. After that their luck worsened. A storm arose, pouring down a continual deluge, blinding their way further.

Though it was not a violent storm, it brought higher waves and a wind that blew them off course. As the weather worsened, so did Grey's temper. They arrived at the mouth of the Columbia two days later than planned.

Chapter III

DUSK WAS FADING into night blackness as Kenna stood by Braic, her hand on his arm, watching her husband and cousin argue with a steamboat captain.

"Will he not even let us dine before making us board another boat?" Kenna asked in exasperation.

"The man hasn't the time. He's losing his race against the calendar."

"I do not understand this race. Why is he in such a terrible hurry to get us to this place called Idaho?"

"Well, uh, it is a bit complicated." He looked around and she thought she detected a little embarrassment.

"He has told you, then, what this is all about?"

"Aye. He's confided quite a bit in me," he said with a touch of pride.

"Then will you explain it to me? First, his demand that we must wed by April and be in San Francisco by June. And now this mad dash for the hills. Why such haste?"

"You'd best ask him," Braic said a bit uncomfortably.

"I have tried," she said. "But he is very vague, and

I feel as if I am being led on some wild chase for no reason at all."

"The man has his reasons. His race against time means great gains if he can win, and great losses should he not meet his goal."

They were both distracted by Grey, who had taken out a flat-folding pouch, from which he drew a number of notes, plopping them into the riverboat captain's outstretched hand. The captain quickly pocketed the money, and Grey slid the pouch back into his jacket. Then he turned and strode down the gangplank toward them with Fergus in his wake. He smiled broadly as he reached them.

"It was a hard task to persuade him, but we'll be setting off as soon as our things and some extra cargo are put aboard."

"We have hardly set foot on ground and now we must board this steamship?" She eyed it uncertainly. It was white, three-tiered, and flanked on either side by black steampipes that jutted skyward. It lay at the mouth of the Columbia like a graceless, squat water beast, so unlike the fluid lines of the *Northern Clipper*. At its end was the huge paddle wheel that powered its movement.

Grey discerned her thoughts. "It is sturdier than it looks. It will go where a clipper can't."

"Will we not at least spend one evening on land?"

"I'm afraid not. We must get to Silver City, and soon."

"Why?"

"It's complicated."

Kenna angrily put her hands on her narrow waist. "I am no fool, Mr. Fauvereau. Yet you three men give not even the simplest explanation. I will not set foot upon that floating barge until you explain."

Grey took a step nearer her. He smiled into her dark eyes. "I have no secrets from my wife. What would you like me to explain?"

"Your haste."

"It is necessary for me to reach Silver City by the first week of July."

"So I have heard, repeatedly."

"I'm sorry, Kenna," he said, his voice caressing her name. "I should have taken the time to explain. I own The Bank in Silver City, or at least half of it. If I do not get back as quickly as possible, the ownership will revert to my partner. I realize that so much traveling, right after your journey to America, is very tedious. If I had any other recourse, I would have taken it."

Kenna was thinking that his appearance did not fit that of a banker. Somehow she had suspected his business dealings to be less appropriate. "You could have explained this earlier," she said softly, walking past him and up the gangplank. He watched her go and smiled to himself, very pleased.

"She'll be learning the truth sooner or later, Grey," Braic said behind him.

Grey raised an eyebrow. "Every word I spoke was the truth."

"Aye," Fergus said, joining them. "But with an explanation and a half left out. I think my young cousin won't be liking it."

"She will not like the truth no matter when I tell her," Grey said, his voice amused, "so for this reason I postpone it. But if either of you wants to tell her . . ."

His voice trailed off and he looked at Fergus and Braic.

"I won't be doing your chores for you." Braic smiled. "But you'd best win her over before you tell her."

"It won't matter," Fergus said pessimistically. "She will be angry whenever she learns of it."

Grey did not hear Fergus's last comment, since his mind was dwelling on Braic's advice. Yes, Braic, he thought. I want very much to win her over. You have no idea how much.

He went on deck once their things were loaded. Coal was heaped into the boiler, steam rose from the shafts, and the paddle began to move. Soon it was churning up the water, propelling them up the Columbia, past the lights flickering from the riverbanks.

"Did the captain object to our boarding?" Kenna asked as he joined her at the rail, remembering the argument and bribe.

"No, he objected to our time of departure. He wanted to leave in the morning. But he was willing to forget his losses for a price."

Kenna looked up at Grey and smiled. "A banker. For some reason, that is the last form of business I expected you to run. You should have told me," she mused.

"Disappointed?" he asked, in a voice that almost sounded hopeful.

"Why, no," she said. "It is a respectable business."

"I do other things than run The Bank, you know."

She waited for him to give further details, but he did not. Instead, he stared at her with a gaze that made her warm. "I hope to get you back home to Silver City soon. This is not how I wanted our marriage to start out."

He slipped his arms around her waist, and she was suddenly very aware of their solitude. She looked up at him in alarm as his mouth came down on hers, his lips softly plying the warmth there. She had no strength to pull away as the steel bands of his arms pressed her closer to him, her hands resting on the thin fabric of his shirt. She could do naught but give into the strange weakness that washed over her.

At last, he pulled back, still keeping his arms around her. His face was very close to hers, and his eyes looked blue-black in the darkness. "It is my greatest ambition to have you, Kenna."

Later that night, as she lay in bed alone in the tiny cubicle that was the only private room aboard the steamship, those words kept repeating themselves in her mind. There was something exciting, yet frightening, about them.

The next morning as they ate breakfast together, Grey was cordial and polite, with no hint of that threatening side she had seen. He looked very handsome in a dark suit that contrasted with his fine white linen shirt. The wind off the river ruffled his hair. He smiled at her as he sipped his morning brew.

"We're making good time. I should have you in Silver City very soon." He spoke so politely that Braic and Fergus discerned nothing in his words, but Kenna felt a blush creep color into her cheeks. He leaned back, satisfied, knowing that she understood the meaning of his words.

The steamship chugged along the smooth-flowing

river, traveling upstream against the tide alongside the thick, wooded shoreline.

And then there was a delay because of a problem with the steam engine, and they had to drop anchor until it was fixed. Grey threw himself into the repairs with such determination that only an afternoon had been lost. But he felt the time slipping away from him and his mood became dour.

Kenna, on the other hand, did not mind the delay. It gave her time to know this man a little more and yet keep him at a safe distance.

In time, they reached the Snake River and followed its eastward course, which eventually took a southerly turn. No lofty pines graced the shores here, with misting drifts on the banks. Instead, they filtered away into canyons so steep that they took her breath away. Sheer rock lunged upward on either side, cutting off all but a narrow strip of sky, and the river grew rough. Water spewed onto the deck, dampening her hair so that escaping tendrils always surrounded her face. She gripped the rails as the ship followed its course.

Grey came to stand beside her. "What do you think of the territory of Idaho?"

"This is it!" she gasped.

He laughed. "Only the beginning."

"Truthfully," she said soberly. "I think it is quite the ugliest land I have seen. Is this Silver City you speak of in such country?"

"No, it is far from here."

"We have already traveled so far! By now I could have been to London from Auchinleck."

"We have days to go, still," he said, looking down

45

the distance of river. "Right now we are going through Hell's Canyon."

"Appropriately named."

"You've seen nothing yet, Kenna."

Eventually, they came out of the canyon, and Kenna came onto the ship's deck in the morning to find the river much smoother, widened out to sloping banks. But there were no trees as there had been in the Oregon Territory. Instead, there were desert prairies, the likes of which she had never seen.

By afternoon, she caught sight of some buildings on the banks, and Grey told them they would be pulling into Farewell Bend. The owner of the Olds Ferry came out to greet them, and Kenna was glad to get off the boat and onto land. But it was not for long. They ate lunch on shore as the captain unloaded his goods and received payment. Kenna walked about, eating salad and potatoes as she read the toll rates. It would cost them twenty-five cents a footman to cross or seventy-five cents with a horse. As she viewed the large but rickety ferry, she was very glad that they would not need it. After half an hour, she reluctantly boarded the three-hundred-ton boat; its shrill whistle startled her. It pulled free from the shore, lighter now with half its cargo headed for territorial outposts. After another seemingly endless journey, they reached their destination, a hundred and five miles from Olds Ferry.

Kenna wearily stepped off the boat, so very glad that the traveling was over. She looked around the banks lined with Russian olive trees, the light green of their leaves in contrast to the darker willows. And she looked out across the vastness of the plain in dismay, seeing miles of washed-out white earth prickled with dots of green sagebrush. The mesas melted into distant mountains that were a blue smear against the horizon. She was assaulted by the heat, and as she stared across the landscape, a hot breeze blew strands of hair about her face. She did not mask her disheartened feelings.

Grey spoke. "It is not as barren as it appears, Lady M'ren," he teased. "You have not seen its best side."

"I can hardly wait," she moaned.

A few buildings leaned sadly together on the bank, and they stepped inside one of these for something to eat. Braic sat next to her; even he seemed discouraged. They ate in silence while Grey inquired about the stage. His sudden shout caught their attention.

"You can't mean it!"

A lean fellow with hunched shoulders and wire-rimmed spectacles sat perched on a high stool, looking in awe at the angry man. "I am sorry, Mr. Fauvereau." He shrugged. "But I have no control over the stage. It will be here the day after tomorrow, if it gets here at all."

"That will be too late! The stage always comes through every workday."

"Unless it's out of repair, which is not the fault of the stage line."

"Damn!" He slammed his fist on the desktop, making a bottle of ink wobble.

He conferred for a time with the stage man before nodding and coming to sit down with them. He leveled a stern gaze at Kenna, looking her up and down. "Can you ride?"

"Aye, and very well," Braic answered for her. Her brother seemed to have caught the enthusiasm of this adventure again.

"You want to take her by horseback?" Fergus McDoo asked in surprise.

Grey sighed and shook his head. "I do not want to, but it is my last chance. With every delay, my calculations have been cut to ribbons. Today is the last day of June, which gives us only three days. The stage could have made it with time to spare, if we left tomorrow, because it travels all day and night. But it won't be here until the second. So unless we leave tomorrow, at the earliest, and travel three full days, we won't make it, and I will have lost everything."

"But what of our trunks?" Kenna asked uncertainly.

"Someone will have to stay here and be responsible for them. The fewer that travel, the faster we can go."

"Then Braic and I shall wait for the stage and catch up with you," Kenna said. The three men looked at each other.

"Kenna," Grey said. "If I do not bring you back with me, I will lose The Bank."

"Me?" she asked in bewilderment.

"Yes. That is why I will lose my establishment. I had to marry to keep my holdings."

"Indeed? So that explains our wedding, and our haste," she said musingly.

"Will you go with me tomorrow?" he asked softly.

She hesitated, then looked at Braic. "Do not be letting him down after all we've been through," he encouraged.

"But I only rode on hunts and picnics on our land," she said uncertainly.

"You also beat me at a race," Braic reminded her.

She looked at Grey, who was staring at her as if he

were willing her consent, and she glanced away. "Very well," she sighed, looking down at her hands folded on the table. "I cannot say I look forward to crossing any more of this forsaken land, but I will not let my weakness stand in your way."

Grey smiled broadly and leaned back in his chair. "I knew you wouldn't let me down."

While the men seemed confident in her decision, she was not. She was pledged to cross this barren wilderness alone with her husband, the stranger.

The stagehouse was not an inn, so they shared a common room set up with extra cots. If the quarters they had before had been unsatisfactory, these were doubly so. Although they curtained off a corner for Kenna, the lack of privacy still grated on her nerves. By the time it grew dark, she found the courage to take off her dress and loosen her stays, but that was all. She lay on the rough cot, feeling alone and desolate.

She had barely managed to fall asleep when she heard her name called from far off. She pulled herself awake as a candle wavered to life. She blinked and shielded her eyes.

"We have to be going," Grey's voice said.

She turned her head away. "No," she murmured. "It's still night."

She felt his rough hands on her arms, pulling her to a sitting position, and she was suddenly quite awake, holding her blanket around her. "All right!" she said, glaring at him till he left. The sun was not even up.

She did a quick toilette with a small bowl of water, removing her slip and looking through her trunk for

49

her riding habit. She was about to put it on when the curtain was thrust back and Grey stepped inside again, the candle casting revealing light. He set it down. She clutched the habit in front of her, looking at him in dismay.

"Mr. Fauvereau!"

"Is that what you plan to wear?" He quirked an eyebrow at her.

"It may not be new, but I always wore it when I rode."

"That's not what I meant. It is too hot. We are crossing through desert. You won't last an hour in those clothes."

"Then what do you suggest I wear?" she asked in irritation.

He tossed something on the bed. "Try those."

She held up a set of men's trousers. "These? They are gentlemen's pants!"

"Not exactly. I had them made to your size. This heavy blue fabric wears like iron; all the railroad men are starting to wear them. They'll hold up to our travels."

"I cannot wear them."

"Would you rather that your tender lady's hide be worn raw by a saddle? As you pointed out, this is not a fox hunt. We will be traveling hard, and I can't have blisters slowing you down. And another thing," he said, stepping near. "You can't wear this either."

He grabbed the loosened ties of her corset, pulling it free and tossing it onto the bed, leaving her in a thin chemise. Her angry shriek echoed through the room, bringing McDoo's snoring to an abrupt hault.

"How dare you!" she screamed at him in fury.

He grabbed her and clamped his iron fist across

her mouth, pulling her to him, his mouth next to her ear. "I dare, because I am your husband, and I am doing what I think best."

Despite her struggles, she could not free herself; when she stopped fighting him, he pulled his hand away, his thumb gently rubbing her silken cheek. His face was very close to hers. "I want you to get there safely. By the time the sun hits zenith, you'd be fainting. Now be a good girl and put on the trousers so we can go."

She stared into the tanned face, venom in her eyes. "I'll put them on, blackguard, only you remember that I'm not your property, no matter what the law says. So keep your hands off me!"

There was such ice in her voice that Grey was taken aback for a moment. Then he smiled at her, that slow, wickedly taunting smile she had seen before. "I'll remember," he said, releasing her so suddenly that she fell back onto the cot.

With a groan, she clenched her fists, watching his back disappear through the curtains. How she could hate this man! She threw off her pantalets, since their bulk would not fit into the trousers, standing with indecision as she looked into her trunk. She pulled out and donned a light linen blouse. Then she put on her hardiest stockings and slipped into the pants. They were nothing like she had ever worn, and as she fastened up the front buttons she felt a wash of embarrassment. She tucked in the blouse and pulled on her riding boots. Then she plaited her hair into a thick braid down her back, deciding rightly that during such travel hairpins would never hold. She felt naked without her corset and slip, and vulnerable without the heavy skirts or full riding pants of her habit. She repacked her trunk, salvaging the riding jacket, then she parted the curtain and stepped through.

Braic and McDoo stopped what they were doing to stare at her. The pants fit her shapely form, cinching her narrow waist with a surprisingly good fit. The soft blouse was in contrast with the "serge de Nimes," or denims as they were called, and Braic let out a low whistle.

"Is that your new riding habit, sister?"

"Courtesy of Fauvereau," she said bitingly.

"Well," Braic said, noticing the delicate curves of his sister for the first time, "I've heard of women wearing a man's pants, and if this is the result, I don't think that I shall mind."

Grey burst out laughing and she glared at him. But during their hasty preparations, he often glanced at her slender yet shapely form.

Braic hugged her farewell, promising to join her within a week. With no aid from her husband, she mounted the horse he had bought her and caught the hat he tossed her. She pulled it on, the wide brim shading her eyes. She thought that she now truly looked like a man, little knowing how wrong she was.

It was still dark, with only a tinge of pink on the eastern horizon. Grey secured their saddlebags and then mounted his own steed. She waved to her brother and cousin as they started their journey, even casting back a wavering smile. She pretended bravery where she felt none. The danger of Grey's presence had been abated by the comfort of Braic's company, but now Grey seemed more threatening to her as she looked at him. His features were silhouetted black against the light of oncoming dawn, the sharp lines of jaw and brow holding her gaze. She was going, alone, into the desert with this stranger who was her husband.

Their horses were laden with bedrolls, saddlebags, and skins filled with water. The saddles, lighter and less ornate than those at Moldarn, sported a horn on the front and were placed over a wool blanket. Inwardly, she was glad that circumstances let her ride free, as she had loved to do in private, rather than in the lady's sidesaddle position. As she rode next to Grey, her leg brushed his a couple of times before she could steer the difficult beast away.

Kenna was well aware of the strong muscles of thigh and arm beside her. In every aspect, he was so different from her; his strong fingers easily held the reins, for example, while she had to work with hers continually. He seemed quite at ease in the saddle, moving the horse along at a steady pace, heedless of rocks and dirt which slid beneath the animal's hooves. He appeared very different to Kenna than the first time she met him on the street in San Francisco.

As their journey had progressed, Grey had removed pieces of his suit, becoming more casual as they traveled. But now, in the heavy blue breeches like the ones she wore, with tall brown boots and a leather jacket, he looked more rugged. And more handsome, if that were possible. He had a wide-brimmed leather hat pulled low that made him look like some wild highwayman. He seemed more at ease in these mountain-man clothes than in the businessman's suit, she thought.

Behind them, the buildings were mere blurs of dark color on the horizon as the sunrise came into full glory. It was breathtaking, and overwhelming. This land was nothing like Scotland.

When they left the Snake River, they left the trees that grew there, and moved into the desert. They followed a wagon trail, their goal the mountains ahead. They crossed over mesas and through a sea of sagebrush. Grey pointed to the mountains.

"Those are the Owyhees. We'll be crossing them."

"It will take days to reach them!"

"Not if we keep up this fast pace," he called back to her.

Inwardly, she groaned. Already she was growing stiff, and her back was beginning to feel the jolts that the horse took. She had not ridden in such a long time.

As the trail widened a bit, they rode abreast again, and she glanced up at him. "Owyhee . . . Idaho . . . the men your people named this land after had strange names."

"They're Indian names. Most of the names in these territories are. Idaho means 'Gem of the Mountains.'"

Since Grey seemed proud of this, Kenna did not say that this desert land looked more like a rock than any precious jewel. She felt she had seen too much of it already.

"Are there Indians still around?"

"Still?" He looked at her in surprise. "All this is Indian territory."

"Are they dangerous?" she asked worriedly.

"It depends on what tribe we run into. But I've got this." He patted his long rifle. "We'd have a good chance of making it with her. I'm a good shot."

"What tribes do we need to worry about?"

"Mainly, I'd say, probably the Shoshoni. In 1860 they massacred the Otter party; it was pretty awful."

"That was only eight years ago!" she said, aghast.

He looked over and grinned at her. "Are you afraid?" She shuddered and spurred her horse a little faster. "Glen must have been right," she murmured.

He caught her words. "Glen?"

"He said that America was full of savages and barbarians. I'm not so sure he was wrong."

"This Glen wanted to dissuade you from coming to America?" he asked in a hard voice. She nodded. "I see. He had an interest in your welfare?"

"He warned me about savages. Perhaps I should have heeded him."

"This man wanted you," he said softly. "He loved you?"

She eyed him suspiciously but said nothing. What did this man know of her past, and how had he learned it?

He would not let the silence lay. "Braic said there was a man in your past."

"My brother speaks too freely," she said stiffly.

"Drink helped him along, and I plied him, so don't blame Braic."

"Why did you ply him?"

"I told you that I wanted to find out about you."

"And are you satisfied?"

"No. I know there was some man in your past, but even when he was drunk I could get nothing out of Braic as to why you left the man."

"You have no right to ask of my past, not even as my husband," she said angrily. "That part of me you have not bought."

55

He stared at her with those eyes as bright as the heather in Auchinleck, and she finally tore her gaze away. Perhaps it was best to give him what he wanted so that he would leave her alone.

She looked toward the mountains, always there yet never growing closer. "The man I loved wed another," she stated in a voice as smooth as if she discussed the weather. "Though he professed to love me, I had no dowry, so he married my friend, who did."

He reached out, lifted a stray lock of hair from her cheek, and tucked it back into the braid. "The man was a fool," he said.

"He felt that pleasing his family and keeping the peace was more important than following his heart."

"You defend him?" he asked in surprise.

She shook her head. "No. I explain him."

"I've been poor, to the point of stealing a crust of bread, and I have been wealthy. I've found little satisfaction in the pursuit of wealth alone. I think that he'll regret following his duty."

"He has already said so."

"He wanted you back?" Her silence was the answer he wanted. "Then the puzzle is solved at last. You accepted my offer to flee not just the poverty, but also the man you loved."

The truth of his words stung. "Must you pry into every facet of my past? Would you know everything of me?" she asked in exasperation.

"None of this is what I really wish to know, Kenna. I need to know if you loved him, and did you give yourself to him?"

In anger, she tightened the horse's reins. The horse shied nervously, loose rock slipping beneath its hooves. The animal backed up, sensing its rider's distress, and in fear Kenna threw her arm out, hitting Grey's chest. He reached out and grabbed her onto his steed as her own jerked into a gallop; in panic, Kenna pushed away, and Grey lost his balance. They tumbled to the ground and landed in puffs of dust; Kenna cried out and pulled away.

"Stop it!" he said angrily as he grabbed her. He pushed her to the ground, pinning her beneath him. "You are my wife," he ground out. "I have a right to learn things about you."

He seemed very hard to her, threatening, as he loomed above her. He came down, his mouth meeting hers in a heated kiss that seemed to verify his words. She tried to struggle, to pull away, but she was helpless beneath his strength. Neither did his mouth release her so that she could gasp for air. Instead, under his heavy weight, she felt herself weaken, almost passing out from his smothering possession of her. When he felt her lie limp in his arms, he pulled away, staring down at her. Her eyes were closed, her lips parted as her breath quickened. His mouth came down again, this time with a beckoning gentleness that demanded surrender.

When at last he released her, she looked up with eyes as gray as moonstones, edged by coal lashes. She blinked hard, sitting up. He caught her chin in his fingers, turning her face to his.

"You need to take greater care in leading your horse along these trails," he said. Then his voice softened. "Understand my purpose in asking, Kenna. I wanted you the first time I saw you. I've had many women before, but none have whetted my appetite as you have. I dislike the thought of another man having any claim upon you. You are mine. The fool who abandoned you has no claim now. I'll never let you go. And I won't share you, either your flesh or your memories."

"Do you think I have no morals?" she said, pulling away and then standing up. Though she was angry still, his words had touched something in her that made her soften.

"I think that you are a woman of hidden passions. No severe clothes or primly pulled-back hair can hide what you are inside. I have learned more from our kiss than from anything you've said. Our desire is mutual, even if you won't admit it."

"Must you say such things!"

"Do you deny it?" he asked softly, a note of surprise in his voice.

She turned on him, passion moving her. "No! I'll not deny it, but neither shall I play the part of harlot! I'll stay the coming of desire as long as I can."

He stood up, thinking her words over as he beat the dust from his clothes. He liked her words. He brushed the dust from the seat and legs of her breeches, and the unfamiliar sensation of his touch made her protest and move away. What was it about this man that so aroused this inner turmoil?

"Damn," he said, yet the word was not spoken with any vehemence. "A lady." That seemed to vent his feelings and he strode toward the wary horses, catching up their reins and bringing them to Kenna. He lifted her into the saddle, his hands lingering on her waist before he mounted his own steed, urging the horses to move.

Kenna stared at the muscular back of the man in front of her; his embrace had evoked such a peculiar stirring within her. He would have her, as he stated, she knew. And that time was drawing ever nearer.

Chapter IV

THE SUN'S HEAT shimmered across the sagebrush. The trail that they had been following merged with a road; rutted with wagon trails and rough, it was still wide enough to make the going easier. They picked up their pace.

The horse's faster gait jolted Kenna's back until she could not stand to go any farther. Grey saw her pull up and he reined in.

"I've got to stop," she said.

"We've only been on the journey for four hours."

She felt embarrassed that she was not stronger. He nodded and dismounted, coming over and lifting her off the horse. "I guess we could eat. We didn't breakfast this morning."

She was grateful for this concession and stretched; every joint ached. She walked around, trying to shake out the stiffness in her legs and in her hands, which had clutched the reins so tightly. Blisters were beginning to form even though she had worn gloves.

Grey let the horses graze on the sagebrush after he took some food from the saddlebags. Kenna quietly

accepted the dried meat, bread, and cheese he offered. He had seen her temper today. Yet, since their
scuffle, she had ridden by his side without speaking.
He wondered if she were still angry.

Kenna eyed him covertly. She had been furious at
the cruelty of his prying and his biting words. Yet,
strangely enough, his explanation had softened her
anger. The desire he spoke of sent a thrill of nervousness through her even now. What was it about this
forceful man that touched her as never before? Men
had courted her from the time she was still a girl,
and she had laughed and turned aside their affection
so that she might make her own choice. With Grey
there had been no choice, yet she did not regret the
decision made for her.

He handed her a canteen of warm water to wash
down the food, and their fingers brushed as she took
it from him. He had been silent since her outburst,
yet still he studied her. Those eyes of his made her
uneasy. Blue was the color of a summer sky or the
heather in Scotland, a color one would think of as
open to understanding. But the blue of his eyes was
the color of dark pools, whose depths were unknown.
And it was that unknown which both frightened and
seduced her.

The afternoon heat was oppressive as they
mounted again; she kept her riding jacket on to
ward off the hot sun. Perspiration made the escaping
tendrils of hair around her face curl, and she brushed
them back with her hand. In the distance, the mountains were almost blue, inviting and cool; she kept
her eyes on them as if they were a beacon. The road
began to climb, winding along the edge of hills as
they began their ascent toward the Owyhees.

They finally dismounted as the sun began to sink behind those grand mountains; Kenna was so exhausted she could hardly stand. Her fingers ached terribly, and the muscles in her back and shoulders had stiffened. She took a sip from the canteen, pouring a little into her hands to rinse the dust from her face. Grey cautioned her not to use very much. He spread out the bedrolls under an outcropping of rock. She forced down a bite of bread, which had grown stale despite being wrapped in a wet cloth when they left, and some meat and water. Then she lay down, too exhausted to move or care about Indians or renegades.

Grey saw to the horses and set up camp before he sat down to eat. He chewed thoughtfully on some jerky as the moon rose huge and round above the edge of the horizon and the stars came out. He spent much of his time watching Kenna. She had fallen asleep almost immediately, the travel more of an ordeal than she would admit. He had seen her discomfort, but time was money and he had to press on.

An owl spread its wings, circling overhead. Its sudden appearance broke his reverie, and he lay down on his own bedroll, letting sleep ease his mind.

The aroma of roasting meat invaded Kenna's dreams enough to wake her from her deep sleep. She looked around and saw Grey bending over a small fire, tending meat on a spit. She sat up and stretched, but every muscle ached in protest. She had been sore yesterday, but this morning her body was stiff. She managed to tend to her needs behind the boulders and rinse her face with a few drops of water before coming back to sit across the fire from Grey.

The sky was lightening, and the day looked to be overcast.

He handed her a hot drink which she took gratefully, sipping at it to take away the chill of the desert night. "How much farther?"

"Two days." He took a long draft of his own drink.

"I cannot believe how huge this country is," she said wearily. "I feel as if I've traveled between Glasgow and Auchinleck several times over."

He chuckled softly. "We've made good time, and you can rest for a week in bed when we get there, if you like."

"I'd rather soak in a tub for that week," she said. "This land has dust, if nothing else. What is that you are cooking?" She eyed the fire suspiciously.

"It's a rabbit I snared."

"It looks like a skinned cat."

He laughed. "You're Scottish, and never had rabbit?"

"I've had it," she assured him. "But the cook always prepared it cut up." Still, it did smell good after the jerky they had eaten, as its juices dripped into the fire, splattering grease.

They ate, then packed and mounted. Kenna's saddle felt harder than before, the heavy denims not enough protection. Her stiff fingers grabbed the reins, the blisters on her hands having come to a head. She was determined to say nothing of her miseries to Grey.

The morning's travel was easier since no cruel sun beat down on them. Instead a cooler wind blew from the mountains as they approached. How moody this land was, she thought. And how unpredictable, just like Grey.

The road they traveled twisted higher into the hills, the horses picking their way along sheer cliff drops down into a canyon.

"What made people move out into this forsaken land?" she asked to break the silence.

"A legend," he answered. "To be exact, the blue bucket legend."

"Go on," she encouraged, her interest up.

"Well, over twenty years ago an immigrant wagon train came down the south side of the Snake River. They made camp along one of the streams in the area, and the children went to get drinking water while the parents set up camp. They brought their blue water buckets back filled with shiny rocks they found on the stream bed."

"And that was how the gold was discovered?"

"No, because the parents paid no attention to the nuggets."

"Why?" Kenna asked.

Grey shrugged. "Too tired, probably. They had traveled for a long way, and all they could think about was reaching their destination."

"I can understand that," Kenna said, changing her uncomfortable position in the saddle.

Grey chuckled. "The immigrants thought of nothing but making it across the mountains before the snow came: Idaho was not settled then and they were headed toward the Oregon Territory."

"But what did they do with the gold?"

"Most of it they threw out, although some made it into a toolbox. But they were just too tired and desperate to notice until years later when they had settled down. It was then that the legend began to spread. The gold rush here began a decade ago."

Kenna looked at him in amazement. "Then this land has been settled for fewer than ten years?"

"Does that bother you?"

"My homeland is so old by comparison, then. Everything in Scotland is so ancient; how will I ever get used to living in a country that is in its infancy?"

Grey laughed. "I appreciate the opportunity to build an empire in a new land. Silver City has been built by men with a desire to succeed."

"Greed, do you not mean? They came here looking for wealth; I assume that they found it?"

Grey nodded. "Yes. The lure of silver and gold beckoned. But when gold was finally discovered, men poured into Idaho. Their lust drives them where nothing else could. But it's not as easy to find in reality as it is in dreams. Mining is rough work."

"And is the lust for gold what brought you here?"

He smiled and shrugged. "Truthfully, there are other things I desire more."

She felt uncomfortable with his words. "But you bank the gold."

"I do, so to speak. But money is not so very important to me."

"Then why this mad dash back to Silver City to save your bank?" she asked.

He was thoughtful for a moment. "I think it is winning that whets my appetite. Only those things that are a challenge are worth winning."

She lifted her eyes to his. "Does that include me?"

He grinned at her, his white teeth contrasting with his tanned face. "You're getting to know me, Kenna."

They rode on in silence, reaching the peak of the hills by early afternoon. The sky was even darker, and there was a light film of rain. It brought out the smell of the sagebrush, an odor like nothing she had smelled before. It sweetened the air as the rain settled the dust. They stopped and ate, overlooking a creek that meandered through the gully, past white-topped weeds and prickly wild flowers. The mountains, still ahead of them, layered into the distance. They were craggy, the ones before them massive brown stone thrust from the earth. The ones behind, more shrouded in mist, were gray.

He pointed to them as he chewed a crust of hard bread. "That's War Eagle Mountain. We'll be crossing over that."

She choked on the water she was drinking. "Cross that! It's the highest peak there!"

"Don't worry, the road is still good."

She had not thought that the roads they had been traveling on were very good, and she did not like the idea of winding around that snow-crested peak. They mounted their horses, and she pulled on her now wet riding jacket, buttoning it up tightly and settling her hat low. Rain, when viewed from inside the warm confines of a house, was enchanting to her. But traveling through it made her long for shelter.

They wound back down to the floor of War Eagle Mountain. The trek took them the rest of the day. As they ended their descent Kenna exclaimed in delight. It was as if they had crossed a border that cut off the sagebrush and began with trees. A gushing stream wound around the foot of the mountains, and lush pines interspersed with aspen, young oaks, and blue wild flowers edged the banks. There was such beauty in this land she had thought so barren.

Kenna pulled her horse in by the stream beneath a

65

copse of birch trees. She dismounted, putting her hands at the base of her aching back. Grey reined in beside her, letting his horse drink.

"Kenna?"

"I cannot go on. I am sorry to be a 'lady' such as you disdain. Every fiber of my being aches, and I cannot bear to get astride that beast again. It's beautiful here. I never thought I'd see beauty again."

"But we could probably go a few more miles. We start climbing from here, and don't stop until we get to Silver City."

She looked at him wearily. "Please, Grey?"

Something in her voice made him weaken. He dismounted. "It'll be dark in a while. A rest will do us good."

She smiled her appreciation and stood by the stream. It flowed between croppings of rock, the soft murmur of its water beckoning to her. It was cool and clear, and she refreshed herself drinking it, since the water in the flask had been warm and tasted of leather.

"I want to bathe," she said. "The grime must be inches thick on me."

"It's ice cold," he warned.

"I won't be swimming in it. I just want to wash off; I think I have the courage for that."

He nodded, and she went off a distance, finding a place where water ran on either side of a flat ledge, the place well masked by trees. Grey busied himself with the horses and bedrolls and started a fire now that the rain was only a sprinkle.

Kenna unplaited her hair and worked a brush through the tangled mass. She pulled off the riding jacket and boots, then unbuttoned the pants and slid them off. Her skin was sore and red where the seams had chafed her skin. She pulled off her blouse, looking sadly at what had once been her favorite. No longer white, it was dusty with streaks from the rain. She tossed it across a low limb along with her pants and jacket. The cool breeze chilled her skin, and it felt delicious as she stepped into the icy water, letting it rush past her swollen feet. She dipped a cloth in the water, wiping off her face and arms. She wished for some scented soap or lilac water, and yet was grateful for the small luxury of being able to wash.

Grey caught a glimpse of his wife through the copse of birch trees and he froze. She was standing in the shallow stream, running a wet cloth along her long limbs. She was clothed only in a sheer chemise whose thin lace straps and short length displayed more of her than he had yet seen. Her hair, combed out from its braid, fell in a dark and tangled mass down her back. She was tall for a woman, and her legs were long and silken as she sat down on a large rock in midstream. He watched, mesmerized, as she finished her bathing. A shudder ran through him, and he jerked his eyes away. He grabbed a rope and began tying it in a triangle around three nearby trees; then he tossed a canvas over it so that their bedrolls would have protection from the rain which was threatening again. He was absorbed in thinking of her when a scream rent the air.

His head snapped up, and he bolted for his rifle, which leaned against a tree, then ran the short distance to the copse. Kenna stood on the flat rock, her fists clenched together in front of her, her eyes wide with fear. By the side of the stream, very near to her, were Indians.

Kenna stared at the two men. Their skins were dark, their hair plaited in many rows daubed with mud, displaying feathers and a few dark beads. The young one wore little more than a loincloth and heavy moccasins and both had bearhide robes. She had seen nothing like them in her life and terror washed over her at the sight of the stone spears they carried. Their faces were passive as they eyed her, and they took little notice of Grey's sudden presence.

Grey took a step nearer and the younger Indian turned his hawklike profile to him. He made several swift motions with his hands, then indicated Kenna. Grey pointed to her, then touched his chest with his fist. They looked at her again, then the Indian made more motions and Grey nodded his understanding. The younger one had turned to leave when the older Indian stopped him with his hand. He pointed to Kenna. He spoke, and the brave drew a knife of sharp stone tied with leather strips to a wooden handle.

"Kenna," she heard Grey's deep voice say with quiet calm. "Stand very still."

As the Indian waded across the stream toward her with his knife, she clenched her teeth together to keep from crying out. Her mind screamed at her to turn and flee before this savage put stone to flesh. But Grey had given her instructions, and she must trust him. She stood rigid, locking her knees lest they give out. The Indian stood before her, his dark eyes looking into hers. She looked back unwaveringly into the ominous face which gave no clue to his thinking. He raised his knife, passing the cruel instrument before her eyes, then sliced it downward, cutting off a lock of hair. Kenna gasped and jerked away. Her heart was racing, and the Indian made

68

the sound of laughter, a brittle noise that scared her still more. He waded across the stream and handed her lock of hair to the older warrior. The latter held the auburn tress up to catch a glimmer of fading light; then his bony fingers stuffed it into a leather pouch he wore around his neck. With no further sound, they turned and left, vanishing among the trees, moving toward the desert.

Grey leaped the stream in time to catch her as her knees buckled. She clung to him, sobs escaping the fists clenched to her mouth. He wrapped his arms around her, feeling her shudder in his embrace. He held her until her shaking stopped. She still could not find the courage to leave the warmth of his arms. Finally she pulled away, wiping at the tears with the back of her hand.

"You all right now?"

She nodded. "You were brave, Kenna," he said. "You're made of tougher fabric than I'd thought."

"That knife . . ."

"The old Indian wanted some of your hair for his medicine pouch. He must have thought that its color was magic."

"How did you know he wasn't going to kill me?" she said, her voice still shaky.

"Those were Digger Indians, on some trek. They went up to old War Eagle, as best I understand. But they were on their way back to the desert when they saw you." He tightened his arms about her. "If they had been Paiute or Shoshoni, we'd have been in bad trouble."

That matter-of-fact statement and the cold air chilled Kenna, and she shivered. Grey reluctantly let her go and gathered up her things, taking her the

short distance back to their makeshift camp. He
threw more wood on the fire, and she held out her
hands to the warm glow. It was growing dark
quickly, and she huddled on her bedroll, pulling her
blanket about her. Grey came and sat beside her, offering her some food.

"You know their language?"

"It's Indian sign. Almost universal. Every tribe
has its own tongue, and it is the only way they can
talk to each other. They asked about you, and I said
that you were my woman."

The fire died down into coals as the rain began
again, and Kenna was grateful for the protection of
the canvas tarp. The sounds of night and the noise of
the rain seemed menacing to her. She moved nearer
to Grey.

"Will they come back?"

He was quiet for a long while. "I don't think so."

There was a flash of light, gone as fast as it had
come, and it was followed by the low-throated rum-
bling of thunder which echoed through the gulley.
Fear made her lunge into his arms and she whispered, "Terror makes me forget my pride!"

He held her close and warm in his arms. He laid
her on the bedroll that was cushioned on fresh pine
needles, and she clung to him. He wrapped his blankets around them, yet still she shivered. His mouth
came down to hers, and he heated her with his desire. The thin chemise was little covering, when she
lay so close to him. Yet she could not find the
strength to pull away, nor did she desire to.

The heat of his kiss warmed her like a swallow of
hot brandy and made her lightheaded, in his control.
She felt herself respond to the touch of his mouth.

The rough blanket fell away as she slipped her silken arms about his neck.

Grey pulled his mouth away from Kenna's. Her body lay enticingly beneath the steel length of his own frame.

"Are you sure you can follow this trail?" he asked quietly.

Kenna stared into the blackness, only sensing the man who lay above her, stalking her desire. "No," she answered. Yet her arms took their own course, pulling his mouth down again to hers.

He slipped his hands beneath her neck, pulling her to him, conquering her, claiming his wife. Yet to her, the conquering was a victory. His touch did not humiliate her, for she sensed her own power as her hands ran down the hard muscles of his back. Desire flared up within her very marrow and she shuddered. It was easy to let all the training of being a lady slip away, as easily as he let his rough clothing slip away. She had always taken the sense of touch for granted, yet now, as their bodies lay together and his rough hands slid the length of her, she came to realize its full potential. Those same hands, despite their size and strength, were gentle with her; experienced, yes, but willing to teach. She moaned softly, her fear driven away by passion. She found no shame in her desires. Her fingers ran through the light furring of hair on his muscled chest, then slipped about his neck again.

"Oh, lady!" He moaned with pleasure as he took her, gently branding her as his. "No longer do I disdain the title!"

Rain fell in veils upon the tiny valley, hissing the coals of fire into death, while other embers, those of passion, blazed into life.

* * *

Kenna awoke to the sound of dripping water in quiet darkness. The rainstorm was over and all that was left was the dripping from the trees and canvas, and a sweet, clean smell. She turned her head slightly to look out the open side and could detect only a faint graying on the eastern edge of the hills. Her husband's arms were about her, arms that were strong and warm and very masculine, warding off the chill that came in the early hours.

The storm has ended, she thought. That storm between them. The violence of passion had managed to bring peace in its wake. The intimacy she had feared proved to be pleasurable. Making love had been an experience like nothing she had imagined. Yet she frowned at the word love. That had not been spoken between them; he had talked of the desire that she, too, longed to have filled. But there had been no mention of that most tender word of all. She had remembered too late to ask for that one word, and now she was truly his wife.

Grey was awakened by a stirring in his arms and a slight pulling away of delicious warmth. He was immediately alert, always the light sleeper.

"Kenna?" he murmured.

She sat up, her head brushing the wet tarp. "Yes?"

He ran his hand up her back, lingering on the softness of her flesh. "Are you all right?"

She sighed and lay back down beside him, pulling the blanket up against the damp chill. "I do not know. You tell me. Am I all right?"

He chuckled softly into the darkness, catching her meaning. "You are more than all right. Quite a lot more. Oh, lady, I was surprised. I had no taste for gentle ladies before. I didn't know what I missed."

"After last night, you can still call me lady?"

He moved his face against her hair, breathing in the fragrance of her. "Always a lady to me, and more."

She stirred, pulling away a little, and he sensed the slight distance she put between them. "You need to hear more than that?" he asked softly.

"Since I have been married to you these few short weeks, I knew that I was to be your wife in every aspect. Still, I was unprepared to become Mrs. Fauvereau. Nonetheless, you have what you wanted from the bargain and maybe even more, am I right?"

"Yes. You have given me more than the bargain entailed."

"You are satisfied then." She said it as a statement.

"No," he drawled slowly. "Satisfied? I am satisfied when the laundryman does my shirts right or when the cook prepares my veal the way I like it. Satisfied is not the word I'd choose. But I think you're using it to make the point that you are not. Am I right, Kenna?"

She was surprised at the depth of his perception. "Yes," she said finally.

"I thought, from all you did and said, that you flew as high as we could soar." His voice was quiet.

"Oh!" She sat up and turned to look at him, but she could barely make out his features. "In that, Mr. Fauvereau, I was well pleased. Even, I would say, more than that. This thing between man and woman is something I had only touched the surface of before. I had no concept of what pleasure there was."

He smiled into the darkness. "This is only the beginning for you."

"No." She stated the word firmly, almost as if he were a child in error.

"What?"

"Even though there was pleasure in this act, I shall not give myself to it again."

This time he sat up to stare at her in surprise. "Why?"

"Because there must be more to our marriage than this. Despite the title, I had no wish to go to court or travel in the company of the rich and genteel. I only wanted to find a man who loved me and wanted to live with me. In Scotland, those dreams were snatched away from me before they could begin. So I set sail for America and nurtured the seed of a dream that here I would find a man who would love me. I feared that you might be a man I could not care for, or perhaps even tolerate, but by whom I would do my wifely duties. But then you came and teased me, and I met you as Grey before I met you as my husband. Braic was quite right when he said I admitted I found you handsome. You were quite everything I had hoped for and knew that I would not have; that is why I cannot."

She fell silent and he said nothing, then, "I still don't understand. You say you can't love me because I am what you desired?"

"I am so embarrassed that I said those things. The words came by themselves."

He reached over, caressing her face with his fingers. "I need to know you, lady. I like hearing you talk of things that are important to you. I need you to explain."

"Don't you understand, Grey? I turned away many suitors, oblivious to their hurt. Yet once I tasted rejection, and it was bitter. With you, I have come farther down this road than with any other, because we became one only hours ago. And now, too late, I can see my folly. I could come to love you. When you take me as your wife, I can put no wall between us to protect me. And that pride which I forgot in fear last night has come back doublefold this morning. I cannot give myself to a man who does not love me."

Again she was embarrassed by her candid words. But once before, she had waited too long for a pledge of love. Grey was silent. She pulled away, numbly wrapping the blanket around her.

"I admire your honesty," she said with a stone-straight voice. She began looking for her chemise, which had been discarded during the night.

Suddenly he grabbed her and jerked her beneath him, his weight pinning her. His mouth came down over hers, and she began to struggle, writhing against his naked chest. But he held her helpless, smothering her with his mouth until she was spent. She lay icily beneath him and he drew back, looking at her in the dull light of dawn.

"Damn you, woman!" he said. "Is that the price? A few words to sell yourself to me?"

She glared at him with venom, regretting that she had shared her deepest feelings. "Yes! Yes, blackguard, it is! And credit has been given once. Just do not try to borrow again on an unpaid debt! Get your hands off me." The last was a command.

"Don't forget that I own you; by law you are my property."

"Then take what is yours, rogue! Only expect no response from me."

His mouth came down over hers, rough, forceful,

75

and demanding. Her lips were bruised, and she fought with all her being to stifle any response that her body might give. She lay like ice as tears stung her eyes.

Grey pulled back, cursing vilely. She chose that moment to jerk free and scurry from beneath the canvas. He lunged for her but snatched empty air. He ran after her white silken body, managing to grab her and pull her to him. She squirmed and fought for air as he held her lithe form next to the steel of his own frame.

"Let me go," she warned in a panther growl, but he would not.

"Don't try to escape me, Kenna! You are my woman, and I will have you." He dragged her back into the tent, throwing her down on the bedrolls where they had become one during the night. "I don't like meeting demands, woman!"

"Then make none of me."

"I am simply to give up the taste of flesh that you offered once, and live without it?"

"There are other women," she managed, a sob creeping into her voice.

"Damn you, Kenna," he said quietly. "I have had other women. But I don't want another. I want you."

"It is only an infatuation. You have won once; why do you want to win again? Always to conquer, never to concede." She was shaking now, and she pulled the blankets tightly about her as she spoke.

"The others were infatuations. But not you. I want you, Kenna." He spoke each word slowly. "If love is what you want, you have it. I admit defeat." He pulled the shivering woman into his arms. Her sharp tongue had dealt more blows than the fouler cursing of spurned harlots, and he was anxious for the battle of wills between them to end.

"Yes, Kenna. I could easily love you. Isn't love the word our actions spoke of hours ago? I have talked of desire, but in this instance love and desire are the same."

Oh, but they were not the same! His words fell short of her expectations, and the safeguard she so needed. Grey talked of desire and love as if they were one, yet to her mind they were far apart. There had been desire in her veins for this man, yet she did not love him. Could it ever come? Love was the caring, tender nurturing of kind consideration. Desire was the want of that person's touch. Desire and love belonged together, but they were not always found together. How could she expect this man ever to love her—to care for her with those most tender feelings—when he said his lust for her was love? He twisted the words until she was not sure exactly what he had said. He surrendered too easily, and her mind thought of another man. Glen had also spoken of love, only to turn from her at the last. Grey had spoken too soon; she could not trust him.

Kenna pulled away from the warmth of his arms, from the feelings he stirred within her. I must not surrender to this man again, she thought.

Grey stiffened as she left his arms, bewildered that she now lay with her back to him. Had he not given her what she asked for? With a curse, he left his bedroll, angrily pulling on his clothing.

As the horizon lightened he went to the horses, getting them ready for the day's journey.

Chapter V

A COYOTE CRIED an eerie howl from a rocky perch and startled a jackrabbit scurrying across the path they traveled. The road ascended, climbing upward into the craggy Owyhees. Kenna loved the woodland atmosphere with the splashing miniature falls that made gulleys in the road. The higher atmosphere gave birth to a multitude of cliff flowers and tansy bush, and the air was sweeter and less dry. The sky was still overcast, but there had been little rain; instead, a wind whipped about them, stinging Kenna's face with sand. She turned up the collar of her coat and brought the hat even lower to help shelter her eyes.

Grey glanced over at her, recalling the pleasures wrought so recently by her soft body. Those gentle curves clung in his memory like the taste of a heady wine. His anger had abated.

He had been furious with her demands. That she would sell herself to him for words of love had kindled an angry flame. Although he desperately wanted to possess her, he was not about to concede to her by lying about his feelings.

Kenna glanced at the man riding next to her and saw that his eyes were on her. She looked away, staring down the twisting road. The words of the night before had become a blur in her thoughts, but there were other sharp memories. She could not forget the masculine roughness of his hands and the heated press of his kiss. His caresses were all she had ever hoped for from a man, yet his words were so wrong. She was wary of her husband. Trust was a fragile thread that must be strengthened over time. I must give him time, she thought to herself. Perhaps when we get to this city in the hills, there will be time for us to work things out.

Two mule deer turned and stared, their tall ears pricked up in the air and their white noses twitching as Kenna and Grey passed by. Farther on, they saw cattle grazing in the mountain foliage and they passed octagonal corrals of rough wood. It was the first sign of other people, and Kenna eagerly hurried her horse along.

They stopped for lunch in a grassy clearing, eating the last of the food they carried. Grey said they would reach Silver City by sundown, and Kenna was relieved. But then her horse threw a shoe, losing it along the way. And the worst of it was that she had not noticed its loss until the mare began to limp. Grey was angry, but kept his temper in check. Certainly he could not blame her that the mare had lost its shoe.

He swore softly as he examined the horse's sore hoof; he had no choice but to tie the lamed animal to his with a lead rope. He lifted Kenna onto his saddle. Mounting behind her, he slipped his arms around her, resigned to a late arrival at Silver City.

"If we can reach the Bronco Stage Station, we can trade the horses and ride into Silver City tonight."

She sighed, weary to the bone already. He tightened his arms, drinking in the feel of her. She leaned her head back on his shoulder, tilting her chin up to look at him.

"I'm so tired, Grey. Is it really so important to be there today?"

"It is. I wish it weren't! If we'd only had fewer delays and more time . . ."

"I keep forgetting how important this is. I'm just sore and sick of moving."

"You've been sturdier than some men I've known. Not nearly the soft lady I'd thought you'd be," he murmured against her hair. "Rest against me; I'll guide the horse."

She closed her eyes and allowed his strength to comfort her as they traveled the winding and rutted road.

Grey smiled as he imagined the faces of the people in Silver City when he produced this beautiful bride. Sadie, Jess, Murphy Duke, and Maryetta. He lingered a bit over that last name. She would not find his bringing a bride to be a triumph. The pretty Frenchwoman who had found his favor often in the past would not enjoy meeting the beautiful Lady M'ren. It would be an interesting confrontation. Maryetta had met her match without even knowing it. He looked down at the woman in his arms who slept in innocence. That word described her well; except in the depths of passion, Kenna was a lady. She would not like meeting the woman who boasted of being his mistress. Perhaps he could protect her from that knowledge until he won her love.

Kenna awoke to coming darkness. She tried to rub the grit from the mountain winds from her face. The fine sand was everywhere, and she leaned forward, blinking it from her lashes. She tried to stretch her back but winced.

"How much farther?"

"A few more bends and we'll be at the stage station. You can rest there for a few minutes until I exchange the horses."

She nodded, too tired to talk. Finally she saw a squat, four-sided building with a flat front. Grey reined in the horse in front of it. He let her slide down, then followed.

A man opened the door and Grey greeted him, as he led Kenna inside. "I need fresh horses, Clem!"

"I can't believe it's you! We been keepin' watch for three weeks now! They give up on you in Silver. Duke's burnin' your deed at midnight." He turned and stared at Kenna, trying to look beneath the grime. "This her?"

"It is."

"She don't look like she's gonna make it." He squinted at her.

"She's tougher than she looks. Now, about horses?"

"I'll get 'em. But you sit your wife down and give her some o' them beans while I'm gone. They're bettin' strong in Silver and half o' them is in a misery 'cause you ain't showed," he said over his shoulder as he went out into the wind.

Kenna was too tired to make sense of the old-timer's words. She sank into a chair and moaned as her saddle sores came in contact with wood. Grey came over with some beans, eating from his own bowl.

"Try to eat," he said. She forced down a few bites and gave up.

"I'm too tired. Can't you go on without me? I'm sure that nice man won't mind if I spend the night."

He knelt down and looked into her face. "Kenna, if I show up without you, I'll lose The Bank."

"I don't understand," she said dully. "It can't be that important."

"It is. If I don't come to The Bank with my wife before today ends, I will lose everything." He touched her cheek. "You've come this far."

She closed her eyes for a moment and sighed. Then she opened them and looked at her rugged husband. "All the days of travel are catching up with me. But I can still go on, if it's so important to you."

He leaned forward and kissed her. "That's my brave lady. It isn't that much farther."

Clem darted into the building. "I gave you my fastest horses. I'll feed and bed down yours once you've left. My money's been on you, Grey, and I hope you win. It's gettin' dark, though, and it ain't easy goin' even in daylight."

"I know the road like my own street. Thanks, Clem, and cross your fingers."

He pulled Kenna to her feet and led her outside, lifting her onto the back of a horse that snorted its excitement to go. "It's getting dark," she said worriedly.

"Just stay behind me. We'll need to go fast, so just let the horse follow my lead."

He mounted up and snapped the reins; his horse darted forward and hers followed suit. Her fingers ached as she tried to maneuver the reins, yet she could not control the headstrong horse as it took its willful lead, following only the flanks of the other horse. She clung to the beast as its hooves thundered beneath her, whipping her through the mountain air.

The cloudy sky cut off any moonlight, and flashes of lightning lit their way, threatening a new deluge. When the rain came down in stinging nettles against their faces, their horses slowed, much to Kenna's relief. Visibility on the road that Grey knew so well was impossible. The horses had to pick their way around the ruts that were now thick with mud.

It was late when they reached the road around the jagged peak of War Eagle Mountain; the going was very slow, the horses' hooves sinking in the mire. Grey urged them on as the rain eased, and the beasts heaved and snorted as they worked against the weather.

Suddenly the road surged downward, winding into a long and narrow valley where lights glinted in buildings, flickering beacons of warmth beckoning to riders. Kenna spurred her horse on, as anxious as Grey to reach this final destination.

The mining town boasted several rows of saloons, but one held a packed house. Every chair was filled, and many people had to stand. Talk and cigar smoke were heavy in the air. The crowd was divided in half by an imaginary line. On one side was a jubilant group, who talked animatedly, voices growing louder with laughter and bits of song. In their center, was a small man clad in a worn black velvet jacket, a scarlet brocade vest, and a fancy neck stock. Small of

stature, with a wiry frame, Murphy Duke was the
most exultant of all. He sat at a table, his legs
propped up to belie his nervousness. His small, close-
set eyes darted often to his pocket watch then back to
the paper in his hands, which would so easily ignite
on the tip of his cigar. Yet he dared not, his eyes
keeping continual track of the time, while he
grinned and ran his hand over his slicked-down,
enamel-black hair. As victory seemed imminent, his
supporters grew more boisterous.

Liquor also moved with ease on the other side of
the room. This morose crowd sat glumly at their
tables, listening to the hubbub across the room and
drinking. There were more souls in misery, especially two who sat at the center table. One was a
woman of slightly heavy build, middle-aged, and
with a prettiness that was somewhat earthy. No
doubt when she smiled that basic something came
through which would make her likable to anyone.
But at this point she had forgotten how to smile. She
wore a yellow silk dress that looked as if it were the
last effort at a brave facade in a losing battle.

Next to her sat a young man who was putting
away more liquor than he had ever consumed. Of
slender build, with brown hair and eyes, dressed soberly, he was taking the loss badly despite never
having placed a bet. He watched as Duke took his cigar, put it to the corner of the paper, and watched it
singe.

"It isn't time yet, Murphy Duke!" he called out
with verve unusual for him. "We've got twenty-five
more minutes left according to the piano clock, so
keep your cigar butt away from that contract!"

Duke glared at the young man, knowing he was no

threat, but he caught the angry glare of the large mob across the room. He made some rude remark that brought a laugh from the rowdy group around him, but laid the heavy parchment down on the table.

"That's telling him, Jess!"

Duke looked back in anger, picking up the deed. "There ain't no use in waitin', Jessie boy! You think he's gonna come waltzin' through those doors before the day's up? It's been a year and he ain't shown. A boy who's supposed to be as bright as you shoulda figured out by now that the bet's been lost." He held it up, the contract catching lamplight, as he touched his short cigar to the already singed corner. The losers gasped as it caught, the fire licking upward as he dropped it onto the table, the contract curling into black ash.

"Just in time," a resonant voice said from the doorway. "I'm glad to have our contract ended, Murphy."

Heads whipped to the doorway and there were loud gasps. Jess bolted from his chair. "It's Grey!"

His name spread through the saloon like wildfire. A great commotion arose, with shouts of protest or joy as the crowd stared at the man leaning casually in the doorway.

He was dirty, in muddied clothes, with water dripping from his hat brim. His face was in need of a shave and his boots were covered with thick mud from pulling a horse through the drenched streets. But, undoubtedly, it was still Grey Fauvereau.

Those who had been drowning their sorrows were now joyful, cheering in ecstasy at this turn of events, while the erstwhile jubilant crowd stood around uncertainly. Murphy Duke stood on a tabletop, spilling drinks in his effort to gain the needed height. He shouted for quiet, pointing an accusing finger at his old partner.

"He may be here," he bellowed. "But that don't mean he won!"

"You don't know Fauvereau!" someone shouted out, and ribald humor came alive in the air.

Duke glared at the crowd, but someone shouted, "Don't leave us hangin'! Did you do it or not?"

Grey gave a curt nod, and a cheer rose up. "Where's the proof?" Duke demanded.

Grey went out the doors and returned leading a reluctant woman behind him. In a filthy pair of pants and hat, with hair falling in muddy strands from beneath the hat and a face splattered with dirt, she quieted the crowd as nothing could have. Two hundred and forty people stared at her in dead silence as Grey led her to a chair where she shakily sat down.

"This is my wife," he said casually. "Lady Kenna M'ren from Scotland."

The silence was broken by a solitary laugh, high-pitched and feminine. Kenna looked up to see a pretty woman dressed in a lovely blouse of starched lace and a full skirt of blue velvet. Her light brown hair was piled on her head, and her pale blue eyes looked with derision at Kenna. No one else laughed, though, staring in silence at the young woman who looked down at the filthy riding gloves she held in her blistered hands. The mud hid the blush of humiliation that spread up her cheeks.

The fair woman came up to Grey, placing her hand on his muddy jacket and kissing him. She pulled back and smiled prettily. "Welcome home, Grey. And congratulations on winning your bet."

Kenna felt a sick wrenching inside, biting her lip and tasting the muddy grit. "Who says he's won?" Duke cried out feverishly. "She don't look like no lady to me!"

"Neither would Maryetta, if she would've come through all those miles in the rain," the lady in yellow silk said, looking at the woman by Grey's side. There was snickering, and Maryetta stared at the older woman who poked fun at her. Kenna only dared a glance, humiliated to tears at her filthy appearance before all these people who were Grey's friends.

"She's a lady, tried and true. She's a daughter of an earl who lived in Scotland."

"When did you go to Scotland?" Duke challenged.

"I didn't. She came to America a few weeks ago."

"Ha!" Duke cried triumphantly. "You was to be wed months ago!"

"We were. By proxy."

Duke squinted at him. "What?"

"We were married in April, in plenty of time, but with someone standing in for each of us since there was an ocean between us. It is all very legal."

"Done all the time in the old world countries," Jess said, stepping forward. Everyone listened to him, thinking him one of the town's best educated men. "Grey is right, it is legal. And since he's here before the fourth day of July, it appears he is the winner."

A cheer went up but Duke waved his arms. "It's a trick! Some dirty dealin' has been done here, and at my expense! There ain't no way that you can prove she's a real titled lady and that this proxy stuff is legal!" He was practically hysterical.

"Actually, Duke, I can prove it all. McDoo will be arriving on the stage with all the papers: her birth certificate which states she is the daughter of Earl and Lady Cedric M'ren, the proxy papers, and the witnessed signatures. I'm sorry, Duke, but The Bank is mine."

A cheer of approval went up again, and then angry shouts for the sheriff to step forward. A tall, lean man in leather breeches came out of the throng where he had been watching the proceedings. Known as an honest man, he had been impartial through all the betting; the crowd turned to him for a decision.

"It appears to me," he said slowly, "That Fauvereau just might have won this bet. But we'd better wait and see what McDoo has to say. He's our town's best lawyer."

"McDoo is pulling for Fauvereau," one of Duke's friends shouted.

The sheriff nodded. "I guess he is. But he's no shyster, and I'll believe his words if he can back them up with documents. I'll ride out to meet the stage tomorrow, just to make sure there's no fooling around." He looked straight at Duke, who was agitated to the point of hysteria.

"It ain't fair! He's just used trickery, that's all! Call off the bet!"

The sheriff leveled a stern glance at Duke. "It's your own fault, Murphy. You bragged about your titled ancestors till this town was sick of it. So when Fauvereau bet that he could win a titled wife and bring her back married, and all in one year, you shouldn't have taken him up on it. But your pride got the best of you, and it looks like you'll be losing your half of the saloon."

Kenna's exhaustion was quickly dispelled by a surge of adrenaline which made her heart race. The words the sheriff was speaking were sinking like lead within her. She saw nothing of the elaborate interior of the saloon with its fine furnishings and thick draperies. Instead her eyes were locked on the huge mirror upon which was lettered in fancy gold writing arched neatly across the glass: THE BANK. Realization felt like the sting of a wasp, the pain of it smarting her very soul.

Grey saw his slender wife, muddied and tired, look suddenly wide awake as she bolted from her chair, heading for the door. He ran after her and the crowd followed, stepping onto the boarded walkways.

"Kenna!" He grabbed her arm and she turned around, swinging her fist at him, which he only narrowly avoided. He had no desire to have a brawl in front of these people who were already laughing at the comical scene. He caught her up, throwing her over his shoulder so hard that it knocked the wind out of her. He marched through the mud, down the street, and the crowd caught up the excitement, whooping and following them, catching up pans and sticks to bang together. When Grey reached the porch of the large, white Idaho Hotel, he set her down. She tried to move away but he caught her wrist, pulling her inside and up the stairs to the second story despite the startled look of the proprietor's wife. He dragged her down the narrow hall, and the noisy crowd outside followed, knowing where his room was. They stood below his window, banging pots and singing songs, as Grey led Kenna into the room, shutting the door. She stood stiffly in the middle of the room, staring at him with no emotion in her face.

"They're giving us a shivaree," he said. "In celebration of our marriage."

She said nothing. She began to shiver with cold and rage, wrapping her arms about herself. He went to the window and threw it open. "Go home!" he called. His fingers quickly lit a lamp, dispelling the dark.

"Don't you want a friendly shivaree?" a shout came.

"I want to be left alone," he called over the din.

"We ain't goin' nowhars! We want to celebrate with you!"

He shook his head. "A round of drinks, on me, for everyone over at The Bank!"

A general hooray went up and the crowd immediately dispersed, though Jess still stood beneath the window. He smiled cockily at his boss. "Anything before I leave?"

"Our horses need seeing to."

"Right away. And congratulations on your marriage."

"Thanks." Grey smiled, feeling the intoxication of winning spread through his veins. He closed the window and turned around to see Kenna staring at him. He felt his euphoria evaporate.

"Kenna," he said in a tone of explanation.

"The bank you own isn't really a bank," she stated. "It is a bar. A saloon."

"I named it The Bank, a good place for miners to deposit their gold. I did not have the heart to tell you I

owned a gambling palace when you thought that
The Bank was really a bank."

"You had to have a wife, a titled wife, to win a
bet," she stated flatly.

"Murphy Duke is an unbearable little weasel, as
you saw. I came to Silver City with dreams, but no
money. He was a miner who had money to stake. He
gave me the money, but I was the one who made The
Bank the best saloon in the territory. Every week, it
pulls in more than his original stake, yet he has refused to let me buy him out. Instead, he sits by while
I do everything that makes it a success. The only way
to get him was through a bet, because he is a compul-
sive gambler. The man is also a braggart, telling
everyone that he is royally descended from a real
duke. When I offered my half of The Bank if I
couldn't bring back a titled bride in one year, he just
was not able to resist. And now I've won!"

She glared at him with venom. "You deceived
me."

He stepped near. "No, Kenna."

She lashed out at him, her fist striking his chest.
"You are a liar!" She hit him again and he stood,
taking her blows. "You parade me before those people when I look worse than I have ever looked, so
that that woman could laugh at me!" She struck
again, hitting him with all her strength. "You
dragged me through all these horrid miles, through
rain and dirt and Indians, so that you could shame
me before those people!"

She gasped for breath and he took her fists, holding them in his own. "I admit your anger is justified,
Kenna."

She moved away from him, sobs emerging as she

91

put her hands to her mouth. He came to her, pulling off her soaked riding jacket and blouse though she struggled against him. He unbuttoned her pants, pushing her back on the bed, despite her cursing and name-calling, as he stripped off the last of her wet clothing. He arranged the sheets and blanket around her as she lay sobbing into the pillow. He stood staring down at her, waiting for her tears to subside.

"You're just tired, lady. You'll feel better tomorrow."

She turned and glared at him, brushing angrily at her tears. "Oh, no, blackguard! Tomorrow I annul this marriage!"

He started to smile, but it faded as he saw she was in dead earnest. "You can't annul a marriage that's been consummated, love," he said softly. Could she forget that wild ecstasy between them?

"Oh, no! Never again, Fauvereau!"

He sat down beside her, stroking her wet hair. "Kenna," he pleaded.

With her last strength, she turned and shoved him off the bed, her violent action surprising him. He watched as she turned away from him, pulling the blankets about her as she sobbed into the pillow, the heartbreaking sound reverberating through him. Her sobs abated as exhaustion overwhelmed her at last, and she sank into a dreamless sleep.

He stood staring down at his muddied, beautiful bride with a feeling of unhappiness. He had assumed that once he had won her over and taken her as his, she would forget his discrepancies. How could he have forgotten what pride she had, and her deep sense of honor?

He pulled off his own muddied clothing, tossing it

in a heap, and climbed into the other side of the bed. He wanted to take his sleeping wife and cradle her in his arms. But even in sleep she was pulled away from him, as if forbidding his touch. He lay on his back after dousing the table lamp and stared into the darkness. Despite his exhaustion, sleep was slow in coming.

Chapter VI

SHOTS, LAUGHING SHOUTS, and racing horse hooves startled Kenna awake. She glanced around a small room furnished with a high wardrobe, night table, and bed with a tall wooden headboard. There was a straight-backed chair in the corner and a long oval mirror with wooden legs opposite it. There was no carpet on the hardwood floor. A delicate lamp on the night table, a porcelain pitcher and bowl painted with roses, and two framed watercolors saved the room from being stark.

She had been too exhausted and furious to see anything last night. She sat up in bed, casting off the patchwork quilt only to find that she was wearing nothing. With a groan, she remembered that Grey had removed her clothes as she sobbed into the pillow. The memory of yesterday's events left a bitter aftertaste. She thrust her mind away from it until she could find the strength to face it. She looked for her clothes, but they were gone, as was Grey. She went to the wardrobe and found a single shirt, which she pulled on. Was this his way of keeping her here, fearing that she might run off if he wasn't watching her? He had nothing to fear from that! The rogue would settle with her before she would think of leaving. Her muscles ached, her fingers stiff as she buttoned the shirt before the oval mirror. Her hair was dull with dried dirt, and her face had a film of grit as well as mud smears. No wonder the woman in the saloon had laughed; she cringed, remembering it. How could he have shamed her and betrayed her in so many ways? She had given herself to him, confided tender things to him, and now she felt unsure. How could she trust a man who was not proving trustworthy?

There was more commotion outside and she pulled back the thick green velvet window drapes. Bright light immediately flooded the room. She looked out on a balcony that faced the main street. The town had come alive with a variety of people milling about, avoiding the horses that raced through the streets. She caught a glimpse of bright blue sky and a few wispy clouds, amazed that the only sign of rain was the drying mud in the street. From the angle of the sun, now quite high, she guessed that she had slept late.

She let the drapes fall back into place as she heard the door open. Grey came in, dressed in clean clothes and looking devilishly handsome. She saw that she'd forgotten how attractive he was—deceptively attractive. She stared at him with cool disdain. He tried a smile.

"So you're finally awake. You slept long, though you needed it." As she remained silent, he continued, "Would you like to bathe?"

She stood, scantily dressed in his shirt, which revealed her long and slender legs, not moving or speaking.

"I'll bring the bath in," he said, knowing that she really did want to wash.

She would show no sign of gratitude, though she anticipated a long soak. It was something she had wanted for weeks.

Grey returned, rolling in the tub. She stared at it in dismay. The tubs at home were deep and long so that one could recline and soak in comfort. But this was not as big as a washtub! It was made of tin, round with sloping sides so that one could sit on the rim, feet in the center, and wash as best as possible. She groaned as she looked at it and her eagerness disappeared. Had she anticipated coming to Silver City to be back in civilization? What a foolish error.

"It's the best we have, Kenna. I'll bring up the buckets of water."

It took three trips with the hot heavy buckets. He let out a breath of relief as he set the last of them down. "I've brought you some scented soap." He handed her a round ball that smelled like lavender. Kenna held it in her palm, staring at him and the tiny peace offering given with boyish pride. It was not enough.

"My brush and comb are in the drawer there. I'll leave you to your bath while I go get you some clothes."

She said nothing, ignoring his casual air. He left, shutting the door quietly behind him, and she finally moved.

She used a whole bucket of water just to rinse the dried mud from her hair, finally lathering it with the soap until the last of the grit was gone. Then she used the rest of the water to rinse off her hair, wet down her body, lather it up and rinse off. The last bucket of water was cold, and she shivered despite the day's warmth as she caught up the towel he had tossed onto the chair. Although her bath had not been the warm soak she had hoped for, it still refreshed her. She dried her hair with the towel, pulled on his shirt again, and brushed her hair. It took a while to get all the snarls out, and it dried by the time she was done. It fell down her back in a flow of silk, back to its auburn color.

The door opened again and Grey came in with a bundle, tossing it on the bed. "I hope these will suit you. You might not like my taste." He smiled at her but she said nothing as she looked through the package. "I had to judge your size from memory," he said, coming near and slipping his hands about her slender waist.

She pulled away from him as if he were a stranger. "Let go of your anger," he said quietly. "You've reason to pout, I'll grant you that. But don't keep it up too long."

"Pouting? Is that what you think I do?"

"So you'll speak now. Good. Get dressed and we can go eat."

"I'm going nowhere with you," she said icily.

He stared at her with iron in his eyes. "Can you tell me how long you plan to stay mad so that I can work around it?"

"I never forgive those who betray me."

"I didn't betray you, Kenna. Would you have given your all to save a saloon? No, but you would have for my bank. You were too respectable for me to rely on."

"So you lied."

"I held out some of the truth and told you some."

"You misled me."

"Would you have given as much as you had if I'd explained that the circumstances were . . . shady?"

"You'll never know," she said distantly.

"I know you're a lady with too much ethics for the race. Tell the truth, Kenna. Would you have gone along with me if you'd known the facts?"

"Had you been gentleman enough to write the truth, that I was the end to a joke, the fool bet upon, I would not have left Scotland."

"The bet was not like that! It wasn't meant to ridicule you; I'm not so cruel as that."

"Cruel enough, Mr. Fauvereau."

"So it's back to that! And will you forget what happened between us, as well as my first name?" There was mockery in his voice.

"I will try."

"You'll never forget, Kenna." He grabbed her and pulled her into his arms, kissing her mouth with all the violent passion he felt. There was no use in fighting this man, or his power that swept down upon her like the attack of an eagle. When finally he released her, she pulled away, turning her back to him.

"I'm not that easy to be rid of," he said. "If you will dress, we'll go to The Bank. They're having a big breakfast to meet you."

"I don't want to meet anyone," she said over her shoulder.

"What will you do, stay in this room forever? Concede to me and put an end to your anger. I conceded to you once," he said softly at the back of her neck. She could feel his closeness and remembered the words he had spoken, words that had come too quickly, and carelessly. Obviously, there had been no truth in anything he had said. "Come with me. I want you by my side. The coach will probably be coming through today."

She turned and looked at him. "Good," she said. "I want to talk to Fergus."

He gave her a funny look. She did not plan to ask legal advice about an annulment! Surely those words had only been spoken in anger, and he did not wish to bring them up now.

"While I'm dressing, will you purchase me some hairpins? I can't go with my hair streaming down my back."

He left and she sorted through the articles wrapped in brown paper. She pulled on a low-cut silk chemise. It barely covered her bosom, and she looked in the mirror at its skimpy fit. It was delicate and beautiful, and she was surprised that he had found something like it in this forsaken little city. She gasped as she held up the corset. Of black silk with slender bone stays, it was decorated with pink ribbons. She had never seen anything like it anywhere. She wondered where on earth Grey had purchased the clothing. The pantalets were very delicate also, and she stepped into them, fastening them at the back as was the fashion. Then she cinched in the ties of the corset, holding her breath. It pinched in her small waist and thrust her chest up in a daring display. She caught sight of herself in the mirror and drew in her breath at the provocative woman it reflected. Her suspicions about the clothing were beginning to jell.

She opened a box to find silk stockings, which she

pulled on under the lace edge of the pantalets. Then she lifted out the shoes. Dainty gray kid with small round buttons running up the sides, they were lower cut and had more of a heel than she was used to. She looked for a buttonhook in the drawer, found one, and fastened them. She was bending over the slip and dress on the bed when the door swung open and Grey stepped inside. She stood up and whirled around to find him frozen in the doorway.

He slammed the door behind him and stood boldly appraising his wife in the slender pantalets and re- vealing black corset. A slow smile came to his face.

"Where did you get these clothes?" she asked, and he did not miss the accusation in her voice.

"At the best dress shop in Silver. Don't you like them?"

"They aren't what I would have picked."

He laughed. "No, lady, they aren't what you would have chosen. But I like them well enough for both of us. Or, rather, I like you in them. You are quite the temptress."

She ignored the enticement of his words, pulling on the slip edged in delicate lace which hid the black corset. Then she held up the dress. Of delicate lawn, it was neither pink nor orange, but the soft color in between. She pulled it on over her head and slipped her arms in. It buttoned up the side and fit her per- fectly. The neck was square, edged with white lace, and insets of the same lace decorated the bodice and sleeves. It was really quite lovely, perfect for her col- oring.

"I knew you would look beautiful in it," Grey said. "I sorted through twenty dresses until I found it."

"I'm surprised at the fit," she said, staring into the mirror.

He stepped behind her and she saw his darker reflection. "I had the seamstress take in the sides so that it would be right." At her inquiring glance, he smiled. "I know you better than you think." He slipped his hands about her slender waist but she moved away, picking up the brush and working with her hair. She coiled it into a soft swirl at the nape of her neck, securing it with the hairpins he had bought.

"Ready?" he asked, opening the door.

She answered by stepping out and letting him lead her down the narrow hallway. It was wallpapered in rose with a red fleur-de-lis design, and illuminated by lamps of tulip-shaped glass. They turned and went down the steep stairwell and through a lobby that was surprisingly well furbished, with a large caged desk. She caught only a glimpse of it as he led her out into bright daylight.

There were men riding by on horses and much tumult. Grey held out his arm, indicating the city. "Well, what do you think?"

"Is it always this noisy?" she said coolly.

"It's Independence Day. They're celebrating and having races."

"Independence from what?"

"British repression. We're celebrating our liberty from England's rule. And our birthday. Our nation is ninety-two today."

"And I wondered why it's barbaric," she said so quietly that he hardly caught her words. She wondered about him. He took all her coldness and rude barbs affably. She would not easily forgive his careless cruelty. She might go with him now and do his bidding, but that was only a facade. Until he could learn the meaning of common honesty and respect for another's feelings, she would not make anything easy for Grey Fauvereau.

Kenna glanced around her. The town was in a long and narrow valley, with streets going up into the hills; there were many buildings, some obviously thrown together in haste. The mountains were green with bush and fir, layers of emerald hue marred by waste from the mines. And these same peaks sloped up on either side, hovering over the town.

Grey led her along a board walkway and then across the street. She saw people stop and stare at her as they whispered to each other. They came to a creek that ran through the town and crossed a bridge.

"This is Jordan Creek. The miners built the town right on the place where they discovered gold."

She said nothing, staring instead at the building they neared. They had passed several saloons, but this one was obviously the most impressive. Its two-story facade was faced in elaborate woodwork with scalloped layers and a balcony of delicate spindles. The steeply slanted roof was shingled. A sign in elegant black etching proclaimed: THE BANK. There were windows covered with decorative shutters, and two double doors dominated the front. These had insets of beautiful stained glass and sported crystal doorknobs. It would have been elegantly impressive in San Francisco, in Silver City it was doubly so. She understood suddenly why Grey had been so proud of it and so determined to keep it. She braced herself against the feeling. She would not allow the man sympathy.

He pushed the door open and she stepped inside. It was twice as beautiful within, the walls papered in dark gold flocking. The long bar was of polished mahogany with a footrail that was graced every few feet with brass spitoons. There was a huge mirror behind a carved facade with bowed cupboards that held liquor bottles and boxes of fine cigars. Sitting on the shelf at the base of the mirror was a large model of a Yankee clipper and a silver money register. Bottles and ceramic jars, doubled in the mirror, peeked between spindles. A burly fellow tended the selling of whiskey, and people sat about in leather chairs or at tables. All the furniture was of the finest quality, and there was woodwork around doors and windows.

There was one long table sectioned off by a low wood railing at which a few people waited. There was much excitement in the air. Kenna surveyed the excited throng with dismay. Grey had said some friends wanted him to come to breakfast. Was he friends with every miner in the city? She never would have left the hotel room if she had known his intent was to display her publicly. Was the man never to be believed? She was ready to leave when they caught sight of her. The talk ceased and heads whipped to the door. The room became dead still. Kenna saw the pretty woman who had laughed at her before and had come to greet Grey with such obvious intimacy. She could not turn and leave now. Instead, she stood elegantly serene, looking back at the crowd. The woman looked at Kenna in bewilderment before the truth dawned. She sat down, her face going a bit pale.

Someone let out a long, low whistle, and Grey smiled. "You remember my wife, Lady M'ren?" he asked casually.

A murmur went through the throng. They stared at the beautiful woman with auburn tresses swept away from a face with high cheekbones and long, stormy eyes. Her gentle mouth was held primly, her hands daintily clasped in front of her. Grey led her to the long table and they watched her accept the chair he pulled out.

The talk came up again, but this time they turned to the discussion of facts. "I don't need to see no papers from McDoo," a man's voice carried across the room. "Here's the five dollars I owe you, Shorty. You win!"

There was some laughter that sent a coral blush into Kenna's cheeks. Apparently one only had to dress like a lady to be considered one.

A woman at the end of the table stood up and glared at the crowd of onlookers. "Mind your business, fellows! This is a lady sitting here, and you have no call to do your antics in her presence."

The men looked away a bit ashamed, and she felt her tensions begin to ease. She smiled in quiet appreciation at the woman, who said, "When you come to the West, it's a different way of life. Men just love looking at a pretty woman. Now you just sit down and relax while I get this breakfast going. Chen!" she shouted. "Bring out the food!" She turned to Kenna again. "By the by, my name is Sadie, and I help manage The Bank for Mr. Fauvereau."

"Thank you, Sadie," Kenna said politely.

At that moment the doors into the kitchen swung open and a line of Chinese waiters emerged with plates of mounded food. She had never seen so much set down at once. All the people began to fill their plates.

Grey introduced her to Jess Banes, a quiet young man in a dark suit who was her husband's assistant, as well as others. He introduced Maryetta Gaylor last. The activity at the table paused as the two women studied each other.

So, Kenna thought, I was not a fool to suspect intimacy between Grey and this woman. Everyone here knows and has been waiting for this meeting. She pushed back an ache that threatened, forbidding it.

"It is nice to meet you," Kenna said with charm.

Maryetta had also managed to gain her composure. The time for falling apart was later. She smiled, forcing her lips into a carefree pose. "We have long awaited your arrival. Welcome to Silver." How could this possibly be the bedraggled, mud-drenched girl that Grey had brought to win his bet? Last night she had been elated at his return, hoping with all her heart that if he showed, it would be without a wife. When he arrived with that poor specimen, she knew that he had only married to win his bet.

How well she knew his desire to win! She had disdained his affection in the beginning, almost longer than she could stand, just because she had sensed that Grey loved a challenge. His bringing home a wife was no different than if he had arrived with a thoroughbred horse. At least, that was what she had believed last night. She had been convinced that their relationship could continue, wife or no. But in the face of Kenna's beauty, she felt that conviction crumble.

Kenna smiled at the welcome proffered by the

other pretty woman. "Thank you. I hope to get to know it." The woman has poison in her eyes, Kenna thought. And why not? It is obvious she has been his mistress. And it has not been a secret; of that I am certain!

Everyone was watching, she realized. They were waiting for the confrontation, and she was left with the choice of either displaying the embarrassment she felt or playing the part of the fool, blind to the truth. Renewed anger filled her and she glanced at Grey. He had dragged her before these people, to bear their stares and whispers. And then he had added the further humiliation of compromising her this way. She was certain Grey Fauvereau had no sense of decency or propriety at all.

Her thoughts were cut short by polite queries from Jess which she answered kindly. The meal proceeded. For Kenna it was difficult to eat. Grey leaned near, whispering to her. "You see? Coming here has not been so difficult."

Maryetta nearly choked on the ham as she saw Grey lean near Kenna, whispering to her. And in return she smiled up at him, her words only for his ears. None of them missed her hand on his sleeve or her innocent smile.

With that same innocence she spoke softly to Grey. "Once again you play me for the fool, seating me at the table with your mistress."

He hardly believed her words had come from such a loving countenance. He set his fork down, shading his surprise.

"Kenna," he said softly.

She took a dainty bite of potato. "I am not so blind,

Fauvereau." Only he saw the steel daggers in her eyes.

He leaned back and smiled at her, his hand slipping beneath the table to caress her thigh so near to his. He knew she dared not quit the game she had started. She was seated too closely to move without getting up.

Kenna fought the electrifying urge to bolt from the table and out of his grasp. All the spectators saw was a husband lean near in concern to catch his wife's words with an understanding nod. No one heard them. "Touch what you can for now, blackguard," she said sweetly. "You'll touch me not again."

Grey pulled his hand away, and a few thought they saw a dark expression cross his brow, but it was gone as swiftly as it had come.

The meal was nearing an end, Grey and Kenna no longer talking, when the doors into The Bank were flung open and someone burst in shouting that the stage had been sighted. The miners poured from the saloon while the meal came to a hurried halt. Grey finished his meal with leisure. "Jess?"

"Yes, Grey?"

"Where is Murphy Duke? I haven't seen him since last night."

Jess smiled. "He tried to shoot out the stained glass in the doors but the sheriff stopped him in time, I am glad to say. He took Murphy's guns away, and after that the poor man spent the night drinking and swearing revenge."

"Indeed?" Grey hid a smile.

"He drank himself into a crying stupor and he's sleeping it off at The Queen's Place."

"He's better off at Queenie's." Grey rose, throwing down his napkin as he discarded further thoughts of his old partner. "Ready, my dear?"

"Yes," Kenna said, standing. She would beat this rogue at his own game. Maryetta stood also, having stayed to the end of the meal. "It was nice meeting you."

"Likewise. I am just so happy for Grey that he was able to use your marriage to win his wager. He is very clever," she said coolly. "But I must confess that I'm not surprised he followed through on this new wild adventure. It isn't the first."

"I'm sure," Kenna said with the smile she endeavored to keep from wearing thin.

"You never can tell with reckless men like our Grey. I would not have thought he would give up his freedom just to win a bet. But you are willing to sacrifice for greater gains, aren't you?" She reached up to remove a piece of lint from Grey's collar with such familiarity that it made Kenna want to grate her teeth. Instead she looked at the woman with clear gray eyes.

"You know him well."

"Yes, I do." Maryetta's smile was gone.

"Unfortunately for me, I'm still learning," Kenna said softly. "But Grey assures me he will continue to teach me." Her words, so innocently spoken, told of hidden intimacies that Maryetta had hoped did not exist. Kenna saw her countenance harden.

Despite the insinuating words she had spoken, Kenna was seething, furious at the betrayals and humiliations heaped upon her. If she could simply manage to control her feelings until she reached her brother and McDoo, then all would be well. Despite the strange circumstances of this marriage, there had been nothing said of all the truths Grey had hidden. Most certainly such deceits would be grounds for an annulment!

There was a sudden noise from outside and a man opened the door. "The stage is in, Mr. Fauvereau!"

"I'm coming. Your brother is here, Kenna. If you'll excuse us, Maryetta, Sadie." He nodded at the latter with a smile. He guided his wife outside, his hand about her waist, chuckling softly. "If I had to place money in a fair fight, it would be on you, Kenna."

As the door closed behind them, cutting off the others' view, she pulled away. "Keep your hands off me!" she hissed. She walked ahead of him, back toward the hotel where they had spent the night. There was anger in her stride, and suddenly Grey laughed. The sound reached her, but she did not grant him the favor of an angry glare.

The stagecoach had jerked to a halt in front of the hotel, its large back wheels coated with dried mud. In front, the team of six white horses stood sweating from the long journey, their leather harness and gear creaking. Goods and luggage were hauled down from the top, the strongbox coming down last of all.

Braic and Fergus stood on the board walkway, stretching their stiff, dust-covered limbs. There was an excited mob around the stagecoach and Braic wondered if Silver City were so isolated that each arrival was always greeted with such a commotion. He caught a sudden movement and recognized his sister, beautiful, in a dress more frivolous than any he had ever seen her wear. He smiled at her as she came into his arms.

Katherine Myers

"Braic!" They embraced, the crowd gasping into silence.

"He's holding Fauvereau's wife!" a miner whispered harshly as if the rest of the throng were ignorant of the fact.

Kenna pulled away as the mob watched Fauvereau's approach. Despite his refined exterior, they were aware of his more ruthless side. Much to their surprise, he stepped up, clasping the young man's hand in a friendly welcome.

"How was the trip?" Grey asked Braic.

Braic rolled his eyes heavenward, then grinned stiffly. "I would rather have ridden horseback than be cramped in that little cell with my knees beneath my chin. I had forgotten how truly awful it is to travel by coach."

Grey smiled. "I've done it before, too. Your stiffness will be gone in two or three days." He turned to Jess Banes. "Jess, this is Braic M'ren, Kenna's brother. And you remember lawyer Fergus McDoo."

"Indeed I do." Jess nodded at Fergus. Then he reached his hand out to Braic. "Welcome to Silver. We hope you'll stay."

"I guess I will." He grinned. "You won't be getting me on that stage again."

The listening crowd gleaned the information that the young man who had embraced Fauvereau's wife was in fact his new brother-in-law. Disappointment filled many who had expected a gunfight or a brawl at the very least.

The sheriff had arrived with the stage and nodded at Grey. Then he took his horse to the livery. Grey awaited his return so they could go to the saloon and settle this matter. Kenna had slipped her arm

110

through McDoo's and was leading him away from the noisy throng. She was talking to him in earnest and he pulled back, looking at her in complete surprise. Grey watched his wife.

"Where has Kenna gone?" Braic asked, looking around for her.

"There . . . with McDoo."

"I've not even had a chance to talk to her. I want to know how she fared on the trip, though from her fair looks, I would guess she did well."

"It was not easy, but she gave it all she had."

"And you arrived in time to save The Bank?"

"Yes," Grey said grimly.

"Then where is your spirit of celebration?" Braic asked in surprise.

"It is gone for the moment. I may have won the gamble but I've lost my wife," he said, nodding at McDoo and Kenna. "I believe she is consulting your cousin about an annulment."

"What?"

"Your sister holds her anger for a long time. She is not about to forgive me for letting her believe that she tried to save a real bank instead of a saloon."

"You did not tell her!" There was anger in Braic's voice. "That was very foolish."

"So I've learned." They had walked away and he stared at Kenna. The summer breeze whipped a few long tendrils loose and she brushed the hair off her fair face. She seemed to plead in earnest with McDoo, who was worriedly arguing with her. "As you recommended, I won her over. I thought it was enough at the time."

"Did you explain about the wager then?"

"Actually, she learned about it at the same time that she discovered the true nature of The Bank."

Braic stared at him in disbelief. "I said to win her over before telling her! Not just to gain her favor and assume she would accept the rest."

"She did not take it well."

"I've no doubt!"

"That is why she is talking to Fergus right now."

Braic ran his hand across his brow. "What will you do?"

Grey's stare hardened. "I won't give her up."

"When she sets her mind to something, hell and tide cannot turn it aside."

"But she has no legal recourse," Grey said softly, still watching the earnest play of emotion across his bride's face. "We are husband and wife in more than name."

Braic's anger abated. "I thought you'd be winning her over soon. Though she'll be hell-bent to not make it easy again."

Grey laughed. "So she's said. You know your sister well."

The sheriff appeared again and called to McDoo, who extricated himself from Kenna.

"Do you have the papers that Mr. Fauvereau has spoken of?"

"I do, Sheriff Sampson. Do you want to see them?" The crowd was gathering again.

"I do. But not here in the streets. Let's go back to The Bank since it is the center of the dispute." Everyone nodded in agreement and headed back to the saloon.

Kenna reached Braic's side and he smiled at her. "Will you come to see what happens?"

She shrugged. "Perhaps I can help him lose."

"You cannot mean that."

"It is what the blackguard deserves," she said, a hard note coming into her voice.

"What he did was out of foolishness, not to be cruel. If he did not tell you that The Bank was not really a bank, or that he bought your title to win a wager, it is because he feared to tell you."

"You knew?" She stared at him incredulously.

"Aye, Kenna. I've known since we started up the Columbia."

"He saw fit to tell you, but not his wife?" Her anger was rekindled.

"Would you have listened kindly to the news that he sent clear to Scotland for you so that you could win a wager for him? You, who despise gambling because it, in part, is what ruined Moldarn? I would not blame the bravest man for shying from the task."

"I hate cowardice. And deceit."

"And Grey Fauvereau?" There was silence for a minute.

They were nearing The Bank and Kenna placed her hand on his arm. "Do not take his side in this."

Braic stared up at the large building. He let out a low whistle. "So this is The Bank. No wonder he wanted so badly to keep it."

He opened the door for her, and she stepped in before him to see Fergus McDoo already seated at a table, drawing out the papers. The crowd milled around, looking down at the case of papers in solemn quiet. Grey sent Jess to rouse the drunken Murphy Duke and bring him round, noticing with pleasure that Kenna had returned.

"Well," the sheriff said. "Explain the proof, Mc-Doo."

"This is the marriage certificate. As you can see, Lady Kenna M'ren was wed to Grey Fauvereau in early April, with her brother standing in proxy for Mr. Fauvereau. Here is his half of the certificate which shows it took place in San Francisco. I witnessed this one—note the signature—and the other one is likewise signed. Each has the stamp of a legal justice."

"Can you explain this proxy stuff?" Sampson said.

"It is all very legal, I assure you, as long as both parties participate in the ceremony with someone standing in the stead of their spouse. Braic M'ren stood in for Grey and a Miss Felicia Layton stood in for Kenna."

"Hmm. Well, strange as it is, that does make sense."

"And it was done in April. That was the bet. That in one year Grey could wed a woman with title. From April till April. And then till July fourth to get her here. Both parties did agree that traveling time was only fair. Here is the wager agreement signed by both Grey and Murphy."

"So he's married," someone who had wagered heavily—and wrongly—said. "That doesn't prove her title any!"

While some had believed upon seeing her that she was a true lady, others suggested that Fauvereau had pulled a clever ruse. Would it not have been more simple to find a wife and forge her identity? Especially since Kenna was such a beautiful woman; her looks added fuel to the speculation that her title was a fake.

Fergus withdrew a birth certificate; it looked authentic and had a seal on it. It showed her name, the date and place of her birth, the names of her parents and her father's title. Then he brought out a copy of the county records in Auchinleck and, last of all, the deeds of title for the Earl of Moldarn. With a nod, Sheriff Sampson turned to look at Kenna.

"I believe you are really Lady M'ren." He addressed the crowd then. "This bet is settled. Grey Fauvereau has won!"

A moan of disappointment escaped many while money reluctantly changed hands.

Kenna smiled sweetly. "May I see you and my husband privately for a moment?" she said, addressing the sheriff.

Grey looked at her uncertainly. He knew how angry she had been. He strode to a door that led into a private, elegantly furnished dining chamber. As she passed by him into the room, he saw that the crowd was beginning to disband, some discouraged losers making hasty exits before debts were called due. Braic and Fergus followed the sheriff into the room and Grey closed the door.

The men looked at her, waiting to see what she had to say. The smile remained on her lips as she looked at Sheriff Sampson. "I did not wish to say anything publicly. But your conclusions may be in error; there is common-folk blood in my veins, despite my Scottish descent."

If Kenna had expected a reaction from Grey, she was disappointed. He stood looking at her, and there was no reading his expression.

"Do you bear the title or not?" Sampson asked.

"I do not." Kenna stood coolly before Grey, their eyes locked.

"Is this the game you play, Kenna?" Grey said icily, and she smiled despite the chill.

McDoo was staring at Kenna. "Lass, you cannot cast doubt on this venture. Do not tease your husband," he said cajolingly. "After all, I am your cousin, if but distantly related. And I have lived my whole life knowing that your father was Thane of Auchinleck, Earl of Moldarn. Will you deny your parentage?"

"No," she said slowly. "I am decended of Cedric M'ren."

"Then why the confusion," the sheriff asked sternly. "What is the truth in this matter?" He did not relish the thought of making a retraction of his earlier announcement.

Braic pushed off the table he was leaning against, nearing his sister. "Perhaps I can help. I am Braic M'ren, Kenna's brother."

"Then explain your sister, if you will. I cannot dally all day with this foolishness!"

"Kenna and I are twins. We are the only offspring of the Earl of Moldarn. I think that is the discrepancy which my sister balks at," he said.

"Twins!" Fergus stammered, his face reddening at the dawning of understanding. "Saints save us, I'm a fool!"

There was sudden concern in Grey's eyes though he gave no other clue to his anxiety. "Why, Fergus?"

"It is quite simple, Mr. Fauvereau." She stepped near, standing before her husband. "Braic and I are the only children and we are twins. Since he is the male, he carries the title of Lord M'ren. I am but his sister."

"You went by the title of Lady M'ren," Grey said coldly.

"Merely a concession. I acted as lady of Moldarn House until the time that Braic would wed. Actually, as twins we have shared the title, but he is the rightful holder."

Grey looked at McDoo, who had gone from red to ashen. "I am so sorry! When you sought my help, I thought of my cousin, the only titled person in Scotland I had claim to. I never glanced at the old Scottish technicalities. I cannot ken the fact that I was so blind!"

"Then Grey has lost his bet?" the sheriff asked.

Kenna looked at Grey. She had to admire the man's composure; he looked as if he had merely lost the ante in a poker game. She did not let her triumph show either. Had her anger spurred her on to actions too rash?

McDoo shrugged helplessly. "I'm afraid it appears so."

Grey never took his eyes off Kenna. She dared not let herself grow uneasy, looking back at him with the same cool appraisal.

"Then it appears that Murphy has won after all," the sheriff said, shaking his head in regret. "If you have the wager contract, McDoo, then Grey had best sign over The Bank. I'll fetch that little weasel Murphy Duke and tell him he's won. How on earth am I going to explain this to all those people?"

"Just a minute, Sheriff Sampson."

He turned to look at Braic M'ren. "Yes?"

"I have my own comment to add. My sister points out this minor discrepancy in title out of anger. She seeks to punish her husband, I think, because she is angry. She disdains this wager and knew nothing of it until last night."

"So?" the sheriff said.

"You've heard of a woman scorned?"

"Braic!" Kenna gasped in anger. "Do you betray me?"

"No, sister dear. I seek to save your marriage."

She glared at him in astounded anger. The sheriff looked at her and then at Braic. "But none of this bears on the winning or losing of the bet."

"Actually it does. You see, as my sister has said, we are twins. But we have always shared the title equally, and she was always known as Lady M'ren in Auchinleck. So despite the fine line, she is Lady M'ren."

"But McDoo says you bear the title of lineage and inherit this Moldarn name. Therefore, Fauvereau loses his wager."

"Only as long as I hold the title. But the minute I release my inheritance, Kenna gains the earldom."

"Braic, no!" Kenna was aghast.

He ignored her. "Fergus, if you'll write up the agreement, I will sign it, and then Lady M'ren will really be Lady M'ren. And Grey will have won the wager after all. Quite simple."

"Is that right, McDoo?" Sampson asked.

He nodded. "That would make it right, sure as sure!" He took out a kerchief and mopped his brow.

Grey came over to Braic. "Thank you," he said quietly. "But no. I can't let you give up everything for this foolishness."

"It is only an action, nothing more. Do you not remember that Moldarn House was put up for sale and will soon belong to other than the M'rens? There is nothing in Auchinleck for me to return to. The Earl of Moldarn comes to an end with us."

Grey looked at him. "It does not matter. That is

the last bit of Scotland you have left. You can't give it up so I can win."

"The decision is not yours!" Braic said, his voice hard as flint. He turned to McDoo. "Draw up the papers now, cousin."

"Braic, I beg you," Kenna said, flying to his side. "Do not do this thing! It will be through my foolish error that you will have sold your inheritance!" He turned from the tears in her eyes, picking up a quill, dipping it in ink and signing the short new contract. Kenna sank down into a chair, her face pale.

"Grey!" Jess burst into the room. "Duke is gone! I checked Queenie's, the hotels and the stable. His favorite mare is gone." He was gasping for breath, as he had run all the way back.

Grey swore softly. "He knew he'd lost and headed for the hills. He wants to get out of signing over the saloon to me."

"Do you want us to look for him?" Jess asked.

He shook his head. "He was a miner before he was a profiteer; he can hide out as well as the best old-timer."

"The snows will scare him out," Sampson said. "Until then, consider The Bank yours." Glad this last bit was finally settled, the sheriff left. Jess followed.

Grey smiled, no humor in his eyes as he walked toward his wife. There was storm in his features; the quiet control of moments ago was gone. She stared back at him, not daring to let him see how weak she felt.

"Have you nothing to say, my dear wife?" His voice was brittle with sarcasm.

She turned to her brother. "I did not mean to lose

your title for you, Braic," she said quietly, shame in her voice.

"I know that."

"You should not have surrendered it so that this gambler might win." She would not look at Grey.

"We owe him his win, Kenna. 'Tis what he paid for."

Fergus stood, blowing on the ink of the contract until it was dry. He put it with the other papers. "It is all taken care of then! I am glad it is over, I am. Kenna, you gave my heart quite a strain by pulling your tricks. What possessed you to cause such havoc?"

"My darling wife wished to punish me." Grey's eyes bore into her. "As Braic said, a woman scorned."

She glared at him but said nothing. Fergus turned to Grey. "That is not all she is up to. My lovely cousin has the notion in her head that she will get the marriage annulled."

"Oh, Kenna." Braic looked at her, pretending shock.

"It is true!" Fergus said soberly. "I spent a quarter hour trying to talk her out of the scheme. But she insists that I proceed, saying the marriage is invalid because you deceived her. We did warn you to tell her the truth in the beginning, so, well, that is your fault in part," he mumbled.

"There will be no annulment! The subject will not be brought up again."

"But she does have every right," Fergus said worriedly.

"Not anymore. Is it not law that upon consummation, the bonds stand?"

Fergus grew red-faced and glanced away from his cousin. "Yes, true, quite right," he murmured in embarrassment.

Color came to Kenna's face also at this, the ultimate betrayal. He had set the trap and she had been caught in its grip. Her eyes said what she thought, although she was silent.

The door swung open and Sadie breezed in with a tray on which sat a whiskey bottle and three glasses. "Hello, gents! I thought I would bring you a toast to celebrate with." She turned to Kenna. "And since this is a gentlemen's gathering, Mrs. Fauvereau, how about if I take you back to the Idaho Hotel? Your trunks have arrived, and I know you'll be wanting to unpack them." She ushered Kenna from the room, ignoring Grey's dour look, and closed the door.

Braic scowled at Grey. "Don't be forgetting that my sister is a lady and that such talk shames her."

"Maybe the lady needs to be taken down from her high horse."

"You've done enough to her, brother. And if you want your marriage to survive, and I know you do or you would have let the annulment go through, then you must learn to make concessions."

"Concessions!" Grey snorted. "I've met your sister's demands. And in return she betrays me and you lose your title."

McDoo harrumphed. "Well, you see, it is not quite as bad as it appears. Now that you have won the wager, as soon as you can get ahold of that little rummy, Murphy Duke, Kenna can sign her title back over to Braic."

"She can?" the two asked in unison.

"Aye. And no one need be the wiser."

"You see!" Braic grinned, his ire gone. "It has all turned out for the best. You have your saloon, I'll have my title back, and Kenna has saved a piece of her pride."

"How do you figure the last?" Grey said, his good humor not so easily regained.

"Well, you drag her into the town to settle your bet, making her a laughingstock—at least in her eyes. But by giving you a bit of the shame, she has made you share in being part of the jest."

"The jest does not make me laugh."

"It never does when you are its end. Be grateful she did not air her words publicly, or the opposition would not have given in so easily. You have still won your bet while she has salvaged her pride. Am I not right, Fergus?"

"Aye. I see it perfectly."

"I wish I did," Grey said sternly.

"That is because you've a long way to ride before you meet Scottish pride with an equal eye," Braic replied.

Once outside the saloon, Kenna took in a deep breath of the summer air. Yesterday's clouds were completely gone, the sky overhead like blue silk. The wet road had partially dried into a scarred and rutted avenue. The sun was warm on Kenna's back and the breeze gentle, yet she felt none of the pleasant summer atmosphere. A cloud of homesickness hung over her. She blinked back the sting of tears in her eyes and gulped in the fresh air. Why oh why had she left Auchinleck?

Sadie smiled at the lady by her side as they wove

their way through town. She was sensitive to the embarrassment Kenna had suffered. So she talked about the town, pointing out items of interest to the newcomer. By the time they reached the hotel, Kenna had regained her composure.

They went through the beautifully furnished hotel lobby and up the stairs. Kenna found her trunks in the room. She unlocked the clasp and pulled out dresses, shaking off the dust that had managed to seep into the trunk and smoothing out the wrinkles. Sadie helped her, noting the fine quality and the age of the dresses. So Kenna M'ren had come because she had few funds. All the more for pride, then.

"I have known your husband for a long time. Ever since The Bank was first started. I came to work for him right at the beginning."

"What brought you to Silver City?" Kenna asked politely.

"Caleb. My husband."

"I do not think I have met him."

"Oh no, honey. He died back in sixty-four."

"I'm sorry," Kenna said, embarrassed at her error.

"No need. He brought us through on the wagon train headed to the Oregon Territories, but gold fever was hitting Silver, and so we stayed. Cholera took him and my little ones."

"You lost children?"

"Two. They are buried by their father in the cemetery on the hill."

"How terrible for you," Kenna said.

"Yes," she said quietly. "There isn't anything so awful as having one of your little babies burning up with fever when nothing you try makes them any

123

better. But I was blessed. I kept my two older sons, and they've been my strength. But the girls, they were little, and Caleb already had bad lungs. They say that this land is hard on the weak."

Kenna bit her lip. How could she wallow in self-pity over her minor problems? She was a weakling compared to a woman like Sadie. "Where are your boys?"

"Martin helps around The Bank and Louis is away at the University back East."

"How impressive! What does he study?"

"He wants to be a lawyer. Imagine that! My son, taking up the law. Mr. Fauvereau helped me send him. I owe your husband a lot. When Caleb died, I had no way to survive. I took in washing but it was not enough. So when he offered me a job at The Bank, I took it. I know that some of the ladies on the hill up there looked down on my doing it. But I've been glad long ago that I did."

Kenna shook out a slip, folded it again, and placed it in a drawer. "I guess there is a side to him I did not know."

"He's had an interesting past all right."

"He has?"

Sadie looked at her in surprise. "Why, Mrs. Fauvereau, don't you know much about your husband?"

"I know he is an American businessman."

Sadie laid Kenna's brush, mirror, and comb on the dresser top. "He is a man who does not talk of his past much, but you being his wife, I thought he would have told you more about himself."

"I'm afraid not." Kenna sighed. "We have been off to a bad start. I wish I did know him better; certainly it would make the way easier."

"That it would. He has had a hard life. Born in England, you know."

"He was?" Kenna was quite surprised.

"Yes. It appears that he was raised on a grand estate in one of those English counties, though I cannot recall which one."

"Is that where he got his money?"

"Heavens, no! His father was a gamekeeper, I believe he said. And he worked in the stables, if I remember right. He talked about living under the superiors, being a servant to those who thought themselves better. But I believe that the old landowner liked Grey; he is ambitious and smart, and so it's understandable. He let him be tutored with his own son. That is why Grey is such an educated man."

"Yes," Kenna said thoughtfully.

"But I guess it was not easy, for he said that the son despised him, ridiculing him before others their age."

"How did you find all this out?"

"Oh, Mr. Fauvereau can do many things. But he doesn't hold more than three drinks well, so he seldom imbibes. A fall from a horse he was breaking dislocated his shoulder, and the doctor poured half a bottle of whiskey into him before setting it. He talked a blue streak to me before falling asleep, and I stayed and listened, deciding better me than somebody like Murphy Duke."

"Very interesting," Kenna said. "Do continue, please."

"I don't know very much more except that he struck his master's son. I guess that the teasing went too far and, being a rash youth, he thoroughly thrashed the source of his ridicule. The English lord was very angry and sent the sheriff after him. His father lost his job and his family their home. It was a sad price to pay, I think. With the law after him, he boarded a boat for China as a cabin boy."

"China? How old was he?"

"Fourteen, if I remember right. About that age."

"So young?"

Sadie nodded. "It was on the ship that he really learned how to work. In time, he handled trade with the captain quite successfully. Then he settled in San Francisco to make his fortune, but found that it had to be made in Silver first. He built The Bank himself, with nothing but a stake from Murphy Duke. And it's done better than most in 'Cisco," she said with pride.

Kenna put away the last of her underthings. So that is why he disdains titles, she said to herself. She looked at Sadie and smiled. "Thank you for telling me this."

"I thought you needed to know." She was straightforward. "But I don't think he has any idea that he told me, so you might keep silent on what you know. He does have a temper, and I don't want to bear it." Kenna nodded solemnly. "I'd best be going, Mrs. Fauvereau. I've things to do back at The Bank."

Kenna thanked her again, for the rescue and friendship, then watched her leave. The trauma of the ride and today's events were still with her, so she pulled the heavy drapes, removed her dress and corset, and lay down on the eiderdown quilt.

Chapter VII

KENNA'S REST was short. She was pulled into awareness by the sound of scraping and thumping and muffled voices. She pushed away the drowsiness and donned a cream silk wrapper. There were more noises and she looked at the second door.

The room had the main entry onto the hall and another door in the middle of the east wall. Before it had been locked. Now she tested it again, surprised when the knob turned under her hand. She opened it a crack and peered in. Braic, Grey, and another man were spreading out a large oval carpet, finely woven in floral print. Once it was in place, they began bringing in furniture: a blue stuffed sofa with wooden arms and legs and a polished cherrywood rocker. Grey placed these with an exacting eye. A lovely secretary and chair were set near the window. Braic unpacked a lamp of etched glass that had a delicately fluted chimney. It was beautiful, as were the other pieces of furniture and miscellaneous items they set around.

"Take that down," Grey said, indicating a picture over the narrow mantel. "Bring in that flat crate out in the hall." She watched him unpack a beveled mirror in a gilt frame which they hung over the fireplace. "There," he said, setting two porcelain candleholders on either side of the mirror and putting in the tall blue tapers. He stood back and looked at the room with approval. "Thanks for your help, Orson." The man nodded and left. "What do you think, Braic?"

"I think it is quite remarkable to change a dowdy hotel room into such a fine sitting room." He lowered his voice a note. "I think Kenna will like it."

"I hope she does," Grey said, and she felt suddenly embarrassed by her spying. "What *do* you think, Kenna?" He turned and stared at her through the dark crack.

Braic looked at the door in surprise. "Sister?"

She pulled the door open, looking at the two and the room. "I could not sleep with all the noise."

Braic smiled. "Well, what do you think? He had them shipped up with us from San Francisco. The supply wagon arrived in town only a while ago."

"It is very nice. Only"—and at this point she looked at Grey directly—"why are we to live in a hotel, Mr. Fauvereau?"

"You disapprove, Mrs. Fauvereau?"

"Actually," she said, strolling over to the secretary and straightening the lamp, "it is a bit odd. You did buy a wife, and a wife is supposed to see to the order of the household, or so I was taught. Yet there is no staff to run, no cook to give orders to, no kitchen, in fact. I came well prepared to take over my duties running a house, yet there is no house to run."

"Kenna," Braic said, his voice suggesting she be tolerant.

Grey was looking at her as yellow afternoon sunlight came through the white lace curtain, outlining her frame. "Don't worry. I'll think of something."

Kenna did not like what his voice suggested. "I assumed that a banker would already live in a house. Oh, but I forget. You really aren't in the banking business."

"I never needed a house. My room here was sufficient, or my office above The Bank. But if you want a house so that you can fulfill your wifely obligations, I will build you one."

She looked at him in surprise, then smiled. "Thank you, no. These rooms really are fine."

"You just said you wanted a house." There was no humor in his voice.

"I think I will settle my own things in my room," Braic said, avoiding the storm as he left.

"I only asked about my wifely duties," she said in a false naiveté that irked him.

"There are only two I need. The rest I can pay others for." He came to her swiftly, with the attack of a hawk. His hot hands slipped around the wrapper, cool beneath his palms. She pulled away before he could kiss her, moving out of his reach.

"Oh, no, black devil!"

"I did buy a wife," he said. He took in her angry stare. "I quote the source."

"Do you really think that what has happened is so unimportant that I will simply forget about it tomorrow or the next day? I am not merely upset at this, willing to hold my anger for a little and then forgive before the week is out. Oh, no! What I shouted at you in madness last night holds in sanity today."

"So what will you do with your anger, m'lady?"

129

There was a tint of sarcasm in his voice. "Will you hold it until it spoils the union? For the marriage stays intact."

"You will grant no annulment?"

"Grant it? I forbid it! Have you forgotten that you signed the contract?"

"How can I," she cried out, "when you flaunt it before my family to shame and humiliate me further?"

"Better now, before your brother and cousin, than before a judge and court."

"You would describe our intimacies before others?" she asked incredulously.

"Yes, rather than have the marriage ended."

She glared at him. "You tricked me, so that once I learned of your other deceits, my fate would be sealed."

He assessed her slowly, the long length of her. "You know your surrender was willing, lady."

A flush of embarrassment heightened her color. She turned and went through the door, shutting it behind her. Grey smiled ruefully at the portal, then rapped on it. "Lady, are you going to honor my two requests and fulfill your wifely duty?"

The door opened a crack and she stood in the narrow opening. She pushed the hair off her neck with her hand, keeping her eyes steadily on him. "I said I'll not give in to your desires, Fauvereau." There was something in the throaty voice that both denied and encouraged.

"My grandmother used to call it cutting off your nose to spite your face, Kenna," he said with a smile. "You punish me by refusing what we both desire. Can you deny that?" His eyes held a challenge.

Kenna's smile met his own. "Above all things I am honest; I won't lie."

"So you admit your desire?" Grey smiled again, reaching up to run his thumb along her jawline.

"Aye. But I will also admit that I have a great deal of willpower." She turned and went into the room. Grey followed, anger quickening his stride. He grabbed her arm and spun her around. "Fine. I accept that. I also have a strong will. We will see who has the greater willpower."

She looked at him in surprise. "You will not pursue me in the physical sense?"

He grinned wickedly. "Exactly. It will be a test. Will you eventually judge my punishment enough and acquiesce, or will I be unable to stand the punishment, and take you by force?"

Kenna gasped. Grey shrugged. "That is the risk of playing deceitful games."

She slipped off the wrapper, pulling on the corset and working the laces as her husband watched. His eyes slid over her as she donned her slip. "So the contest has already begun."

She turned and glanced at him with feigned innocence, then put on the dress. He stepped near, helping her fasten it. She looked up at him. "But didn't you say two things?" It was as if she had just remembered his earlier words. "You have pleaded too ardently for the first, but said nothing of the second duty requested. What is it?"

"Will you grant it?"

"Blindly? Tell me what it is. Do you wish your laundry done or letters written?"

"Vixen," he said softly, leaning near. "I think you are the one who is deceiving me."

She pulled back primly. "Just tell me what you want done." She was very secure in her position now, knowing that he had no right to ask again for what he had once requested.

"Will you grant it, I ask again?"

"Perhaps."

He studied her, his eyes narrowing a bit. "I want you to give me something."

"What?" She was becoming impatient.

"I want a son," he said casually.

She looked at him in amazement. "Sometimes, Grey Fauvereau, I think you mad! Do you try to dupe me as though I were a simple maid?"

"All wives willingly give their husbands children."

"True," she said slowly. "Yes, I will give you a child."

"You will?" Now it was his turn to be surprised.

"Yes," she answered, leaning near for a moment. She looked into his face. "The prize will be given if you win the game. But if not?" She shrugged. "And how long will this game ensue? A year? Two or three?"

She went out the door and into the hall. There was determination in her stride, disguised by the softness of curve and feminine dress. He grinned, then hastened to catch up with here.

"Where are you going?"

She glanced up as if surprised that he was still with her. "I thought I might walk around the city, if one can call it that, and see what there is. The task should take me all of twenty minutes."

He opened the lobby door and they stepped out

onto the porch. "There is more to Silver than you would think at first glance."

"From the way you talked I had expected another San Francisco. This could fit in its pocket."

"Ah! But it makes up in roughness what it lacks in size." He smiled at her. "It's like the gold found here, unrefined but promising."

"What is that?" She pointed at a gathering of people involved in activities.

"Races and competitions. In celebration of independence."

"Yes, I'd forgotten. Independence," she murmured. "Would that I had the same cause to celebrate."

Before he could do more than scowl, they had reached the hammering nails competition. When the winner, a wiry old man with a sure eye, was called out, a new competition started in which miners matched their skills at boring blast holes into rocks. As Kenna watched in amusement, she felt the infectious excitement of these people. Rough miners and ladies in refined dress cheered on the competitors, and children ran and laughed. There were a number of families, and some women pushed babies in prams.

Kenna saw Braic and the pretty young woman to whom he was talking so gaily. It was Maryetta. Braic caught sight of his sister.

"Kenna! Have you met Miss Maryetta Gaylor?"

The women smiled politely. "I didn't know until we had spoken for a time that Braic was your brother," Maryetta said. "I was very pleased to make his acquaintance. He assisted me through the crowd."

Kenna did not miss the woman's hand on her brother's arm. Did she wish to make Grey jealous, or was she interested in Braic? And did Grey materialize because she was thinking about him?

"They are selling lemonade there," Grey said. "Let's get some." His casual air led Kenna to believe that he still found the meeting of the two ladies amusing. As the four stood sipping the cool ade, several young men gathered around Braic, eyeing him. He nodded congenially.

They wore canvas or denim breeches, suspenders, and clean work shirts. Most had their hair cropped short above the ears, and several had handlebar moustaches. They felt no embarrassment at obviously sizing up Braic. Finally one ventured near.

"Is it true you are a Lord?" Emphasis was played on the last word. They all waited for his answer.

"Not anymore," he answered casually, glancing at Kenna and Grey with a smile. "That was only in Scotland, and now I am in America."

A young fellow with red hair stepped closer. "The nearest thing to royalty we've had in Silver City has been Murphy Duke." Someone snorted but the young man continued. "He's got a hundred tales about his grandfather being a true duke and all that."

"Well," Braic said slowly. "I think that when a man boasts of ancestors, the best part of him is buried underground."

This sank in for a moment, and then after serious study of the statement, the young man stuck out his hand. "The name is Lester. These here are Ray, Simon, Bill, and Joe." Braic shook hands with all. "What you planning on doin' here?"

"Get a job if I can. I've had some experience with raising sheep." This made a further impression on them and they spirited him off for deeper conversation, leaving Maryetta to find other interests.

Kenna went for a walk and Grey followed her. There were houses built up into the hills and along streets. Many had porches with narrow railings and windows with shutters cast wide. There were wood picket fences and straight, two-story buildings.

"It appears that there is a good deal of enterprise in this town."

"We've a brewery, three blacksmith shops, four lawyers, two doctors, a tin shop, and six general merchandise stores."

"A regular city," Kenna said flatly.

"Oh, that isn't all. We have a feed store, an excellent bakery, a photograph gallery in the planning, a bank, a jail, a post office, and an ice house."

"How impressive."

"Do I detect a note of sarcasm?"

"What am I doing in this place?" she asked, half to herself. "I am hundreds of miles from anywhere, in a place that is built into the mountains in a manner I've never seen, not even in the hill country at home." She looked at the town that was interspersed with trees and at the small cabins built along the meandering stream bank.

He pointed out grander houses built up on the hills, and she had to admit they were lovely, and a contrast to the rest of the town. Two-storied, they were decorated with beautiful wooden spindles and gingerbreading.

"I've never seen the like. It looks like wrought-iron trim, yet it is made of wood."

"Exactly. It was far too costly to transport the heavy wrought iron back up into these hills. So we hired expert wood carvers to do the work; there's nothing else quite like it."

She pointed to a beautiful white building with a bell tower, arched doorway, and arched stained glass windows that caught the afternoon sun. It stood on a stone base and appeared to stand above the whole city. "You did not mention the church."

He shrugged and smiled. "For the pious ladies in town."

"You do not go?"

"I haven't."

"How about this Sunday?"

He smiled wickedly at her. "You wish to reform me?" He slipped his hand about her waist. "There are better ways for you to reach me, Kenna." His words were bold and sent a flush through her. She pulled away.

Grey caught the whiff of scent still lingering in her hair from the lavender soap. He was drawn to her by more than fragrance. They turned back, passing houses built on rock wall bases with boardwalk porches. Most had steep shake roofs and slender chimneys.

When they arrived at the Idaho Hotel, they went into the spacious lobby. It was dominated by a large desk decorated with pigeonholes and wrought-iron bars like those in a bank. There were huge ledgers and a kerosene lamp with a hooded copper reflector. Behind the desk was a tall stool.

They stepped into the dining area where they

found Braic standing by the bar. Above it was a large painting—a nude in muted colors against a dark background. Cupids offered the lady roses and grapes; Kenna thought it quite inappropriate for a hotel. The walls were covered with bordered cloth and there was a player piano installed with its own kerosene lamp. Double windows, tall and narrow with wavery panes, looked out onto the hilly landscape. There were wooden tables to seat six, lamps, clocks, and an ice chest. This last was six feet tall with decorative tin on wood and wide double doors sporting latch-drop handles. The kitchen was off the dining area.

Kenna sat down at a table near the window, pushing aside the stiff, tatted lace curtains. Grey and Braic followed suit.

"Would you like to eat?" Grey asked.

"It is six o'clock if that wooden clock is right. Unless you have another meal planned with your friends."

"No. This is fine. The food is good here."

A lady in a black dress and white apron came out to take their order. When she left, Braic looked at his sister. "What did you think of Miss Gaylor?"

Grey put down his drink of water. He looked at her. "It is hard to make a judgment when I do not know her," Kenna said.

"You've met her twice," Grey stated.

"So she had said," Braic commented. "I thought her quite pleasant. Do you have no opinion of her?"

"I'm sure she does." Grey smiled. Did he bait her?

"Well?" Braic encouraged.

There had never been dishonesty between herself and her brother. "I do not care for her, Braic."

137

"You do not? Why?"

"Because she is Grey's mistress," she answered coolly, sipping her drink.

Braic's good humor disappeared as he stared at the two. "Is that true, Grey?"

Grey shook his head. Kenna looked at him. "You deny it?"

Her words were cut short by the arrival of platters thick with sliced beef, potatoes, breads, and steamed vegetables. The minute the waitress left, she turned to him. "Would you lie about the obvious?" Her words rang sharp.

He leaned his arms on the table to be nearer to her. "You err, my dearest wife." There was a mocking note in his voice. "You state that she is my mistress. That is quite untrue. You, Kenna, are the only woman I give that title to."

She drew back, busying herself with dishing up food. "You toy with words, kind husband." Her mocking matched his own. "You cannot deny that Miss Gaylor was more to you than a friend."

"True," he said coldly. "But that is past, as is Glen Kinross."

Braic almost choked on his drink. Grey shrugged and smiled, flashing white teeth against a tanned face. "I simply point out that it is best to bury the past."

They ate in silence. Afterward, Grey went to The Bank and Kenna retired to the new sitting room. It was really quite lovely, and she took the time to examine the items on mantel and table. She would not allow herself to show pleasure in front of her husband, for her anger still burned. But in truth she found his taste refined. This was a room she could enjoy, and she no longer felt disappointed that she had no house to live in. Grey would not learn of her feelings, she decided. They had a long way to go in this marriage.

Kenna stepped out onto the balcony, watching the stars come out over the jagged hills. A cool breeze touched her and she leaned on the rail, looking over the long ravine that formed the valley. As it darkened, lights began to glow warmly in windows throughout the hills. There was something about this rugged, mountain-dominated country that reminded Kenna of her homeland.

She went back into the sitting room, seeking out a comfortable chair to read for a while. But she found her eyelids growing heavy despite her earlier nap. Just as she was pulling on her soft blue silk nightgown, she heard the sitting room door open and close. Kenna turned to see Grey come through the doorway. He smiled appreciatively at her.

"Back so soon?" There was no happiness in the statement.

He stepped into the room, pulling off his boots and putting them in the base of the wardrobe. "I thought I would turn in."

She looked at him in surprise. "Here?"

He looked about the room as if to discover her meaning. "Where else?"

"There is only one bed." Her voice was cold but he ignored it, staring instead at her soft shape outlined by the silk. Kenna felt bare beneath his perusal and pulled back the sheets, slipping beneath them. "So obviously you cannot sleep here."

He smiled wickedly, shattering her security. "It is my bed, too."

She had been plumping her pillow and stopped in the action. "But what of our agreement?"

"If you mean your statement that we will no longer live as husband and wife in the physical sense, remember that I didn't agree to it. I simply acknowledged your intentions. I never said I would cooperate."

He removed his gold cufflinks, unbuttoned his shirt, and peeled it from his body. She pulled her eyes from the handsome display and sat in bed, her hands folded primly before her. "You simply mean to share this bed as if we were happily wedded?"

"I do."

She lifted her eyes in protest, only to see him remove his breeches, and her protest faltered. His name gave no clue to what he was: black hair, blue eyes, tanned skin and strong muscles that tapered to a narrow waist and slim hips; a light furring of black hair on his chest. There was nothing gray about this man. He was too bold and darkly brash for that! Kenna pulled her eyes from him, the traitorous blush creeping up her cheeks. She had touched him in darkness and felt his caress before dawn, but she had not seen him in daylight. Nor had she realized his beauty till seen in the bath of amber lamplight. Perhaps her determined goals would not be so easily attained after all.

Grey chuckled softly at her uneasiness and climbed into bed. Kenna snatched the sheets to her and pulled back to her side of the mattress. "Sir! You are as bare as the day you were born!"

"That's how I sleep."

" 'Tis indecent! Have you no nightshirt?"

"None." He lay on the pillow, his arms beneath his

140

head as he stared at the ceiling. His naked chest was exposed. "What do you suggest?"

"That you find a bed elsewhere. What about the rooms above your saloon?"

He turned his head to look at her. "Do you want it obvious to all that my loving wife won't let me share her bed? You would fail your duty as wife-in-name by doing that, and ruin my reputation."

"What reputation?" she asked in exasperation.

"Everyone thinks I am quite the resourceful gentleman to have won a titled wife of such beauty. Imagine the disgrace if it were known that you reject my offering of intimacy?" He reached out, fingering a lock of hair that caught gold from the lamplight. "You still refuse it?"

"I do!"

"Then there is nothing left but to keep up appearances. I must at least sleep in our room."

"Then have a cot brought in."

"There is no room."

"Room can be made."

"No." He lifted up on his elbow to look at her, casting enticing shadows about them. "What's the saying? Now that we've made our bed, we must sleep in it. And that's exactly what we'll do." The tone of his voice left no room for argument. He turned and blew out the lamp, engulfing the room in blackness. "Go to sleep, Kenna."

"I cannot." Despite her earlier fatigue, she was now wide awake. "This arrangement will never let me sleep. Do you expect me to lie here knowing that at any time you might approach me?"

"You can trust me," his voice said into the surrounding dark.

141

"Trust you! That is the last thing I should do, Grey Fauvereau." She turned on her side, as far over to the edge as possible, her sheets and coverlet tightly about her. She lay very still, unable to sleep. Grey, it seemed, managed to fall asleep rather quickly. She could hear his heavy breathing in that slow, relaxed way which made her long all the more for rest. Yet just as she was near nodding off, he stirred, moving closer to her. Finally she slept, waking with the first light to find herself wrapped in the warmth of his arms, his bare chest against her back. She could not bring herself to leave the comfort of the bed, so she sank back into sleep.

The next day she bought Grey a present. It was a silk nightshirt.

Braic was hired by The Bank to help with renovation of the second floor. The job was temporary, but other offers seemed to be abundant. Once his wise remark about ancestry had *been* spread, he became well thought of in town. The acquaintances made on Independence Day had become friends. He was accepted at their tables and was good-humored about the frequent mispronunciation of his name. The Americans tended to call him Brake.

Kenna discovered Silver City even had a local territorial newspaper. *The Avalanche* boasted that it was a publication of the highest caliber throughout the West. Apparently it serviced a large portion of the territory, although the first copy which Kenna read left her quite disconcerted.

On the second page was an article about the arrival of Lady and Lord M'ren. It recounted the wager between Grey Fauvereau and Murphy Duke, the winning of said wager, and the disappearance of the disgruntled Mr. Duke. It spoke briefly of Braic M'ren and his affable, levelheaded nature, then went on to praise Mr. Fauvereau's lovely and spirited new bride.

"This is foolish nonsense," Kenna stated over breakfast. Her eggs grew cold while she read. "Have you seen this, Braic?"

"Aye. It is last night's edition. It appears that Joel Malvern was quite taken with you."

"Who?"

"The reporter who wrote that for the society section. Look at the by-line."

"I think that it is embarrassing to have our concerns aired so freely, especially by someone I have never met."

Braic smiled. "You made quite an impression on him for having never met him. 'Lady M'ren is one of the loveliest women ever to grace the Idaho Territories, graceful in stance and nature, with a fair brow and gentle eyes.' Wasn't there something else about your hair?"

"Please stop quoting."

"I think he referred to her tresses of molten auburn, wasn't it?" Grey asked.

"That's it! It sounds to me like he has a longing to be a poet," Braic added.

She frowned at them before drinking the last of her milk. "Better a poet than a journalist. I've read many papers both in Glasgow and London, and even on the society page a reporter was not granted the license that this one has taken. I am humiliated that he would ramble on describing us for three long paragraphs."

"Actually," Braic said, "The paragraphs were yours. There were only two lines donated to describing my wonderful countenance."

Grey chuckled and picked up the paper. He looked down at the small ink drawing depicting Kenna's fair features. It was actually quite a surprising likeness. "The picture is good. I think the resemblance is remarkable."

"Well, I don't mind the drawing very much, though when it was done I've no idea, I never posed for it."

Grey folded the paper, intending on keeping it for the likeness at least, and Kenna gave it no more thought.

As time passed, she found herself even more the center of attention. She was invited to several teas and discovered that the ladies of Silver City were friendly and genteel. They did not look down on her because her husband ran a saloon, rather, they thought highly of him because it was one of the most profitable establishments in town. Also, she learned, they thought of her marriage circumstances as quite romantic. Grey was esteemed as one of the most charming men in Silver's society. In the eyes of Silver City, the Fauvereaus were a happy, loving couple. Kenna successfully hid her frustration at their sleeping arrangements.

The gift she had given Grey, the white silk dressing gown, still lay folded in his bottom drawer. He had smiled at her, thanked her for the gift, then put it away. Kenna was still waiting for him to use it. In the meantime, she spent her hours reading or sewing late into the night. She retired only when she was sure exhaustion would put her right to sleep, and napped during the afternoons. Still, the fact that he shared her bed made sleeping difficult. His arms were always willing to pull her close in the deepness of her dreams, and his warmth enticed her sleeping form next to his. She wondered if this were part of the game, his continual nearness in the double bed which seemed too small. But he appeared so innocent in sleep, arising with each dawn refreshed and happy, that she thought not. Little did she know what an accomplished actor her husband was.

Grey managed control of the game by sharing her bed with pretended ease. He was quite aware of the effect on his bride as he came to lie beside her beneath the comforter. But did she realize how she affected him? Several times he had entered their rooms to find her in the act of dressing, her slender limbs sheathed by a slight bit of material. Afternoon light or golden flame would accent that skin whose softness begged for his touch. And because he lay naked beneath the covers, the gowns she wore to bed were little better. Soft, silky things, they beckoned to him, and frequently he held her, aching for her. She lay so well within his arms when she slept, it seemed a sin to participate in this unwholesome abstinence. Yet when she was awake she would push out of his embrace. And now she stayed up late into the night, and once he found her napping during the day. He remembered too well her passionate response; surely she must also remember or she wouldn't need ruses to avoid him. Perhaps he was closer to winning the challenge than he realized, and the bending of her will to his was not to be long in coming.

The challenge wrought so easily between husband and wife in hurt anger was losing its appeal.

Kenna stepped off the board walkway, lifting her skirts, as she walked across the street. She looked at the large two-story building across from the Idaho Hotel. The top story's balcony was dressed with decorative spindles and a sign indicating it was a Chinese laundry. The arrow showed the laundry was on the downstairs side, while another sign indicated LAW OFFICES OF JUDGE EDWARD NUGENT.

Kenna stepped through the narrow door into the laundry. Her senses were stung by the spicy scent of incense emanating from a small, pot-bellied brass dragon on the counter. Silk lanterns hung overhead. An old man stood behind the counter. He was small, with a wiry frame and black eyes faded with age. His whitened hair hung in a long braid down his back, and he wore a black silk hat on his head.

"May I help you, Lady Fauvereau?" He spoke surprisingly good English, not the sing-song pidgen English of the chef and waiters at The Bank.

"Yes, Mr. Weng. Here are my husband's shirts and collars; I would like them laundered and pressed." She handed him the items. Kenna had only been here once before and she had found the soft-spoken old gentleman to be wise, as his age suggested.

"Very good, Lady Fauvereau. They will be done by the morrow." He rang a bell and a woman parted the curtains. She was young and quite beautiful. Her long blue-black hair fell in a straight sheath down her back, and her almond-shaped eyes were black as onyx. She wore a simple silk dress which did not manage to hide her lustrous skin and fair features.

146

"This is my favorite granddaughter, third child of my fourth son. Her name is Mai Lei."

Kenna smiled. "Hello, Mai Lei."

The girl nodded shyly and gathered up the shirts, hurrying into the back room.

"She is lovely," Kenna said.

"True. But her beauty is well earned, for she is as fair within as out. I would say it is the same with you, Lady Fauvereau. Your beauty, I think, comes from within as well."

"Thank you," Kenna said almost shyly as she took the laundry ticket with its foreign writing.

She stepped out of the building and into the summer sunshine. Next to the Chinese laundry was the county office building, which also housed the newspaper offices of *The Avalanche*. As she was passing by, the doors opened and a young man stepped out, almost colliding with her. He mumbled some words of pardon, looked up, and stammered in recognition.

"Why . . . Lady M'ren! I do beg your pardon!" He pulled off his hat, staring at her. "Please forgive me for my clumsiness."

"That is quite all right," she said, turning to walk across the street. Kenna found him by her side.

"Let me escort you across the street."

She looked at him and suppressed a smile. "I have crossed it once today already and it was quite safe."

He smiled. "Yes, of course it was. May I introduce myself? I am Joel Malvern; I work for *The Avalanche.*"

She stopped in her stride to stare at him. He was a young man in a neat pinstriped suit and starched collar. Wavy brown hair shaded his brow and pale eyes.

"So," she said, continuing her walk, "you are Mr. Malvern. I have wondered when we should meet."

"You have?" he stammered in pleased surprise.

"Yes, I have. I read your article on the society page."

"Oh." His voice trailed off. "I hope you did not mind." He seemed very concerned, and the lashing she had prepared for the imagined Mr. Malvern evaporated.

"You took considerable liberties, sir. You took it upon yourself to tell the public of our private affairs—"

"The whole town knew of the wager!"

"And to describe me in detail although we had never met."

"I knew all about you!"

She looked at him severely. "You could not know all about me. Certainly you know very little of me."

"I know you are a fair and lovely woman," he said softly. "I only wrote what I saw. But if it offended you, I offer my deepest apology, Lady M'ren."

"I am Mrs. Fauvereau now, Mr. Malvern," she said, approaching the general store that was next to the Idaho Hotel. It had a square front facade and wrought-iron guards across the windows. She stepped up onto the broad porch with its square front pillars and he watched her go inside. Joel Malvern was more impressed than before by Grey Fauvereau's wife.

The store was full of a hundred purchasable items. There were barrels of flour, molasses, brown and white sugar, and coffee beans. Wire baskets were filled with brown and white eggs priced at three dollars per dozen. Kenna was astounded as she looked at the foodstuffs and their extravagant prices: pickles at three dollars a gallon; cheese, seventy-five cents a pound. She looked around in amazement. Grey handled the money and she had had no idea of the soaring prices in a mining town where goods were scarce. She saw a barrel of cranberries labled thirty-five dollars per keg, while butter was hardly reasonable at a dollar thirty-five a pound.

The proprieter came up to her. "Why, hello, Mrs. Fauvereau. Welcome to our store."

"Your butter is one thirty-five a pound!"

"But I'm running a special on lard. It's only seventy-five cents a pound."

"How do people afford to live in this town?"

He chuckled good-naturedly. "Because they make so much money. This city is made of gold and silver. Gold dust is abundant; it is eggs that are scarce."

She looked around at the dry goods: gray blankets, buck gloves, picks, shovels, and mining boots. They were all equally overpriced. She ended up purchasing paintbrushes and watercolors and paper, all high-priced but not as expensive as the goods that were in constant demand.

That night at dinner as she and Grey sat alone in a corner of the hotel dining room, she told him of her conversation with the store owner. Grey nodded. "It's quite true. The profits miners make are cut by the expanded cost of living in Silver. Everything from eggs to whiskey at The Bank to the ladies on Long Gulch Creek are overpriced."

"What was that last?"

"Sorry." He smiled. "This is a town filled with rough working men."

"It is so openly accepted in town?"

"Mother Mack's and The Irish Queen's are part of business, just like any establishment; only the ladies that live on snob hill disdain it. It's one area of Silver I wish you to stay away from. It's a rough section of town, and there are brawls and other unpleasantries." He smiled at her, then handed her a small box. "Let this take your mind off of it."

"What is this?" she questioned.

"A gift."

"Why, Mr. Fauvereau! Do you try to win me over with gifts now?"

He raised his eyebrows in surprise. "That *is* a thought. Well, you gave me a gift—that handsome silk nightshirt."

"Which you never wear."

He smiled long and slow, finished off his drink and said, "This is in return payment."

"Wearing it would be payment enough, sir."

He laughed. "Open it."

She looked down and picked up the card of folded parchment. Inside was a poem.

Her air had a meaning, her movements a grace.
You turned from the others to gaze on her face;
And when you had once seen her forehead and
  mouth
You saw as distinctly her soul and her truth.

Kenna looked up, her eyes quiet. "That is quite beautiful."

"It's by Elizabeth Barrett Browning."

"I did not know that you read poetry," she said.

He leaned back in his chair. "There is a great deal you have to learn of me, my wife."

She opened the small box and gasped. Inside, against black velvet, was an ivory cameo. The woman, whose face was turned three-quarters away, had fair features and hair fading away into the ivory. She looked like Kenna.

"How . . . where did you get this?"

"From our best jewelry and silverware store. I commissioned it from a man who is a genius with a jeweler's tool."

"But the likeness . . ." Her voice faded as she stared down at the beautiful ivory edged in a fine oval filigree of looped gold.

"I saved the etching from the paper."

"Yes, of course." She pinned it at the throat of her gray taffeta blouse and then smiled at her husband. "Thank you, Grey." She leaned near, kissing his cheek, and as he turned to seek more, she pulled back.

After dinner, they went to their rooms, where Kenna was eager to try out her new watercolors and Grey spent his time working over the books he had brought home from The Bank. Several times his attention was drawn away from the neat rows of digits to the woman who was so involved in applying paint to paper.

Many women had been as easily read by him as the tidy numbers on the tally sheet he looked at. But Kenna did not add up with such ease; she eluded his calculations. He had won her over when they had traveled alone. He had given her the avowal no other woman had ever gotten and yet still he had difficulty with her. Since their arrival to Silver, there had been no talk of loving. Grey did know that pride was the prickly thornbush that separated them. He saw it all clearly now, remembering what it had been like to have his pride trampled; he could still taste the bitter injustice. Had he thought a titled lady would not feel the sting of embarrassment? Or had his inner, sightless mind only perceived her as the means to an end?

He lifted his eyes to Kenna again, closing the ledger. Her title did represent what he had hated. Was that why he had so carelessly used her? He had not known what a woman she would be. He smiled to himself. You, Grey Fauvereau, are in love with your wife.

Kenna finished the picture, a cool lake on a meadow's edge. She had seen it many times in Scotland. She felt a presence standing close behind her and glanced up.

"It's very good."

"Thank you," she said, putting down her brushes.

"Don't stop; I didn't mean to distract you," he said, leaning near as if to examine the art, yet taking in the smell of her hair.

"I'm done. I am afraid that lack of practice has made me awkward with the brushes." She sighed, picking them up to wipe them clean.

"Well, I am quite impressed. I did not know you were talented."

She looked up shyly before wiping the brushes on a rag. "I like to do it. There was so much work to do at Moldarn that I hardly found the time."

"You did work at Moldarn?"

"Surprised?" She put away her paints and paper. "You, more than many others, know what our circumstances were. You loaned my father a great deal of money."

He shrugged. "That told me nothing of you."

"Well, Braic did the land overseeing himself. He worked with the sheep and managed the books. It was quite a difficult job with so little help."

"But what about yourself?"

She opened the door to the balcony. "I did much of the gardening. You would be surprised at what I can produce. I also saw to the upkeep of our house. That was no small matter, since it had many rooms." She stepped out into the night breeze. Grey followed her.

They stood at the railing, looking at the scattering of lights across the narrow valley, the mountain darkness peaceful. Above them were a million stars. The absence of the moon made the blackness like velvet; Kenna was well aware of the man next to her. There were strengths in her husband which she admired and yet was cautious of. Too easily she could slip into his arms.

Kenna's fingers slid to her throat and she touched the beautiful cameo. This tender action had reached her more than she wanted to admit. Grey slipped his arm about her.

"I like the valley when it's quiet like this."

"It isn't that quiet," Kenna said. "There are lights blazing at the saloons." They could barely see The Bank in the distance.

"That is good for business," he said, leaning nearer. Since she did not lift her face to his, he satisfied himself with putting his head near her own. To any passerby, they would appear a most loving and contented couple.

"Grey, could you tell me where there are some good dress shops?" The ladies at tea had already recommended several, but she could think of nothing else to say.

"Dress shops are not on the list of things I know," he murmured against her hair. "Why?"

"I thought I would order a few things, and since you procured that dress and those fascinating undergarments, I assumed you might know."

"Well, Maryetta owns and runs a dress shop."

"Oh?" Kenna pulled back a little. Then she pulled back further as a new thought struck her. "You didn't buy my things there, did you?"

"The woman who heads all of the sewing and designing is called Madame LaRue. She is French, and quite talented."

"But it is Maryetta's shop." It was a statement.

"Yes. Yes, it is." Grey was very matter-of-fact.

She moved completely out of his reach. "And did she help you pick out my dress and undergarments?"

He looked at her, silhouetted by the light from their rooms. "Why does the origin of the dress concern you?"

"Your previous mistress chooses your wife's clothing. How convenient. But then, she would know what you prefer in corsets."

He laughed softly, leaning over her. "If Maryetta had picked out your dress it would have been of black crepe. And your chemise? I dread to think!"

She glared at him. "Your laughter demeans me, sir."

His smile faded. "Madame LaRue helped me judge your size but I chose each piece. I knew you would look beautiful in that dress." He stepped nearer, slipping his hands about her waist, pulling her to him. "So you see, you judge me in error."

"It was still her shop," she said coolly.

"Don't fight with me about this, Kenna," he said softly, bending his head down to take captive the softness of her mouth. The heat of his kiss spread through her like a brushfire. His hand entangled itself in her hair. He claimed possession of her until she could do nothing but surrender. When, at last, he released her, she barely had the strength to stand. She rested against the railing, panting.

Grey stood staring at her, his face hidden in the shadows. She moved through the door; he followed. When she turned to look at him, she was the picture of serenity. "Will you be retiring now, Mr. Fauvereau?"

"Yes," he said huskily. "I will."

"Oh." Kenna turned and looked at the row of books, picking out the one she had been reading the night before. She sank into a chair and opened it. Then she looked up, almost as an afterthought. "Good night, then."

Awareness dawned. She fully intended to read into the late hours, as always, until he was asleep. He had not gained one single advantage toward winning her over.

"You mean to read into the night, again?"

"It is a very interesting novel."

"I do not think its appeal is as strong as your fear of our marriage bed." His voice was cool.

"Let us just say that its appeal is greater than yours," she said coldly.

"If that were true, you would not find yourself wrapped in my arms every morning. Admit that you responded to that kiss. If your pride will allow it."

She came angrily to her feet. "Do not boast of your manly prowess before me, sir!"

"I don't need to boast of something you're well aware of! At least admit that my naked body waiting for you each night makes you come to bed so late?"

"Indeed it is! I am not accustomed to such indecencies!"

He smiled slowly, wickedly, looking like a handsome devil. "That did not scare you when we were alone in the mountains."

"I was afraid! I sought comfort, heedless of the results. Would you mock me about a time when I was terrified?"

"And can you forget that passion followed, and you had the final choice?"

Kenna groaned and turned away. There was no arguing with the man. He was impossible. She felt his hands on her shoulders, slipping down her arms. He kissed the side of her neck, sending a shudder of weakness through her. Grey pulled her back against him, the strength of his muscles at her back. "Let this turmoil end" he said against her skin, his breath sending a new rush of sensation through her. "Surrender so we can be at peace."

Kenna drew on inner strength, pulling away from him and sitting down in the chair. She picked up her book and pretended to seek out the page she wanted. Grey stood staring down at his wife; her eyes were cast to the open book, her lips thinned in sober self-control. Only the coral blush on cheek and brow gave her away. At last she looked up and found his eyes boring into her.

"You are a hard woman, Kenna." He snatched his

hat from a chair and strode out of the room, slamming the door.

Kenna threw the book down and went into the bedroom. She looked in the mirror, catching sight of the cameo. Carefully she unpinned it, looking at its detail. Tears threatened as she put it into the small jewelry case she had brought with her from Scotland. She lay across the bed, burying her face in the thick quilt, crying out her frustrations. She could not surrender. Once she had given her love, and it had been rejected. Then she had given herself to this new lover, and in return she had been hurt. How many times had Father said, "Fool me once, the shame is on thee; fool me twice, then shame on me?" The sobbing eased her ache and she slept. When she woke later, the long tapers in the parlor had burned out and one of the lamps had been extinguished.

She rose, dousing the rest of the lights and undressing in the darkness. The clock declared early morning, and still Grey had not come home. She climbed into bed, staring into the blackness, listening for sounds of his return. But he did not come, and once again she cried herself to sleep.

Chapter VIII

MORNING LIGHT filtered through the lace curtains. Grey stood in the doorway between the sitting room and the bedroom. He was watching his wife, who lay still in the innocence of sleep. Her hair was a dark and tangled mass spread across her pillow, and her lips parted with slumber's breath. He felt a longing to pull her into his arms, to feel her softness within his embrace. The black lace of her eyelashes against her cheeks shut away the stone color of those eyes that he saw reflected condemnation, pride, severity.

The sound of drawers slamming shut startled Kenna into wakefulness. She stared at Grey, who was pulling clothing from his drawers, and banging them shut afterward.

"What are you doing?" she managed.

He turned, pretending to notice her for the first time. "Oh. Did I wake you? I just needed to pack some things."

She lay back down, looking at him. He was clothed in a leather jacket and breeches tucked in dark brown boots. He looked rugged, his black hair showing beneath a wide-brimmed leather hat. She watched as he tossed clothes carelessly into a carpet-bag. "Going away?"

"Yes, as a matter of fact. I assume you won't miss me."

The sting of last night's words felt less sharp in morning light, but she still remembered them clearly. "Where are you going?"

"To DeLamar. It is a little mining town back in the hills. We'll go there for a trip someday."

She was aware that he did not ask her to go with him now. No doubt he felt her nature too hard and her tongue too sharp. "How long will you be gone?"

"Ten days at the least." He shoved his clothes down into the bag; why did she have to look so enticing?

"Is it far away then?" She stretched her arms over her head.

"No." He slammed the case shut. "But I have business there; I own a saloon in DeLamar that I'm selling. I'll be meeting the buyer and making some changes in the place before I sell it."

She brushed the mass of hair away from her face, looking at him through half-lowered lashes. "Have a nice trip."

There was something soft in her voice, hinting of invitation. But as he stared at her, he was uncertain. The last thing he felt like facing this morning was rejection. He turned and went out the door, shutting it behind him.

Kenna moaned softly, and turned onto her side. Why did he have to look so devilishly handsome at so early an hour? Certainly he must have had as rough a night as she! On second thought, she retracted the idea. Nothing bothered the man. He fell asleep with

Katherine Myers

ease each night beside her, so why should it have
been any different in his office? Or had he slept at
The Bank? She remembered Maryetta Gaylor's continual hovering. The woman still acted as if she were
Grey's woman. Kenna pushed away the niggling
doubts. Perhaps his absence was exactly what she
needed to get her thoughts in order. Maybe she
would not regret his departure after all.

But as the days dragged by, Kenna forced herself
to admit that his continual presence had been affect-
ing her. His current absence was only a temporary
reprieve; when he returned to Silver City, she knew
that he would also return to her room. Could she go
on pretending, when the game was growing tire-
some?

At the time she had taken the proxy vows in marriage to a stranger, she had chosen to honor the debt
and to take up the duties of a wife to the American
businessman. How had things gone so awry? Would
it be possible to set things right, to salvage her pride
and the marriage?

There was no turning back; Grey was her legal
husband and no annulment could be obtained. She
had chosen to marry this stranger because it had
been her only hope. There could have been no further
happiness back in Scotland, and the union offered
freedom from financial burdens. Too long she and
Braic had struggled to find enough money to pay
their debts. Now, for the first time, she was no longer
plagued by money worries. If she wanted a new
dress, she could buy it; and she did not need to choose
between paying exorbitant prices for food or going
without.

No, Grey was her husband, and whatever their differences, she must honor her marriage contract. There could be pride in taking on that which was one's obligation, she decided.

The logic of her thoughts reassured her; she did not need to love Grey or to give him her heart. That was not in the bargain. But she very well might be willing to take on the role of being Grey's wife.

She spent several hours a day during the afternoon painting her watercolors. There were teas to attend and dinner invitations. With Grey out of town, she received even more invitations from the women concerned with her welfare. But many Kenna declined. She prefered a quiet dinner with Braic, or by herself.

One evening, as they sat at the corner table in the dining room, Braic asked, "How are things going, Kenna? Between you and Grey, that is."

"Quite well now that he is not in town."

Her brother chuckled. "Things still touchy then? I thought you would have forgiven him by now."

"I am a far ways from that." She sipped her hot drink.

"Nessie would have called it 'banging yir head agin a stone to be rid o' the ache.' "

Kenna laughed at the sound of the familiar brogue. "Yes, she would have. Though I do not believe she would have sided so easily with the foe."

He sobered. "Is that what you are believing?"

She smiled at him. "No. I think you have my best interest at heart, or so you believe. I have come to understand that you think I would be happy if peace were made."

"You know you would."

"I know that he would be happy."

"And you would not?"

Kenna shrugged. "This challenge between us is leading me down a trail that is unknown; I am unprepared for the consequences. The only end that I see is in surrender; in all things he must win, and I find fault in that ambition."

"He is a good man. If that is his worst fault then half the world should be so cursed."

"It is his ambition always to win that I disdain. That is what dragged us hundreds of miles to this forsaken place and in the end lost your title."

He looked at her in surprise. "Has he not told you, then? Hmmm, I see that he hasn't. The title is not lost to me. Cousin McDoo assured us that as soon as this Murphy Duke signs over the saloon, you can sign a paper turning the title back over to me."

"I can! Oh, Braic, you do not know how that eases my heart. That blackguard! Why did he not have the kindness to tell me when he knows that I have mourned my folly?"

"I think he strives to rid you of some of your prickly pride," he said thoughtfully. "Yet it is his own pride which trips him. Father would have called it ram's pride."

It was a term her father had used for two people who knocked heads together in confrontation, just like the warring rams on his property. "True, on both our sides."

"It is that pride that you admire, Kenna. It draws you to the man. You cannot love a man who has a weak will. Can you be forgetting Glen Kinross so soon?" he said softly.

"No. You may be right. But there is always something we clash over that destroys any effort at peace. I do not wish to surrender to his terms."

"Has he not already met you halfway? In his winning, you would not be the loser. I have seen your pensive moods since his absence. It is said that separation brings the kindest memories. Have you not thought of him at all since his departure?"

"I have. But, then, thoughts are subject to will, and Grey Fauvereau is not."

The following day, Braic and Kenna rented horses from the livery and went for a ride into the hills. It was refreshing, and Kenna felt uplifted. She had given a great deal of thought to her brother's counsel and began to look forward to Grey's return. In the meantime, she kept busy.

Once, in her dreams, Grey had come to her, his eyes teasing, entreating. And Kenna had been powerless to resist him. Her whole being had longed to go to him, to be pulled into his warm caress. But there was a dark chasm between them, bottomless and uncrossable. The more she yearned for him, the wider the dark crevice.

Braic's words came back to her: "In his winning, you would not be the loser." What purpose did the conflict between them accomplish? There could only by further difficulties if she sustained her anger against Grey. The deceits he had played upon her could not easily be forgotten, yet that did not mean she could not work at the marriage. There was no future in her continual remembering of the past. It was time that some sort of compromise be reached, she decided.

On the tenth day, Kenna awaited his arrival but was disappointed. When she extinguished the last wick, she still listened for his footsteps. But Grey did not return and she was unable to get information from Sadie or Jess who knew nothing of his whereabouts.

Grey returned at a time she least expected.

Kenna and Ella Farwell were walking along one of the shop-lined streets of the city, two weeks after Grey's departure. It was a warm day with a blue sky full of cotton clouds, and the two talked cheerfully about their purchases. Mrs. Farwell was the young wife of Captain Farwell, stationed in Silver City from Fort Boise. Despite being only two years Kenna's senior, she had three small children. Kenna liked her very much. After breakfast the two ladies had gone shopping, and Kenna had purchased a pair of kid riding gloves, a silk fan, a reticule, and a new brush and comb set. She had also ordered several dresses made. The quality of clothing and accessories were surprisingly good, and the price was exceedingly high. But for the first time in several years Kenna did not have to worry about that. She had money from the sale of the Moldarn furniture and the advantage of Grey's credit in town.

The ladies stopped at a milliner's shop that displayed such pretty hats in its plate glass window that they stepped inside. There was a delectable array of sporting veils, feathers, silk flowers, and ribbons. They tried on many under the solicitous eye of the proprietor. The hat that caught Kenna's eye was of very finely woven straw. It had a wide brim and tied under the chin with thick ribbons of ivory satin. She tried it on, tilting it slightly, and tying the bow to the side. With a smile, she turned for her friend's inspection.

Ella laughed. "That is my favorite of all! Oh, Kenna, get that one."

The owner smiled. "Lady M'ren has excellent taste. Not too gaudy, that one." A frail man with oval spectacles, he wore a pinstriped suit and a silk tie.

Kenna turned back to the mirror. "Do you think I should, Ella?" She had already bought several frivolous things.

"The sun here is terrible for a lady's skin. You wouldn't think so, being so high up into the mountains. But you cannot be careless, especially with your fair complexion."

The owner nodded in agreement. Lady M'ren did have the most lovely skin beneath that mass of burnished hair. Not white or ruddy, as often seen with her hair coloring, rather, it was a light golden color that complemented her beauty.

"Very well. I shall take it."

"Would you like it boxed?" the man said, eagerly stepping forward.

"No, I shall wear it."

"Very wise. The sun is hot today. Now just let me write up a receipt. That will be seven dollars. Do you wish me to credit it to your husband?"

Inwardly she cringed at the exorbitant price. Even in the days when her family had been better off, she had never paid that much for a hat. But instead of grimacing, she opened her reticule and handed him the proper amount of money. "I'll just pay for it myself," she said. It would be best if Grey did not receive a bill of seven dollars for a mere hat.

The proprietor saw them to the door. He was quite thrilled. As soon as he spread the word that Lady

M'ren had purchased one of his hats, he would sell half a dozen just like it. He rubbed his hands together in anticipation of the profits.

Kenna and Ella stepped out of the shop, and their discussion ended in midsentence as they caught sight of Grey on the street corner, not two shops away. He was talking to Maryetta, who stood looking up at him, her arm through his. Though Grey's face was unreadable, Maryetta's was turned up to his in innocent coquetry. She leaned near, smiling so prettily at him that Kenna gritted her teeth.

"I did not know that your husband was back in town, " Ella said.

"Neither did I, " Kenna answered, a bit too indifferently.

"Oh," Ella said, embarrassed.

Grey nodded, pretending polite interest in Maryetta's words, though he was eager to seek out his wife. And then he looked up and saw Kenna. She stood on the walkway, wearing the soft peach-colored dress he had purchased for her. She held some packages which were tied together, and she wore a wide-brimmed straw hat with ribbons. A slight breeze stirred the brim of the hat, and loose strands of her hair entwined about the satin ties. He stood staring at her, time holding still for him. She looked at him, her features calm, her eyes cool as stone. He found himself striding toward her, unaware of the woman left to trail awkwardly behind him.

"Hello," he said with cool ease.

Kenna said nothing. Ella Farwell tried to smooth over the situation. "We did not know that you had gotten back in town. You must have just arrived."

"Oh, no," Maryetta said with pretended innocence. "He got in last night."

Ella glared at the dressmaker. Like most women in town, she disliked the flirt. Grey paid no attention. Yet he noticed the spark of fire in Kenna's eyes. "Have you no greeting for your husband?"

Before she could answer, Grey took the packages from her and handed them to Ella. Then he slipped his arms about her, his face swooping beneath the brim of her hat, his mouth finding hers. Before she could protest, Kenna found herself being kissed with eager tenderness. The assault of his mouth was so persuasive, so enticing, that she was swept away from the walk in front of the narrow shops.

Passersby stopped to gawk in amazement at the prettily romantic sight. One of these was Joel Malvern. How he wished he were holding Kenna, instead of the ruffian gambler. At last Grey released her and she took a step back, gasping for breath.

"Grey! How could you, in front of all these people?"

He smiled lazily. "I missed my wife," he said. "There is no law against that, is there, Ella?"

"Certainly not," her friend replied in kind.

"And now, if you will excuse me ladies, I have plans to take my wife to lunch." He retrieved the packages from Ella Farwell and slipped his arm around Kenna, leading her away.

They walked along together and Kenna glanced up at her husband. "Sometimes I think I shall never understand you, Grey Fauvereau."

"You have our whole married life to learn to," he said.

"I doubt it will last that long," she said with anger

in her voice. Had he gone to see Maryetta last night instead of coming to her? The thought filled her with unhappiness.

He raised an eyebrow in surprise at her comment. "Are you mad with me?"

"Mad? Why should I be mad?" Kenna said, growing furious. "You are gone for weeks, return to town and seek out Miss Gaylor upon your arrival, then assault me with your kiss on one of the most public streets in town!"

"I sense you're really mad about Maryetta being with me this afternoon." Grey was thoughtful. "Did it upset you when you saw us together?"

"That I should believe my husband out of town, only to run into him on a street corner, with his mistress? That I should be publicly humiliated as she informs us that you sought her out last night, when I did not even know you were in town? Certainly not." Her voice was sweetly understanding.

"Jealous, Kenna?" He sounded pleased.

She stopped in her stride to glare at him. "And to think that your absence did nothing to enhance our marriage. Now that you have returned I find things as annoying as before you left."

He chuckled. "I wouldn't want a marriage that had no spirit."

She groaned and quickened her pace in an effort to move away from him. Why did she let the man bother her so? He lengthened his stride and stayed with her.

"I didn't get into Silver until nearly two o'clock this morning. I rode most of the night so that I could come back to my bride, from whom I felt I had been separated for too long. But being the courteous husband that I am, I did not wish to burst in on her in the middle of the night. So I slept in my office at The Bank."

She looked at him to see if he was telling the truth, and could find no evidence of a lie. "I see," she managed.

"I was very tired and slept in late. I didn't bother to eat, only to bathe and shave. I was on my way to you when Maryetta engaged me in a discussion about something I don't remember. Unfortunately, my bride chose that exact moment to happen upon me."

Kenna was silent. He looked at her expectantly, his black hair catching a glint of afternoon light and his eyes darkly blue. His face was even more tanned than before, adding to its handsome rugged lines. Grey smiled, flashing white teeth at her as he continued his piercing stare. Why must his looks be so devilishly appealing?

"Mr. Fauvereau," Grey said playfully. "I apologize for misjudging your character." He paused but she said nothing. "I realize that you really are a sterling fellow and have only the most tender concerns for me." She still refused to answer his baiting. "And I will not doubt you again." He leaned near, as if playing the second part of his act. "It is quite all right, Mrs. Fauvereau. I forgive you."

Staring at him from beneath the brim of her hat, Kenna would not surrender to his humor. "You are a wicked devil, Fauvereau," she said. "But I will forgive you." She walked off.

Grey stared after her before stepping out to catch up with her. "You forgive me? For what?"

Kenna paused and looked up at him with innocent

composure, her face close to his. "For all the difficulties and embarrassments you have caused me."

He leaned in closer, his mouth longing for hers. "Is that for just today, or the last two months?"

She looked thoughtful for a moment, then glanced at him with those flint-colored eyes he found so piercing. "I haven't decided that yet."

They found themselves before the hostlery and he led her into the cool, dark exterior that smelled of horses and hay. "Would you like to go on a picnic?"

It sounded wonderful to Kenna. "Yes. I would like that very much." Since when had the thought of such a small thing as a picnic managed to lift her spirits so? Could it be the return of her husband which made thoughts of small things pleasant?

Grey stroked the nose of the bay mare, leading her from the stall. The strength of his hands was fascinating to Kenna as he gentled the animal. He had an easy way with animals, she thought, as his lean fingers stroked the horseflesh. He buckled the cooper around the mare's tail, securing the harness in place; then he guided the animal back between the buggy shafts, working on either side to fit the long poles into the leather loops. He pulled back the long leather straps, hooking them into place, and then he patted the mare's rump in acknowledgment of her cooperation.

He came toward Kenna, now turning his attention to her. Slowly his hands came to her waist, in the common movement that a man used to lift a woman into such a conveyance. But there was nothing common in his touch, for his hands lingered about her waist. She could do nothing but look up at him, caught in the web of his stare. Sounds from without were muffled, the quiet of the livery broken only by the soft neigh or stomp of horses. All about them were the musty shadows that made a public place suddenly very solitary, and intimate. There was one window, small and high-placed, through whose dusty pane light filtered. Distorted by the thick glass, it played its magic; straw was turned from brown to blond and Grey's features were edged in a line of gold. The darkness hid his expression, and a thrill of excited fear ran through her.

"I have thought of you often," he said in a quiet voice that threatened her in some way she could not interpret.

Slowly he bent his head, until at last his lips brushed her own. He did not immediately press his advantage, for his lips spoke to her of invitation, enticement. Kenna's eyes closed, eyelashes fluttering to her cheeks, as surrender wrote itself upon her. She had no will to resist, no strength to pull back. The softness of his mouth spread heat through her, rekindling that which had once before been lit. His arms slid about her, pulling the litheness of her womanly body into the muscle of his own. The fever of his touch inflamed that which she had worked so hard to encase in ice. Fingers of fire scorched through her dress as if the fabric had no more substance than air, and she was rendered helpless by his kiss, which threatened never to end. She felt herself drowning in the hot pools in which his unspoken demands had submerged her. Her lips were bruised from his passionate assault. His eyes were black in the shadowed light, taking in her quickened breath and parted lips. His desire for her was a shudder of heat, she the only draft that would slake his thirst.

His arms were still tightly about her, and the lightweight fabric of her dress was little protection from the steel muscles of his chest, clothed only in a soft chambray shirt. The softness of her breasts, the lithe curves of hip and thigh, were pressed against him in a way that brought Kenna's mind reeling back to earth once the enchantment of the kiss had worn away. She wanted to flee. But his hands would not release her; they held her as tightly as bands of iron.

With a movement she least anticipated, he swept her up onto the seat of the buggy and climbed into the other side. The conveyance dipped then sprang back; the horse pranced, anxious to go. Kenna sat primly, her hands in her lap, and he took the two reins between his strong fingers. He clicked and they moved forward through the door of the livery. The shadowed intimacy of the place still lingered about them. She could not help but notice that Grey's eyes were dark with desire, even though his features were calm. And Kenna's appearance betrayed her even more. Though her posture was meek, her eyes were cast down out of emotion rather than modesty. The bright flush coloring her lips the shade of rose petals also tinged her cheeks in a lighter hue. Her mouth was not held in her customary sharp line of primness; rather, her expression seemed bewildered.

Gaily the horse trotted off down the street past shops and houses. Lightweight, the narrow vehicle sported black rods on either side that fanned out to the arched top. It was trimmed with a nickel railing in front and a wooden holder which held the buggywhip. It seated only two people, and his thigh pressed against hers; to them both there was nothing

172

casual in the contact. The thin steel rims began to gather speed, and Kenna watched the wooden spokes spin. The side and back curtains were rolled up and tied, the cool air swirling about them; overhead, the leather top shaded them from the sun. The rutted ground vibrated the wheels as the horse quickened its pace, its tail swishing and the harness bells jangling. Grey reined in in front of The Bank, jumped down, and handed her the reins. He went inside, returning moments later with a large picnic hamper. During that time Kenna had managed to control her emotions, and she was less flustered. He took up the reins again, and they sped away.

The wind whipped strands of her hair and plucked at the ties of her hat as they reached the end of town and cut off on a dirt road that wound up into the hills. The road led far above the town and up onto a gentle plateau; at last the buggy came to a stop and the horse snorted, looking back at them. Grey jumped down and tethered the horse to a tree, then came around and grasped Kenna about the waist, swinging her down. He did not immediately release her.

She looked up into his face. "We lunch here, then?"

"Yes, m'lady," he murmured, not releasing her from his stare or his hold.

"How pleasant," she answered softly, holding onto the brim of her hat before pulling out of his grasp. She looked over the land. At this height, she could see the entire city, nestled so tightly into the long valley. And the mountains which jutted skyward were clothed in green, pines as well as leaf trees amid patches of bush. Wild flowers dotted the land-

173

scape, and the beauty of the hills was marred only here or there by mining scars. Beneath it all, the jagged rock of the mountains showed. Directly below them, yet still far away, were the houses scattered across the side of the valley.

Grey spread out a checkered cloth and opened a basket of food. They were surrounded by fir trees and yarrow bush, and the land sloped gently away before them. Kenna picked a few wild flowers and watched two butterflies dance around each other before flitting off. She sat down on a log by the tablecloth and watched Grey pull out cold chicken, cabbage salad, rolls, and cherry pie. He served her a plate and handed her silverware wrapped in a linen napkin.

She studied him. The man was a puzzlement to her, unlike any man she had ever known. She ate quietly, looking across the valley. The clouds had become tinted with blue as they scudded across the sky, and a wind stirred the pines. Kenna tried to act casual, as if his presence did not affect her.

"How was your trip to DeLamar? Successful, I hope."

"Yes. I sold the saloon there and made a profit on it."

"I hadn't known that you had owned more than The Bank," she said, biting into a roll.

He shrugged. "I have a number of investments. But I didn't want to be traveling back and forth between Silver and DeLamar." He nodded at the land. "Do you like this spot?"

"Yes, it's beautiful up here, and the view is spectacular."

"I am glad that it pleases you. I bought it a couple

of weeks ago." Kenna looked at him in surprise. "You did?"

"Yes, ma'am. I am going to build you a beautiful house up here; I've already ordered most of the furniture from San Francisco so it will be here before snowfall."

Kenna looked back down the winding road. "This is quite high up isn't it, Grey?"

"It's above any other house so far. But the privacy will suit me." He looked at her with those startlingly blue eyes. "It has been my fondest desire, since meeting you, to take you somewhere far away. I now find the Idaho Hotel too public for my tastes." He leaned back, looking at her.

Kenna did not want to meet his unspoken challenge. She looked across the land. "In some ways this reminds me of Auchinleck."

"That is one thing which has drawn me to Silver. I felt akin to it as I had to no other place since I left England. Perhaps that is why I settled here."

"You are from England?"

"I was raised there," he said.

"One would think that you were born and raised in America. You have no accent."

Grey shrugged. "I worked hard to erase it and to be an American."

"Why didn't you tell me that you were from England?" Kenna made no mention of her conversation with Sadie. "It is really amazing how little I know about you."

"My life in England was not a happy one. My father was gamekeeper on the estate of an English lord. My family was always subservient to them, no matter what. When I found myself in a fight with the man's son, I refused to let him whip me as if he were the better. I fought fair and beat the coward. Unfortunately, his father couldn't see any fairness in that. He sent the law after me. I narrowly escaped, by hiring on as a cabin boy on a ship."

"What of your family?"

He frowned. "My father was dismissed, and so of course he lost their house and holdings. I lost touch with them for a long time but finally found them. My father died several years past, but I can now at least send money to my mother. I believe the rest of the children have left home now; I have lost touch with my brother and two sisters."

"I am sorry," Kenna said softly.

Grey shrugged and smiled at her. "That is all in the past."

"But you still have harsh feelings about what happened. Is that why you so despise nobility?"

He looked at her for a while. "My family and I ate the dust of the genteel for a long time. The constant inequality made me want to fight. Yes, perhaps all of it accounts for my outlook."

"What about Braic and myself?" Her voice was quiet.

His countenance softened. "I like your brother more than you know, Kenna. I think he is a fine and fair man, one that I would gladly call my brother. Maybe the financial difficulties made him more of a working man, or perhaps he has been bred differently. I don't know. But, still, I like him and have thought highly of him from the start."

"I am glad. There have been few, layman or lord, who have been able to find fault with my brother." She paused for a moment. "Yet what of me? How often, since the beginning of our journeys, have you called me lady, and I have seen that you hold the word in disdain." She began to return the dishes to the basket.

Grey studied her. "I do not disdain you," he said tenderly, reaching out and caressing the line of her cheek with his finger.

Kenna stared at him. His eyes were fastened on her. The wind was growing stronger, whipping up the brim of her hat and tugging at the ribbons. She moved away to stare down into the valley. Grey followed. She felt his heated presence behind her, his arms enfolding her. Kenna turned to him, her hands against the fabric of his shirt. He pulled her to him, his hands sliding up her back, pressing her softness against him. His hands slid up, tangling themselves in her hair, bringing her lips to his. The heat of his mouth branded her own, yet she was helpless to resist the assault on her senses. Slowly she slid her hands up his shirt, entwining her arms about his neck. She pressed back her own urgent answer, unable to stop the blaze of feelings. How she wanted this dark tempter to hold her and claim her. His caresses pushed all reason from her mind, and his touch swept her away.

The sky was darkening and the clouds roiled angrily. Wind whipped her skirts about their legs and tugged at her hair. But it was not until the kiss had ended, the heat ebbing away, that the two felt the cold drops of rain against their skin. Kenna ran to the carriage where the horse snorted nervously, and Grey caught up the cloth and basket, tossing them and himself inside. He clicked the reins and Kenna stayed close to him, her hands about his arm, as he guided the horse down the narrow road. Once on the main street, he whipped the horse to speed until they arrived at the hotel.

Grey lifted her out, gathering up her packages, and tossed a young man a coin and instructions to return the carriage to the livery. He led his wife inside and up the stairs. Once in their rooms, Kenna lit a lamp, for although it was afternoon, it had grown very dark outside. Thunder rolled through the narrow valley, and knives of lightning split the darkness. Rain streamed down the windows in a watery veil, and the solitude of the afternoon struck them. There was tension between the two who stood staring at each other. The intimacy of the moment increased as Grey stepped near. Carefully he untied the ribbons of her hat, which had become entangled in her hair. He tossed it on a chair. Her curls had come unpinned and fell in auburn disarray. She looked more alluring to him than ever before. His fingers fumbled with the delicate pearl buttons at the throat of her dress and she leaned into him, her mouth very near his own. She looked up into his face, her eyes showing that she chose the course yet was still unsure why she must surrender.

Grey did not hesitate in his task, determined that he would have the vixen who had so plagued his thoughts. Having succeeded with the buttons, he turned her around to work with the ties at the back of the dress. Outside, there was a crack of thunder so loud that Kenna jumped, then leaned back against her husband. He slipped his arms about her, his mouth near her ear.

"Are you afraid of mountain thunderstorms?" he murmured.

Her breath had quickened at his touch and she

closed her eyes, "There is more to fear within, than the thunder without," she said quietly. His touch made her shudder; having removed her dress and untied the ribbons on her slip, he busied himself with the ties in her corset. He cursed the difficult clothing; giving up for the moment, he pulled her to him again to satisfy his claim with a kiss.

The storm grew fiercer without, rattling the windows as rain pelted the panes. A draft swept beneath the door, swirling about the lamp and extinguishing the light, leaving them in darkness. Their clothing lay strewn about the floor as the dim light clothed them; Grey lifted her silken form in his arms, carrying her to the welcoming comfort of the bed. They escaped the chill air within the heat of eiderdown mattress and quilt and he pulled her close.

Kenna slid into the heat of his arms, relieving at last her longing to be held.

"Oh, Kenna!" he moaned, holding her to him. "Why did you make this all so difficult? I don't want this contention between us; we were meant to lie together like this. Could your surrender have been such a concession?"

Her mouth sought his in reply, for she had no answer to his query. All she knew was that she wanted him to take possession of her. She lay back in his arms, limp beneath the spell his touch cast. Her head was tipped back, the tangle of her hair entwining itself in the brown shadows. Her throat was arched by the tilt of her head, the ivory flesh vulnerable. He bent his dark head, his mouth leaving a fiery tremor where it touched and teased. Kenna's eyes, which had gazed upward, slowly closed, her lashes fluttering down. The roughness of his manly hands, contrasted by the gentle

179

touch, traced the lines of her body as if they revered the sculpture of her woman's form.

There was a flash of lightning, a split second of silver light that sheathed them before the world turned dim again. Three counts, and thunder rumbled across the valley, rattling the windowpanes. In that sudden burst of light, Kenna saw a glimpse of the man she lay with. His image stayed with her long after the light was gone. She discerned the chiseled features, the indigo of eyes, the raven mane; broad were his shoulders, and strong, as if meant to carry her burdens. Long and well-muscled, his arms were on either side of her, straight and powerful, as if he were her protector. Dark hair furred his chest; slowly Kenna reached up, placing her hand against him, feeling how foreign and yet intriguing was his male body. She had long known men were different. But what interest the difference could arouse, and what passion it could inflame, she had not fully realized until now.

Grey looked down at the woman beneath him, her flesh tawny in the shadow. Lightning flashed again, turning her skin golden. She stared up at him with acceptance and anticipation etching her countenance. Never before had he seen those eyes turn to the soft gray of a dove's breast. He bent his head to hers, kissing her brow and mouth, her eyes and throat. It was as if he meant to drink her in. A slight shudder ran through Kenna and she slid her arms around the lean ribs, pulling him down to her. She knew then there would be no one else to give her what she wanted.

Grey was oblivious to the angry rain as he laid claim to the one possession of life that he really wanted.

The mountain thunderstorm, which had thrown its wrath against War Eagle mountain and the silver valley, left the valley drenched, and the roads thick with mud. In its passing, a rainbow arched in perfect splendor across the width of the ravine. It left streaking rays of sunlight to filter down onto the small mining town, piercing rain-washed glass panes.

Kenna stirred as the watery sunlight slid into the room. She was aware of the warmth, the heat from the golden man who lay next to her. Yet as she glanced around the small room, the intimacy of dark pleasure seemed nakedly exposed. Where was the darkness of rain-streaked windows and clouded thunder? She moved deeper into the comfort of her husband's arms. Kenna felt him stroke her hair and she lifted up, looking into the blue depths of his eyes.

Grey studied her as he might a reverenced Old Master's painting. His wife lay with her arm beneath her head, most of her hair swept upward, spilled into a tangle across the pillow. He studied the line of jaw, no longer held squarely determined; there was no lifted eyebrow, only the soft arch like the line of a bird's wing. No mocking, no reprimand, no reserved manner tainted her countenance. Instead he saw eyes softened by the loving union they had shared.

The sheet was draped about her, the folds calling attention to the curve of her body as she lay on her side. He reached out, running his hand along the length of her bare arm. He leaned over her, kissing the exposed nape of her neck. A shiver with the memory of his touch, ran through her and she tingled. She lay back and smiled softly; he was very near to her, bending in for a light kiss. His lips held no demands, the kiss was one of tender appreciation.

"I can hardly believe how in awe of you I am," he said in a quiet voice. "It has been a long wait for this."

Kenna lowered her eyes, offering no answer. She had given up her vows to resist him, to turn aside his advances and attentions; yet in her imaginings she had envisioned herself coming to him in solemn duty. What torrent had caught her up and swept her to him, helpless as a leaf fallen into a rushing stream? How could she forget that only this afternoon he had humiliated her publicly, a course he seemed to follow regularly? Kenna had wanted the giving to be her decision, to be doled out as she saw fit. Yet today she had been forced to surrender to him, not by her own decision, but rather by the need she had so strongly felt. Desire had made her body betray her, and she felt irritated by the power he held over her.

Grey observed the expressions crossing her face, and he instinctively sensed that not all was set right, as he had earlier hoped. He reached out, his hand caressing her side before it slowly moved the length of her, following the valley of her waist and the curve of her hip. It rested there, heat moving through the sheet to brand her skin. He smiled at his wife.

"It is best that this game between us has come to an end," he said.

She looked at him with an unwavering stare. "Is that what you think all this has been? Simply a game?"

"What else would you call it?"

"A challenge, a conflict, an endeavor to salvage my pride." She was very serious. He looked at her for a long moment and then laughed, the sound echoing through the small room. "And of course you find humor in the hurt you have caused," she said, turning away from him to lie facing the wall.

"I am the one who has been hurt!" he said in amazement, as if she were blind to the truth.

Kenna turned her head and looked at him over her shoulder. "You?"

"Yes. You refused to let me touch you because you wanted to punish me, to make me sorry that I had ever brought you here because of a mere bet." His voice softened and he moved closer. "Well, you got what you wanted. I was unhappy when I was with you because I couldn't have you, and I thought about you all the time I was away."

He bent his head and pressed kisses upon the bare flesh of her back. She pulled away, to lie flat on her back, grasping the sheet tightly about her. He leaned near. "Will you deny you wanted this?" His voice was wickedly soft.

"No, I shall not deny it, and perhaps I should have continued my refusal," she said, the brighter sunlight bringing a closer inspection of the truth now that their passion had fled with the storm.

He looked at her in amazement, wondering how his words had stirred such anger. He did not know that Kenna was berating herself for the passion that she had let sweep her away; there was no control when she was with this man!

"Kenna, I thought that all was forgiven; are you still angry with me for past happenings?"

She thought of Maryetta pressing herself against Grey's arm, and later the public kiss on the streets of Silver. Could she continually forgive him for the humiliations which he brought her? She had spoken words of forgiveness when he explained the situations, yet did she dare trust the black-haired man who had come into her life with such impropriety?

All cajoling humor was gone from him, his patience frayed. "Damn it, woman! There is no reaching you with words, is there? Only with passion. Nothing I can say can arouse true compassion from you. Perhaps I should stop talking and return to the one thing which can bring a response from you."

Before she could take a breath, he lowered himself to her, kissing her with demanding vigor, bruising her lips. Anger made his touch rough, his kiss forceful. The power of his passion caught her up, inflaming her flesh as well as her inner self; she tensed beneath the onslaught of this aggression and against the reactions of her own body. When he finally pulled back a few inches, his face still above hers, her very being quaked and she pressed her lips together so that she would not betray all that she felt.

A slow smile spread across his face, for he read what she tried to hide. "You'll never convince me that you don't long for the same thing that I do. It's the only reason this ridiculous fight has come to an end. Can you deny that?"

Kenna's breath came in short, sharp gasps; his presence overwhelmed her. She fought for the strength not to surrender to him again. "Passion, yes. But it is not the only reason."

"What other, then?"

She sat up, forcing herself to be calm. "I made a decision while you were gone." He said nothing, and so she pulled the slipping sheet more tightly about her, choosing her words carefully. "I decided that it was time I honor our contract, and take up my duty as your wife."

"Duty!" The word exploded from him.

"You see," she said quickly, as if discussing business matters, "I willingly signed the contract. I knew that I must come to America and be the wife of the man I married." She took a breath, feeling his eyes boring into her. "I decided while you were gone that it was time I accept this marriage, and be willing to work at it."

He lifted a mocking eyebrow, his features hard. "A great concession, my beloved bride." His voice teased her as he leaned near, one arm going on the other side of her. Kenna was at the very edge of the bed, trapped by the twisted sheet and his arms. "While I was gone I, too, made a decision. It was the same as yours."

Kenna looked at him, unsure of what he meant. He smiled slowly, his heated stare grazing her body. "I decided that this foolish separation had gone too far, and that it was time you took on your responsibilities as my wife. You will grace the home I build, preside as my hostess . . . " His voice trailed off.

"And?" she questioned.

"And be my wife in every sense," he said, pulling her beneath him. "It's good, then, that you are willing to take up this wifely duty, as you call it."

Panic filled her as he sought what she was now reluctant to give. A duty, a contract to honor, no problem. But this heated, desire-filled yearning could upon no pretense be considered the dull responsibility that the word duty suggested.

"No! Stop, Grey," she cried, fearful of this new path he led her down.

"I have no mercy for you, vixen," he growled as his lips traced a fiery line upon her throat and his hands gently caressed the softness of her breasts.

He was stonger than she, the gentle force he used too persuasive, she succumbed to his demands. He kissed her until she grew faint, and when he pulled away she caught her breath. He looked down at her, his face very close.

Kenna looked up into his indigo eyes. "You are cruel," she said softly.

"Yes. But it was brought on by your own words. I would not have had it this way. I only want you to come to me willingly, with no talk of debts to be fulfilled." He kissed her again, his actions growing tender.

Kenna felt the trap of his words and his touch. How could she ever commit herself to this man, when she was so unsure of him? And how had her own decision to accept and work at this marriage, turned out to be what this dark aggressor desired?

All thoughts were jolted from Kenna's mind as he placed a line of kisses across her breasts and arms. She closed her eyes, lying submissively beneath his touch as her fingers entwined themselves in the pillowcase, tightening into fists. Her body tensed beneath his patient touch, small gasps coming from her lips.

Grey watched her hands as they tensed into fists, betraying all she felt; it increased his pleasure and he turned his attention to becoming the master, ruling her body in a way he could not rule her mind.

Chapter IX

IT WAS NOT LONG before construction began on the house on the hill. In the weeks that followed, the Fauvereaus often visited the site, watching the raw pine frame being hammered in place. Kenna anticipated living there, wanting the privacy that only a house could give. Grey had become more considerate, courting her with patience and charm; his good humor had returned now that Kenna was his wife in every way. And she had come to see that her decision to honor the marriage contract had been for the best, despite the tension she felt beneath the surface of their relationship. Still, she hoped that there was some chance for their future.

They stood on the hill, his arm about her slender waist, as they viewed the pine skeleton of their home. Kenna walked toward the steps, imagining it.

"Can we have a rock wall here in front, a low one? And can we fill the space with flowers?" she asked thoughtfully.

"Whatever you would like."

"We could plant shrubbery. Perhaps a lilac bush

also. And iris. Yellow and purple ones. That way, when they bloom we'll know it is spring."

"Iris doesn't start to bloom here until early July." He smiled.

Kenna shrugged. "Then we will know it is summer when they bloom." She went up the steps, pretending to open the front door. "Can we have crystal doorknobs throughout the house?"

"I will get you crystal doors, if that is what you want." He was standing very near. "I have no protest about catering to any of your whims, Kenna."

His voice was so serious that she turned to look at him. His arms automatically encircled her, his mouth swooping down to claim hers in a torrid kiss that left her dizzy. When he pulled away, her eyes were still closed, and as he stared at her, they slowly fluttered open. "Can we have a bay window?" she breathed, never taking her eyes from his.

Grey laughed as he guided her through the house, his hand at the small of her back as he remembered what the soft skin felt like, under the dress of lawn and a corset with bone stays.

Kenna excitedly described the curtains she wanted, a watered-silk wall cloth she had in mind for the parlor, and etched glass lamps she had once seen. Grey nodded, smiling, all his attentions on her, while he took mental notes.

August scorched its way into the valley and the heat was oppressive. Kenna could not believe that a town so high in the mountains could be so sultry. But the thin atmosphere lent itself to pale skies and hot sunlight. Mornings were the only comfortable time to be outside, and Kenna loved the soft, clear hours, dressing and going out early each day. She and Braic frequently walked through the town together, then one morning she found herself confiding in him.

"Sometimes I feel so unsure of this marriage," she sighed.

"I thought things between you two were better," Braic said.

"Yes, they are. Grey shows much consideration and has tried to smooth things over between us. But I do not know if there can ever be complete peace in this marriage."

"Have you not forgiven him for his transgressions?" Braic asked.

Kenna thought of his many deceits. "I have forgiven him, although I cannot forget."

"If you do not forget, you do not truly forgive," Braic reminded her.

"I suppose that is true. But I am wary. How can I trust any man, when I have been betrayed so much in my life?" She thought of her father, and how he had practically sold her to Grey. She thought of Glen and then of Grey, and the tentative trust that had been continually trampled down. "You are the only man who had been loyal and honest with me."

"Grey has his faults but he is a fine man. And I have known from the beginning that you could come to care for him. From your first meeting, you never showed the polite indifference that might have been expected upon your meeting a proxied husband. Grey Fauvereau evoked a response from you, and whether it was anger or not does not matter. He reached you and made you answer him. The fact that he found you beautiful, if also prickly proud, secured your fate. I do not believe that there is anything which Grey wants that he does not eventually get.

Give the marriage—and the man—more time. He is good for you; his strong will may be the source of your irritation, but it is also something you need. Weak men have never been for you, my sister."

Kenna looked at her brother. "You admire him a great deal, don't you?"

Braic nodded. "I do that! I could not be happier with the choice of man."

"Even Glen Kinross?" she asked.

"Yes, even him. When he decided to marry Sue-Anne, I was hurt. I had felt he was the very best for you. But now I realize that it is best mere mortals don't decide such things. I'd have been wrong." He looked at her. "Despite what troubles plague your marriage, remember that the course could never have been easy because of the circumstances. Give Grey a chance to win you over completely, and do not keep your heart from him for much longer. He is the man for you, and I have no doubt of it."

Kenna's brow knit in worried puzzlement. "I do not know if I can follow your advice. I want to trust him, but his word has not always been true. I just keep thinking, what will he do next that will cause me humiliation or hurt? You make it all sound so easy, but it is not so."

"Trust is a fragile thing. But it can never gain strength unless you are willing to expose it."

Kenna smiled at her brother. "You are such a philosopher," she said. At least there was one person she could trust. Braic had always been there with his quiet support and she was glad to have it.

"Will you try to follow my advice?" he asked.

"I will try," she said. "Although what comes about

in this marriage will depend further on the actions of Grey Fauvereau."

Braic nodded and smiled at her. "That is true. And neither he nor I can ask for more than that." The two of them walked toward The Bank, where they were to meet Grey for the afternoon meal.

There was the sound of a gun being fired and shouts of excitement as they neared. The crowd that had gathered moved hastily back against the buildings and Kenna saw Grey standing in the middle of the road. Opposite him, across the street from The Bank was a small fellow, holding a gun from which smoke curled. He was filthy, with a beard and hair greasy with dirt.

"That," said Grey in a loud but steady voice, "was not called for, Duke."

"It's Murphy Duke!" Braic said. "At least it must be. Grey has been waiting for him to come out of the hills."

"It is," a bystander confirmed.

Kenna remembered the nasty little man who had given Grey such difficulty her first night in town. "I hardly recognize him! He is filthy."

"Been living up in the hills with the miners, I reckon," a spectator said.

Grey took several steps as if to approach Duke, but the little man waved the gun menacingly at his opponent. "Stay back!" he cried, his voice high-pitched.

Grey held a gun of his own by his side. In his other hand, he held a document. "Come sign this, Duke. Then you can go back to Queenie's."

"Sign over my half of the saloon, just like that? Just lose everything I own on account of some stinking trick?" Liquor still tarnished his senses.

191

"I'm willing to pay back your initial investment. It is here in the contract."

"You tricked me!" He looked at the crowd of spectators. "He tricked me!" He found no sympathy there.

"Duke," Grey said in a chilling voice. "Sign this or I am going to kill you."

Duke squinted at him through swollen eyes, straightened to his full height, and made a threatening movement. Grey whipped up his pistol and fired a shot right between Duke's legs. The blast of gunfire echoed through the street and dust rose from between the man's legs. He staggered.

"You could have killed me, you idiot!" There was surprise in his voice, and the crowd laughed.

"Not yet," Grey said coldly. "But unless you get over here and sign this, I'm going to whittle away parts of your worthless hide with my bullets. Come sign this!"

Duke's eyes were scared but he would not give in. He lifted his gun, waving it in the air. "You cheated me!" His voice was nearly a sob. "You stole my saloon!" He steadied the gun with both hands and the crowd scurried away to crouch out of range of the unreliable gunman. He pulled the trigger and his hands lifted up as the shot resounded.

The bullet whizzed past Grey. There was the sound of shattering glass. He glanced behind him to see the shattered stained glass window in the right door of his saloon. He swore. "Damn you, you little weasel! That glass came from San Francisco and cost fifty dollars. It's coming out of the money I owe you once you sign this!" He aimed slightly to the right of

Duke's head and a bullet whizzed by the scared man, pinging off a post.

Murphy Duke was shaking, but stubborn. He swore vilely at Grey to hide his fear, and again the crowd lunged to safety as he lifted his gun. They did not fear Grey's aim, only the drunkard's.

Kenna leaped forward, running toward Grey. "Stop it! The fool will shoot you!" she cried.

Grey turned, startled. "Braic!" he shouted. "Get her away from here!" Duke's shot rang through the air, the bullet hitting a mark too close for ease.

Braic grabbed tightly to his sister, dragging her away. "You are insane, Grey Fauvereau!" she shouted at her husband. "Will you be so reckless as to gamble with your life?"

Grey ignored the desperate tone in her voice. This was one contract which he needed to bring to an end. And he was doing it in the only way he knew. "Do I need to take aim between your eyes, Duke, or shall I shoot off one of your legs?"

Murphy Duke's eyes narrowed and he licked his lips nervously. "How could you have cheated me, Grey? We were partners for nearly three years!" His voice took on a wheedling note.

Kenna saw the sheriff walk up and she hurried over to him. "Thank goodness you are here! Grey and that Duke fellow are shooting at each other."

"Yes. Well, I figured it might come to this. Grey will settle it."

She looked at him incredulously. "You aren't going to stop them?"

He shook his head. "We have a way of settling debts here, and mostly it works out fine to let the men take care of it themselves. We don't have any fancy English laws here, ma'am."

"I guess not!" she said angrily.

Murphy Duke was squirming miserably. "Why don't we just call the wager off? I won't say you lose and you won't try to cheat me of my partnership. You can still run The Bank and I'll be the silent partner, just like it was before."

"I am losing what is left of my patience. Are you going to sign or do I shoot you?"

It was then that Murphy Duke saw the sheriff. "Ralph! Good thing you got here. Fauvereau has been shooting at me with his gun, trying to force me into signing that cheating contract!"

"Well." The sheriff shrugged. "Better do it."

"You gonna let him shoot me!" Duke screamed hoarsely, his face beaded with perspiration that left streaks in the dirt.

"He's got the right. He won the wager fair and square. He brought back Lady M'ren and had all the papers to prove it." The sheriff nodded at Kenna, and Duke glared at her as if she were the cause of everything. Then he waved his gun threateningly at Grey.

"I ain't never giving up my saloon!" He fired two shots. The second bullet lodged too close to Grey. Kenna groaned.

In desperation she turned to Braic. "Stop it, please!"

Braic walked across the road toward Duke, who warned him with his gun, but he paid it no mind and turned to look at Grey.

"Will you stop this shooting, Grey? You cannot settle a disagreement this way, with a doctor picking lead out of both of you."

A murmur of laughter swept the crowd. Grey smiled icily at Duke. "If this coward is willing to sign the contract."

"Never!" Duke bawled, pointing the gun at Grey and pulling the trigger, only to hear the empty click of a hollow cartridge.

"Now," Grey said, aiming his gun, "this foolishness is over and I am going to make you sign."

Braic was to Murphy Duke's left, slightly behind him, so Grey pointed his revolver to the right. He took aim at a large cast-iron frying pan which hung on the wall of the cookware shop behind the two. He pulled the trigger. There was a loud crack and the bullet slammed into the iron with a noisy ping before ricocheting off.

The force that struck Braic knocked him backward, and he fell against the board walkway.

It took long seconds for the raucous crowd to see the end destination of Grey's last bullet. Kenna screamed, before the sound died away she caught up her skirts, running across the street. Grey was dumbfounded. He saw Braic sprawled awkwardly across the boards, and Kenna kneeling beside him. He looked down at the revolver, its muzzle still hot from the fired bullet. He dropped it to the ground as he ran to Braic, pulling the young man into his arms, holding him; his own tears coursed down to the sound of Kenna's quiet sobbing.

"Get Dr. Phillips," the sheriff directed Jess. Then he leaned down to offer help but Grey shook his head, lifting Braic with him as he stood. He carried him into the saloon, unaware of his crimson-stained clothes. They hurried into a back room and Grey laid him on a long table. The sheriff grabbed a towel and pressed it against the wound. Sadie ran in, assessed the scene and provided some whiskey. If he woke, he would need it. Kenna took a towel and placed it beneath his head to cushion the hard table. Sadie made her sit down; the girl was in shock. Braic's lashes fluttered and he opened his eyes, trying to make them focus. Sadie made him take some whiskey. This done, he lay his head back, looking at his sister and brother-in-law who leaned near.

"What have I done to you?" Grey said brokenly.

Braic managed a wan smile. "Don't be blaming yourself, my brother. It was the fault of the stray bullet." He painfully turned his head to look at Kenna. "And don't you be blaming him either, sister."

"Braic," she said, tears on her cheeks.

"I love you, Kenna," Braic said, his voice growing softer. "And so does Grey."

His eyes closed just as Jess and the doctor ran into the back room. Dr. Phillips bent over Braic, turning him to look at the wound and listening to his shallow breath. He was aware of Kenna's tortured stare as he tended the young man who was bleeding to death on the table.

There were a few rasping, labored breaths and then, at last, his chest lay still.

Jess caught Kenna just as she slipped, unconscious, to the ground.

When Kenna awoke, she was disoriented. Slowly she looked around at the concerned faces hovering over her, and then her eyes were drawn to the still form that lay on the table. Grey stood by Braic's body, his hand on the hand of her brother; his head was bent in misery and his muscles were tense as if he were trying to will life back into Braic.

Kenna moaned and she pushed herself to her feet; Jess steadied her. Slowly she moved toward Braic. "No," she said, shaking her head in disbelief. It was as if the cord which had bound them together since birth had been severed. She could not feel his presence, feel the sharing she had known her whole life. Her fingers touched his face, her shocked brain insisting that he only slept. Braic could not be dead!

Even as her mind denied the truth, her heart acknowledged it. Her chest ached with the pain she felt and she bent down to him, pressing her cheek against his brow. "No, Braic," she whispered. "Please do not leave me! You can come back, I know you can!"

There were hands on her arms, strong hands pulling her away. She resisted the force, finally turning to the person who was drawing her away from her only brother. Slowly she looked up at Grey.

"Come away now, Kenna," he said, his voice hoarse.

She jerked away from him as if his touch burned her. "Why did you do it? Why did you not listen to us when we asked you to stop? Did you care nothing for his life?"

Dr. Phillips was near her, his hand on her arm. "You are in shock Mrs. Fauvereau. Come sit down and let me give you a draft of something to calm you."

Kenna paid no attention to the doctor; her eyes never left Grey. At last he spoke. "I am so sorry . . . I did not know. I fired the gun so far to the side."

She hated the pain in his face; she saw the hurt he

felt. She did not want to feel sorry for him. Her own grief washed over her in waves and her vision blurred.

"Mrs. Fauvereau," the doctor said, "it was an accident. The bullet ricocheted."

"An accident, yes," she said, sobbing with misery. "But a needless one! He would not heed my words. He would think of nothing else but his bet and his saloon! It is his reckless way . . ."

She could not speak as sobs wracked her body and blinded her. Grey caught her in his arms, tears shining in his eyes. "Yes," he whispered, unable to say anything else as grief constricted his heart.

Kenna jerked herself from the comfort of his arms. She wanted nothing from him! "Kenna . . . Kenna," he moaned, grabbing onto her so that she could not escape him. She struggled in his arms, not wanting to see the pain he suffered, not wanting to hurt for him, also.

She struck his chest with her fists, hitting him with all the strength she had left. "Why did you not stop!" she screamed. Her sobs choked her and she could hardly breathe; he stood still, taking the blows that she inflicted. He did not feel the physical pummeling; his own suffering was too intense. Finally she had no more strength, and she stood still, sobbing out all the unhappiness which smothered her.

His arms encircled her but she pulled away, staggering back. The doctor caught hold of her and led her to a chair; she sank down as a great weakness overcame her. Grey stood staring at her, tears coursing down the lines of his face; his expression displayed the misery which overwhelmed him. He slowly walked away with the gait of a man drunk with grief. He was desperate to escape the vision of what he had done.

Kenna did not watch him leave; she would not reach out to him. She could not. Instead her eyes went to Braic, and she wept.

The room was very dark. The furniture was shadows against the darker walls; muffled sounds penetrated through the door along with a crack of light. There was one candle lit, its wavering glow the only light that Kenna could tolerate. She stared at the long table draped with a sheet. Candlelight glimmered off the waxen features of the shell that had once been Braic. Kenna still could not believe it.

Sometimes she rocked back and forth, her arms wrapped about herself as she sought warmth. Despite the August heat, she was cold. And empty; a part of Kenna M'ren was gone. When she and Braic had been only eight, and had found themselves trying to understand the bewildering loss of their mother, he had explained it. She had always seemed older than he, yet in this matter he had a simple understanding. Kenna still had difficulty comprehending it. When they found themselves without a mother's guiding touch, Braic had made things seem light. Through their growing poverty and the eventual death of their father, through the struggles of trying to run Moldarn themselves and the ache of rejection, Braic had laughed at pessimism. When they lost Moldarn, his dauntless courage had nearly failed him, but he pulled through at last. Through it all, she had never been far from him. Though they had been separated at school, there had been letters and holidays to buoy them up. But this was a separation which she could not comprehend, or believe. Braic could not be dead.

Yet his form, so radiant with life, lay solemn in death. The unfairness, the bitter cruelty of it, struck her.

Kenna did not see Grey again. She did not ask where he was. Although the doctor, Jess, and Sadie were concerned about her, she had insisted on returning to the dark room downstairs.

Kenna remembered her father's long vigil by her mother's side. Kenna understood she needed this time to sit by Braic's body, to absorb the reality of his death. Had they taken him away, she could never have fully believed it. Yet now she could face it and perhaps accept seeing him lowered into the cold earth. The rage she felt surged through her. At last the deep misery came.

There was a quiet knock at the door and then it opened. Sadie slipped inside, bringing a tray of broth and tea. She set it down, coming over to sit beside Kenna. She slipped her arm about her comfortingly. After a long time, Kenna spoke.

"Where is Grey?" It was the faintest whisper.

"He's in his office. He has gone through two bottles of whiskey." Sadie was silent for a while. "I've never seen him cry before."

For the first time, Kenna turned her mind to Grey. She had seen the misery in his face, the wretched despair at what he had caused. But she had no room in her grief to pity him.

Sadie sighed. "It was an accident, Kenna. Caused by a foolish stunt, yes. But Grey would have rather cut off his arm than hurt your brother."

"I know." It was a mere exhaled breath. Kenna's

chest was heavy as she breathed slowly. "But he could not heed my pleading. He was careless, reckless with his own life. But my request that Braic stop him brought my brother in line with the bullet."

"Now listen to me," Sadie said sternly. "It was not your fault that Braic was shot. Nor was it Grey's. It was just a terrible accident that took him, just like the plague that took my husband and babies. And if I believed that I could have done more and did not, then I might well have given up and been buried with them. Feel your pain, Kenna, and then let go of it. The hurt will stay a long time, but sooner than you think you will be able to live with it."

Kenna brushed angrily at the tears she could not stop. Sadie looked at her. "Do you hold Grey responsible?"

She was quiet for a very long time. "Yes," she whispered at last. "It was his disregard for caution, the careless gamble with his life that is at fault. I know how miserable he is. And I know that when this numbness leaves me, I shall feel nearly as much sorrow for his pain as for mine. But still I blame that reckless streak in him that he would not temper."

Sadie took her hands, holding them in her own. They were icy and she took the cup of hot drink, wrapping Kenna's fingers about it, making her drink. "Will you let me take you home now?"

Kenna shook her head. "I will not leave him for a while yet. In Scotland, we spend this last time with those we love."

Sadie understood. She slipped out the door and up the stairs to check on Grey.

Kenna sat staring into the darkness for a long while. She knew that inevitably she must see Grey.

But the pain was too fresh, and she realized that there would be accusation in her eyes. Already she had spoken cruel words, born of this new anguish. Could she keep herself from saying everything she felt?

Quietly she went to the back door that opened out onto the alleyway behind The Bank. She stepped outside, closing the door behind her. The sky was clear and black, stars standing out like hard chips of light. Overhead the moon was a silver crescent and the air was still.

Kenna walked down the alleyway and onto one of the roads that led out of Silver. She did not know her direction, only that she needed to walk. There was more pain behind her than she could endure.

The road twisted away between buildings and past houses until it narrowed to where hillocks guarded either side of it. Pines and birch trees shadowed the road with dark lace.

A Chinese funeral procession traveled down the same road in a long file. Pretty silk lanterns hung from thin poles like large fireflies suspended in the air, and their glowing light was a pleasant contrast to the cold moon's rays. Long streamers fluttered from poles and decorated carts. Mai Lei Weng sat in the cart next to her grandfather, pulling her quilted jacket about her. She did not like the long ride to the Chinese cemetery, especially at night, so she thought about a new dress. It was not the slender shell of silk she was allowed to wear, but one from the rich ladies' shop. It had a full skirt and soft ruffles, but the color was not yellow. Yellow was the color of mourning. Glancing about, she could see every person wearing some yellow item to show grief. It was foolish the way white women swathed themselves in black from head to toe. Everyone knew that you wore your brightest to send your lost one off on the last journey.

Mai Lei brought her mind back to the dress. It could not be yellow, even though she looked fair in yellow. She changed its color to pink and added white lace and a sash. There was a twinge of guilt as she realized that her mind should be on mourning, but Great Aunt Leung had been too hard of nature and quick to pinch.

The queue was passing by someone walking in the same direction as the procession. Grandfather Weng made a sound, then clamped his lips into a tight line. Mai Lei glanced at the old man, knowing his eyesight was keen. Who had he recognized, walking in the shadows?

Kenna plodded along, barely aware of the long column of Chinese mourners. Their lanterns lighted her way, yet their eerily pitched wailing songs haunted her. The last cart stopped with a lurch beside her, the red lantern on its tail swaying. The mule who pulled it turned to look woefully back.

"Lady Fauvereau," a quiet voice said. "Would you like to ride with us for a while? We are traveling in the same direction."

She looked at the old man who had alighted beside her. Kenna felt weary, and she took the hand he offered, feeling its strength as he helped her into the cart. Mr. Weng and Mai Lei sat on either side of her as the man urged the mule to shorten the distance between themselves and the other carts.

Grandfather Weng looked covertly at the lady, but discerned that she mourned too much to see what went on around her. His fourth grandson had come into the shop, his chatter highly pitched with excitement. There had been a shooting, an accident, in which the young Mr. M'ren was killed. It was said that his sister's husband had fired the gun. Weng had not believed the story. But later in the day he heard the truth about the shooting and all that had happened. He felt sorrow for the Lady Fauvereau and her husband. But they had to learn to accept fate whether it was foreordained or merely chance. Unhappily the white foreigners had much difficulty understanding this.

Pah! They understood little about living, accepting, and mourning. He glanced again at the lady. Perhaps this one knew. You must cry with the going of the one you loved, and wail if your pain was great, but then you must bear the burden. Grief was a private thing, and if one could not withstand it in dignity, then it was best to go off and be alone. He looked at Lady Fauvereau with new appreciation. This must surely be what she was doing; there was much to admire in this woman.

Mai Lei had heard the tragic story today, repeated more than once, and she had felt saddened. Lady Fauvereau often brought her laundry to their shop, and she had always been courteous. She smiled kindly at Mai Lei and spoke to her in a friendly way. Too often the women in the town had snubbed Mai Lei. It was as if her beauty had made her Chinese heritage all the more repugnant. Mai Lei had long ago decided that she could not be blamed for her pretty features, almond eyes, and long flow of silky black hair. If the gods had smiled pleasantly on her, then why should she bear her beauty in humility as if it were a curse?

Kenna shivered as the heat of the summer day was replaced by the cool mountain air. She wore only the apricot-colored dress that Grey had bought her. There was no shawl to keep her warm so she wrapped her arms about herself. Mai Lei noticed the shiver that went through the lady. No doubt it was shock and sorrow that made her shudder. Did Lady Fauvereau have a destination, or did she simply flee the misery? Mai Lei was filled with curiosity but dared not ask. She looked once more at the shivering woman and then at her own quilted jacket. It was her favorite, yellow, with a fanciful design of embroidered braid in red, blue, and gold. Mai Lei hesitated only a minute before shrugging it off and helping Kenna slip into it. Grandfather gave an approving glance as he halted the cart near the burial grounds.

Slowly, Kenna turned to look back, and caught a faint glow of Silver City's light over the distant hills. It was not far enough away. She slowly dismounted from the cart. Numbly she looked at the old man and young girl who stood by her.

"Thank you, Mr. Weng," she said softly.

"You could return with us just as easily as you have come this far," the old man said in his raspy voice.

"I must go away for a while," she said sadly.

"I understand. There will be honor in this course, and you can return stronger."

Kenna looked at the old man. How could he understand what she did not? He reached under the seat in the cart and brought forth a box. He threw back the lid, hoping that no one saw him. He brought out a small sack of coins, feeling their weight in his work-roughened palm. It was to be his gift to Great Aunt Leung. Yet, as he thought about it, he decided it was better that they aid the living than solace the dead. He slipped the pouch into the jacket pocket. He remembered that Mai Lei's mother had made delicious tarts filled with meat and rice and delicately formed sweetmeats. They could sustain this girl on her journey or they could travel with Great Aunt Leung. He thought for a moment, quickly weighing importances. Great Aunt was well fleshed and certainly would not starve. Perhaps, without the sweetmeats she had so loved in life, she might meet her forefathers with a smaller girth. He took out the food, wrapped it in a large kerchief, and closed the lid. Only he and Mai Lei would know the box was empty. He tied the cloth and gave it to Kenna. She nodded and turned down the road which traveled away from the Chinese cemetery.

Mai Lei watched her go. She slipped her hand into the old man's. "Grandfather, is it wise to let her leave?"

"She is learning what we civilized men have known for centuries. Sometimes you must escape *with* pain before you can escape from it. If she goes into the mountains and struggles with her grief, she can conquer it and return home stronger. If she mourns in the quiet of a white woman's parlor, it will turn bitter and poison her strength."

"The mountains are dangerous when you are by yourself," Mai Lei murmured.

"They will teach her."

"The air is cold."

"Cold can purify."

Mai Lei watched the small figure disappear in the distance. She could think of no argument to make Grandfather go fetch her.

Afternoon sunlight filtered through the leaves of the quaking aspen trees that covered the hills. A summer wind cooled the heat. Small animals scurried beneath the protective brush, and birds chattered in the high branches.

Kenna's eyes were cast down as she followed the dusty trail of the wagon road. She stumbled once, then caught herself. The narrow road followed a shallow stream which chortled over mossy rocks and grass-covered banks. She had walked for a very long time, and her feet were bruised, the hem of her dress soiled. During the night she had walked until exhaustion drove her to sleep on a grassy spot sheltered by two large boulders. Sitting atop a small knoll the next morning, she ate the food Mr. Weng had given her. She cried for a while and then washed her face in the cold water from the stream.

During the first day, she heard the approach of riders; hiding behind some large rocks by the side of the rutted stretch, she saw horses galloping past as if in frantic pursuit of something. She caught enough of a glimpse for her to recognize one of them, a man who worked as a tough at The Bank. Were the riders looking for her? The thought paralyzed her with fear.

She would not let them take her back; she could not face Grey. Did she hate Grey Fauvereau for causing the death of her dear Braic? No, she did not hate him. But oh, his foolishness, his flamboyant pursuit of winning! She hated *it*. But when she could go back to him again, she did not know. She had to reconcile one other truth: she was the one who had sent Braic into the path of the bullet. She would not think about that now, for her heart fairly ached within her breast and her breathing grew labored.

Noon found her skirting a small mining town to find a wagon trail that led up into the hills. She breathed easier with the town, and people, behind her. Walking, she ate the last of the sweetmeats. As she traveled farther back into the mountains, she stopped often to drink from the stream that followed the road.

Jeb Denner opened his eyes and peered at the light that filtered through the straw of his hat. He pushed it up on his head and looked across the forest that sloped up to the Golden Girl mine. Something had disturbed his nap, and although it had not been horses, there was some sound that had caught his ear. Craning his neck, he caught sight of a traveler, alone and on foot. His interest immediately trebled. Sunlight glinted off burnished tresses that fell in disarray down a slender and straight back. He got to his feet and hurried toward the road in an attempt to see more of the woman who passed by. He caught sight of a pale dress and a quilted silk jacket, but the face eluded him.

"Hold up!" Jeb called, running down the hill and onto the narrow road.

Kenna heard someone call out and she turned in surprise. Did the young man running toward her shout at her?

Jeb hurriedly reached the woman, coming to a sudden halt by her side. He did not hide his admiration as he looked at her fair, dirt-streaked face. Wide gray eyes stared back at him and he studied the fevered eyes and mouth. Jeb pulled off his hat to show matted hair. He grinned at her.

"Hello, there, miss. Where are you heading? You ain't lost, are you?"

Kenna looked away, feeling too weak to carry on any idle chatter. She continued on her way but found her path suddenly blocked by the young miner.

"This road don't lead nowhere but up into the hills. There's some mining camps along the way, but that's all. You sure you going the right way?"

With a sigh, Kenna turned and went to the small stream that ran along beside the road. She withdrew a handkerchief from her pocket, dipped it in the water, and held it to her hot face. The cold water refreshed her and she stood, finding a helping hand at her elbow. She looked up at the young man who gawked at her.

Jeb smiled in a way he thought charming, seeing that the face was even prettier once she had washed away the dirt. He felt a thrill of excitement. His partners Brody and Coop left him to watch the mine while they enjoyed the pleasures of town, yet here a pretty girl had just happened into his hands. He could not understand his good luck.

"I got food up at my camp, and something to drink. Nothing hard, I'm out of that for now, but strong coffee. Would you care to rest a bit?" Jeb was very eager.

Kenna looked at the young man. He seemed amiable enough, and the thought of food made her realize that she was hungry. Perhaps if she could eat something and rest for a while, she would regain her strength. Kenna nodded and the miner grinned at her, taking her arm and leading her up a wooded incline.

Though the man introduced himself as Jeb Denner and talked in a friendly way, she did not wish to give her name and would not answer his questions. When they reached his camp she sank down on a log, staring into the coals of a fire which he stirred up beneath a blackened coffeepot. He dished up a plate of beans and salted pork and brought it to her.

Kenna managed to force down a few bites of the overseasoned food. He poured her a cup of coffee but it was only lukewarm and bitter. She asked for water instead and he eagerly brought it to her. He sat down across from her, watching the way she daintily ate the coarse fare.

"What are you doing way out here? You must have come from Fairview, is that right?"

She shrugged noncommittally and continued to eat. He stared harder at her. This young woman was quite a puzzlement. He had been to Fairview enough to know that if she had been in town, it had not been long. He would have remembered a beauty like her.

Kenna set down the half-finished food and stood, her hands smoothing the soiled dress. "Thank you," she said softly. "I had best be going."

Her voice did not sound like the voices he was used to. "I can take you back to Fairview if you want, if you can stay around for a bit," he said, his eyes glancing over her as he licked his lips nervously.

She turned and started down the wooded hillside, and Jeb hurried to catch up with her. "You don't look like any of the girls I know down in town. Maybe you are new at Gert's or The Silk Stocking?"

His words made no sense to Kenna's fevered mind, yet she sensed a subtle threat. The way his eyes raked over her body and the menacing smile made her hasten toward the road.

Jeb caught her arm, turning her around and stopping her progress. "You ain't just leaving! Stay with me for a while." He leered at her. "Gert says I'm the best there is. I'll treat you real good 'cause I do believe you are the prettiest little thing I've laid hands on in a long time."

She stared at him, the gray of her eyes stone cold. "Take your hand off me."

There was such command in her voice that Jeb instinctively removed his fingers from her arm. As she turned and headed down the hill, a flush of red anger spread up the back of the miner's neck, and he ran after her.

"You ain't going nowhere!" His hands clamped onto her arms and he pulled her to him. His lips sought hers, bruising her mouth as the smell of sweat and soil assaulted her nostrils. She fought against him, but she was weak and he was determined. When he released her, she staggered back, gasping for breath. She knew she had little strength left to fight him.

"Please," she managed, brushing aside the mass of hair from her brow. "I'm not what you think. I'm lost. My husband and his men are looking for me." Kenna's head was pounding and she swayed slightly. The miner smiled slowly.

His hands pawed at her and the delicate dress fabric gave way at the neck, exposing her flesh. She began to scream, the sound tearing through the silence of the hills. She could not escape; and his weight pressed down on her.

Suddenly she found herself free as he was jerked to his feet. Jeb gave a squawk of protest as he found himself suddenly facing Brody. Kenna sat up, shakily trying to pull the tatters of her dress together. But the damage was acute and she pulled the quilted jacket about her.

"Whooo-wee! Jeb does have the damnedest luck!" a heavyset bearded man said.

Another man, dark of face and feature, stepped up to her, "Where'd she come from, Jeb," he said, without taking his eyes from Kenna.

"She just come walking down the road. I was working and thought I heard something. She was walking along there all by herself."

Brody reached out with a finger, lifting her chin. He took in the bright lips and flushed cheeks, the creamy skin and the mass of auburn hair. "My husband and his men are looking for me," Kenna stammered.

Brody was a strongly built man; his hair was dirty, and his clothing soiled. Yet it was his eyes, so darkly cold, that scared Kenna. No pleading words would touch him. She took a step backward, swaying against the wave of faintness.

"My husband is a powerful man," she said. "He would easily kill any man who harmed me."

Brody ignored her words. He caught her wrists and pulled them apart, his eyes roving over her body. The jacket gaped open, revealing the torn dress and too much of her skin. He dragged her struggling, toward the campsite next to the mine.

"Brody!" Jeb called. "I'm the one what found her!"

"You can have her when I'm done."

Kenna began to scream, her free hand clawing at

the fingers that manacled her wrist. Her efforts were useless, and he lifted her into his arms. She fought him, her fist striking his face and head, but he ignored the blows as if they were a child's.

The crack of a rifle shot echoed through the air, and Brody stopped in his tracks. He and the other men looked down the hill to see a wiry frame leveling double barrels at them.

"Put her down," a reedy voice called.

Brody hesitated and there was another crack, close to his feet. He stared back at his opponent, realizing his gun was still in the wagon. There was one more shot, again very nearby. The stranger quickly reloaded.

"If you prefer, I can just shoot your feet off, then she'll be put down."

Brody released his hold on Kenna and she slipped to the ground; she needed no urging to hurry down the hill. "Now," the stranger said. "You there take off your boots and socks." A wave of the gun got rid of any hesitation. "Throw 'em down the hill. That's the way. Now, unbuckle them pants and slide 'em to your ankles."

There was more hesitation and the stranger fired a shot at Jeb's feet; he yelled and hopped back. "You crazy?" Coop shouted, unbuckling his pants. The others followed suit.

"Who are you?" Brody growled.

"Just a passerby." Kenna's rescuer looked at the three in their long handles and snorted derisively. "Ain't you a fine lot? Now me and the little gal is going to bid you farewell, and we don't want you following us, hear? I didn't shoot your kneecaps off 'cause I was in a good mood. But you try to follow and I kill you dead. Come on, girl."

Kenna hurried after the stranger while Brody cursed vilely, struggling into his pants. There was a wagon at the bottom of the hill with a team of two horses; the stranger told her to get in and ran to the other wagon not far away. The stranger quickly released the two horses, slapping their hind quarters to send them running off, then hurriedly returned to the wagon, hopping in and snapping the reins. They were well off down the road when the men reached the bottom of the hill, swearing revenge.

The team was fast despite the heavy load, and the road sped away beneath them. "Ha!" the stranger said. "Don't you worry none. There ain't no way them louts will catch up with us!"

"Thank you, " Kenna managed. "You saved my life."

The stranger shrugged. "Ain't often you hear a woman screaming way out in the woods. That kind of miner gives the good ones a bad name. I should of shot that dark one through."

Kenna managed a smile, brushing her hand across her brow. After several miles had been put between them and the miners, the driver reined in. "You are swaying like you're ready to keel over. You sick, girl?" Kenna felt cool fingers on her brow.

"Why, you are burning right up! Here, climb down and come round to the back of the wagon. You'd best lie down in the back."

Kenna complied, lying across some sacks of grain. The stranger tucked a blanket around her and used another beneath her head.

"What you doing way out in these hills with a fever? Did them skunks kidnap you?" The stranger looked down but there was no answer. Kenna's eyes were closed; she had sunk into an exhausted, sick slumber.

"If this ain't the oddest bundle you've ever freighted, Sierra," the stranger said, climbing back into the wagon. "Geddup, Jezebel, Salome. Let's make home afore nightfall."

Chapter X

GREY STOOD STARING out the second-story window of his office; his eyes looked across the familiar hills that merged at the edge of the valley. Cold came early in the mountains, the first snows in late September. But autumn sunlight had melted it away except in crevices and shadowed spots. Not the lusher greens of dripping forests that Grey had seen, but rather the strict beauty of a hard land.

He watched the sun melt into the horizon, lying like burnished locks across the hilltops, the color of Kenna's hair when it caught light from the setting rays. Grey cursed softly as she came, unbidden, as she had a thousand times before, to his mind. He turned away from the window.

Jess watched his boss come back to the large desk and sit down in the comfortable leather chair. He lit the long, thin cheroot and watched the smoke curl upward; it was a habit Grey had only recently acquired.

His boss finally spoke. "So give me the reports."

Jess cleared his throat. "Nothing much. Three claims for the reward that didn't pan out."

"You really checked them thoroughly?" Grey interrupted.

"Yes. And rumor has it that Tracker Jack has been following a trail clear back to San Francisco. Maybe he just decided to go on to 'Cisco because he'd gone so far, we don't know." Jess hesitated.

"There's something else, isn't there?" Grey asked.

Jess nodded. "Dobry the scout just got back." Grey leaned forward across the desk and he hurried on. "There is no word or sign of her among the tribes, the Paiute or the Shoshoni."

Grey leaned back again, grinding out the cheroot. Jess could sense his disappointment. He looked with sympathy at his boss. "You know it's best that the Indians don't have her," he said softly.

Grey gave a curt nod. "Did you pay the scout?"

"Yes. He deserved it. There aren't very many men you could hire to go into Paiute or Shoshoni country."

"Then that's everything?" Grey asked.

"Yes. Except for that newspaperman Malvern. He's waiting outside to talk to you."

"Give me five minutes," Grey finally said. "Then let him in."

Jess left quietly and Grey sat thinking. He had refrained from comment as he listened to Jess. He dreaded the reports: rumors that a white woman was held captive by Paiute warriors, or that a woman fitting Kenna's description had arrived in Weiser, or that she had been found in a cat house in Dewey. And every rumor was like the smell of bread to a starving man, yet when he followed each trail it evaporated to nothing in his grasp. It was as if she

217

had simply disappeared from the face of the earth. It seemed a good possibility that she was dead.

There was a slight knock and the door opened. Joel Malvern, reporter for *The Avalanche,* stepped inside. Grey watched as the slender, boyish-looking man seated himself in front of the desk.

"Is there any information on your wife, Mr. Fauvereau? I heard that the Indian scout got back in town today."

Grey looked at the reporter. "No news."

"That's too bad. I'll mention that in the paper."

"I'd rather you did not write articles on every detail of these circumstances."

The younger man narrowed his eyes a bit. "The public has a right to know the news."

Grey looked long and hard at the young man until Joel pulled at his stiff collar. "I detest your continual prying into my private life, Mr. Malvern." The hard sound of his voice struck Joel.

"You did not object when I wrote articles about Lady M'ren's disappearance and the reward you are offering."

"I only allowed it in hopes that the publicity would find her. So far it has been completely useless! And your frequent articles filled with nothing but speculation as to her disappearance are in very poor taste. I demand you cease your articles about Kenna."

Joel's face was flushed and he stood. "You have no right to keep news from the public!"

Grey also stood. "And you have no right to use your column as a soapbox for your affections for my wife."

Color drained from the reporter's face. "Do you accuse me, sir!"

"It is obvious to any person capable of reading between the lines that you are enamored of my wife," Grey said quietly. "I can't blame you for that, since any man could easily fall in love with her. But for you to declare your feelings openly, in a territorial newspaper, leaves us both looking like fools."

"I didn't know it was so obvious," Malvern stammered.

Grey eased up then, feeling that he had been too hard on the younger man. He had vented feelings too long suppressed. "Maybe it is only obvious to me, Joel," he said kindly, using the man's given name for the first time.

The younger man looked up and nodded. "I apologize, sir." He turned to leave. "Please let me know if you learn of her whereabouts."

Grey watched the door close, then his eyes focused on the letter on his desk. Fergus McDoo had given it to him today; the San Francisco office of his legal firm had forwarded it to Silver City. He opened it again, rereading the contents.

Dearest Kenna,

This letter is to inform you of the death of my wife, SueAnn. It was rather sudden—a horseback riding accident—and has left her family stunned. To be brief, I must tell you that I will be leaving for America next month. I must get away from Scotland for a while, since I have no happy memories left. I want to seek out you and Braic, and I hope that you will not mind a visit from me when my ship docks in San Francisco.

During the past few weeks, my mind has constantly wandered back to the time that you,

Braic, and I roamed these hills in our youth. Suddenly Auchinleck has lost its charm for me, for I see the two friends that I love most in every glen, every wooded copse or hillside burn. Do not think me too forward in my writing, my dear Kenna, but understand that I am a man who grieves, not only for this sudden accident which has made me a widower, but for the youth gone from us. If Providence wills, I shall meet you and Braic when I come to America.

Forever yours,
Glen Kinross

Grey's grip tightened on the letter until he squeezed it into a ball of paper. He knew Kinross was the man Kenna had once loved. And now he was widowed and coming to America; no doubt he would try to win Kenna back. And she would seek refuge if she were offered the comfort she needed. Perhaps Kenna had already made it back to San Francisco and had chanced to meet Kinross. If that were the case, he would never see her again.

He sighed and looked out the window one more time. Darkness had spread its cloak across the valley, the sunset only a streak of fire along the hilltops. It was the night that bothered him. Where was she in all that blackness which engulfed his world each evening? Was she frightened, was she crying for him or cursing him? Grey could not blame her for despising him enough to run away. He had killed the only family she had. Would she look at him with more hatred in those eyes that love had not yet softened? The misery he had felt at Braic's death was a sword which had taken on a double edge with her disappearance. After days of carrying the burden of misery, his heart began to harden against the pain.

Grey pulled on his coat and caught up his hat. He blew out the two desk lamps and left his office. The Bank was doing good business, but he avoided the cheerful hubbub and slipped out the back door. Going to the livery, he saddled his horse and let it meander homeward, his mind haunted by other things.

As he passed along Jordan Street, Grey caught sight of a familiar house. Warm yellow light beckoned through white lace curtains. He wondered why such a simple thing as cozy lamplight should make him feel overwhelmed with loneliness. He brought his horse to a stop in front of the house and sat staring at the little dwelling.

The door opened and Maryetta stepped out, casually resting one hand against the porch beam. She looked quite lovely, wearing a soft blue evening dress with her hair falling freely. She smiled slowly, just as if she were expecting him.

"Come inside. Your dinner's getting cold."

Grey dismounted, wrapping his reins around the gatepost. Maryetta's eyes roved over the masculine form that carelessly pulled open the gate and moved toward her. She pushed open the door, letting the warmth of her comfortable home invite him inside. He sat down on the couch, tossing his expensive felt hat onto a nearby chair as Maryetta leaned against the door to close it.

"You aren't exactly dressed to receive callers, Etta," he said, taking in the flimsy silk she wore. He knew she hated it when he called her that, and he studied her as she did nothing but smile at him.

221

Maryetta shrugged. "You've seen me in less." She went to a sideboard and poured him a drink. She leaned against his knees as he sipped, her heady perfume reaching him.

Grey glanced around the small, expensively decorated living room. It had been a long time since he had been in her house and he noticed stained glass lamps, the velvet couch and chairs, and the expensive inlaid fireplace screen, all of which were new.

He handed her the glass. "I had no idea that the dress shop was doing so well."

Maryetta shrugged. "Come into the dining room. As I said, your dinner is getting cold."

He followed her in and sat down at a beautiful mahogany table set with delicate china. Maryetta pulled her chair next to his and slid her place setting over. She rang for the cook, who served them. The fare was delicious and Maryetta was charming, chatting gaily about social and political events while Grey ate.

"You certainly have become far too sober about everything, Grey. I can hardly recognize the man I knew." She pouted prettily. "You used to have a great deal more to say."

He tossed off the last of his wine and put his napkin by his plate. "You say it all too well, Etta. I had forgotten what a master of conversation you are."

Maryetta laughed and came to stand before him, the flimsy material outlining her womanly shape. "I hope you have not forgotten other things that I am good at."

She slipped onto his lap and slid her arms about his neck. His demanding mouth sought out hers in a heated kiss impassioned by denied longing, and she clung to him. A bold knock at the front door broke into their intimacy, and Maryetta looked up nervously.

"Hadn't you better answer that?"

She smiled down at him, stroking his hair. "I could not possibly care who it is. Everyone I care about is here." She moved in to kiss him again, but the knocking was repeated, more insistently.

"I hate interruptions," Grey said softly. "I'll go get it."

"Oh, no!" Maryetta bolted to her feet. "You stay here and relax. I'll be only a moment."

She hurried from the room, and Grey leaned back in the chair, smiling. He could hear a man's voice and then Maryetta's cajoling. There was the sound of light banter and then the door closing.

As Maryetta returned to the living room, she saw Grey pulling on his coat. "Thank you for dinner. Give your cook my compliments."

"You cannot be leaving!" She put her palms against the lapels of his coat, changing her tactics and pouting at him. "Grey Fauvereau, you should be ashamed of yourself! Here I have been patient as a saint waiting for you to throw off this blue misery, and you plan to up and leave? You take off your coat and sit back down right this minute or I won't speak to you again, ever."

The pretended innocent air that he would have found charming a year ago left him unstirred. He bent down and kissed her cheek. "Good night, Maryetta."

She threw her arms around his neck, pressing her body against his. Her mouth assaulted his in a pas-

223

sionate, fierce kiss. She finally pulled back. "Will you deny that you enjoyed that?"

He shook his head.

"Can you forget all those nights you spent in my arms? I was your mistress, Grey Fauvereau. And I gave you pleasure long before you brought back that high-bred whore! Tell me that you find me attractive, that you want me," she murmured, her mouth still against his. When he did not answer, she looked into the handsome face. "Say that I am beautiful, " she demanded.

"Yes," Grey said. "You are beautiful." He caught hold of her wrists, pulling them from around his neck. "But you are not Kenna."

She shrieked at him, enraged, as he went through the door, shutting it between them. The sheriff was sitting on the porch.

"Evening, Grey."

"Good evening, Ralph. What are you doing here?"

"That's a good question. I thought I was supposed to be coming here for dinner."

"Oh. I think I ate your dinner," Grey said, embarrassed. "But I'm leaving if you want to go in."

"No, thanks." The sheriff headed towards his horse.

"I'm sorry about this, Ralph. I didn't know."

The sheriff mounted his horse. "No problem. Any news of Kenna?"

"No," Grey said quietly. "Nothing at all."

The sheriff looked on sympathetically as Grey mounted his own horse. "If there's anything more I can do, let me know."

"You've done everything you could do, Ralph. But thanks for the offer."

Ralph nodded and the men headed out in different directions. Grey cursed himself. What had made him go to Maryetta's place? He had had reason enough to seek comfort. But there was only one woman who could comfort him, and he could not find her. It had been a mistake being with Maryetta; he had known it from the moment he had entered her house. Never again could he settle for plain bread since he had tasted cake. She had held no charm for him; her musky perfume had made him long for the lighter scent that Kenna wore. Her hourglass figure made him want to hold the softer curves of his wife. And Maryetta's curls, lovely as they were, made him ache to entwine his fingers in curls of a more burnished color.

His horse had reached the edge of town; he urged the animal up the steep road that led to his house on the top of the hill. He felt deep pride every time he returned to the elegant two-story house with its bay windows, wide porch, and carved upper balcony that sported an elegant facade beneath the steep gable.

He led his horse into the carriage house, unsaddled it, and gave the animal water and oats. Then he slipped into the house. The servants had left lights burning for him, as they often did, and he picked one up as he went upstairs. Quietly he stepped into the huge master bedroom, tossing his coat across a chair. He looked at the large brass bed with its thick velvet quilt. This room was serene and reminded him of Kenna.

Through all this time, the house had been a lifeline for him. Every day he had come to the site to watch the workers build his home. Sometimes he had even helped with the work. The house was a labor of love, for with every board put in place or nail hammered in, he thought of his wife. Grey associated the house being finished with Kenna's return. He was consumed with building the house, with having their home ready for her. Once it was built, he did not lose faith. Instead he threw himself into finishing it. No expense was spared as carpets and cabinets, furniture and fittings were chosen. The things from the Idaho Hotel were brought over, and he turned in his hotel keys. But with each beautiful thing added to the house, Grey's misery grew. His certainty that he would never see Kenna again increased.

Despair overwhelmed him, and he took his things to the wardrobe, hanging them up. Kenna's clothes hung in the closet, waiting for her. He reached out and caught one of her gowns in his fist, pulling it from the hanger. He lay down on his bed, still holding it, staring at the filmy cloth. He pressed it to his face, catching the delicate scent that still lingered in the fabric.

"Kenna," he said softly. "Come back to me, Kenna."

The lamp grew dim, finally flickering out and plunging the room into darkness. As Grey lay in the emptiness of the bed, the blackness about him, he took comfort from the soft cloth. He fell asleep, Kenna's silk gown in his grasp.

A huge oak tree spread its gnarled limbs over the wide spot in the stream. Its roots surrounded a large boulder as if the two had grown together. Kenna sat atop the rock that had been heated by slanting afternoon rays and leaned her back against the oak.

Kenna was surrounded by a forest of quaking aspen, the sunlight making the leaves appear like yellow paper; birds pitched their songs at different levels to fill the air with gossipy sounds. The wooded beauty calmed her heart as it had often done in the past.

How long had she been here? She was not quite sure. Before, time had always been important to her. But with no mantel clock or calendar, no breastpin timepiece to glance at, she had no sense of time at all.

Months ago, she had opened her eyes for the first time in the small cabin. Kenna remembered her eyes focusing on the rough furniture, the black stove, and the pine shelves. The one-room house had smelled of burning wet wood, onions, and earth; light had come in through one small window covered by an oiled animal skin.

She had pulled the torn quilt about her, glancing down to see herself clothed in a rough flannel gown that was a hideous shade of green. A movement caught her eye, and she saw a wiry little figure turning over hotcakes on a blackened griddle. The stranger turned and stared at her before flipping over the cakes.

"Ain't got no coffee," a rough voice said. "Don't buy it at seventy-five cents a pound. Got root tea, though. Do you want some?"

Kenna struggled to sit up in the bed, steadying herself against the dizziness that threatened her. "Thank you. That would be nice."

The miner dished up the hotcakes. "Thought you'd never get rid of that fever. It broke last night, though, so I figured you'd be coming round. If you can sit up to the table, you can have some of the cakes."

Kenna studied her rescuer for a while before rising from the bed and making her way to the table. "You are a lady, aren't you?"

There was a spurt of laughter from the other. "I ain't been called that for years. My name's Sierra Nevada."

Kenna looked at the woman with short-cropped hair clad in men's breeches and a work shirt. "I'm Kenna Fauvereau."

Sierra had looked up, surprised; then understanding dawned on her face. "So! You're the one they's looking for. Now all of this makes sense." She had dished up the hotcakes and topped them with maple sugar, then poured two cups of root tea. Sierra shoved the plate toward Kenna. "You'd best eat. You been without food for three days now, 'cept what broth I could coax into you."

Kenna looked at the woman with the throaty voice who so adeptly took on the disguise of a man. "I have been here that long?"

Sierra nodded, taking a mouthful of the hotcake. "You been sick all right. But you must be feeling much better. There ain't more than a handful who are keen enough to tell I ain't no man. And I'd 'preciate it if you would keep the facts to yourself. It makes it much easier living out here as a miner if the men you got to work with think you are one of them."

"I guess most men don't expect to see a woman in a man's clothes."

"Ain't that the truth? They always expect to see a

woman wearing a dress. Most men can't see past the ends of their noses."

Kenna had eaten one of the hotcakes. "This is very good."

"Sourdough. Shorty Johnson left it to me in his handwritten will, the sourdough starter, that is. He'd been using the same starter, feeding it and using it for five years 'fore he died. Then he left it for me to use and I've had it nearly two years."

"I've never heard of that," Kenna said, drinking the last of the root tea in her cup.

"I can show you how it works when you're feeling better. But you're looking a bit peaked to me. Do you want to lie down again?"

Kenna nodded and made her way to the small bed. But Sierra, after seeing to her horses and dogs, came back to talk, as if she were a little lonely. Kenna smiled at the odd little woman. "I want to thank you for saving me, Sierra. That was very brave."

Sierra shrugged. "Them dirty riffraff ain't got no cause to bother a lady like you. I hate them kind anyway."

"Still, if it hadn't been for you I could have died at their hands or from the fever. I hope you will let me pay you back."

"What you got in mind?"

Kenna looked at her in surprise. "Well, I don't know exactly. Maybe I could help out with your work."

"You?"

"I'm tougher than I look."

Sierra studied her for a while. "Did you know they been looking for you in town?"

"They are my husband's men. I'm sure that Grey has them searching everywhere."

"What did your husband do to you that made you want to run away? He must be an awful man."

"No," Kenna said quietly. "He is not an awful man. But what he did was awful. He killed my brother."

Sierra sat back in startled silence. Finally she looked at Kenna. "Did he hate your brother?"

"No." Kenna sighed. "It was an accident brought on by a foolish whim. I know that Grey loved my brother and that he must be suffering. But the pain of losing Braic at his hands has been more than I've had the strength to withstand. So I walked out of Silver City and ended up here."

"You ever going back?"

Kenna was quiet for a long time. "I don't know. I can't think about it now."

Sierra cleared off the table. "Can't say that running away is the best way to handle pain. I'm more for fighting it straight on."

"In this I am a coward," Kenna whispered. "I cannot face Grey and speak words of comfort with accusation in my eyes. Neither can I stand meekly by and watch my brother buried in the earth. I have been brave about many things but now my courage fails me." She brushed at the tears which spilled too easily.

"Somehow that all makes a kind of backwards sense," Sierra said gruffly. "You're welcome to stay here long as you like. This cabin ain't much, but it do got two beds and a stove. When you're well, you can help out by working in the cabin. Maybe later I can teach you how to mine a bit. It ain't rough as every-

one acts." She studied Kenna. "Don't expect you'll
be able to hide out here long, though. With a reward
to get you back, everyone in the hills will be looking
for easy cash. And the first glimpse a passerby gets
of your hair and dress, he'll be coming for you."

Kenna remembered the conversation as she
leaned over the clear pool of water that lay trapped
by a log at the base of the oak. She looked at her reflection. Short, burnished locks framed her face and
curled down the nape of her neck. Rough blue overalls and a flannel work shirt hid her soft frame, and
a hat succeeded in hiding what was left of her feminine image. At first she had been unsure about trim-
ming her locks. But there was no water, save the
stream, in which to bathe, and her hair had become a
tangled mess. Also, every passerby or local miner
had to be avoided. She became tired of darting into
the cabin or hiding in the animal shed. Determined,
she had taken the shears to her hair, with Sierra's
help.

Kenna stared down into the pool and at her shaded
image. The tangle of curls that framed her face was
not unattractive. When Sierra had gone to town for
supplies, Kenna had given her the money in her
jacket pocket to buy her some men's clothing. Although she did not really look like a man, she did re-
semble a handsome youth. She cast aside the hat she
often wore and she smiled at her changed reflection.
With each passing day, she had a growing desire to
stay in the hills.

Working in the solitary rough environment, she
felt a subtle healing. At first, Kenna had often felt
despondent and listless. But in time, she felt herself
accepting the circumstances of Braic's death. She

gained control of her feelings and knew that when she met Grey again, there would be no accusation in her heart.

She mourned for Braic, missing him in a hundred ways. But when she thought of Grey, her heart felt like a stone weight in her chest. Did he suffer? Did he miss her, or had he found solace elsewhere? Soon, she must return to him. Could she simply walk back into Silver City after all this time and assume he had not changed? Now that she was almost healed, Kenna felt the weight of this other problem. She did not see how their differences could be resolved. So, she stayed.

A soft wind stirred the leaves of the aspen, making a gentle rustling sound. Kenna had spent her time not only cleaning Sierra's messy cabin and making breads and soups, but also learning the art of mining. Sierra was a patient teacher, and Kenna had been surprised how much she learned from the lady miner. Living in limbo between her past and future, Kenna felt herself beginning to long for reality again. She looked across the wooded hills, so beautiful in afternoon light, and caught a glimpse of snow patches that had remained in shadowed areas. The first snow had fallen three days ago and, according to Sierra, they were heading for a mild winter because the snow had come in late September and had melted almost immediately.

The sight of the snow depressed Kenna. The thought of winter made her feel homeless. She looked down into the reflecting pond as a waterskipper suddenly raced across it, blurring her image. She brushed angrily at the tears which burned her face.

"Feeling poorly again?" Sierra Nevada said, coming up behind her and sharing the rock.

Kenna looked up at her friend. "I haven't done this for a while, have I? I thought I was getting better."

"You were, for a while. But you been awful mopey the last few days."

Kenna leaned her head against the tree, overcome with despair. "Winter is coming, Sierra. There will be more snow and winter will be here." Kenna closed her eyes against the sweep of misery. "What am I going to do?"

"About winter coming?"

"Yes. About the winter coming," Kenna whispered, "and about my having a baby."

Sierra sat thoughtfully quiet. At last she said, "You sure?"

Kenna nodded, opening her eyes. "Yes. I thought at first it was shock. But the past few days I have been more aware than ever of the subtle changes in me. This baby must have been conceived the first time. Of course Grey Fauvereau would do something like this to me!"

She blinked back the last of her tears. Sierra looked at her. "So what you going to do?"

Kenna shook her head.

"If you are ever going back, you'd better do it soon. The snows come and you'll stay. And my old cabin ain't no place to have a baby. You may have cleaned it up shinier than it's ever been before, but still, the floor's dirt and the cracks let in the cold."

"I know I can't stay here, but how can I go back?" Kenna blinked hard lest the tears return. "Can I simply go to Grey and say that I've decided to come back now that I know I carry his child? He may be a reckless man, careless of consequence, but he is also proud. Perhaps in his eyes I have shamed him. If this is so, he will not eagerly accept my return."

"I got to go to town in a few days. Why don't you come with me then? Maybe you can ride the stage to Silver and stay with a friend till you can talk to your husband. It ain't that you can't stay here. I've come to be quite fond of you, you know," Sierra said gruffly. "But you ain't content no more. Now that you are over grieving, your heart wants to go back."

Kenna nodded. "I do have a friend there," she said, thinking of Ella Farwell. "She would let me stay at her house until I could see Grey again." She glanced at her reflection and the short locks. "I'm not sure he'll even want to see me again."

"Well, you'd best find out."

"Yes," Kenna said, half to herself. "I will find out."

Yet all day long, as she kneaded the bread and cleaned the small cabin, thoughts of Grey Fauvereau came unbidden to her mind. The memory of him haunted her. Two days later, she went to the stream to work it for gold as if the cool, fresh air could chase him from her thoughts.

The rushing stream ran over the flat pan, sifting through the silt and rocks. Sierra Nevada had already found gold in the brook. Now it was a process of working the stream in both directions until the area of the find was determined. Then they would go up into the hillside and, by drilling and testing, they would pinpoint the mother vein. Sierra had said that she was betting the large, visible quartz ledge was holding the main core of gold.

Glancing up toward the hills, Kenna hoped that there would be an untapped vein and that she would find something to show Sierra.

The lady miner had left only half an hour ago in search of her horse. Somehow the old nag had gotten out of its wooden corral and wandered off. Kenna was sure Sierra would find it easily and be back soon. She was startled to find a nugget in the pan. Hastily she picked it out, hardly able to wait to show Sierra her easy find.

The man crouched in the aspens, peering through the cover of trees at the stream bank. His eyes were fastened steadily on the woman below who panned gold with surprising adeptness. There was no doubt in his mind that the miner so intent on working the stream was a woman. A man's overalls, belted too narrowly at the waist, did very little to hide the softer curves. Slender, delicate hands quickly scooped up wet soil. He watched as she paused to remove the floppy-browed hat. Sunlight glinted on soft auburn curls, the tendrils curling in disarray at nape and cheek. The man felt the quickening of desire as he looked at her.

Kenna's thoughts welled over into memories of Grey. She was overcome with an aching desire to feel the comfort of his arms about her. How she needed him to hold her! She fought the feeling, shoving the pan into the stream bottom. Curse you, Grey Fauvereau! her mind cried; angrily, she sifted through the silt.

The wind swept down from the mountain and a shadow fell across the stream. A man stood staring down at her, a grin on his unshaven face.

"Hello, Mrs. Fov'roe. Remember me?"

The tin pan dropped to the stream bank as Kenna slowly stood up. It took no effort to recall the man who had threatened to rape her.

"Mr. Brody, isn't it?" she said coolly while her mind raced on. Why had she left Sierra's gun back in the cabin? And where was Sierra? She should be back by now; Kenna glanced at the stream between them.

"I didn't know you'd remember my name. Ain't that friendly." He looked at her, openly appraising what he saw. "Who would think that a rich lady would be hiding out in the hills this way? Your husband don't know where to look. His men have been searching every town and coach for months now, and here you are, hiding in the hills. Course, they been looking for a lady in a fancy dress with long hair. It was smart, whacking it off and dressing like a man."

"I suggest you get out of here," Kenna said, staring at him with obvious dislike. "The miner who works this claim will be coming to join me, and he'll be bringing his gun," she bluffed.

He grinned at her again, showing yellowed teeth. "Oh? I thought that he was out chasing after his horse." He enjoyed her startled expression and her effort to hide the fear she felt. "You see, it was our plan to have Jeb lead the nag off so the fool would traipse after it. He and Coop will take care of him for what he did. And I will take care of you."

Kenna turned and bolted toward the cabin as Brody lunged across the stream after her. The water only slowed his progress for a moment; she heard his racing footsteps close behind her. He jumped to tackle her; she leaped to the side and he grabbed empty air before he hit the ground. When he got to his feet, he could not see her. He listened for the sound of running feet but heard nothing and decided she was hiding. Quickly he wove his way among the trees, his feet stepping on a carpet of new-fallen leaves.

Kenna's heart was pounding in her breast as she listened for the rustle of leaves. Her back was against a fallen log, her face pressed against damp soil. There was the smell of moss and decaying bark in her nostrils, and she strained for any sound. Perhaps he had moved on, she decided, lifting herself up as quietly as possible to peer over the edge of the log.

He turned at that moment and saw her. Before she could flee, he was on her like a stalking cat on a mouse. Her scream echoed through the forest as he caught her wrists in his brutal grasp, jerking her to her feet. But this was not the girl, weak with fever, that he had dealt with before. Her foot kicked his knee and he nearly lost his balance as he grunted in anger. Still he did not release his hold. All her fighting was useless against his greater strength.

He leered at her, leaning close until his breath was a hot stench against her face. "I can see why he is willing to pay two thousand dollars to get you back. And I aim to collect. Just as soon as I get payment from you first."

"Grey will not pay you if you hurt me. He will kill you," she said, icy hatred in her voice.

He looked at her with pale eyes, cruelty in their depths. "I ain't afraid of him. And I take what I want, whether it's a claim or a woman." He pulled her to him, his lips coming down on hers in a wet heat. Kenna fought against him and the nausea which threatened to make her ill. When he let go, she pulled away, repulsed at his touch.

Brody grabbed her arm, dragging her behind him toward the cabin.

"Damn if you don't got more fight in you than ten cats!" he said, picking her up but finding that this only gave her more of an advantage in striking him. Finally he pulled her to him, crushing her efforts. "Will you stop, woman! I ain't going to hurt you," he explained patiently. "You and me are just going to roll around together in this cabin, and then I'm going to take you back. Now, if you will just help out, Mrs. Fov'roe, I'll go easy on you and we can get you back to your husband. It's just a matter of time till some bounty hunter gets here anywise. When I caught rumor of a young boy pretty as a girl, I figured it out, and I'm sure others in town are doing the same thing. So you just cooperate and there won't be no problem."

He had loosened his grip on her and she slapped out, striking his face so hard that her palm stung. His surprise hardened to anger as she bolted away. Kenna felt him grab a handful of her hair, jerking her to a stop. She cried out as he pulled her around, his face ugly in anger.

"You had your chance, rich lady! And now you are going to pay the hard way."

He threw her against the cabin door, shoving it open with his weight and pushing her onto the narrow cot. But she was off again as fast, catching up a heavy cast-iron pan. Brody paused a moment, surveying her awkward weapon.

"One step nearer and I'll smash this on your

238

head!" Kenna threatened, lifting it up with shaking hands.

Slowly, he reached into the deep pocket of his coat, his voice cursing foully. He pulled out a knife with a stubby but sharp blade. "Damn you, lady. Put that thing down or I'm going to cut you up."

Kenna glanced at the cabin's only door. Brody was standing in front of it, blocking her escape. "You'll have to kill me before I let you touch me!" she cried.

"I may just do that," Brody said through clenched teeth, the knife glinting wickedly in his fist.

The door was suddenly shoved open, slamming into Brody's back and sending him stumbling forward. Before he could lift himself up, a man flew through the air to land full force on his back. Kenna stared in shocked silence as meaty hands grabbed the miner's throat, pounding his head against the floor. Brody ceased to fight as he was beaten into unconsciousness.

A hulking man stood up, looking about the cabin for other foes. Large in frame and feature, his hair was a rumpled thatch of blond and he had a square jaw and blue eyes. He turned his gaze on Kenna, looking her up and down.

"Are you hurt?" Kenna detected a mild accent, Nordic in flavor.

She shook her head. "Is he dead?" She pulled her eyes from the miner's limp form.

"No, I do not think so. Mostly he will wake up with a sore head." He looked at the frying pan she still held hoisted in the air. "And you can put that thing down. I will not hurt you. I am not a bad one like him." He nodded at Brody.

"Who are you?"

"Ulrik." He stepped near, looking her over. Then he touched her arm as if testing it for muscle.

Kenna pulled her arm away, taking a step back. "What are you doing?"

"Making sure you are a lady." He reached into a pocket and pulled out a piece of paper, unfolding it. Glancing back and forth between the paper and Kenna, he smiled. Leaning forward, she caught a glimpse of an etching of her.

"Ya. Well, when I heard of a boy pretty enough to be a girl, I decided to come see. You may have cut your hair and you may be wearing men's pants, but I say you have the face and arms of a woman. And now I will take you with me."

Kenna took a few steps backward, glancing about for another object with which to defend herself. "You stay away from me!"

"I told you before, Lady Fauvereau. Ulrik is not a bad man. I will not hurt you. You understand, ya?"

With that he strode forward, grasping her wrist in his oversize hand. But Kenna did not come along as easily as he had expected. She struggled and cursed him, determined not to go with him. Seeing that there was no progress to be made this way, he picked her up in his arms as if she were a child, holding her wrists together in one fist so she was helpless.

"Put me down! You are making a mistake, you oversize buffoon!"

He strode away from the cabin down the hill towards the road. "Ulrik makes no mistake, Mrs. Fauvereau. You are the one the reward is offered for, and your husband wants you back." He looked through the pines and aspens at the road. "Yo! Ferd, Levi!"

Two men jumped down from a wagon, eyeing the

struggling Kenna with growing interest. "Who is this?" one asked, stepping near.

"This is her, ya?"

"This is a boy!"

"No, it ain't," the other one said slowly. "Look past the clothes, Levi."

Ulrik set her into the back of the wagon and she immediately bolted out of it. He caught her and shoved her back, climbing in after her. "Get this rig going!"

The two hopped aboard, snapping the horses to action. As the wagon headed off down the road, the speed was too great for her to jump out, and she sat eyeing the Swede with open dislike. After bearing such hostility for a few minutes, he looked at her, appealingly. "I do what is best for Ulrik and for you," he said firmly. "A lady does not belong in a mining camp."

Kenna looked away, watching the pine trees and rocky hillsides whip past.

Silently she cursed her husband. How dare he send bounty hunters after her, placing a price on her head! If he had wanted her back, why had he not come himself? Instead he had endangered her life by sending men like these to search for her.

Perhaps they would take her straight to Silver City, and to Grey. No matter; as long as they were only interested in the money, there was hope for her safety.

The rig rode at high speed all the way to Fairview slowing its pace as it passed through. On the outskirts once again they picked up the pace.

The wagon finally turned off, following a jagged road into the woods. This was not the way back to

Grey; they had left the road which led to Silver City. Her hope turned to despair and she laid her head on her arms.

Ulrik watched her, seeing her fear and unhappiness. He felt remorse at being the one who had brought this about. Embarrassed, he looked away toward the granite hills which appeared to swallow up the winding road. Maybe selling this woman back to her husband was not such an excellent idea as he supposed.

Chapter XI

A TINY BIT OF SUNLIGHT shone into the windowless. shed through the cracks in the walls. It lay in a distorted pattern on the dirt floor and Kenna stared at it until the image blurred; then she leaned her head back against the rough planking.

When they had arrived in the miners' camp, they were joined by three other men. The miners, who were only just starting to work this claim, had pitched several tents and built a small shed to lock away food. Kenna averted her eyes from the venison and fowl which crowded the shed, hanging from its rafters. At first, the miners let her join them around the campfire, but she had grown uncomfortable at the men's stares. She wondered what use her cropped hair and men's clothing had been, since they detected her gender so easily.

"It don't bother me none that you ain't in a dress," said one young man in worn denims and red suspenders as he moved near, catching a tendril of hair that had been lying prettily on her cheek. He rubbed the softness of it between his rough fingers and she turned her head away. The miner was undaunted.

"You must be awful special to get bought back for two thousand dollars," he confided.

Kenna's head snapped around, her eyes narrowing. He was so interested in studying the softness of her lips and on making plans to seek out a kiss that he was unaware of the large form hulking behind him. Thick fingers came to rest on his shoulder and he jumped to his feet, staring at the Swede.

"I'm just talking to the lady."

"Ya. Just talking, but talk that is not very nice."

The miner licked his lips nervously. He would be insane to fight this giant, so he pushed back his pride and tried to reason. "Ain't no reason we can't enjoy her company, you know." The others gathered around. "Ain't you ever wanted to hold a sweet thing like her? We can share her just like we are going to share the money. I say that the rest of the men here got a strong urge to feel this lady's flesh, and the majority rules."

Kenna chose that moment to make a dash for her freedom, spurred on by his words. If she had not distracted Ulrik he would have knocked the eager fool out. As it was, she leaped into the forest before someone noticed and all of them bolted into the underbrush like baying hounds after a doe.

Kenna was swift and sly, having often played the child's game of fox and rabbit in the woods which surrounded Auchinleck. She leaned against a huge maple tree, listening to the miners thrashing noisily past her. When she heard them down the hill, she turned and tracked back toward their camp. Cautiously, she crossed the clearing, then the stream. Quickly she ran into the trees. As she stopped to catch her breath, she heard footsteps. Turning, she saw Ulrik just as he grabbed her. They tripped and fell, but he moved to cushion her landing. He helped her to her feet but did not let go of her.

"Now, Mrs. Fauvereau, you got to stop running away."

She tried to pull her wrist free. "I'll not go back to that camp so that I can be molested by those miners."

Ulrik looked at her seriously. "They only talk rough. You do not need to fear. I am a strong man, ya? I will not let them hurt you, so you come back now and no more trying to run away."

He had dragged her back to camp, and poured her some coffee. It was so strong that she could not drink it. Instead, she sat staring miserably down into the tin cup as the others returned. They stopped in their tracks at the sight of her.

"How'd she get back here!" the one named Ferd gasped, out of breath.

"I found her," the Swede said calmly. "She doubled back across the camp just like a fox. Sly and smart like a fox, and scared like one too. Joe made her afraid by talking like that. Now there will be no more bad talk, ya? We make two thousand dollars for her going back to Mr. Fauvereau unhurt." He looked at the young miner. "You heed?"

Joe nervously rubbed his hands along his pant legs, looking from Ulrik to Kenna. Fear of one and desire for the other made him take on the appearance of a nervous ferret. "I say we vote on this here matter."

"Ya, good idea." Ulrik pulled out his gun. "Any man who votes ya, I shoot his leg off. So now, vote."

The miners all looked uncomfortably at each other

while Joe looked nervously at Ulrik's pointed pistol. "Listen," the one called Ferd said. "For the money we get, I say leave her be. Two thousand split five ways is four hundred. You could make a lot of visits to Stella's or Mother Mack's, Joe. 'Sides, maybe he wouldn't pay us no two thousand if we'd been rough on her. Them reward notices says 'unharmed.' It's only a thousand for word leading to her or the return of her body."

"Yep," Levi put in. "Two hunerd dollars don't sound near so good as four."

With that, they all agreed to leave her alone. They also decided to keep her locked up in the meat shed since it appeared that she could outrun them all. Although Kenna hated the filthy shed, she knew she was safer out of sight of the men, especially Joe.

But being locked away was terrible. She spent a lot of the time listening to the men's discussions. It appeared that Joe felt that if Grey Fauvereau had two thousand dollars to offer as a reward, then he ought to have five thousand to pay for a ransom. But once again his plans ran up against the stalwart Ulrik. Still, Kenna worried that now she was being held for ransom. Certainly Grey would not pay five thousand dollars for her return. If he didn't, she would be at the mercy of Joe and the other men.

That night she was given a dirty wool blanket that smelled of smoke. The hard earth floor and single blanket were little comfort, and she thought with longing of the cots in Sierra's cabin. She did not sleep easily, and during the night she was startled awake by voices outside her door. She could hear someone unlocking the door and then Ulrik's voice.

"What? Uh . . . naw!" Joe said. Then, louder. "I'm

just checking on her!" There had been the loud thwack of fist to jaw, a thud against the door, and a moan which faded away to silence. Then the door had been pulled open and a candle had been lit.

"You all right, ma'am?" Ulrick said, looking at her pale face and eyes wide with fear.

"Yes," she managed.

With a nod, Ulrick shut the door, sliding the bolt back into place. Then he dragged Joe's unconscious form back to his bedroll. As difficult as Kenna's situation was, she felt grateful to the giant Swede. He was as good as his word, and she knew that he would not let the others hurt her. After that she slept better.

They let her come out for a breakfast of fried venison and biscuits, and she avoided Joe, who wore a bruise along his jaw. Ulrik allowed her a skimpy toilette at the stream; with his back turned to her, he made her talk to him the whole time to be sure she had not run away.

But after that she was locked back in the shed. She had been able to do little at the stream to improve her appearance; sleeping on the dirt left her hair dimmed with the earthy dust. Tears she could not fight back left streaks on her face, and her hopes were as soiled as her body.

At noon, she was brought a plate of half-cooked beans and mold-splotched cheese. She was also supplied with a bucket of water and a dented tin cup. The confinement in the small prison left her nervous and bored. She tried reciting poetry memorized at girls' school, but this soon left her even more unhappy. Finally, she fell asleep as the bits of sunlight changed their pattern on the floor with the aging of the afternoon.

The door to the shed slammed open and Kenna was startled into awareness. She looked fearfully at the form silhouetted in the doorway; with bright sunlight behind him, she could only see his dark outline and she blinked, raising her hand to shadow her eyes. Slowly she rose to her feet, staring at the man who stood with clenched fists at his side.

"Grey!" she gasped.

Kenna found herself in his strong hold, his hands on her arms as he looked down into the upturned face. His grip tightened and he began to shake her. Kenna's head snapped back and he stopped, staring down at her; she made no sound except the quickened rasp of her breathing. Grey slid his hands up to her head, entwining his fingers in the short curls. He lifted her head, pulling her to him until she leaned against him. He held her to him with the same strength which had vented his violence. She felt the smooth leather of his jacket and his soft linen shirt against her face.

How long he held her and how long she reveled in his embrace she did not know. But when he released her, she was the target of his fury again. He grabbed her wrist and strode from the shed.

The miners all stood looking expectantly at Grey. "This her?" Ferd ventured.

Grey gave a curt nod. "You can come to my saloon in town and collect payment. You'll be able to get it in gold dust or bank notes, whichever you prefer."

Joe stepped up. "How do we know we'll get the money?"

Grey looked at him in a way that made the young man uncomfortable. Joe was glad that he had not harmed this man's wife; Grey Fauvereau would be a dangerous foe. "My word is good."

His movements were angry as he lifted Kenna onto his horse and then mounted in front of her. He spurred the horse into action; the men watched them disappear into the down-thrusting hills.

The ground sped away beneath the large brown stallion. Kenna had to encircle her arms about Grey so she wouldn't fall off. His broad back protected her from the rush of wind. Fall weeds, red, brown, and yellow, colored the craggy hillsides as the horse raced down the twisting road. She could not see Grey's face, only the nape of black hair whipped by the wind; but she could sense his anger. She could not fathom all she felt at being with Grey again. In the sudden weariness that comes from emotional exhaustion, she laid her head against his strong back.

Grey felt Kenna's head against him and he felt an ache which spread through him like an echo through a hollow cave. He felt her arms about him and her body pressed against his back, and he was overwhelmed by the contact.

How had she survived? He could not believe the conditions she had chosen to live in rather than return home. He was filled with anger and frustration. Why had he been so foolish as to build the house, anticipating her return?

He felt cold with fear when he thought how close he had come to ignoring the miner who had arrived at The Bank with word about Kenna. He had checked out false claims too many times. This informant tried to boost the price, which made him suspicious. Not until he stood staring at her small, startled face streaked with dirt had he believed it. She had cut off her hair and was dressed like a man in order to hide from him. How much she hated him! he thought.

As the sun sank behind the mountains which were purpled in shadow, the windows in the valley reflected the molten glow. Kenna realized that they had ridden for some time, as evidenced by her discomfort, yet it seemed a short distance now that she sat so close to Grey. Watching the landscape slide away, feeling the wind on her face, she felt strangely peaceful. She was with her husband again even though her thoughts separated her from him.

On the outskirts of town, Grey headed to a steep road which Kenna realized led in the direction of the land they were building on. When the two-story house with its ornately carved gables came into view, Kenna sucked in her breath. It was just as she had imagined. The large front porch extended from the rest of the house, and its gracious front steps were overhung by a small, ornately carved miniature gable. Two large windows of fine leaded glass stood on either side of a heavily carved wooden door; the front section of the house was walled with overlapping scallops. The second story had a balcony with a delicate rail and an arched facade of carved spindles. The larger back section of the house was set with a smaller gabled end also facing forward. Beneath it was a beautiful bay window with a decorative glass arch. The roof was steeply slanted to deal with the heavy snows, and three chimneys thrust upward from it. A low rock wall surrounded the house, and flowers and shrubs grew within. Every detail, from the carved porch posts, to the starched lace window curtains to the newly planted rail ivy, was perfect. Grey reined in the horse, dismounted, then helped her down; he wrapped the reins around the banister and stroked the tired animal.

"This is the house we were building," Kenna said hesitantly.

"Yes. This is it. It may not suit your taste since you were not here to help decorate it."

"It is quite more beautiful than I had imagined," she said softly.

Grey smiled and bowed mockingly, sweeping off his hat to indicate the door. "After you, m'lady."

Kenna looked away, embarrassed, unsure of him. She went up the stairs and he opened the door for her, letting her step inside. The interior was quite as beautiful as the outside; the entryway led immediately to the wide staircase which was carpeted and sported a fine mahogany banister. The walls were papered in a delicate, subtle blue print on an ivory background. To the left was a door, slightly ajar, a library or office. To the right was the dining room, with large windows facing east and south, curtained in heavy white lace. A large oval dining table and chairs of oak graced the room; beneath it lay a plush Chinese rug in maroon and indigo. North of the dining room was the kitchen, and she caught a glimpse of the large black stove and wooden cupboards. Yet it was the dining room which held her attention, with its beautiful china cupboards and stone fireplace. The room located along a hallway which passed the stairs appeared to be a large parlor, but she could see little of it through the doorway. Her eyes caressed the beauty of the house; the polished wooden floors and carved door molding, the etched glass lamps and silk prints which hung on the wall. She was fearful to praise it because of Grey's mocking remark.

Voices arguing in Chinese could be heard; two people emerged from the kitchen, their talk ceasing when they saw Grey. One was a small man with a long black braid hanging down his back; his age was indeterminable. The other was a pretty young girl who resembled Mai Lei Weng.

"Ah, Mr. Fauvereau! Dinner is ready. We were just debating when you might return," the man said.

"This is Wu. He cooks and takes care of the garden and firewood," Grey said to Kenna. "And this is Ling Ti. She does the house cleaning. This is my wife. You can serve us now, Wu. I'm sure Mrs. Fauvereau will be wanting a bath drawn afterward, Ling Ti."

Neither looked at her oddly, despite her strange attire. Instead they hurried to their tasks. Ling Ti brought out beautiful china and set the table; the linen napkins, silver, and crystal were of excellent quality. Grey seated Kenna, and Wu brought in steaming bowls of chowder, rice, sliced ham, and milk gravy, along with braided rolls, yams, and fried greens. Once the food was brought out, the two servants discreetly left. The sight of such delicacies after the mean fare she had lived on left Kenna very aware of her hunger. She sampled everything and enjoyed the meal as best she could under Grey's continual stare; he paid little enough attention to his own plate. She tried to ignore him but she grew uncomfortable. She was quite aware that her filthy appearance was in considerable contrast to the elegance of the room and she summoned all the poise she could find. Finally she put her fork down and looked at him.

"Yes, Grey?"

He stared at her, his eyes hard. "Hasn't it bothered you to live like that?"

"I was held prisoner for a while with no chance to bathe; I slept on a dirt floor and was not supplied with a change of clothing," she answered calmly. She continued to finish her meal.

It was impossible for him to keep his aloof manner now that she had spoken more than a few words. "Where have you been?"

"In the hills above the mining town."

"I was told you were living with a miner," he said coldly.

"Yes."

"Who is he?"

Kenna put down her fork, completely losing interest in the meal. "He is a she, actually. Her name is Sierra Nevada, and she dresses like a man so she can be a miner. Sierra saved me from some rough miners, and then she took care of me. I was quite ill with a fever."

Grey looked out the window. Darkness had fallen across the hills, and Ling Ti came in to light more of the lamps. "Would you like me to draw your bath, Mrs. Fauvereau?"

"Yes, thank you," Kenna replied. Ling Ti left and Kenna looked about the room avoiding Grey's stare. She wanted to tell him why she had left, but she could find no words to explain clearly. Ling Ti came to get her. Grey followed her with his eyes, turmoil within him. She was different, stronger, he reflected. But then hate had a way of hardening a person.

Whether she hated him or not, he felt both relief and anger now that she was safely home with him.

Ling Ti led Kenna into the bathing chamber at the back of the house. It was paneled in wood and dominated by a large porcelain-coated, claw-footed, cast-iron bathtub. A tall water pump leaned over it. There was a small stove against one wall to heat steaming buckets of water. A window, placed high on the north wall, was of dark green and gold stained glass. A wide cabinet with glass doors held thick towels and jars of scented soaps and bath oils. Kenna stared at everything in amazement.

Ling Ti lifted the large buckets of hot water, filling the tub and testing the temperature. "Is this not a grand bathtub? It was brought all the way from San Francisco on the freight wagons that cross the Nevada Territories. Wu says that it cost nearly eight hundred dollars to buy it and ship it."

"Yes," Kenna said, gazing at it. "It is quite an impressive tub."

Ling Ti opened the linen cabinet and took out a fluffy towel, washcloth, and scented lavender soap. She set these on a nearby stool and then poured in crystals which foamed in the water. "Will this be everything?" she asked.

"Yes, thank you. Oh, Ling Ti. Are you related to Mai Lei?"

"She is my older sister. My grandfather Weng owns the laundry across from the Idaho Hotel," she answered proudly.

"Yes, I know him." She remembered their kindness the day she had run away; she smiled at the girl. "Thank you, Ling Ti."

Kenna cast away the filthy clothes, and stood before the tall oval mirror at the far end of the room. The signs of her impending motherhood were more obvious than she had earlier thought; the changes were delicate yet unquestionable. She sank into the tub; the hot water felt wonderful to her. She smelled the scented soap, then eagerly sudsed her hair. As the dirt soaked from her, so did the tensions. She rinsed her curls, then leaned back in the tub. Steam clouded the mirror and window as she closed her eyes. It seemed years since she had last soaked in a full-size tub back at Moldarn.

Grey reentered the house, having seen to the care of his horse. His feet led him toward the bathing chamber. He wanted to be aloof but his mind raced, knowing she was there. He could not resist her presence: a moth to the veritable flame, he thought grimly. His hand reached for the glass doorknob.

Kenna was startled from her solitude by the sound and sight of boots entering the chamber. They were beautifully tooled brown leather; her eyes focused on them as the relaxation of a moment before was replaced with tension. The tub was deep and she was grateful, sinking down until only her shoulders were above the water. Her eyes followed him as he sat down in a chair in the corner. He spread his legs out in front of him, the expensive boots leading up to leather breeches; his shirt was of the finest linen, casually open to reveal the light furring of black hair. He was more tanned than she had remembered, and more handsome. His raven hair was still in disarray because of the ride; remembering how it felt in her hands filled her with a sudden rush of

emotion. She glanced away, busying herself with
scrubbing her nails. When Kenna glanced up again,
she saw that he was still staring at her with those
eyes as blue as deep water. There was something in
his look that she could not interpret. She watched
him pull out a thin, square-cornered cheroot and
light it; the smoke danced in a ribboned pattern,
twisting upward. Never had she seen Grey smoke before; this new habit made him seem even more a
stranger. She wrapped her arms about herself defen-
sively.

Grey leaned back in the chair, his eyes on his wife.
He sensed her discomfort at his presence. Soaking in
the tub, she took on a different appearance. She was
not the filthy woman in boy's clothing he had
dragged back with him, nor was she the Kenna he
had known. Heat and his presence made her creamy
skin blush coral. Her granite eyes contrasted beautifully with their fringe of black lashes. Her lips were
soft, parted as she breathed the steamy air, and her
erstwhile matted and dull hair now fell in curls
about her face, shining like blackened copper in the
lamplight.

No longer was she the formidably aloof titled lady.
Before him sat a girl, shy of bathing in front of him,
her woman's body protected from his gaze by the
water. As he sensed her vulnerability, his desire for
her increased.

His voice startled her. "Get out and dry off. The
water must be getting cold."

It was, but she had no desire to rise up naked before him. "Have you nothing better to do than watch
me bathe?" she demanded.

He grinned at her, his teeth flashing white in his

tanned face, but there was no humor in his smile. Devil! she thought.

"No," he said slowly. "I've nothing more interesting to do. Certainly you do not begrudge your husband's attentions while you bathe?" The mocking in his voice struck her. She felt a dredging of sorrow at his bitter tone; he must hate her for running away.

"There is no robe for me to put on," she said quietly. "I forgot to ask Ling Ti for one."

Perhaps this would send him out so that she could leave the tub and dry off. But instead of leaving, he went to the linen cupboard and opened the glass doors. Her hopes were dashed as he reached to the bottom shelf and pulled out a silk gown with a pleated bodice. Did this man have every action planned so he might best her in all things? He tossed it across the edge of the mirror stand where it hung in shimmering folds, far from her reach.

"Damn it! Get out of that water," he barked. Kenna jumped at the hard crack of his voice. "That water is cold and you will get a chill." As she hesitated he commanded again, "Get out."

Kenna caught the towel from the stool and concealed herself from his view as she stepped from the tub. Drying off proved difficult for he stared at her intently, perceiving what she tried to hide. He leaped forward, snatching the towel away, the cheroot falling from his fingers to smolder on the varnished floor. The curve of her abdomen was slight, yet still it was there, and her breasts were a little heavier.

"Damn, Kenna! You are with child!" he said.

She angrily snatched up the gown and pulled it on, shakily buttoning the bodice.

He was angry that she was having his baby! Had she so completely misjudged Grey Fauvereau? She looked up at him. "I am sorry if you are unhappy about it but there is nothing I can do," she said coldly, before she left the room. She hurried back through the kitchen and dining room and then on up through the stairs. Grey was in her wake. In the hallway she stopped, looking at all the doors.

"Where is the blasted bedroom!" she cried angrily. She leaned against a beautifully papered wall, exhausted and unhappy, tears shimmering in her eyes.

Grey leaned next to her, his arm against the wall, and she wondered how a man not a great deal taller than herself could loom so powerfully over her. "Kenna," he said softly, his breath brushing her cheek. "I did not say that I did not want the baby. Contrary to what you think, it gives me great pleasure; I have always wanted a child. It's just that even knowing you carried my baby, you chose not to return here! Would you have continued to live in that wretched condition with the child to accomplish your revenge?" His voice was so accusing and unhappy that Kenna could not answer. How could she tell him that she was planning to come home? He would never believe her.

Grey hit the wall in frustration. "And then we rode on horseback all those miles. You could have lost the baby because of that. I am still not sure it didn't hurt you."

Kenna clamped her lips together lest they tremble. Grey slipped his arms about her, picking her up. He carried her to the end of the hall, where he pushed the door open into a large room whose huge bay window looked out onto a balcony. He kept his arms around her as he let her feet slip down to the floor. She felt soft against his rugged form. Grey looked down at her, brushing his face against the damp silken curls. He felt his resolve to be indifferent melting; if he did not tear himself away, he would say all the things he felt so deeply. But he had no strength to leave.

Kenna did not look up at him but neither did she pull away. At last she spoke. "You must leave me here alone, Grey."

He pulled back slightly. "Why?"

She glanced up at him, her eyes brimming. "Because I must cry and I cannot bear for you to watch," she whispered.

Grey reached down and pulled back the thick blue and white quilt, helping her to climb between the sheets. Then he covered her and left.

He stood outside the bedroom door. Kenna's sobbing was quiet and quickly spent. When he went back into the room, he saw she slept as if completely exhausted, the last of her tears shimmering on her lashes. He blew out the two bedside lamps, sheathing the room in darkness. Then he left the room, seeking out the guest chamber.

The lights were slowly extinguished by the servants. One, in the back of the house, glowed late into the night, until it, at last, was also put out.

Chapter XII

KENNA AWOKE to the sound of icy rain lashing against the windows. The forbidding moan of wind and the icy streamers on the windowpane could not dampen her happiness. Despite last night's tears, Kenna felt nothing but pleasure at being back. The exhaustion of the previous day was gone, and she sat up in bed, looking around the bedroom. She sat in a large brass bed with an eiderdown ticking and pillows; the quilt was a beautiful thing pieced from velvet in shades of blue and white. There was a huge oak wardrobe against one wall and, opposite, a matching dressing table with a mirror of beveled glass. Draped across a high-backed rocker in one corner was a beautifully stitched lap quilt. She recognized two of her watercolors expertly matted and framed above the marble fireplace mantel.

Kenna slid from the bed, walking around the room to examine the white etched glass lamps, the dressing table topped with her brush, comb, and mirror, and an inlaid jewelry box. Her fingers brushed the delicate blue print on the wall and she looked out the lace curtains to the balcony with its arched facade.

She drew in her breath at the spectacular view of the soaked hillsides and valley.

She moved to the wardrobe, opening it to see if there were something to wear. There were more items than those she had earlier possessed; several dresses were new, and lovely sheer gowns hung together with her own. She counted a dozen hat boxes stocking the top shelves, although she had had only two hats brought from Moldarn and one bought in town. In the bottom of the wardrobe, she found her shoes as well as a delicate pair of dancing slippers she had never seen. She moved back to the dressing table, finding a box of ribbons and combs and other feminine items.

Had Grey built this house for her, waiting for her return? It was as if he had put each thing in its place with the certainty that she would come back to him. She opened a leather, brass-bound trunk at the foot of the bed and found her paints and books. She put down the lid, thoughtfully.

She washed at the porcelain basin, then pulled on a slip and pantalets and selected a dress from the wardrobe. Stepping up to the dressing table, she brushed her curly hair into a soft mass that framed her face. Then she patted her cheeks and bit her lips until there was more color in them. The soft green dress she had chosen hid the changes in her body. She stood before the mirror, examining herself. How wonderful to wear a dress again and to look like a woman.

There was a sharp knock at the door before it opened; Kenna turned to smile timidly at Grey. His heart quickened as he looked at her; he steeled himself against the emotions he felt. He did not return the smile, and hers faded.

"Do you want breakfast?"

She nodded and he walked her downstairs to the dining room. Wu was just dishing up a large plate of fried eggs. There was also toast, ham, and milk. Kenna sat down and Grey served her, scooping two large eggs as well as ham onto her plate and then his.

"The house is quite lovely," Kenna said. "I haven't seen it all. I want to look around after breakfast."

"Fine." He poured the milk into two tall glasses, setting one before her. "Just don't leave the house."

She looked up at him in surprise as he ate a piece of ham. He took his time before continuing. "I would have said something about this last night but you were too tired. I don't want you roaming around aimlessly. You need rest after your ordeal, and I need a respite from searching for you."

Kenna stared down at the eggs, which grew less appealing every minute. Pride, not love, colored his words, she thought.

He softened his tone as he continued. "I do not blame you for running off before. You had reason enough with what I did." Kenna looked up but he turned his own gaze away. "Just don't be running away again. Will you eat those eggs! The damn things are getting cold," he said tersely.

Kenna savagely cut off a piece of egg, the white runny with unset yolk, and almost immediately she was on her feet running toward the bath chamber. When she emerged, Grey was standing by the door. He handed her a damp cloth which she took gratefully, then he guided her back to the dining room. The table had been cleared. She sat down, pressing the cloth against her face until the feeling of nausea disappeared.

"I'm sorry, Kenna. I didn't think the eggs would make you ill."

"It's all right. This is just part of having the baby; it has happened before." She well remembered the mornings of grabbing for a dry crust of bread in the hope that it would settle her stomach.

"I plan to have Dr. Phillips come by today," he said, pulling on his coat.

"I don't need a doctor yet," she said, but let the subject die when she saw his face. Had there been such a determined streak in this man before? She sighed as he left with no kind word or caress. Perhaps he had only brought her back to save face. He held her in judgment for staying away so long, especially because of the baby.

She went into the library. An oversize desk with a leather chair was backed against the window so it could catch the light. Deep drawers held paper and stationery as well as ink and pens. A porcelain wheel for wetting stamps, two silver pens in their holders, and a large oval wax seal sat on top of the desk.

It was obviously Grey's room. Kenna timidly sat in the high-backed chair; the smell of leather touched her as she examined a letter opener and the desk lamp of heavy brass. She could sense Grey's personality here and it intrigued her. After a while she left the library to seek out the parlor.

It was a much lighter room with French doors opening toward the rear. Heavy ecru draperies were pulled back on either side and a thick carpet of a darker hue was spread across the polished floor. She recognized the furniture from their hotel parlor room. The chairs, delicate tables, and desk were charmingly displayed against elegant wallpaper of ecru-colored fleur-de-lis on cream satin. There was an expensive cast-iron stove, tall and ornate with a floral leaf design picked out in silver on the front; the practical combined with the fancy.

She spent the rest of the morning looking around while Ling Ti checked on her several times to see if she needed anything. Kenna found that the rooms upstairs were equally well furnished and that there were several guest rooms with extra beds. One of these appeared to be used by Grey. She thought of the times at the hotel that he had insisted on sharing her bed. Now he willingly stayed in a spare room.

By lunch, all trace of her morning sickness had vanished. She had just finished two cucumber sandwiches and a glass of juice when she heard voices in the entryway. She strained to catch the conversation as Grey and Dr. Phillips entered the dining room.

"Bill, this is Kenna." He looked at his wife. "Do you remember Dr. Phillips?"

"You seem familiar to me, doctor, although I don't remember exactly when I met you," Kenna said.

The doctor smiled; he had attended her brother the day he died. "It was probably at a party or someplace like that."

Kenna nodded as they sat down. "I've asked the doctor to join us for the noon meal," Grey said, and she signaled Wu to bring in more sandwiches as well as cold ham and carrot salad.

The doctor was quite personable, and Kenna felt at ease with him almost immediately. He was per-

haps forty-five, with wavy black hair and impressive
muttonchops, clean features, and deep eyes. "Grey
tells me you are going to have a baby, Mrs. Fauvereau. Do you have an idea when?"

"Yes," she said. "April third if I go the full nine-
month period."

The doctor ignored Grey's surprised look. Kenna
knew that he was calculating back to the first time
when he had taken her and she ignored him also.

"Grey says he would like me to deliver your baby.
Would you prefer a midwife?"

"No, Dr. Phillips. Actually, you remind me of my
family doctor back in Auchinleck."

"Fine. Then I'd like to start by taking a look at you
to make sure you are off to a good start. Grey told me
that you've had a rough time the past couple of
days."

Kenna nodded a bit shyly and they went upstairs
to her room. "I have nausea often in the morning, although I've heard this is common."

"It is," he said, opening the door. "There's a good
chance it will be gone by next month."

Dr. Phillips treated her very carefully, and as he
checked her over, she asked questions. Having them
answered by the doctor was a great relief.

He patted her shoulder in a fatherly way. "Everything is fine and I concur with your dates. You can
expect a spring baby and you shouldn't have any
problems. Try to get lots of rest and eat three times a
day or more, if you feel like it. There isn't much meat
on you, so maybe we can fatten you up during this
confinement."

They found Grey standing in the hall, leaning

near the door. Smoke curled from his cheroot and he
looked at the doctor.

"She is fine, Grey. No need to worry about anything." Kenna glanced at him; had he expressed
worries to the doctor? "Make sure she eats and
sleeps, which she will probably do on her own, actually. Gad, Fauvereau! When did you take up that
nasty habit?" Dr. Phillips looked at the cheroot. "If
you are concerned about your wife's health, don't
puff on that thing around her. In fact, if you care
anything about your own, you should stop.

"Why?"

"I don't know, exactly. But it doesn't seem right to
me to be taking smoke inside you, and it certainly
isn't good for her morning nausea." He turned to
Kenna. "Just enjoy living in this beautiful new
house, and don't let him bully you. He's very glad to
have you back," he added confidentially. "I'll let myself out."

He left, and Grey's angry stare followed after him.
But after dinner, Grey did not light his cheroot nor
did he at any time afterward, though Kenna watched
for the habit to return.

Although he was always polite, as the days passed,
he was distant; the beautiful house became wrapped
in dour silence. Grey refused to let go of his anger
concerning her actions, especially now that he had
learned she was carrying his child. The fact that he
had had to search her out was an irritant to him,
while a different fact continued to bother Kenna.
Once again Grey Fauvereau had paid for her; he had
brought her back with his money—openly displaying
the fact. She hated being owned by him, bought once
again by his gold. Her earlier euphoria of returning

to the safety of the beautiful house had begun to evaporate.

Above all of this, however, was the one terrible thing which stood between them: the death of Braic. She had wanted to talk to him about what she felt. She remembered how she had blamed him for her brother's death. Yet she had come to accept part of the burden of guilt herself. Knowing the truth, however, did not make it any easier. And Grey gave her no chance to talk about it, keeping himself distant, as if coming close to her would make an opening for words to come, especially those words which would speak of things that hurt.

Airy morning sunlight entered Kenna's bedchamber, and the sky outside was blue, a change from the steady rains of four days. Checking the time, she was surprised to see it was not as late as she had first thought, and she hurriedly dressed, happily thinking of the sunny parlor where the morning light would be ideal for painting.

Grey had already left for The Bank, so when Ling Ti came to check on her, Kenna just requested scones and tea. She set up her easel and began painting; both Wu and Ling Ti checked on her frequently. Had Grey instructed them to keep an eye on her because he feared that she would really run away again?

"You need not worry, Grey Fauvereau," she said aloud as she brushed a blue sky to life across the canvas. "I would not let you shove me out of this house, let alone run away from it."

She had barely finished her landscape when she heard the insistent rapping of the front door knocker. Ling Ti had gone to pick up supplies in town and she could see Wu in the distance as he harvested the last of the garden, so Kenna put down her brushes and went to the door. She pulled it open as the caller poised his hand to knock again. It took her a moment to recognize that he was the reporter from the local newspaper. He stood staring until he realized his rudeness and snatched off his hat.

"Lady M'ren! Perhaps you remember me; I am Joel Malvern."

"Yes, Mr. Malvern. What can I help you with?"

"May I come in and speak to you? I promise not to take up much of your time."

Kenna was unsure, but he seemed so intensely earnest that she let him in and led him to the parlor. "Won't you sit down?"

"Thank you." He sat on the edge of a tapestried chair as if he were nervous. "Is your husband home?"

"He's at work," she said, still standing. "You did say you would keep your visit short," she encouraged.

"Yes, pardon me! I just cannot believe you are back!"

Kenna looked at him, then went to clean her brushes, worrying that perhaps she should not have let this man in. Certainly Grey would not approve.

"Have you been back long?"

"A couple of weeks."

"Two weeks! Why hasn't your husband sent out word that he found you? There are still bounty hunters looking for you; he should have at least cancelled the reward. Lucky thing that I came up here on a hunch. Tell me, Lady M'ren, where were you?"

Kenna slid the brushes into their places, then she

turned to look at him. "I did not grant you this interview, Mr. Malvern, nor did I invite you to my home. Certainly you cannot be so rude as to delve into my private life with full intent to quote me!"

"No, of course not!" He was instantly on his feet. "I did not mean you to think I was interviewing you; it is just a relief to know that you are safe. The whole town has despaired of ever seeing you again. If you prefer, I will say nothing except that you are back home and look well."

Kenna sighed. "I do not mind your printing that."

"Will you at least tell me why you haven't appeared in public since your return?"

She looked at him, exasperated. "Mr. Malvern, please!"

"I ask out of concern rather than curiosity. I would hope that your husband isn't keeping you a prisoner." The startled look on her face made him hurry on. "If you should wish to leave, I'm willing at any time to help you escape him."

"Mr. Malvern, I hardly know you well enough for you to speak this way. And my husband—"

"Your husband is a hard man," he said harshly. "I have long admired you from afar, Lady M'ren, and I feel that I know you well."

Kenna said nothing. He pulled out a pocket watch and looked at it. "I have taken up too much of your time. Don't bother to leave your painting, I'll let myself out. By the way, you do lovely work." He nodded at her watercolors, then left.

The sun slipped behind a cloud, dimming the room. It did not matter, since she had lost interest in doing more.

After lunch she lay down for a nap, and when she

awoke she read until early evening. Despite the beauty of the house, she felt tired. Joel Malvern's question haunted her. Did Grey keep her as a prisoner? Kenna wondered if she could survive the long months of her pregnancy confined in the house.

She dressed for dinner, putting on a pretty gown, one Grey had purchased for her. It had a slightly full cut with pleats, and the fabric was lightweight blue lawn over a heavier underlayer. It was enhanced by silver threads and ribbons of the same hue. As Kenna viewed herself in the mirror she was quite pleased; she tied a silver ribbon from her dresser box at her throat, and smiled at her image. Certainly Grey could not dismiss her, no matter how dour his mood. Little did she know just how ill-placed that mood would be.

An hour past dinnertime, Wu was trying frantically to keep the food warm without overcooking it. Kenna stubbornly refused to eat even though she was hungry. At last, she heard his carriage pull up and she quietly waited for him in the dining room.

Grey wrenched open the front door, letting it slam behind him. Striding into the dining room, he immediately saw Kenna, looking unusually lovely. He threw a newspaper down on the table and shouted for Wu and Ling Ti. As they hurried into the room, his steel gaze fell on them accusingly.

"Why did you let Lady Fauvereau have callers? Who let in that reporter?"

Wu immediately answered although in his excitement, he spoke Chinese. "I let Mr. Malvern in," Kenna said quietly, sitting down.

"You?" He dismissed the servants with a glance

and turned back to Kenna. "Why did you let that poppinjay in the house?"

"Ling Ti was shopping and Wu was in the garden when he came, so I answered the door. I could hardly refuse him entrance."

"Why not?"

Kenna rang the small bell to signal that dinner should be served, and Wu hurried in with steaming platters of sweet chicken and rice. "Should I have slammed the door in his face?"

"Yes."

"Oh, Grey!" She laughed softly, refusing to be baited by his anger. She filled her plate, as she had already waited too long to dine.

He was baffled by her cheerfulness. Had Malvern succeeded in lifting his wife's spirits? "Well, *The Avalanche* has come out with a special edition just to let everyone know you're back!"

She looked at him in surprise. "How long did you wish to keep it a secret? Would you have had me deny that I was back?"

"Don't be flippant! It was senseless of you to grant the man an interview."

Kenna's good humor was gone. "I did not grant him an interview, and I made it clear to the man that I would not answer his questions."

Grey unfolded the paper, showing her the bold headlines before reading it to her. " 'At last Lady Kenna M'ren (Fauvereau) has returned to Silver City. Although she has been back for two weeks, Mr. Fauvereau did not bother to rescind the reward or inform *The Avalanche* that she had been returned to him.' "

271

"That's quite true," Kenna said, savoring the steamed rice.

He skipped farther down the column. "Listen to this: 'It appears that Lady M'ren is in good health, looking quite as lovely as she did before her disappearance, even though her hair has been cut short. Her spirits seem excellent, despite her ordeal and her confinement in Mr. Fauvereau's house. Why he decided to keep his wife's return a secret, and keep her secluded at his residence, one can only speculate.' " He threw down the paper in disgust.

"Your dinner is getting cold," she said.

"Is that all you have to say?"

"What would you have me say, Mr. Fauvereau? That I am sorry you brought me back and that I am sorry you must keep me locked in the house? What a difficulty for you!"

"I don't keep you locked up."

"No? Then why did you tell the servants to dog my every step and why have you told no one that I am back? Joel Malvern asked if you were keeping me a prisoner, and I should have told him yes! No social gathering am I allowed to go to, no ride, no stroll through town. Indeed, I am a prisoner, all but chained here. You yourself rebuked the servants for admitting a caller." She threw her napkin down, standing up from the table. "Mr. Malvern offered me his assistance should I wish to escape, perhaps I should give the offer some thought."

He stood also, facing her. "Of course! Run away into the hills again! Bear the infant in filthy squalor and raise the child in a crude mining camp." His voice was sarcastic and angry.

She looked at him with an unwavering gaze. "You are so cruel," she said slowly.

"I, cruel?" he asked with bitterness. "You dole out punishment with skill, don't you? Well, I will not tolerate any more of your justice. You signed our marriage contract, and despite all that has happened, I won't allow another breach. Neither will I pay any more money for your return."

"No, of course," she said bitterly, his words having hurt her. "I have cost you too much already."

"I did not say that."

"It is the truth! This union was a terrible mistake," she said, her voice quivering. "I should never have blindly signed myself over to you. And you should never have trapped me into this bargain. Running away was the smartest thing I could have done!"

Kenna turned and ran up the stairs, and into her bedroom. She pulled off the evening slippers, flinging them against the wardrobe. It was clear to her that his desire to keep her was only to salve his hurt pride. Now that she was with child, she had not the emotional strength to deal with that. She would not ask for his forgiveness. Angrily she pulled off her bracelet, throwing it on the dressing table. Then she tugged at the ribbon around her throat as the door banged open. Grey stormed into the room.

"Don't talk of running away from me, Kenna. And if that fool, Malvern, tries to help you, I'll kill him." Kenna stood staring at him, overwhelmed by the strength of emotion she saw in the man.

"Then do not keep me prisoner here," she said quietly.

He stared at her for a long time. "I won't have you

running away from me again. I won't give up what is mine." His eyes caught the shimmer of silver at her throat and he took the end of it, sliding the ribbon from around her neck. In a sudden movement he grabbed her hands, entwining it about her wrists, binding her with his tightening grasp. "You are tied to me with ribbons of silver, Kenna. Silver that has passed between our hands," he said chillingly. "I bought your title with silver and in the bargain, I gained a wife." He lifted her wrists in their silken trap, looking down at the woman pulled close to him.

Eyes gray as dove's wings stared up at him, unwavering despite his harshness. Amber lamplight glinted on her hair, inviting his touch. It was more than her beauty that moved him. The power she wielded had a sharper sting than blade or bullet, for she could always leave him—perhaps forever.

The anguish he had suffered when she disappeared, the madness of losing her, had caused too deep a scar. Many nights he had dreamed of her so vividly that he would arise in the darkness and go to her room. He had wanted only to hold his sleeping Kenna, to speak comforting words. He had determined that, if she returned, she must forgive him for that foolish shot fired in recklessness, and he must forgive her for leaving him to suffer more for his deeds. Had she meant to punish him, or had she not been able to stand his presence after what he had done? Either way, the first step would not be easy nor the first words. And now she was here—and his anger impeded him. He pulled her to him. "You have sold your soul to me, Kenna. And your body."

His mouth swept down on hers, crushing her lips as the steel bands of his arms encircled her, binding her even more tightly to him. His hands were harsh against her, his mouth demanding; she had weakened under the demand of his touch. He released her, letting the silken ribbon fall from her wrists.

"Do not tempt me with your threats of leaving me," he said softly as his voice threateningly caressed her. Desire demanded that he take her, but uncertainty made him turn away.

Kenna watched her husband leave, her eyes lingering on the broad muscles of his back till he was out of sight. Would she ever understand this man? Had it been so long ago that he had won her over on a summer afternoon when rain had traced a path down the windowpane? Now he was a stranger who spoke of owning her and the title, of buying her very soul. Yet the kiss had held more passion than revenge.

"You battle yourself more than you battle me, Grey Fauvereau," Kenna said.

A few moments later, Kenna heard the sound of hooves outside, and she went to the window, peering out. She caught a glimpse of Grey on horseback as he spurred the animal on, heading away from the house. She lay awake in bed that night listening for the return of horse and rider or the subtle sound of his footsteps in the hall as he went to the guest room. But she listened in vain.

The next morning she awoke later than usual to find a smattering of snow on the ground and the sky a bright blue. She searched through her wardrobe for something to wear; most of the dresses had been fitted for her small waist with no notion of her impending motherhood. Finally she pulled on one of her favorites, made of a soft brown fabric with heavy lace insets in the bodice. There were shadows under her eyes and she did not look as pert as usual. She went downstairs to the dining room, halting when she saw Grey sitting at the table. He was casually attired, and looked even more darkly handsome than usual to her. A steaming cup of hot coffee sat before him, and he was reading the morning edition of *The Avalanche*. He looked up at her, obviously taking in her pretty appearance; he pulled out a chair for her, and Kenna sat down as he rang for breakfast.

She selected some fried potatoes and eggs. "I thought you would be at The Bank today." She was wary of his mood this morning.

"I took the day off. I thought we might go to town."

Kenna put her fork down and looked at him in surprise. "Oh? Well, that would be nice." She wondered why he had conceded so easily.

There was a knock at the door and Ling Ti admitted Dr. Phillips.

"Hello, Bill. Come in and join us," Grey called.

The doctor entered the dining room and, smiling at Kenna, took the seat opposite her. Kenna returned the smile. "Will you share breakfast with us?"

"Thank you, no. I will have coffee." He accepted a cup, then looked at Kenna. "I was at this end of town so I thought I would check in and see how you are doing. How is your morning nausea?"

"It's almost gone. I've been following your instructions about what and when to eat, and I think that helped," Kenna replied.

Dr. Phillips took a drink from the cup, savoring the hot liquid. "That's good. You do look a bit pale this morning, though and there are shadows under your eyes." He leaned forward and examined her more closely. "Have you been sleeping well?"

"Usually," Kenna said, taking a bite of potato. She had no intention of admitting in front of Grey that she had spent a sleepless night because of their quarrel.

"Are you getting plenty of fresh air?"

"Well, no. I don't go for walks," she said, looking down.

"Gad, Grey!" he said, turning to her husband. "Don't tell me that the article in *The Avalanche* was true? You aren't keeping her locked up?"

"No, of course not."

"This girl needs to get out of the house. I can understand protecting her from the gossips in town; that is why I agreed to say nothing of her return, but you can't keep her locked away forever. Let her start getting out. She needs to go for a walk every day so she won't look so pale."

Grey finished his breakfast. "I was staying home today so that we could go shopping; we need some things. I'm not quite the ogre you and *The Avalanche* suggest."

Dr. Phillips laughed. "Ha! I don't think you are an ogre, Grey." The doctor turned to Kenna. "Don't let him bully you, my dear. Put him in his place and demand that he let you start doing things."

He stood up and she smiled at him. "I'll try." She also stood, and he noticed her dress.

"Very pretty, but too tight." He reached for the waistband. "This is too constricting. Forget your waistline until after the baby comes."

"Most of my clothes were made to show off a narrow waist, doctor."

"You have no appropriate clothes?" He turned and frowned at Grey.

"We will have her fitted today," Grey answered hastily.

"Good. Well, I'll be leaving now," he said, patting Kenna's shoulder. They bade him good-bye, and Grey looked at his wife as the door shut.

"That man is too prying!"

"I like him," she said, unable to suppress her excitement about going to town. "When shall we leave?"

"Whenever you like."

"Right now."

He felt a sudden surge of guilt seeing her anticipation; it had been wrong to confine her. "That's fine. Get your wrap."

Kenna hurriedly fetched a short cape of brown velvet with a bonnet to match. Each was lined with ecru satin and the latter had added ruching. She looked quite lovely, and Grey's eyes admired her though he said nothing. They stepped out into the crisp bright morning, and Kenna waited while he brought the carriage around. His hands lingered about her as he lifted her up before he entered his side of the carriage. A flick of the reins and they were off, the cold air giving color to Kenna's cheeks.

Below them, the city lay surrounded by melting snow, the road a muddy slash. The horse gingerly pranced into the center of the city, and Grey pulled the carriage to a halt before a store that boasted: HOUSE PAPERS AND FURNISHINGS.

"What errand do we have here, Grey? The house is all but finished," Kenna said.

"Well, I thought we might remodel the dressing room off the master bedroom," he replied.

She puckered her brow. "Yes, well, but it is too small for a guest room, I think."

"True. But not for a baby's nursery."

Kenna looked at him in happy surprise. "You want to turn that room into a nursery? Why, that is splendid!"

"It was built into the house as a nursery, but I set it up as an extra dressing room. I had no idea we would be needing it so soon."

The idea immediately appealed to Kenna. She never used the room because the main wardrobe and her dressing table were in the bedroom. It had easy access with only drapes to divide it off. It would be perfect. He helped her down from the carriage and led her into the shop.

The proprietor hurriedly came forward. If he felt any surprise at seeing the much talked about Mrs. Fauvereau in town, he did not show it. He immediately brought out his best samples and the couple sat and looked through the stock.

"It would help if we knew whether this baby were a girl or a boy," Kenna half-whispered.

"It will be a boy," Grey said confidently.

"Oh? You know something that Dr. Phillips and I do not?" she said, raising an eyebrow at him.

"Yes," he said leaning near. "I know it is a boy because it is my child."

Kenna groaned. It was that same insufferable self-assurance that she had observed during their first meeting in front of the Gentlemen's Club. "You might find yourself surprised, Mr. Fauvereau."

"So might you." He smiled wickedly. "Have you forgotten your family tree? You might very well have twins."

Kenna looked up at him, startled, as if the idea had never occurred to her; he could not help laughing. Her eyes were stern. "Only you could laugh at the thought of such a plight! I am hardly ready for one child, not to mention two."

"I quite like the idea myself; it would give this town a new topic of conversation."

Kenna ignored him, selecting a yellow print. "I like this. It is cheerful but not too bright. And if we run wood trim around the wall, we need only paper the top two-thirds." She turned to him for his approval.

"Yes, that would be handsome," he agreed enthusiastically, totally occupied with the curve of her cheek and the flutter of lash.

They next looked over fabrics for the curtains, and Kenna selected white linen with knots of yellow woven in. The proprietor assured her that his man would be out on the next day to measure. They ordered a milkglass table lamp and an infant dresser and then left the store.

Wherever they went, people looked at them with interest and surprise as they recognized the lovely, supposedly reclusive Mrs. Fauvereau.

Kenna and Grey entered the last of the furnishing shops. There they found the cradle they wanted. It hung between two solid stands and rocked quite gently when touched; it was beautifully carved of fine maple, and brass rivets edged the top arches. It was exactly what Kenna wanted and Grey gave no second thought to the exorbitant price. They also bought a larger crib at the same place. The enthusiastic storeowner was most solicitous and assured delivery on Thursday. As they were almost ready to leave, a shelf of toys caught Kenna's eye.

"Look at these, Grey. Let's get the baby a toy."

He smiled down at her as if the childish whim pleased him. "I thought you said only five stores ago that you were not ready to have this baby," he said quietly.

"Yes, I did. But spending all this money on baby things has turned my head around. Look at this." She held up a toy soldier sewn from felt and linen; it sported a tall fur hat and brocade vest. "For your son," she said, the silent challenge in her eyes. She tossed it into his hands and he looked down at her.

"For our son, Mrs. Fauvereau." He handed it to the storeman. "Here, send this up with the furniture."

"Very good," the man replied. "Two doors down is a shop that sells infant sacques and such," he said helpfully.

Grey nodded his thanks and led his wife from the store. "Do you want to continue shopping?"

Kenna shook her head. "I would rather not get everything at once. It will give me something to do over the next few months, now that I may go out of the house on my own." She hesitated for a second. "You are allowing me out on my own, aren't you, Grey?"

Grey peered into her bonnet, taking in the face prettily framed by satin ruching. "Yes, Kenna, I am. Although the privilege has a condition."

She lifted dark eyes to his. "Do state it, sir."

"I want your promise that you will not run away."

She turned her face slightly away, the bonnet's brim hiding her expression. At last she turned back. "Aye, Mr. Fauvereau, I promise."

"That's a good little wife," he said, leaning down and lightly kissing her lips. But his tone was not condescending, and neither was his kiss. Instead it spoke of something sultry, wielding all the more power by what it promised.

Grey smiled at her. "Since you aren't interested in looking at baby things, what do you want to do?"

"I want to eat. The clock in the store said a quarter past one."

"Very well," he said with a nod. "If you've grown weary of spending my money, we can stop to eat."

"Don't worry," she replied. "I am quite willing to resume after lunch."

They enjoyed a light lunch at the Idaho Hotel. Everyone they met was congenial and told Kenna they were glad she was back.

"I must confess I was nervous about coming to town, but everyone has been quite pleasant, though who knows what will be said at the local gatherings."

"There is little they can say since they don't know anything," Grey said.

"No one has made reference to my hair, except Mr. Malvern," she said.

"They will," Grey said, finishing his mutton. "You will have probably started some rage and the other women will be cutting theirs off."

"They would be foolish."

"Actually, I have grown quite fond of those curls

282

trailing on your nape and cheek." He reached forward, fingering a curl near her ear.

"I had no way to keep it clean, living up in that cabin," Kenna said, feeling suddenly shy.

"I thought you cut it to hide from me."

She shrugged. "Maybe in part."

He leaned back in his chair, studying her so openly that a tinge of coral crept into her cheeks. Under such heated perusal, Kenna lost interest in the last of her veal. Just then the waiter brought her the French pastry she had ordered earlier.

She looked at it unenthusiastically. "What's wrong, Kenna? You were anxious to order the pastry."

"Perhaps my appetite for sweets was larger before I ate lunch. I was quite hungry when we came in." She picked up her knife, slicing it in two and putting the larger piece on Grey's plate.

"Now that is a wifely gesture," he said.

"You disdain wifely attentions, Mr. Fauvereau?" she asked.

"Indeed, wifely attentions are what I have longed most for these past months. It has been my greatest woe that I have received none."

She chose not to read a double meaning into his words. "Then eat your pastry."

He poked at the cream-filled dessert with his fork. "It is not pastry I have had a hunger for," he said softly.

When they left the hotel, they headed for the street that sported a number of ladies' dress shops. "Which one do you want to go to?"

Kenna took no notice of Maryetta's shop as they passed by, pointing instead to a small shop squeezed between two large buildings. "Ella Farwell said that she bought most of her confinement dresses there, and that the woman does nice work."

They went into the small, overcrowded shop. There was an air of busy industry as two girls in the workroom sat sewing tiny stitches. A woman bustled up to them and smiled broadly; she was short and matronly, her hair pulled up into a cap. She wore a work apron full of small sewing necessities.

"Are you Madame DeLaney?" Kenna asked. "I am Mrs. Fauvereau and I wish to purchase some things."

Madame DeLaney expertly covered her surprise at having the famous lady M'ren in her shop. What an advertisement this would be for her store if the well-known lady bought her gowns!

"Welcome to my dress shop." She beamed. "What would you like to see? I have some sketches of lovely gowns, copied from the latest styles in Paris."

A half a year behind, Kenna thought. But in this remote town, fashions were always behind the times. "Actually, I have heard you make some very nice confinement dresses," she said kindly.

"Why, how lovely for you, my dear," she said, truly happy because this meant a whole new wardrobe for the lady. "I do have a number of lovely confinement styles, and I can easily add in whatever changes you desire. I can even put in touches to follow the latest trends."

Madame DeLaney pulled out her special files with sketches of the dresses Kenna could choose from. They pored over pictures, and Kenna was pleased to find that most suited her taste. They had elegant touches but were not gaudy or overdone; she selected a number of styles that she preferred and Madame DeLaney set them aside.

"Now," the seamstress said, "if you two will step into my fitting room I will take our lady's measurements and she can choose fabric."

They stepped into the narrow room and Grey took a seat while Madame DeLaney unhooked Kenna's dress. "This dress is not good to wear, Mrs. Fauvereau," the seamstress clucked.

She tossed Kenna's clothes across a stool and busied herself with her tape measure, heedless that Kenna was dressed in only a sheer slip and chemise of lightest linen; both Grey and Kenna were aware of her lack of clothing. There was a tiny edging of lace around the square-cut neck and armholes and delicate pleats covered the bodice, falling open below the bosom. Kenna as well as Grey was very conscious of the slight curve that spoke of motherhood. There was a standing mirror in the room, and he stared at the double image of his wife. Kenna stood stiffly as Madame DeLaney measured her, and then Madame DeLaney slipped through the curtains to gather up some bolts of fabric.

Grey sensed Kenna's discomfort. "Husbands often view their wives like this."

She looked at her husband's reflection in the mirror, speaking to it rather than to him. "But we have not been wife and husband for these past months."

He leaned back in the chair. "I think your new form is attractive Kenna."

Self-consciously, she smoothed the fabric over her rounded abdomen, and Grey cherished the movement. Madame DeLaney reentered the dressing chamber carrying the material.

"I have one of the finest cloth selections in Silver," she said proudly. "And you are lucky, since your confinement will be only in the winter instead of spanning two seasons of extreme weather. This way you can select heavier fabrics to carry you through the cold season." She draped Kenna with some topaz-colored cloth. "Aha! I knew this color would be good on you. What about the sacque set? I can edge it with satin ruching."

"Yes, that would be fine," Kenna answered.

Madame DeLaney held up a bolt of green then tossed it aside. "Pah! All wrong. Look at these wools." She draped the soft, warm cloth across Kenna. The first was light brown and the second a dark, dusty mauve color; she fingered them.

"These are fine wools. I haven't seen the like since leaving Scotland."

Madame DeLaney nodded. "They would make nice day dresses. It gets awfully cold around December and January. And how about these patterns? I can put a lace inset in the brown one, using this heavy crocheted lace."

Kenna nodded, gaining a respect for the madame's tastes. Grey looked on with interest. What other men might have found boring, he enjoyed, for it gave him ample opportunity to watch his wife covertly. They selected a number of fabrics and matched them with patterns, and every so often Kenna would glance at Grey to make sure he did not mind. He only nodded and smiled his consent as Madame DeLaney displayed more goods.

Madame DeLaney held up an evening dress design. "Of course, m'lady will need this for the social events. These short sleeves are quite acceptable if one wears them with the long kid gloves."

Although Kenna liked the pattern she could see no fabric that suited both the style and her coloring. Then Madame DeLaney held up her finger. "I have the perfect thing! I was going to save it, but for you I will get it. Mary! Fetch me the special satin," she called.

Her assistant hurried in with a shimmering bolt of ecru satin, a finer weave than was often seen. "See? Is it not perfect? The other shops have been clamoring to get it but only I have the right supplier. And this lace will match perfectly, do you not think? Also, this ribbon as trim."

Kenna nodded and the woman beamed. "Now, what about slips and camisoles?"

"Put in what you think she will need, Madame De-Laney. I trust your judgment. But for now I think my wife grows tired. If you will total the bill, I will help her dress."

"Yes, of course! Fittings can be tiring when one is in a delicate way." She hurried from the room, and Grey picked up Kenna's dress, helping her slip it on. His fingers hooked the back and lingered for a moment.

She turned to him. "I think we have ordered too many, Grey. It is more than I wished to spend. Let me cancel some of them."

"No, Kenna," he said. "I prefer that the mother of my son be dressed in lovely things."

"But the cost!"

"Have you forgotten that I paid two thousand dollars to get you back? In comparison, the few hundred I have spent today is nothing."

"No," she said, stepping back. "I have not forgotten." Must money always stand between them?

She turned to put on her cape and bonnet and he studied her for a moment before going to settle the bill with Madame DeLaney.

Maryetta Gaylor could not believe her good fortune when she turned the corner and saw Grey's carriage parked in front of Madame DeLaney's shop. She gave no thought as to why it was there, only hurried into the store.

As the bell above the door rang, both Grey and Madame DeLaney looked up; Maryetta feigned a look of innocence. "Why, Grey! What a surprise to find you in this little dress shop." She smiled prettily, coming up to him.

Grey wondered how she could have missed his carriage, knowing it so well. "Hello, Maryetta."

Maryetta glanced around the shop without making the move obvious. Seeing no Mrs. Fauvereau, she felt elated. She smiled coquettishly up at Grey, slipping her hands about his arm.

"You've been quite naughty, Grey, spending so much time at The Bank! All work and no play, you know," she said, ignoring Madame DeLaney's frown.

Grey looked down at Maryetta. He was startled to find himself thinking that she did not have an honest emotion in her. What had he found so appealing a year ago? Kenna either said what she thought or kept silent. He doubted that she was capable of the foolish flirting which Maryetta did so easily.

Finding no response from Grey, she pulled back a bit, turning to Madame DeLaney. "I heard you got a bolt of that French satin, though how you managed to get it, I cannot guess. Anyway, I have come to buy it from you."

Madame DeLaney did not like Maryetta Gaylor, but she hid her distaste. "I am sorry, but it is not for sale."

"Come now! I am willing to pay you twice what you will get for it sewn up in dresses. You cannot resist so lucrative a business deal," Maryetta said assuredly.

"But the satin is no longer mine," the madame said. "It has been purchased by Mr. Fauvereau."

"Grey? But why on earth should you want that fabric?" She ignored her intuitions and looked up at the handsome man beside her.

"Why, for an evening dress for Mrs. Fauvereau," Madame DeLaney replied. She nodded toward the dressing room, and Maryetta turned to see Kenna standing in the doorway. "You see," the seamstress hurried on, "they have asked me to make all of Mrs. Fauvereau's new wardrobe."

"Oh?" Maryetta said, regaining her composure at seeing Kenna looking so calm and pretty in a brown velvet bonnet and cape. Hastily she tried to put together the story of Kenna's return; she would have to seek out Joel Malvern and glean what information she could. But Madame DeLaney was speaking.

"Yes," the older woman said, unable to hide the gloating tone in her voice. "I am making her a whole new wardrobe, many new confinement dresses."

This news was a second stone cast at Maryetta. She rudely studied Kenna's body to see if Madame DeLaney spoke the truth.

Kenna stepped forward, smiling graciously. "Hello, Miss Gaylor, how are you?"

"Quite well, thank you. It is quite a surprise to see you back. Wherever have you been?"

"I was staying with friends."

"Oh, I see. And now you are shopping. What fun! I guess one cannot believe everything in *The Avalanche*, that bit about Grey keeping you locked up."

Madame DeLaney drew a shocked breath but Kenna said nothing, smiling as Maryetta realized her tasteless breach. But the woman was still too upset about Kenna's return to pay attention to social graces.

"Well, my congratulations on having a baby. I am sure that Madame DeLaney will make you some nice things." She turned to the older seamstress. "Be sure and cut them wide, with lots of pleats and ample seams to let out. In the confinement dresses I've made, I found it was necessary, for motherhood will tend to make her blow up quite large."

Grey stepped up to his wife, sliding his hand to the small of her back. "Actually, I think that I am an excellent judge of ladies. My senses have certainly grown more acute this past year. With Kenna's height, I doubt that she will carry my son in a bulky manner." He smiled down at her in a way that made Maryetta grit her teeth. "Even now she does not show her expected motherhood." Kenna pulled slightly away. She did not need Grey to defend her against this woman!

"That is quite what I think, Mr. Fauvereau," Madame DeLaney said. "And I have outfitted half the expectant mothers in Silver. If you will come sign this, then all will be in order," she said, turning away from Maryetta with a sniff.

Grey went to the desk and checked over the list while the two young women stared at each other. Maryetta forced a smile. "I must compliment you on how brave you are in the face of all this. I mean, first being forced into a marriage to settle a bet, and then being dragged here and losing your brother, all in such a short time!" Her voice was sympathetic, but Kenna did not miss the narrowing of her eyes. "And now, to find yourself expecting, it is quite unfortunate. Ah, but then that is the plight of being a woman. When one marries, one is subject to bearing a man's child; this is the reason that I have not married. I have heard from a number of women—many who come for fittings confide in me—that having a baby is the worst pain on earth. It must be dreadful for you, knowing you must face that. Of course," Maryetta said conspiratorily, "I have heard that there is a powder you can buy at the Chinese tea shop next to The Golden Slipper. It can, well, you know, get rid of the problem."

Did Maryetta actually pretend embarrassment at speaking of the subject? Kenna felt more intense dislike for this woman than ever before. "Thank you for your concern, but you see I am quite thrilled to be having Grey's baby. We have been buying baby things all day, even though the time is not close."

"Do you mean you are not in the least bit worried? Why, last year five women died giving birth."

Did Maryetta's voice sound hopeful? Kenna glanced at Grey. When would he be finished? "No, I am not worried. Between Grey and Dr. Phillips, I will be well cared for. And as I said, I am happy to have Grey's baby, since he wants it so."

These last words seemed to fray Maryetta's nerves to the core, and she could no longer smile at the woman she hated. Instead, she looked at Grey as he and Madame DeLaney came back. "Well, I must be going. My shop is very busy this time of day. It was pleasant seeing you again, Grey. Do take care of the little wife," she said in a tone of dislike.

The three watched Maryetta leave, and Madame DeLaney snorted in distaste. "What a dreadful woman! You pay no attention to her, Mrs. Fauvereau, 'blow up quite large,' indeed! Her dresses are overpriced and her taste is outlandish. Why, only last week she showed up at the Woodvilles' party wearing pink crepe tied up with black satin bows. Black satin, if you can imagine! Certainly, a true lady like yourself will pay no heed to that one," she said.

Kenna nodded. Now a mere dressmaker came to her defense against that woman! "Thank you, Madame DeLaney. And I'll expect the dresses by the end of next week."

"No later than that," she assured.

"Would it be possible to have a couple of the simpler dresses done in two days?" Grey asked. "I'd rather she be out of her regular things as soon as possible."

"Yes, of course. I'll have them ready if you come back Thursday for a fitting."

They agreed to that and then left the shop. Once in the carriage, with stores speeding past, Grey breached the silence.

"I am sorry about that confrontation with Mary-etta."

"I did not need you to speak on my behalf to that woman. I can defend myself against your mistress!"

Grey looked surprised that she would rebuke him for his defense of her. "She is not my mistress," he replied, his anger kindling. "Don't refer to her that way again. And as for defending you, I was only doing what any husband would have done!"

Kenna said nothing as they rode along in silence. How had their pleasant shopping spree been ruined? It was that detestable Maryetta, she realized. She was at every turn eager to claim Grey. And once again, she had made Kenna react irrationally.

Grey glanced at his wife; silently he cursed Mary-etta and all the things that had hurt their marriage. He thought of Braic's death and how, through his own foolish action, it had been the most disastrous happening in their lives. Until now, he had refused to talk about it. Perhaps the time had come, he thought, the tension within him lessening at the decision.

Kenna's anger abated as she took in deep breaths of the fresh mountain air.

Grey led the horse down a different road, one that wound into the hills across the valley from their home. The carriage halted as the road ended abruptly. Before them was the cemetery; it was located on a gently sloping hill and surrounded by a black wrought-iron fence. There were rows of marble tombstones, some of the older ones leaning together as if in whispered conversation. Weeds grew in abundance around some, while others were well cared for and planted with flowers.

Kenna sat still as stone and Grey looked at her. "I want you to come with me."

She shook her head. "Kenna," he said softly.

She would not look at him, nor at the gravestones.

"I want you to come with me," he said again, his voice saying more than his words.

"No," she said. "I'm not ready to come here. I don't want to see it." He reached over and took her hand into the warmth of his own.

"All this time, it's been like when he was away at school. We spent many years at different schools and didn't see each other. So though I missed him, it was my happiness to anticipate the holidays, and his letters. It hasn't been so very different now as then, except the letters never come."

"You are a strong woman, Kenna. You helped your brother run Moldarn, and then you sailed across the ocean to marry a man you did not know. You have strength."

"Not in this. I ran away so that I should not have to face his being buried."

"But now you are back," he said gently. He lifted her down from the carriage. She leaned against him, feeling weak. But he would not let her be weak; he opened the gate.

Inside, he led her past tombstones with writing worn away and newer upright stones. She would not read the epitaphs but could not keep from reading names.

Halfway up the hill was a tall marble stone with a rounded top. No verse spoke of his sudden death, only the dates of birth and death. And above, in block print, was chiseled: LORD BRAIC CEDRIC M'REN.

Kenna could not keep tears from coming. More

than anything, this spoke to her of the reality of his death. She leaned one hand against the stone, and wept.

Grey's arms ached to reach out to her, to shield her somehow from the pain. He turned away, sitting down on a large piece of rough granite, the grave of some unknown miner. Sunshine lay warm across his back, but all he felt was his helplessness in the face of Kenna's sorrow.

At last the tears abated and she brushed at them. She turned to find Grey sitting on a large piece of granite, slumped in misery.

Grey heard her approaching footsteps. He could feel her standing behind him. "I'm so sorry," he said hoarsely. "I killed Braic through my foolishness. You begged me to stop, but I could only see the challenge. I never thought that the bullet would ricochet that way. I killed a man I loved, and, Kenna, I swear before God, if I could change things, or take his place, I'd do it."

The autumn afternoon was filled with sunlight and a gentle breeze; overhead a flock of birds headed in a southerly direction. Kenna held out her hand, hesitantly reaching out until her fingers softly stroked his black hair. Her other hand came to rest on his shoulder, giving quiet comfort. She spoke softly.

"I must bear part of the burden, for it was I that sent Braic into the path of the bullet."

His heart ached within his chest in response to her words; for the first time the guilt he continually carried eased slightly.

Chapter XIII

BY LATE FALL, snow was frequent in the mountain valley. Yet Kenna did not find it oppressive, for often sunlight caught the edges of frozen snowflakes, splitting away in crystal shards. The land became enchanted before her eyes, and she was sensitive to the miracle of life, whether it was the season or the feel of movement within her own body. She became well accustomed to the thought of motherhood.

Something changed that afternoon in the graveyard when Kenna stood before Braic's grave, but she was not sure exactly what. Things were better between them now, and bitterness no longer tinged their conversation. But there was still distance between them. Kenna sensed, however, that the coming of this baby would narrow the gap. The baby's cries would fill their silences.

Lovingly, she straightened the bright yellow cover on the baby's dresser top. The nursery was only recently finished, and she was quite pleased with the colorful wallprint and draperies. The furniture was all in place, and under it the soft, flowered carpet. The toy soldier she had made Grey purchase stood guard by a lamp, and the drawers were filled with pretty baby things. There were still more items to purchase, but Kenna took her time to find just the things she wanted. She renewed her friendship with Ella Farwell, and they often went shopping together. Kenna discovered that she was readily accepted back into Silver City's social register and frequently invited to brunches or teas. Any queries by the curious were squelched by the leading ladies of the town's society. Several matronly women felt it their responsibility to take the nice young woman under their wing.

Kenna smiled and brushed at a stray curl. She was not as frail as they thought. Grey had been right; she was strong. And she was capable of fighting for the marriage she had once run away from. Patience and determination were her weapons, and she had all the time in the world to reconcile with him and dispel his black moods.

After much study, Kenna finally hung three watercolors she had painted for the room on the wall above the baby's crib. There remained only a few last minute purchases which Kenna put off, knowing that the time was still months away.

"Mrs. Fauvereau," Ling Ti called out, hurrying upstairs. "You have a visitor."

Kenna was not expecting anyone, nor had she heard the door knocker. "Who is it, Ling Ti?"

"A Miss Gaylor. I showed her into the parlor."

"Tell her I will be down momentarily," she said, hurrying into her bedroom. Hastily she combed her hair and smoothed her dress. She wore a simple but pretty day dress designed by Madame DeLaney. Her expectant motherhood was noticeable, and she in-

stinctively wished to arm herself in finery before
meeting her smiling foe.

She went downstairs into the parlor to find Maryetta sitting primly on the settee, wearing an elegant
dress of peacock blue and a hat sporting feathers
dyed to match. It was a bit overdone for daytime,
Kenna thought. Maryetta took in Kenna's appearance just as avidly.

Though dressed simply, Grey's wife entered the
room with color in her cheeks and a slight smile on
her lips. Her hair was short as reported. This was the
first time Maryetta had seen her without a bonnet.
Her trailing curls made her look younger in the afternoon light. Her impending motherhood was now
obvious, but she carried herself gracefully, as if she
bore a gift rather than a burden. Maryetta felt a stab
of hatred, but she smiled at Kenna.

"My, you are showing, aren't you?"

"Hello," Kenna said, seating herself. "This is an
unexpected call."

"Do forgive me! I should have sent a note to let you
know I was coming instead of dropping in."

"That is quite all right. I was just finishing up in
the nursery. It has been a pleasant task to get everything ready."

"How quaint! I'm sure I should go quite mad with
nothing to do but set up a nursery and wear baggy
confinement dresses."

Kenna laughed. It amused her that Maryetta's
forced politeness was wearing so pitifully thin. "Certainly you are too busy to come by only to give me
condolences. Why did you come here?"

Maryetta reached for a hatbox sitting on the floor;

she handed it to Kenna. Surprised, Kenna opened it. Inside lay a handsome man's hat, and she took it out.

She looked at Maryetta. "A gift for Grey?"

"No," Maryetta said slowly. "I'm just returning it. Grey left it at my house the other night."

Kenna leveled dark eyes at her. "If you are trying to make me jealous," she said softly, "the task is one too large for you."

Maryetta's smile disappeared. "Don't tell me that the little wife is willing to turn her back on what goes on? That is just too self-sacrificing of you."

Kenna leaned back in her chair and ran her fingers around the wide felt brim in a way that thoroughly annoyed Maryetta. "It does not matter what words you use." She lifted her eyes to look at the woman. "Grey is still my husband, and you have no claim on him."

"No claim!" the other scoffed. "He was mine two years before you ever arrived here. You poor little fool. Grey married you to settle the bet, to win the saloon. He only wanted your fancy title—little good it does you—because he certainly didn't marry you for love!"

"Yes, you are right," Kenna said. "Grey did marry me for my title to win the bet. I do not deny it nor do I mind it, for he came to love me once we were wed. Neither does it bother me that you were once his mistress, because that was before he knew me."

"He does not need you!" she hissed.

"I am his wife and carry his child," Kenna said calmly. "You have neither his name nor his son."

"You deserted him when he was at his most desperate, and he came to me for comfort," Maryetta said. She looked pointedly at the hat as if it were proof.

"Well, I am back now."

"But he still wants me."

"No, I don't think so," Kenna said slowly, "for if he seeks you out, why do you feel the need to bring his hat to boast of your possession of it?"

Maryetta stood, two bright spots of color stained her pale cheeks. "I hate you," she said bitingly.

"I know," Kenna replied. "And I pity you for it." She did not need to invite Miss Gaylor to leave, for she hurried from the room and out of the house, her expected victory turned to ashes.

Kenna sat back down in the chair, staring at the fine man's hat in her lap. The clock on the writing desk ticked loudly in the silence, and the hope she had felt these past days faded. She could stand her ground bravely and face the foe until the battle was over, but afterward she felt the scars. Doubts circled like scavengers. Which did Maryetta use as a weapon, deceit or truth? Her fingers tightened on the brim of the hat. It was time she let Grey know how she felt about this woman from his past.

Grey opened the front door and stepped into the quiet house. Often he was greeted by Kenna's humming or the clatter of plates on the table as the evening meal was readied. But the silence that met him impelled him down the hall, searching for Kenna. He found her sitting in the parlor, looking as if her mind had traveled miles away; she did not hear his footsteps.

He felt a strong desire to bend down and kiss her hair. But as always he restrained himself. The wounds were not by any means healed, though the first step had been taken in the cemetery. Since that time, they were able to talk more easily though he was still unable to express his deepest feelings.

He stepped near and Kenna looked up; he smiled at her. "Was that Maryetta's carriage I passed on the road?"

Kenna slowly stood up and faced him, her eyes gray as stormclouds. "Yes. She brought back your hat. You left it there the other night."

With a sudden movement, she lashed out with the hat, striking him across the chest. She did not cease with one blow; instead the hat became some imaginary whip she lashed at him. Grey could only stand and stare at such ineffectual abuse, astounded by her emotion.

He caught her wrist in his hand, staring at the offensive weapon. "Why are you trying to bludgeon me with my hat?"

She glared up at him. "Then you admit this is your hat!"

"I admit that. Does it make me guilty of some crime?" There was humor in his voice, which further annoyed Kenna. She turned away from him, looking out the French doors.

"Kenna?"

"We have nothing to discuss."

"No? A man walks into his own home and is met with anger for no clear reason except that Maryetta returned my hat."

She whirled about, glaring at him. "Of course, you would think it just a courteous thing for her to do. After all, you are the man who married me for a bet and dragged me halfway across the world to fulfill it!"

"Does that still bother you?" he asked with interest.

"Only when combined with proof of your other deceits," she said icily.

He studied her for a moment. "I assume this is in reference to Maryetta," he said slowly.

"How astute!"

"Why did she come here?"

"To return your hat, of course," she said, the forced sweetness of her voice belying the bitter emotions.

He stared at the cause of his troubles, recognizable despite the now battered crown. "How did she get it?"

"You left it at her house the other night," Kenna said.

Grey's eyebrows shot up in surprise. "I did?" The smile that spread across his handsome face irritated her to the extreme. "But how could I? I have not been to her place in months. I wondered where that hat went to. My dearest wife, I have not been to Maryetta's house since your return."

This statement only seemed to make Kenna angrier. "She said that you went to her all the time I was gone! I should have realized that to a man like you, once a woman is out of sight, she is out of mind."

His words were spoken softly, almost teasingly. "Jealous, Kenna?"

She turned on him, her eyes narrowing like a cat's. "Jealous!" she cried, stalking him. "Jealous of a blackguard, of a rogue like you?" Kenna grabbed the hat viciously, slashing it across his chest. She pummeled, furiously.

He grabbed the ruined hat from her, throwing it

on the settee, and pulled her to him, holding her tightly. Hot tears scalded her cheeks. She hated him for making her cry, for seeing her this way; he had made her vulnerable and she was helpless to do anything but let him hold her.

"Damn you," she choked out.

Grey reveled in the feeling of her, and in her need of him. She had seen him weak, desperately in need of her forgiving, and for the first time he no longer resented it. His fingers stroked her hair, and his voice made soft sounds of comfort. He kissed her hair, breathing in its sweet fragrance; for a long time he had ached to hold her, to give comfort and love.

Finally she looked up, and he pulled out his white handkerchief, wiping away the tears that stained her face. Her feeling of humiliation showed in her face.

"There's nothing wrong with crying, Kenna," he said kindly.

He bent and kissed her tenderly. "You have every right to be angry. You are carrying my son, and my name."

"I told her that," Kenna said quietly.

"And did she tell you that in a moment of desperation I came to her house once for dinner and that afterward I left right away? Did she tell you I never came again because she was not the woman I wanted?"

Kenna stared into the darkened depths of his blue eyes. "No," she whispered. "She never said that." There was silence between them, then, "It is hard for me to fight you when you hold me so, Grey."

His mouth came down on hers, crushing her lips desperately. His arms tightened, pulling her against his steel frame, demanding that she submit to him.

303

One hand slid up her back, finally entangling his fingers in her hair; he allowed her no retreat. The wave of heat that swept through Kenna left her weak as her arms slid around his neck helplessly. Her mouth answered his own with unconscious longing as the dark desire for him took hold of her.

Grey was the one to pull away. He glanced down at the soft curve of her abdomen, and worry crossed his brow. "I hope I did not hurt you."

"It takes more to hurt the two of us than a kiss," she said, both to reassure him and to invite him to continue.

But his desire for her abruptly waned. What if he hurt the child during this longed-for intimacy? And deep in the back of his mind was the plaguing thought that he could lose her forever if something did happen and she risked her life to bear his child. He pulled away from her.

"How soon do we eat?" he asked casually.

Kenna observed the curtain fall in place within her husband, and she felt an empty echoing inside. For once she had breached his reserve; she had glimpsed the old Grey, the one she had known before Braic's death. She fled from the parlor and up the stairs, seeking refuge in her room.

Lying on her bed, she brushed at the tears that ran down her cheeks. She ached to be held in his arms again, yet she was at a loss. How could she ever understand that man? Could she believe him that he had not been with Maryetta? Why had he rejected her? Did he still hate her for leaving him after Braic's death? She was miserable, and did not understand how all could be made right again after this devastating rebuff.

Downstairs, Grey ate dinner alone, pondering the vagaries of pregnant women. It did not occur to him that she would misinterpert his constraint. He would claim her again, in time, but until then, he intended to make her love him and yearn for him as he did for her. Love was the bond that would keep her from ever leaving him again.

In December, The Bank did little business because of the snow, so Grey did not spend many hours there, afraid he would be trapped in town, unable to make the steep grade during a storm. It was a pleasant time for them. Grey was more at ease with Kenna now than at any time since her return, never hesitating to bend and kiss her when he entered a room and found her there. Each found comfort in the other's presence.

Kenna was never long out of his sight. Sometimes he would watch her paint watercolors of winter scenes, or help her make the Scottish cookies that were a favorite treat. Other times they sat together in the parlor, each reading a book in companionable silence.

All was silent and still after the storms abated, except for lines of blue-gray smoke rising to the clouds. It was not the only indication of life, for soon windows opened and doors spewed forth children. Cold did not intimidate the people who lived in these mountains.

Grey took Kenna for a ride in the sleigh, and they passed many others whose sleigh jangled merrily with bells. They visited friends, shopped, and went to several dinner parties. But she loved the sleigh rides best. She kept a secret within her heart. Grey was changing, renewing his headstrong joy of life.

The day before Christmas The Bank was closed. The Fauvereaus were throwing a ball; the saloon was emptied of all tables, and the chairs were pushed back against the walls. Kenna supervised the cleaning, with Sadie's help; Grey kept a close watch that she not overdo things. She was watching the workmen bring in a long banquet table when she caught sight of a large man; she took in a shocked breath as the man set the table down.

Ulrik pulled off his stocking cap, nodding embarrassedly. "Hello, Mrs. Fauvereau."

"Ulrik, isn't it?" she asked.

"Ya, it is!" Color came into his ruddy cheeks, a blush of nervousness at seeing the woman he had taken captive. But she looked quite lovely in a pretty dress of mauve wool trimmed with pink braid. A soft lace shawl was draped about her, intended to conceal the fact that she was expecting.

"Are you working here?" Kenna asked with a smile.

"Ya. Mr. Fauvereau, he gave me a job here at The Bank. I take out those who have too much to drink. They do not give The Bank any problem now, since Ulrik is stronger than anyone."

"What happened to your reward money?" she asked quietly, keeping the conversation personal.

"Well, some goes home to my mother in Sweden, ya? And some goes to buy a horse and wagon for Ulrik, and some goes for a bad claim already run out before I was fool that bought it. So now I work for Mr. Fauvereau because I would not be a good miner anyway."

Grey came up to them. "Ulrik is a good worker."

Ulrik looked pleased, pulling on his knitted cap. "Work is good for a man. And now I must go cut down the Christmas tree. I will get the largest one I can find, ya?" He turned and hurriedly left.

Grey leaned on the counter, looking at his wife. "You do not mind that Ulrik works for me, do you?"

"No, not at all. He was the one man who protected me from some of the others. I have always been glad that he was the one who ended up with me, since there *was* a bounty on my head," Kenna replied, remembering the fear and anger she had felt at being pursued by bounty hunters.

Grey looked at her in surprise. "Do you begrudge the reward that I used in getting you back?"

"You put a price on my head," she said slowly, coolly, lifting up her dark gray eyes with slow precision.

"Ah, but m'lady," he said softly, leaning near so that he might smother her with the force of his presence. "You were the one who fled. I only used the best possible means for getting you back. I willingly paid the price."

"A great financial loss."

"I did not say that."

"Once again, I cost you precious money, and once again, you paid it," she breathed, wishing he would not lean in so close to her, trapping her with his presence. She hated the truth—that money had played its part in their marriage from the beginning.

Grey would not be baited into an argument. He smiled wickedly at her. "It does not matter one whit that I paid the money. I would pay it again, pay even double, to get back what is mine. And you are mine,

307

Kenna," he said softly, his voice encompassing her. "You carry my child."

With that he quickly bent his head, brushing his lips against hers before she could protest. Then he left her to finish his work.

Kenna sat down on a chair, smoothing the soft wool of her dress. She watched Grey instruct the others in where to place the boughs of pine and wild holly; she began to see his sense for organizing, and she understood why his saloon had been such a success. Jess brought in a box which he opened; it was filled with long red wax candles. Sadie brought over a tray of glass candleholders, freshly washed. They proceeded to set these among the boughs on windows and tables.

Kenna studied her husband: his sober discussion on where to set the banquet table, his firm resolve as to where the good linen had been stored last year, his sudden laughter at a muddy dog bolting through the open door. She watched his back muscles tense as he lifted one end of the heavy oak table, and she looked at the dark and handsome head nod in agreement.

The back door banged open, and Ulrik stomped his feet to get the snow off. He then proceeded to drag in the largest pine tree which could have been brought in through the door. There was a great deal of discussion as to how a stand should be made, until at last the tree stood in the center of the empty floor. There was applause as it was pushed upright, and then yards of flannel were wrapped at the base; the smell of pine began to fill the room.

"What a lovely tree, Ulrik," Kenna said, picking out an apple to tie on with a long piece of green flannel.

"It was the very biggest one I could find and chop down in one hour," he said, grinning broadly.

Sadie, Jess, and Grey also converged around the tree, dipping into the crates full of apples, nuts, cranberries, and paper ornaments. Kenna tied some thread around a large walnut and reached up to tie it on a branch high above her head, a more difficult task than she first suspected. Suddenly darkly tanned hands above hers took the string and quickly tied it. She looked up to see Grey standing close behind her, tying the final knot.

"Thank you," she said.

"You are quite welcome." He handed her a paper ornament, more easily attached to the tree.

Kenna busied herself with stringing cranberries, not an easy task, she discovered, for the needle would not willingly go through the hard things. She heard laughter and looked up to see Grey watching her.

"No luck at that?" he asked.

In frustration, she handed him the bowl of cranberries and the needle. "Why don't you try it?"

It soon became her turn to laugh, for although he managed to string a few, he broke more. "Maybe they should be cooked," he said.

"None of this makes sense to me," Kenna said. "At home we never did this. Instead we had different traditions, like a yule log."

The thought of Scotland and Christmas saddened Kenna. She thought of Braic with a mellow sadness, recalling the childhood memories of Christmas and Moldarn. I'll never see either of you again, she whispered to herself.

She did not let her melancholy show, instead

smiling brightly as Sadie brought out a tray laden with popcorn balls and sugar-coated cookies. The last of these trimmings were carefully placed on the tree; by midnight most of the edible things would be gone.

Grey took Kenna home so she could rest for the afternoon. She rose before sundown to dress. Happily, Kenna put on the lovely evening gown created from the ecru satin; Madame DeLaney had actually made the dress in two parts. The bottom was a full skirt with a drawstring waist so that she could adjust it for comfort. Over this she pulled on the polonaise, as the seamstress had called it. The blouson top was high-waisted and softly draped midway over the skirt, caught up on either side so that it had soft folds front and back. Kenna fastened the tiny buttons down the front, straightening the draping of ivory lace that crossed over the shoulders. The sleeves were short, edged by the same pleated lace that trimmed the blouse's hem. She pulled on long kid gloves of softest ivory and turned to examine herself in the mirror.

She was quite amazed. The dress almost completely hid her abdomen, the drapery enhancing the lines of her body. As she admired herself in the mirror, Grey's image came up behind her. He looked exceptionally handsome in a suit of black broadcloth, well tailored to his frame. The jacket was cut away in front, revealing a white silk shirt worn under a black and silver waistcoat with oblong silver buttons down the front. His black silk cravat was perfectly tied. He wore the clothes with a casual air that enhanced his look.

He stepped behind her, his hands slipping up her

arms. "You look quite beautiful, Kenna," he said softly.

She smiled at his reflection. "So do you."

"Men aren't supposed to be beautiful."

"No? Handsome, then." Kenna did not mind calling him beautiful. "You do look very handsome. And we had best go. The guests will be coming soon."

He nodded, picking up her heavy cloak and putting it around her shoulders; turning her about, he fastened the frogs at the neck. They went downstairs and outside where Grey helped her into the waiting sleigh, wrapping the fur rug about her. Then he climbed in and snapped the reins. The horse started off, and they traveled down the road, to the jingling of sleigh bells.

When they arrived at The Bank, Grey carefully lifted her down, leading her into the saloon. Kenna caught her breath. The saloon had become an empty ballroom with a huge decorated pine tree standing in the center. Many candles were lit, their flames doubled by reflections in the mirrors and the polished wooden floor. The air was filled with the scent of pine and wax and the delightful aromas which came from the long banquet table covered in Irish linen. A grand feast was laid out buffet style. There were great platters of sliced meats and a variety of breads. There were fancy puddings and pies, and tiny cakes from the finest bake shop in town. The bar offered every desired drink as well as candied liqueurs of a milder nature for the ladies; there was a selection of rummed coffees as well.

"It is all quite amazing!" Kenna exclaimed. "If it were not for those letters written on the mirror calling this place The Bank, I would completely forget where I am!" Kenna remembered her anger the first time she had seen the golden letters, her fury that Grey had deceived her. She ignored the memory, determined that nothing would spoil this holiday.

He slid his hand to the small of her back, looking down at her. "Yes, Sadie and Jess have done quite a job with the place." He sent an approving nod at the lady mentioned, who looked lovely in a blue silk dress.

The people began to arrive, and they greeted them as musicians hurriedly took their places, striking up a pretty waltz. It was an odd combination of instruments: piano, banjo, violin, and mouth organ.

There was dining and dancing and Kenna loved it all. She was swept away in Grey's arms. The lights sparkled, glistening in the stained glass; dancers swirled about them, the gay colors of ballgowns whirling like flower petals. Grey watched as Kenna danced with other young men. He felt a touch of jealousy, watching them look at his wife with adoring eyes. She danced with her cousin, Fergus McDoo, and with Joel Malvern. When the music paused, Grey stole his wife from the younger man's hold and he led her in graceful movements across the floor as the music commenced again. His face was close to hers, his expression somber. No one doubted looking at them, that they were meant to be together.

"I thought I would never get to dance with you again. Each time I headed in your direction, a new song would start."

Grey did not take his eyes from her. "The fault lies in your appearance, m'lady."

She looked up at him, concerned. "It does?"

"You look beautiful tonight. How can I blame anyone who wants to dance with you? I know how unhappy I would be if I knew that all I could have of you was a dance."

A tender smile kissed Kenna's lips. "Do you know something? When we first met, on the street in front of that club . . ." Her voice trailed off.

"Yes," he prompted.

"Well, when I met you, I knew there was something special about you that drew my attention."

"Oh?" He raised an eyebrow in surprise. "As I recall, you put me in my proper place quick enough."

She laughed. "I did, true! But it made it very hard for me to meet my husband. My feet were dragging every step until you invited us to enter that room. I will never forget how I felt when I saw that you were, in fact, my husband."

"You were angry with me, I recall," he said, amused.

Kenna shook her head. "I had so many emotions. Anger was only one of them."

Another barrier dropped with this admission.

The time slipped by, with Kenna in the comfort of his arms, gliding to the music until she was tired to the very core. "I think my dancing slippers are worn thin," she murmured.

"Then I had best let the princess rest." Grey smiled teasingly. He led her to a chair and brought her a plate filled with sliced meets, nutbread, and apple pie.

"I cannot eat all this," she said.

"Then I shall help you." He went back to the table and returned with another fork.

By the end of the evening, when the candles had burned down into sculptures of melted tallow, the guests left with praise on their lips for the elegant evening. When the lights were doused, Sadie and Jess left and Grey took Kenna home; they were pleasantly tired as the sleigh pulled up in front of the house. He helped her out, then got back in the sleigh.

"Go on in; I'll just put this in the carriage house and unharness the horse."

Kenna stood on the porch and blew on her hands. "No, I can't. Just hurry back."

"Why?"

"I have my reasons."

"It's freezing out here, Kenna."

"That is why you had better hurry!" she said brusquely.

Grey stared at her for a moment, then snapped the horse into action. There was no arguing with Kenna when her mind was truly set. He did the chore quickly, returning to find her by the front door, the cape wrapped tightly about her.

"What is all this about?" he demanded.

"Quick, let's go in. It's cold out here."

Grey opened the door, waiting for her to enter, but she shook her head. "No, you must go in first," she said, pushing him in ahead of her. She shut the door behind them and he turned to her.

"You are acting strangely; will you explain?"

"What time is it?" she asked, hurrying over to the fireplace and holding out her hands to its warmth. The house was dimly lit, and the coals glowed hot in the grate.

"Well after midnight."

"There, I knew it. Quick, shout 'first-footing.' Don't look at me as if I were daft, just say it!"

He studied her, then said, "First-footing. Is that right?"

"Well enough, though you should have shouted it. But with Wu asleep, perhaps it's best you didn't." She went to the sideboard and poured him a drink. "Now take this, and without a word."

He swallowed the drink, then set the glass down. "I take it that this all has to do with some Scottish custom."

"Yes, it does! The first person to enter the house on Christmas morning is to be the first-footer. And since it is after midnight, it is Christmas morning. Custom has it that it should be a man with black hair—it is true—he is the most desired. It means that the household shall be blessed with luck all year long. Upon entering, he is given a drink—oh yes, and one other thing I had forgotten! He is to give the household a gift to ensure future happiness for all."

He shrugged helplessly. "I have no gift for the household," he said solemnly. "You did not tell me to prepare for this."

"A gift can be simple. A kind word, a stick of wood for the fire." She bent down, putting wood on the fire until the hot coals leaped upward, reflecting red glints in her hair. "And that is another superstition, you see. The fire should not be allowed to go out at night; bad elves will come down the chimney and dance in the cold ashes." She laughed, turning to him. "Do you think me foolish for observing the traditions of my childhood?"

"No. It's charming."

It was a magical moment between them. "Sometimes I miss Moldarn so," Kenna said softly. Then she looked up and smiled. "Let us not change the subject of your gift for the household, lest ill luck fall upon us."

"What do you suggest?"

"Since I am the one who holds the household keys, you can give me a gift," she said.

"What would you like?"

"I should like you to carry me upstairs to bed."

He laughed, scooping her up in his arms and easily ascending the flight of stairs. He went into the large bedroom, laying her down on the bed. "Tell me, is this the last of your Scottish Christmas traditions?"

"For tonight," she replied impishly, sitting up and struggling to remove her dancing slippers. Grey's hands took over, working the buttons and sliding the slippers from her feet. Then he unhooked the evening gown and chose a nightgown for her.

Kenna placed her hands at the small of her back, and Grey looked at her in concern. She looked so young. Without a woman's evening gown and gloves, without the extra armor of her title, she looked like a mere girl. He set her down on the bed and pulled up the covers.

"Merry Christmas, Grey," she murmured, closing her eyes.

He bent and kissed her. "Merry Christmas," he answered, turning out the lamps and leaving the room.

It grew so cold during the night that when the household awoke they found the windows painted with crystalline frost. Outside, trees dripped with frozen tinsel. The snow was no longer a fluffy covering; it had hardened to a brittle crust of white, and lanes were slick with ice.

Kenna awoke early, thrilled that it was finally Christmas. She did not let the memories of Moldarn sadden her. She dressed hurriedly and brushed her hair before going downstairs. Much to Kenna's surprise, on the dining room table was a stack of gifts. Grey came downstairs to find Kenna adding her own presents to his stock. He greeted her with a kiss.

"Do you want to breakfast before we open them?"

"No. At Moldarn, we always opened the gifts first," she said. "Unless the Fauvereau traditions are different."

"Our family traditions will be what you make them," he said.

"Then open this," she said, handing him a round box tied with fabric strips.

He did as bid, lifting off the top. He could not keep from laughing as he took out a handsome felt hat with a wide brim, an exact duplicate of the one she had destroyed.

"I thought I owed you a new hat," she said.

There were many boxes for Kenna to open. One held a new mirror and comb set with a brush and porcelain hair-holder jar. Another, an ermine muff, thick and handsome. There was a fan of black feathers on carved ivory, and a necklace of black jet diadems spaced with silver beads.

"Grey!" she exclaimed. "This is all quite too much."

He said nothing but opened another box, which held a handsome brush set that could be mounted on the wall. Kenna had bought it hoping that it would take its rightful place in their room. He leaned over and kissed her, then handed her the prettiest wrapped present of all. "Don't shake it," he cautioned.

Carefully she opened the gift to reveal an exquisitely painted china music box; it played the Minute Waltz as a sculpted couple danced in a circle.

They gave Ling Ti a bottle of scented rosewater and a pair of short kid gloves. Wu received a carved tobacco box.

They were eating a large breakfast when Grey suddenly stood up. "I forgot one of your presents," he said.

"Oh, no more, please! You have given me enough for ten Christmases, you know."

He went into the kitchen. "I'd better show you this," he threw over his shoulder. He returned with something in his hands. It was a kitten with long white fur and a blue ribbon tied around its throat. Kenna took it from his hands, cuddling the soft little thing.

"I do want this gift," Kenna said, stroking the fur until the cat purred. "However did you know I would like a kitten?"

"I think it was when a mouse ran across the dining room floor and you went pale."

"I'm not afraid of mice," she countered.

"Then I'll take him back where I got him."

"No. He will keep all the mice away. When he gets bigger." She would not surrender the kitten.

Cats sold for five or ten dollars because mice tended to run rampant through Silver City. Nearly every home and store had its own mouser, although there had been no problems yet in the Fauvereau house because it was so new.

"What will you call it?" he asked.

"Chablis," she said. "I had a cat I loved when I was a little girl; my father brought it back for me from France. So to me all white cats should be Chablis."

After breakfast, Kenna tied on an apron, dragging Grey into the kitchen with her. "What are we doing in here?"

"We are going to make my favorite candy. None of the confectioners had it, so I bought the ingredients instead."

She took a board from the cupboard, rolling out the dough on it and then cutting it into squares. These she arranged on a tray, letting Grey sample one.

"Quite good," he said.

"We had marzipan every Christmas. I made it yesterday because it must stand for a day. The secret, as cook used to tell me, was to beat the egg whites stiff. Then after the ground almonds and confectioners' sugar is put in, it must be kneaded. Here." She handed him a tray. "Put those small cakes on it."

"You baked these yesterday, too?"

"Yes. Another tradition. I make them with caraway seeds."

She filled one dish with glazed almonds and another with mint wafers. In addition, Wu had made chestnut balls and rice cakes. Everything was carried out to the table. By late morning, they were receiving Christmas well-wishers; one of the first was Dr. Phillips.

He brought his wife, a young woman Kenna's age whom she had met socially a few times. They had been married only a little over a year.

He smiled at Grey and took Kenna's hand. "We are sorry we missed your party last night, but Mrs.

319

Newcomb's baby finally decided to arrive." He looked at Grey. "Tell me. Did you build this house clear up here to test my nerve? It took three tries to get up the road with that ice on it. I hope this baby comes on a sunny day."

"The worst will be over by April," Grey assured him.

"Just make certain you give me ample notice," the doctor answered.

Kenna gave the Phillipses one of her watercolors, framed, which pleased them very much. Then Fergus McDoo arrived bearing fruitcakes. Grey promptly gave him a case of Scotch. Kenna had a pleasant conversation with her cousin; she gave him a standing invitation to dinner on Wednesday nights.

By afternoon the house on the hill had hosted many vistors. As night came, Kenna and Grey found themselves alone. She looked out the window at the glow of orange sunset across the mountains; as the light faded, the sky deepened from orange to red along the edge of jagged horizon, silhouetting rooftops and lacy black branches.

Grey took a seat next to her. "Did you get everything you wanted for Christmas?"

"All your gifts were wonderful." Her voice trailed off as if she had more to say but lacked the words.

"You wanted something else?" he asked.

"Yes."

"Tell me and I will buy it."

"You cannot buy it. But you can give it to me." Kenna's courage wavered.

He looked at her. "What is it you want, Kenna?"

She turned to the window. All was blackness without. "Do not hate me for running away from you."

He did not answer for a long time. "I don't hate you for running away. I know why you did, of course. I never blamed you for despising me for killing Braic. I believe you have forgiven me. So how could I hold a grudge because you hated me after it happened?" His voice was hoarse with suppressed feelings.

Kenna turned to look at the stone profile. "How could you know? I have not told you. The truth is this, Grey. I ran away because I would not have you see the hurt I felt, nor try to speak words of comfort when I had none to give. You would have seen only accusation in my eyes." She put her fingers along his jawline, turning his face to hers. "Tell me what you see in my eyes now?"

Grey stared down into a face tender with caring, eyes dark with emotion. He could say nothing.

"Give me what I want on this day of celebration," Kenna said. "Come back into the room that should be ours."

He stood and walked away, his back to her. Kenna pushed away the ache that threatened her. "I can't," he said, pain in his voice. He turned and looked at her. There was misery in his face. "I lost you once, Kenna. I lived through hell. All the time I want to touch you, to lie with you in my arms. But women die in childbirth all the time here. I won't risk losing you."

She went to him, taking his strong hand in hers. "Your child is well within me. Nothing can take him from us, nor me from you. I shall never leave you again, Grey Fauvereau."

"Still, I won't risk it."

"Then at least share the room. It should be ours."

She wanted him to take the next step toward reconciliation, but she saw it would be futile to argue. She turned and went upstairs. She felt suddenly exhausted, emotionally overwhelmed. She exchanged her brocade dress for a silk nightgown, and sat down at the dressing table to brush out her hair. The door opened and Grey entered. His arms were filled with his clothes, and he moved toward the wardrobe. Kenna helped him put the things in the empty space next to her clothes. When this was done, she blew out all the lamps save one while he tossed his clothes across a chair.

The large brass bed welcomed them. Kenna lay in his arms, letting his warmth encircle her. There was such comfort in this for her that she could not imagine how she had survived the bleak months past. Something eased within Grey also as he held her. Kenna took his large hand, placing his lean fingers on her abdomen. Carefully she moved his hand until he felt his child stir. They shared in feeling the movement, a subtle peace engulfing them both.

Chapter XIV

THE SCOTTISH TRADITIONS for the New Year were as important to Kenna as the Christmas ones. So she made a late supper of meat pies, scones, small buttered pancakes topped with preserves and ginger wine. She decorated the table with a centerpiece of evergreen boughs to symbolize long life, coal for a warm house, and a loaf of bread for a full larder. From her earliest memories the New Year's table was set in just such a fashion, and afterward a tray of black bun pastries was served. McDoo, Sadie, Jess, and Ulrik were invited; a strange lot, still, there was more camaraderie than at a social dinner party. McDoo said he had not felt so at home since leaving Glasgow.

In January, an expressman for Wells Fargo arrived with the much overdue mail. The letters were brought in by pack mule, and their cost rose in direct proportion to the difficulty of delivering them.

The last day of February there was a brawl at The Irish Queen's on Jordan Street near Long Gulch Creek. The fight resulted in Murphy Duke receiving a knife in the ribs, placed there by one Davis French, who had since made a quick departure from Silver City.

As March wore on, bare patches of hard earth could be seen beneath dirty snow. Never had spring been more anticipated. But by the end of the month, that proved to be a false hope.

One morning the world was once again blanketed in white and snow still fell. Grey did not go to the saloon even though Kenna told him she would be fine. The Chinese servants were gone overnight for a wedding, and he refused to leave her alone. The sky was still dark as Kenna stood in the kitchen, an apron tied about her. She scrapped butter from the hard, square pound until there was enough to spread on the flat muffins. Then she poached eggs and brewed tea. She stopped often to place her hands at her back, the burden growing heavy for her to bear.

They sat together in the library while Grey went over his accounts and Kenna finished the baby quilt she had been working on. One side of the quilt was pink, the other side blue. When she finished it, she unpinned it from the frames to show it to Grey.

"I know it does not look like such a great accomplishment, but it was a lot of work." She displayed both sides. "See? It does not matter which we have, girl or boy."

"But it will be a boy," he said teasingly. "And what a shame to frame his face in pink."

Kenna sat down, smoothing the quilt and folding it pink side out. "But I would like a daughter."

"We can have a daughter after this one."

"Oh?" she said, changing her position since she was so continually uncomfortable. "I may not wish to go through this again. I am so tired of being like this. Won't this baby ever come?"

He closed the ledger and put down the pen. Then he came over and sat by her, taking her hand. "April is still two weeks away. When the snow melts, we can go into town."

"The only thing I want is for this baby to come." She sighed wearily. "And for the snow to stop."

By noon the road to town was completely obliterated by the smothering snow. Kenna made Grey's lunch but did not feel like eating herself. Early in the afternoon, he sought her out and found her in the parlor, staring at the silent fall of snow. He sat beside her until his worst fears were confirmed. Kenna was in labor.

"I'm going for Dr. Phillips," he said calmly, rising to get his coat.

Kenna's hand stopped him. "No. You can't leave me here alone, Grey. I can face anything if I am not alone."

"Then I'll hitch up the sleigh and take you down to the doctor's."

"Have you seen the road? There is no trace of it," she said quietly. "We could be killed trying to maneuver through the snow, and I am in no condition for a wild sleigh ride."

Grey sat down and looked at her. "This baby was conceived that night in the hills, just before Independence Day. This baby shouldn't be coming until April second."

Kenna smiled at his reasoning, as if calculations on a page were true to reality. "Then I must not be having the baby yet."

He saw the absurdity of his statement. "And what if you are?"

"Then I guess I will just have a baby."

Grey picked her up and carried her upstairs to their bedroom. He laid her down carefully. His hands were gentle as they removed her garments and put on her nightgown.

"I think you should just lie down and rest," he said.

"Yes," Kenna sighed, shutting her eyes as he pulled the covers up. "Maybe this will all go away."

Grey sat in the bedroom, watching his wife nap. He had fetched a book from the library, a medical book that Dr. Phillips had loaned him. One long chapter dealt with childbirth; the doctor knew the difficulty of the winters in Silver City. He had given the book to many families whose child was to be born in the winter; the pages fell open to the proper chapter. Grey held the material near the one lit lamp, drinking in all the words. Some things he went over many times until they were memorized.

Kenna slept fretfully, stirring in her sleep or moaning softly. Outside the wind howled, slashing the snow at the windows, leaving them coated and opaque. Yet the isolation, the feeling of complete aloneness, filled Grey with calm.

Kenna gasped softly, her eyes opening; she could hear wind moaning as it circled the house. The room was dark except for a single lamp by the rocker. Grey sat looking at her. He came to sit on the edge of the bed.

"Tell me how you are," he said.

"Oh, I'm not unwell," she said, smiling with an attempt at humor. Her smile immediately faded, and

Grey put his hand on her stomach, feeling the tightening.

"Kenna," Grey said, "I am sure this baby is coming."

She tried to stay calm. "I don't know what to do."

"You don't have to do anything. The baby will come on its own."

A wave of pain swept through her; all her courage fled. Panic rose upon her like flood waters. She gulped for air until the contraction passed, leaving her weak. She had been brave until the pain came. But suddenly she found herself in a whirlpool of fear.

Grey took her cold hands into his. "Kenna, look at me. I want you to tell me the truth. Do you trust me?"

She looked into his face. "Yes."

"Then listen to me. I will take care of you. Both you and the baby will be fine. I promise."

Kenna's stare did not waver; he was her lifeline. She sensed his serenity, and it calmed her. When the pain came again, she gritted her teeth and closed her eyes, as though squeezing out the hurt. But for all her courage, the pain only increased until she lay writhing on the bed, grabbing the brass rails on the headboard until her hands were white. Never did she scream or even cry out. She could not inflict that on Grey. Yet always he was there, brushing the hair from her forehead, stroking her, murmuring words of comfort. He went to the nursery to gather some light blankets and to the linen cabinet for towels. He refilled the pitcher with water and took off his cravat. Kenna's eyes followed him as he moved silently about the room, placing things where he could reach them easily.

He rolled up his shirt sleeves, a drop of sweat trickling down his back; he was too warm and Kenna too cold. Her fingers were like ice. He kept them in his own warm hands; he wrapped hot towels around her feet. When the pains were closer together and lasted three times as long, Kenna felt a terrible panic. Yet Grey was always there, touching, talking, allaying her fears.

Snow still fell as the thin afternoon light ebbed into darkness and the moaning wind stopped. Grey lit lamps to dispel the gloom.

Kenna took a choking breath and pushed. Her body took over with an incredible, pulsating urgency. Despite the pain, she worked with strong determination, Grey encouraging her efforts; there was no time for fear. She barely comprehended the moment she pushed her child into the world.

The baby caught its breath and its thin wail filled the room. Grey grabbed a ribbon from the dressing table and tied off the cord, exactly as instructed by the book, and with his straight-edged razor cut the bond between child and mother. With towels, he rubbed down the baby until the crying infant was pink with color, the music of his newborn cry an anthem in the silent house.

By ten o'clock, the night of March twenty-third, the storm had abated, the clouds miraculously vanishing. Overhead, the sky was clear with stars like bright chips of glass. Kenna had changed into a clean gown and was propped up on fresh bedding. In her arms, she held a son.

The baby was tiny. She had not imagined a human could be so small, with perfectly formed fingers and soft round toes. Baby feet were fat, she saw, and baby ears like the sweetest petals. She stroked the red hair that lay on his head like fine silk. Eyes of slate blue blinked and looked at the blurs of light.

Grey came back in and, bending, kissed Kenna with all the loving gratitude he felt. "Thank you," he said huskily, looking at his son.

"I should thank you, Grey Fauvereau."

Grey took the baby, pulling back the blanket. This produced immediate disfavor as his son cried in protest. Kenna watched as the long fingers of her husband diapered and dressed the baby in a gown. He rolled up the long infant sleeves and Kenna smiled.

"When I bought that gown it seemed so tiny, and yet now it swamps the baby. I did not know that he would be so small. This is all such a miracle to me."

"I am sorry it is not the girl you wanted." He handed the baby back to her. Kenna untied her gown and put the infant to her breast.

"I should not change him for any other," she said, stroking the soft hair. "And we shall have a girl someday. Perhaps many. Never have I participated in anything which deserved such acclaim. Now I know why women speak so much about this accomplishment."

"We need to name him, you know. I've been thinking about Braic."

Kenna looked at him, and this time her heart forgave him completely. "I've been thinking of Cedric."

"Then Cedric it will be." He sat down next to her, slipping his arm around her, and the three of them were a family bound by silver ribbons of love.

Cedric lay in Kenna's arms, partaking of his evening meal. The sun had not yet set, and the room was filled with dust-colored light. Kenna rocked her baby, holding him close against her as he nursed. She traced the tiny pearl that was his ear and touched the velvet cheek; to her he was still a miracle.

Dr. Phillips had arrived two days later, when the snowy road was finally accessible, and Grey had proudly led him into the bedroom and presented Kenna holding the new baby in her arms. The doctor had clapped Grey on the shoulder and checked the baby over, declaring him to be perfect. He did not need to tell the parents that, for they already knew it; they both believed that no child had ever been born that was as beautiful as their first baby.

Often Grey would hold his son, lifting him up to the light for proud examination. He marveled that this child was so complete, and so tiny. Yet every day Cedric grew, nursing at Kenna's breast; Grey loved to watch them.

For Kenna, the miracle was more than just the birth of her son. Now she looked in awe at her husband. He had guided her through the most fearful, most exhilarating experience of her life with a calm, reassuring strength that made her see him in a new light.

Grey came into the bedroom and looked at Kenna as the afternoon light spilled across child and mother. She looked content, happy in motherhood. And there was something else; it was the way she looked at him. Kenna's eyes said that she loved him. So far neither had spoken the words. He thought she was more beautiful than ever before. Her hair had grown down to her shoulders, and today she had pinned it back on either side with silk roses. Pink tinged her cheeks, and her eyes shone gray as moonstones; it had not taken her long to regain her slender figure, although she retained fuller womanly curves because she nursed the baby. The lace blouse she wore was open, revealing creamy skin as the baby's head lay at her breast. Grey leaned over her, slipping his finger into the infant's palm, watching the small fingers encircle his own. They rested in this special grasp against the swell of Kenna's breast. She smiled up at her husband and he bent down, kissing her.

"I think you are so beautiful," he said. He was obsessed with thoughts of her; he had to drag himself to work, and often stayed at home. Today he had done nothing but follow her around the house. But Kenna did not mind.

He was the one who seemed beautiful to her, with his black hair catching the glint of filtered light and the line of his jaw pleasing to her eyes. Cedric had fallen asleep, and still she looked at Grey. There was something unspoken between them, a wordless contentment; all the hurt between them had faded, and they both acknowledged it today for the first time.

Grey bent and buried his face in her hair. He could not bear to have her see the effect she had on him. At last he stood, and Kenna rose to place the sleeping baby into the cradle on her side of the bed.

He came to her, and his long fingers slipped the buttons back through their loops until her blouse and skirt lay in a pool of lace on the floor. She stood before him in a thin silk chemise, vulnerable yet enticing. She took a step back, her limbs tingling.

He knew her well by now. "Does this frighten you?" he asked softly.

"Yes," she answered. "It has been a long time. We are strangers in this one thing."

He understood. His fingers unbuttoned his shirt, and he cast it across the chair. The other clothes were as easily discarded, until he stood before her, a Greek statue of flesh instead of marble. Muted light shadowed the angles of his straight body. Kenna stepped toward him. She held out her arms and he crushed her to him, his mouth capturing her own in a storm of passion. He thirsted for the heat of her, but it was she who jerked the ribbons of her chemise loose to remove the last barrier.

Grey picked her up and carried her to the bed. He towered above her, his eyes tearing into her. "I have wanted you more than life," he said. "My soul died of thirst for you, Kenna."

Her hands slid over the taut muscles of his back. She looked up into his tortured face. "Then let me give it life again," she whispered.

Grey buried his face in her neck, his hands clinging to her. She twisted his heart with her plea. She rested her face against his hair, smelling plowed fields and late wheat. Did he not understand that he was the very earth to her?

He kissed her throat and her face and her eyes. "I would go to hell for you," he moaned.

She entangled her fingers in his hair, tightening her grip. "I want you nowhere but here, beside me! Grey, do not punish me further," she cried, feeling bewildered by the intensity of his emotions.

"What do you want, Kenna?" he asked, his mouth sweeping across her, leaving the scar of his kiss.

She lay beneath him, her body beckoning him to take possession of her. "I want you to love me," she moaned.

"Oh, Kenna," he said hoarsely, his arms pulling her to him, crushing her against him as if in proof of the statement to come. "I love you!" He would not let her go or loosen his hold, as if his body willed her to understand. He could not qualify the statement by other words; instead he repeated it again and again.

It was the nourishment Kenna's soul needed; strength flowed back into her veins, bringing her to life. She slid her arms around his neck as she slowly opened her eyes to gaze into his tormented ones. She believed him; at this moment, whether he spoke from passion or from the heart, she needed him more than words. She pulled him down to her, her mouth seeking out his in a declaration of surrender that demanded he be the conqueror.

Kenna smiled down at Cedric who lay in the pram as she stopped by the two-story drugstore. Inside, there were many things to see; rows of medicines in small dark blue bottles lined the shelves. There was a large mortar and pestle on the counter, beside which sat brass powder scales. A sign boasted PATENT MEDICINES, and another, TEETH PULLED—LOW FEES. Kenna examined some bottled scents imported from New York, and after selecting one and paying the druggist, she and the baby left. They walked for two blocks to the confectioner's shop where she bought some chocolates to take to Grey. Realizing it was nearly noon, she headed toward The Bank since she had promised to meet him for lunch.

She strolled along in the summer sunshine, catching the appreciative glances of many men. Kenna knew she looked lovely in a dress of taffeta plaid; red and green ribbons crossed over a dark blue background. The top was a fitted jacket that sloped to a vee in the back. She straightened the fold-back cuffs edged with lace and touched the hat she wore. It was a pretty creation of straw with a turned-up brim; dark blue ribbons and white lace decorated it, and her hair was dressed in ringlets in the back.

As she walked down the street toward The Bank, she noticed construction going on across the road. The framework was done, raw pine stretching skyward as the exterior was hammered into place by a large crew of men. She stopped in front of the double doors of the saloon, and Grey stepped out.

"I saw you coming, through the window." He bent and kissed her cheek. "You look lovely. Is that hat new?"

She smiled up at him. "Don't you recognize it? It is one of the hats that was stored in the wardrobe. But until now I didn't have a dress to match."

"Very fetching!" he commented, seriously. "Too fetching for you to be walking down the streets in this rough town."

"Oh, Grey! Who would bother with a woman pushing a baby pram?" She laughed.

"Me, for one," he said, then smiled down at Cedric. "How is my boy?" He played with the baby's hand.

"What is that across the street, where all the building is going on?" Kenna asked.

"Haven't I told you?" he said, a scornful sound to his voice. "That is the framework of The Silver Empire, supposedly the grandest saloon and gambling house to come to Silver City."

"But it is being built right across the street from The Bank!"

"Supposedly for friendly competition," Grey said, smiling with a sardonic twist.

"Is the owner trying to run The Bank out of business?"

"I haven't met the owner yet. Apparently, he is supposed to arrive soon. But, to answer your question, I think that he is."

"But why?"

"I don't know. I assume it's because The Bank has such a good reputation. My place is known for excellent liquor and straight playing. Maybe it is just like having a reputation for being a good gunslinger: everyone is out to beat you."

As the days passed, there was much speculation about the owner of the new saloon, and why he was building it across from The Bank. But no one knew anything for sure until rumor said that the man had arrived in Silver City and would attend a ball given in his honor by Frederick O'Shay, one of The Silver Empire's new investors.

Grey drove home early to get ready for the ball, as anxious as the others to meet his rival. Kenna watched him change his linen shirt for a silk one. "Shall we stay home tonight?" she asked, standing in front of him.

"I thought you were looking forward to this."

Kenna was having second thoughts. "I've never left the baby for such a long period of time before. Maybe we should just stay home."

Grey smiled at her. "I want to go."

She finished buttoning his shirt for him, then

looked up into the handsome face. "Then we won't stay late."

"No, we won't stay late." He slipped his arms about her, kissing her in a way which firmly branded her as his.

The O'Shay mansion was lit with hundreds of candles, the ballroom decorated with silk streamers. Musicians played airy melodies, and the strains wafted into the front hall as Kenna and Grey entered. He handed her cloak to a servant, then took her arm admiringly. She wore a white muslin gown embroidered with colored thread. Four rows of scalloped ruffles graced the bottom, and the waist came to a vee in the front. She had regained her slender shape, and the dress enhanced her narrow waist; the long sleeves fit closely, coming to a point at the wrist, and lace edged the neck.

"I am always amazed by you," he said in approval. The candlelight glinted on her burnished curls, caught back on either side by fresh pink roses.

She lifted her eyes to him and smiled flirtatiously. "Why, Mr. Fauvereau, the things you say," she teased.

He led her into the ballroom, where couples glided and turned to the music. It was a truly grand ball, as out of place in Silver City as a diamond in a brass setting. But none of the guests noticed, preferring to be swept away into the world of refined society. Heads turned to look at the striking couple as they entered.

When the music stopped, they were approached by their host, Frederick O'Shay. He was a wealthy mine owner whose company, the Calaveral, had invested some of its capital in the new saloon and was eager to see Grey's reaction to the competition.

"Good evening," Frederick O'Shay said. "Let me introduce you to the owner of The Silver Empire. This is Glen Kinross."

A gasp escaped Kenna.

"Hello, Kenna," his familiar voice said. Stunned, Kenna could only convulsively clutch Grey's arm as he turned to them.

He was formally dressed in a black suit and cravat over a silk shirt; the candlelight darkened his sand-colored hair. He looked only at Kenna, smiling. "At last I get to see you again."

Kenna was completely taken aback. "I can't believe you are here. When did you arrive?"

"Last week."

"How wonderful! When do I get to see SueAnn?"

His expression changed subtly. "I am a widower, Kenna. SueAnn died just last year in a fall from her horse. Didn't you get my letter?"

Grey looked innocent as Kenna shook her head. "No, I didn't. But mail is often hard to come by up here. I am so sorry to hear about SueAnn." She touched his arm and then looked at Grey.

"Glen, this is my husband, Grey Fauvereau."

Grey offered his hand. Kenna turned to Frederick O'Shay, who was looking on with curious attention. "Glen Kinross is also from Auchinleck. We knew each other as children."

Glen gave a stern smile. "So you are the lucky man who married Kenna."

"Yes, I am," Grey said. "Tell me, what made you bring your business to Silver City?"

"The Silver Empire is yours!" Kenna interrupted in surprise, this second shock registering. It dispelled some of her pleasure at seeing Glen again.

Grey's wariness was understandable. She was beginning to share it.

"Aye, it is," Glen said proudly.

"What made you build here?" Grey asked.

"Well, after my wife died, I left Scotland and some unhappy memories. When I arrived in San Francisco, I met a man who had plans for a saloon in Silver City, and I won his land rights and backing in a poker game. Not very highbrow, I admit, but gambling is my weakness. I was assured that a saloon would do well in this town, so I've come to finish building it."

"Grey is the owner of your competition, The Bank," Frederick O'Shay said.

"How interesting," Glen replied, although he did not seemed surprised. "Well, certainly you don't mind a challenge?"

"Not at all," Grey said with a smile.

He looked at Kenna as if forgetting that Grey existed. "Perhaps you would be gallant enough to let me have this dance with Kenna. It has been a long time since we have seen each other."

Grey bowed slightly, and only Kenna caught the slight mockery in his glance. "Not at all."

As the music began, Glen caught her into his arms, leading her onto the floor in a sweeping circle. "You are so very beautiful," he breathed. "You have changed a lot, Kenna, in just a year."

"A lot has happened in one year," she murmured cautiously. "Did you know that Grey and I have a baby?"

Glen was quiet for a moment. "No. That was the one thing I failed to learn."

She was startled by this cryptic statement and

338

what it implied. "Our son's name is Cedric. He is a beautiful child."

"So everything has changed," he muttered, almost to himself.

"I want to know about Braic," he said abruptly.

An imperceptible shadow crossed her face. She looked away as his gaze bore into her. "I heard about it," he said quietly.

"It was very hard, losing Braic. He was so dear to me." Her voice was hushed.

Glen's arm tightened about her waist. "Kenna, how can you stay with the man that killed Braic?"

She looked up at him. "Grey is my husband, and what happened was an accident."

"I've heard the details." His voice was sharp. "It was still his fault."

Kenna stopped dancing. "Say nothing against Grey," she said, her voice level and quietly commanding.

Glen's body urged hers back into movement lest they create a scene. He looked at her thoughtfully. "You have always been loyal, Kenna, even when that loyalty was ill-placed. However, I have always honored your wishes."

Her countenance softened. "There should be no anger between us."

"There was when you left." He smiled ruefully. "You said you hated me."

"I had been hurt."

"I know. I should never have married SueAnn. She was a nice girl, but even before she died, I knew I was unhappy with her. Oh, Kenna! Why did you come to America? If you had only stayed in Auchinleck as I told you to, Braic would still be alive, and you would be my wife. We would both have had everything we wanted."

"You don't really know that, Glen. You made your decision. I cannot regret mine, for I have a husband who loves me, and a son."

Glen stared long and hard at her. "The baby could have been ours. Cedric should have been my son, just as you should have been my wife."

"Don't say such things," she whispered, uncomfortable with his words.

"Will you deny that you miss Scotland, that you long to be back at Moldarn?"

"No, I don't deny that. But my home is in Silver City now. Tell me, do you know who has bought Moldarn?" She hoped to change the subject.

Glen shook his head. "My Uncle Edgar tried to buy it, but it had already been purchased. I don't know who the owner is."

The thought of foreigners living in Moldarn filled her with sorrow.

"I told you that you belong in Auchinleck, and with the people who are your own kind. We Scottish have a strong bond that pulls us to the land. You belong there, with me." His voice was impassioned, and he stopped abruptly, as if he realized he was imposing on their shared past too much.

"I miss Braic," he said instead, his voice husky. Here was a topic with which he could subtly undermine her feelings for her husband.

Instinctively she knew it. "You mustn't blame Grey. He suffered over Braic's loss even more than I. It has been terrible for him. He is such a fine man. Please get to know him."

Glen shook his head. "I could never come to like the man who took you away from me."

She smiled at his childish statement. "Poverty and debt drove me from Scotland. Grey was my refuge."

The music stopped, and they found Grey by their side. Without a word, he took his wife off as the music struck up again, gliding her possessively across the floor.

"The man held you too closely," Grey said sternly. "It was inappropriate even for Silver City."

"He is just an old friend," she said with a sigh.

"Who has conveniently shown up after his wife's death."

"Tell me about the letter he sent me."

Grey raised his eyebrows innocently, but she persisted. "I perceived at his mention of the letter that there was more to it than a letter lost in the post. Tell me the truth."

"Madam," he replied sternly, "I pity our son if he should ever try to sneak anything by you when he is growing up. Yes, Kenna," he confessed. "His letter did come. But until he mentioned it, I had forgotten all about it."

"What did you do with it?"

"As I recall, it got thrown away."

"What?" she asked indignantly. "It got thrown away? And by whose hand? And for what reason?"

"You are angry," he said, his fingers tightening about her waist.

"Yes. It was an intrusion upon my privacy."

"That never occurred to me at the time. When the letter arrived, you were still missing." His quiet voice contained an echo of his anguish as he recollected the incident. "The letter came at a time when I felt utterly desperate. There wasn't one clue to your whereabouts; I was beginning to feel completely helpless. So when I finally found you, I'm afraid the thought of Glen Kinross's misguided letter was not uppermost in my mind. I had literally forgotten about it."

Kenna was silent. Never before had she really understood what it must have been like for Grey; perhaps she still did not know. Guilt washed over her, tinged at the same time with resentment. She hated still feeling remorse for what she had done, when Grey had caused the problem in the first place. It colored her pleasure at being out with him in company which already was tense with subtle, but ominous, undercurrents.

Grey, sensitive to her sudden withdrawal, released her readily—but with mixed feelings—to Joel Malvern's request for the next dance.

She needed a respite from these invasions by the past, both his suffering and Kinross's appearance.

But Grey found himself practically by Glen's side watching Malvern dance with Kenna. "So you are the man who stole Kenna—away from Scotland," Glen said, looking at Grey with open appraisal.

"And you are the man she left behind," her husband stated.

Glen seemed surprised. "She told you about me?"

"Kenna and I have no secrets," Grey answered, drinking the punch in his glass.

"Don't be so sure," Glen said obscurely.

"Kenna is a woman capable of confidences."

Glen watched Kenna. "Aye. I think you are right. In any event, you are a lucky man."

Grey, too, was watching her. "I know."

McDoo, also nearby, chuckled at the conversation, for the first time catching their attention. "Well," he said, shrugging, "we have a saying where I come from, in the outskirts of Glasgow, it is. 'He who would win the race should not stand debating the outcome after the gun is fired.' "

"Is that pertinent to anything?" Grey asked, annoyed.

"It is basic Scottish sense," Glen said.

"Well, I didn't know we raced. I won Kenna long ago."

"The race is for business," Glen said, his tone of voice contradicting the words. "I plan to run you out of business."

"I have never lost in a business venture yet," Grey said, smiling devilishly, as he did not consider Glen's competition worth worrying about. Yet he was certain Glen's appearance in Silver City was not a coincidence, and that it had as much to do with winning Kenna back as with destroying her husband.

Kenna and Grey left early. She was concerned with nursing the baby, and he was just as happy to get her away from the insidious presence of Glen Kinross.

At home, the baby was only just beginning to fuss for his late feeding. Kenna tossed off the gown and sat with a shawl around herself and the infant. Grey watched her nurse their son, sitting near as she rocked the baby, his mind absorbed with other thoughts.

"I have not seen you so bemused for months. What bothers you?" she asked, already knowing the answer.

He hesitated, then spat out, "That damned Scotsman!"

"McDoo?" she teased.

He stood up and looked at her. "Kenna," he said.

"Sit down, Grey," she responded, resting her hand on his arm as he complied. "Do you remember when you asked me if I was jealous of Maryetta?"

"Yes."

"Well, now you understand how I felt."

"There was no reason for you to be jealous of Maryetta! She means nothing to me. My feeling for her became nonexistent the moment I met you," he explained reasonably.

"Exactly." Kenna put the baby back in his cradle, tucking the blanket about him. "You are my husband. You are the man I am married to, and the man I love."

He groaned and pulled her to him, leaning his head against her. She stroked his hair, running her fingers through the black thickness. "If this is what you felt about Maryetta, I wonder that you did not use a whip instead of my hat!"

Kenna laughed, her sound a soft spill of music into the darkened room. His arms pulled her to him, and he stood, kissing her lips with all the passion that loving her demanded. The bruising kiss made her swear she would never leave him; the heat of desire throbbed like the thud of a heartbeat between them. He swept her into his arms, carrying her to the bed, stripping off her remaining underthings to reveal her naked beauty.

"You asked me once if I had known the love of another man. I do not mind the question now. No man has loved me like this, save one. If I could write I would say you were as a poem and use some graceful words. But my thoughts do not come together for it, so I must write my sonnet to you this way." She caught his hand, pulling him down to her.

They made love in a frenzy which lifted them up on soaring wings. The fierceness of his passion poured over her like molten wax, sealing her commitment.

The heatedness of his desire intrigued Kenna. Had his jealousy of Glen fanned his need? She was reminded of his will to win in all things; what if this new intensity was fired by the competition between him and Glen? She longed to trust Grey completely, with no conflicts or uncertainties.

It struck her suddenly that all her qualms centered around Glen Kinross. A chill coursed down her body as she wondered whether Glen's appearance in Silver City was solely by chance, as he claimed.

Chapter XV

THE SILVER EMPIRE chose Independence Day for its grand opening, allowing all the ladies in town to tour it before the general public. Kenna thought it was not as nice an establishment as The Bank because of its gaudy furnishings. Nonetheless, she congratulated Glen, since it was important to him.

There was much revelry and noise in the streets in celebration of the holiday. The Fauvereaus stayed home, having a quiet supper together and enjoying each other's company. After dinner they went into the parlor. Grey read the newspaper to her as she watched Cedric, who lay on a quilt, examining a spoon with intense fascination. Chablis lay in Kenna's lap and she stroked his satiny fur.

A knock at the door interrupted the peaceful interlude. Grey went to answer it, and Kenna heard a gruff voice demand, "You this Fauvereau fella?"

There was a pause, and then Grey said, "Yes, I am."

Curiosity made Kenna join them in time to hear the visitor say, "Well, then, I come to see your wife."

Kenna delightedly ended his stoic uncertainty by

346

saying, "Well, Grey, don't just stand there. Open the door and let her in." She slipped past him and embraced the wiry little miner. "I am so glad to see you, Sierra Nevada!"

Sierra seemed almost embarrassed and said gruffly, "I just was thinkin' to check if you was all right."

"I am just fine." She slipped her arm about Sierra and led her in. "I was so afraid that those miners hurt you. When I was attacked, I was afraid they were going to try to kill you."

"Heck, I'm too quick for fools who're still wet behind the ears!" she cackled, at ease with Kenna once again. "I knocked one in the knees and crippled him up, and the other one I crowned with a beating stick until he cried out for mercy. They ain't given me any trouble since then."

"Well, I am very glad to hear it! Oh, I'm sorry. Grey, this is Sierra, the lady who saved me." She turned to the miner. "This is my husband, Grey."

"We met at the door," Sierra said. It was apparent she was not too sure about Grey.

"Have you eaten?" Kenna asked.

"I had some home-smoked jerky."

"Oh, that's not enough," Kenna said. "Come in and sit down at the table."

Hurriedly, she dished up a plate of roast beef, potatoes, cooked carrots, and apricot cobbler. She brought this back to Sierra just as Grey brought in Cedric, who had started to fuss.

"This is my baby," Kenna said. "His name is Cedric."

"Ho!" Sierra laughed. "You did have a baby! I

could of never guessed, taking a look at you. He's a fine son."

"I think so," Kenna said proudly. She sat in a rocker, nursing the baby as Sierra ate.

"I couldn't come look for you when the snows was so heavy," she said between mouthfuls. "Had to wait for the thaw. Nobody'd seen you in Fairview, and I was afeared Brody got you. Then when Independence Day come, I decided to ride on to Silver and see if I could find out anything about you."

"I'm glad you did," Kenna said. "I want to tell you how grateful I am. You really saved my life."

Sierra embarrassedly wiped up the last of the gravy with her bread. "It wasn't nothing."

Later she held the baby, awkwardly grinning down happily at the infant. Kenna insisted that she spend the night, and the next morning, she was already up when Kenna came down.

"Ain't never slept in no soft bed like that one," she commented.

After breakfast, Sierra insisted on leaving; she did not want to be away from her claim too long. Kenna put her arm around her. "Do come again, will you, Sierra?"

"If I can."

She went to her wagon and climbed in. Grey handed her a pouch heavy with coins. "I want you to have this. For what you did for Kenna."

"I did it 'cause she was a good girl who needed help. I ain't taking no money."

"Please," Grey asked. "Kenna means more to me than anything. Without your help, she might have been attacked—or killed. It is a debt I have to pay."

His pleading smile won her over. She took the

money and put it inside her jacket. "You ain't such a bad guy after all. Kenna thinks real high of you, too, you know."

He smiled up at the little miner. "She told you that?"

Sierra shrugged. "She moped around awfully bad for you while she was with me. She was planning on coming back to you before she got nabbed by those money-seekers."

His smile faded and he nodded solemnly. "I wish I'd known that long ago."

"Watch out for that little gal, now," Sierra said. She clicked the reins, and the horses headed down the hill.

Grey returned to the porch, where Kenna waited. He slid his arm about her waist, pulling her next to him. "What did Sierra have to say?" Kenna asked.

"Something that I wish I had known from the day I first got you back."

"Oh?" Kenna looked up at him. "What is that?"

"That you were planning on coming back to me."

"Yes, I was," she answered after a quiet pause.

"Why didn't you tell me? It would have made everything so much easier," he said.

"Would you have believed me if I said I was planning to come back, that I was miserable and frightened, and knowing I was with child intensified it all?"

"Yes!" he said, then paused. "Did you only want to return because of the baby?"

"Oh, Grey!" Kenna sighed. "That is exactly the question I knew you'd ask yourself. And why I held off my return so long. If you had understood me better, you might have saved your money."

"I would have spent every penny I own to get you back," he said, circling both arms about her waist as he stood strong behind her. "But knowing that you wanted to come back would have made everything between us much easier."

Kenna leaned her head back against his chest. "But we are so much stronger because of what we have gone through," she murmured.

Grey laid his face against her hair.

Three days later Kenna went shopping. Her last stop took her to the Chinese laundry, where a huge man in Oriental garb lifted a heavy cauldron. She had seen him before; his formidable size caught most people's eye. He did the heavy work at the Wengs' laundry.

As she went inside, she was courteously greeted by Mr. Weng. "Good day, Lady Fauvereau. Your husband's shirts are ready." He handed them to her.

"Thank you," she said, never forgetting the kindness of the old gentleman during her deepest sorrow. She smiled at Mai Lei just as the door opened.

It was Glen Kinross. "Why hello, Kenna."

"Hello, Glen." She smiled, handing Mr. Weng his payment.

Glen looked at the Chinese man. "Do you have that laundry statement ready on the linens at The Silver Empire?" His eyes wavered to Mai Lei as if he was entranced by her natural beauty. The girl smiled back at him, then lowered her eyes.

"Right here, Mr. Kinross," he replied, abruptly cutting off the silent interaction between the two.

Kenna was just leaving the establishment when Glen caught up with her. She, too, had seen the look in Glen's eyes as he had studied Mai Lei. "Don't be hurrying off, Kenna. I haven't seen you for a long time."

"Why, Glen, you have seen me at least five times in the last month."

"But each of those times you were with other people. I hardly think a social gathering is the best place to renew an old friendship."

The morning sunshine felt good to Kenna, the mountain breeze cool against her cheek. She gazed up at the man whose fair looks she had once found so appealing. "Then come to dinner tonight."

"Thank you, no."

She raised an eyebrow. "We have an excellent cook, so I won't be the one poisoning you."

"No, it's not the food I fear. It is your husband's stares that will be poisonous."

"Oh, Glen!" she sighed exasperatedly. "You have not even tried to get to know my husband. I assure you he is a gentleman."

"How can you even speak kindly of him when he married you to buy your title? You do know that is exactly what he did!"

She stopped and looked at him, her expression disdainful. "Yes, I know." She continued walking.

"You know! That's all you can say?" he questioned, ignoring her delicate warning.

"Your loyalties take you too far, girl. You would be true to a man you married, even if you hated him."

"But I don't hate Grey. Even if he did marry me for my title, once he met me he fell in love with the woman. So in this case, the end has come to justify the means."

"And you are satisfied with this end?"

"Yes, I am," she said, her voice soft but sure.

"Even though he killed Braic!"

Kenna turned and looked at him, her stare hard as stone; she strode away, angrily. Glen caught up with her and grabbed her arm.

"I'm sorry, Kenna. Do not be angry with a brash man."

"Your words are cruel to me. Grey did not kill Braic. It was I," she said quietly. "It was Grey's gun, but I begged Braic to stop the shooting. I am the one who sent him into the bullet's path."

There was silence between them, he was uncomfortable with her confession. "Do you blame me for Braic's death?"

"No, Kenna! Never."

"Then do not blame Grey."

She resumed her walk, Glen close beside her. They were quiet for a while and then he said, "Kenna. I'm sorry."

She looked up, resting her hand on his arm. "No apology. Let's not speak of it again."

"I'll do anything for the girl I love."

Kenna shook her head discouragingly. "I give up on you."

"What have I done now?" he asked helplessly.

"You must not talk to me that way. I am a married lady."

"Married or not, you are the woman I love."

"Then take my advice?"

"What is that?" he asked, donning his Scottish charm.

"Find a nice girl and settle down. There are many

lovely young women in Silver City who would be glad to marry a successful businessman."

There was no humor in his countenance. "No, I am afraid not. There is only one woman that I want, and she is with me here."

Kenna laughed. "How can you be so serious? Where is the Glen Kinross I knew in Auchinleck who danced with every pretty girl at every ball?"

"He grew hard when the woman he loved left him."

"Oh, no," she said. "I know you too well. You will soon be glancing at the girls despite your sober countenance. Maryetta Gaylor spent most of the ball at the O'Shay mansion on your arm. And I have seen her with you more than once," she teased.

No playful words roused him from his serious mood. "Did you know that Maryetta was once your husband's mistress?"

She looked at him in dismay. "When did you let your words become so cruel? You are angry with me for marrying Grey, yet you married before me! And now you hold it against me that I do not love you anymore! You are a stranger to me."

"I'm the same man, Kenna. I only try to open your eyes. If the news about Maryetta and Grey is a shock to you, I am sorry."

"It is not a shock. I have known about it for a long time."

"Then you are not the Kenna I knew and loved! You turned against me because of circumstances, but you so easily accept the philanderings of this man."

"I have not held his past against him, nor has he mine."

353

"But he has so much less to forgive!"

Kenna shook her head. "The past matters nothing to either of us. Don't you see? I love Grey."

She left him abruptly, out of impatience with his refusal to give up the past. Restlessly she wondered why it was so difficult to tell her husband the truth that she freely admitted to another. She was able to let go of the past, to acknowledge that Grey was her future. She loved him. When it had happened, she could not guess, for there had never been two people with so many things against them from the very beginning. Yet something held her back from admitting it to Grey. Perhaps it was because he had not expressed it but once to her.

She sighed with frustration. One man was chary with the words of love she longed to hear, while the other offered what she did not want.

Kenna spent several days at home. Her conversation with Glen had left her unsettled. Kenna contented herself with staying at home for a week and painting. She treasured the hours spent with Grey, especially in light of Glen's quicksilver moodiness. Grey was spending many hours at The Bank, taking Glen's challenge seriously. The Silver Empire began to wage war against the customers still loyal to Grey's place. Each establishment lowered the prices of drinks per round and finally per glass. Glen brought in some musicians and German hurdy-gurdy girls who would dance with a gentleman for only a nickel; it usually cost fifty cents in most establishments. Grey hired John Kelly, an extremely talented itinerant musician, to play his violin every night.

The competition between The Silver Empire and The Bank raged on, receiving notice in the newspaper. Grey's saloon managed to hold its own with surprising tenacity, working harder than ever to keep every customer. The Bank was not immediately put out of business as hoped for by the owner and backers of the Silver Empire.

August came, vicious in its heat. Shops in Silver City often closed in the afternoon, since many patrons chose to stay home and nap. By evening, the air cooled off considerably because of the mountain breeze, and Silver City came to life. All the saloons did a steady business.

Kenna chose to do her shopping in the morning. She was in a dry goods store when she met an almost unrecognizable Mai Lei. Mai Lei wore a soft blue dress of lawn edged in white lace. Her hair, usually straight and undressed, now trailed in long ringlets down her back, and she wore a hat with feathers and blue ribbons.

"Hello, Mai Lei," Kenna said. "You look quite lovely!"

Mai Lei smiled, obviously pleased. "Thank you. This is a new dress. I will have to tell Grandfather because he thinks so highly of you. He says I should not wear the clothes of the Americans."

"Oh," Kenna said. "I think you look very pretty in western dress. I was just going to the Emporium; would you like to come?"

Mai Lei looked surprised. "No lady in town would offer to go with me there. The ladies do not like the Chinese." Still, her voice was hopeful.

"I like the Chinese," Kenna said. "Now let me order these items and we can go."

She gave her list to the dry goods owner, and they left. Mai Lei seemed very happy. "What are you going to the Emporium for?"

"I saw some jet combs in the window I would like to buy. Have you seen them?"

"Oh yes. I have stopped to admire them many times. Only Grandfather says a person should not linger over things that can't be had. I have asked him for a western dress like this for a long time, but he has always said that Chinese must dress like Chinese. But if the dress was given as a gift, am I not entitled to wear it?" She stopped, afraid she might have said too much, but Kenna just smiled at her. She knew very well what it was like to have a young heart bound by difficult circumstance. She wondered who might have given her such an expensive present. There was something ominous in Mai Lei's eagerness to become so quickly Americanized. That, however, was none of her business.

"Why don't you come up to the house this afternoon to show Ling Ti? I have more errands to run, but we can have lunch when I get back."

"Oh, that would be quite nice!" Mai Lei said. "Ling Ti says only good things about you to Grandfather."

"I like your grandfather," Kenna said.

"He thinks most highly of you. Perhaps, when you see him, you could tell him there is nothing wrong in my having a dress like this?"

"Perhaps I can," she answered, smiling.

When they reached the Emporium, they looked at the selection of combs and agreed that the ones with

jet beading were the prettiest. Kenna bought two
sets and, as they left the store, she handed one to Mai
Lei.

"You are giving this to me?" the girl said in aston-
ishment.

"Yes, I am."

"Lady Fauvereau, you are the most kind American lady I have ever known."

Kenna smiled. "You come by for lunch today;
don't forget."

"Oh, no. I will be there!"

That afternoon, the two girls and Kenna sat down
to a lunch of cucumber sandwiches, stuffed tomatoes,
and tea. The talk was pleasantly idle, and sometimes
Ling Ti would forget and speak Chinese, but Mai Lei
always answered her in English. Kenna saw how important it was for Mai Lei to be accepted as a west-
erner. The overnight change in the girl left her with
a feeling of disquiet, but there was nothing she could
pinpoint. It was best, she reasoned, leaving the girls
to tend her son, not to interfere.

One evening, when Grey was detained going over
the books at The Bank, Kenna sat on the balcony
outside her window to catch the evening breeze; Cedric was asleep and Chablis sat on her lap, his tail
switching back and forth. Kenna wore a white lawn
shirt with ribbon edged on the bodice; it was the
coolest blouse she owned, and she had left some of
the buttons at the throat undone. She looked down
on the lights of the town glinting gold, like nuggets
in sand. The road that twisted up to the house was a
dark thread barely discernible in the night, but

Kenna glanced at it often in hopes of seeing Grey return home.

The sound of hoofbeats caught her attention, and then the form of rider and horse.

"Who do you wait for, Juliet?" a voice questioned. It was not the tone and inflection she had expected.

She lifted a hand to shade her eyes. "Glen?"

"I knew you were waiting for me."

She peered over the balcony. "What are you doing here?" she asked, surprised.

"Why, I've come to see you, bonnie lass!" he said, throwing his arm out.

"Have you been drinking?" she questioned.

"Not very much. Certainly not enough to make a Scotsman drunk." He looked up and light from above glanced off his features. "You are mighty fair to look upon, but I'd rather not worship you from afar. Could you come down and talk to me?"

"All right," she said with a smile, for he sounded so much like the old Glen Kinross of Scotland that she could not turn away.

When she went outside, she found his horse already tethered. He was sitting on the steps and she sat beside him. "I haven't seen you for a while."

"That's because I've been avoiding you," he said.

She looked at him in surprise. "But why?"

"It is hard knowing that I lost you. I don't want to give you up, Kenna."

"You aren't giving me up," she said kindly. "I will always be your friend."

"Pah! Friendship is moldy bread to a man starving for love. I don't want you as a friend. I want you as my woman."

He looked at her, but her face was turned away,

the shadows harsh on her soft jawline. "If this is how you are going to talk, then I must go back inside."

"I used to be able to tell you anything, Kenna. Do you remember how we talked for hours. Sometimes I think about home, but you always come to mind. You and the homeland are the same thing to me; I should never have left Scotland. Don't you miss it, Kenna?"

"Yes. I miss the heather in summer and the mountain tarn on our property; I could see that small lake from my bedroom window, and it always shone like a jewel. I miss the storms, too, strange as it seems. They were wild and frightening and I loved them. Yes, Glen, I long for Scotland."

"You never should have left," he said. "As I told you before, it is in your blood. Scotland and I are a part of you; you cannot separate yourself from the past."

She turned and looked at him. "I already have. I am a part of Grey and he and Cedric are a part of me; my future is here, with them."

"It hurt me to hear you say you love that man," he said harshly. "I spent many hours thinking about it, and I have come to realize how much I hurt you by marrying SueAnn. Does it make a difference if I tell you I was wrong, that I never should have done my family's bidding?"

"Oh, Glen!" she sighed. "Must you continually dwell on that! I have told you as firmly as I know how that what was between us is over. It is best you put this obsession away. When we were young, you were always the leader. You had to be right in everything and were slow to forgive. Braic and I loved you, but I learned early that you had the strongest will. Perhaps you did make a mistake in marrying SueAnn, but she loved you and you were everything she wanted. Now that she is gone, and I am married to Grey, you must let go of the past and think about your future."

He turned and looked at her, his eyes like darkened ice. "I have no future without you. There is nothing else I want. Come away with me; I will love your baby because he is a part of you. We will have children of our own, and I will take you back to Scotland. I'll buy Moldarn if you want, only come with me."

She looked at him, unhappy that her words should fall against his unyielding will. "You haven't heard anything I said. Listen to me now, because I do not want to speak about this again. I do not love you anymore. I am in love with Grey, and he is the only man I want to be married to."

He stood frozen, staring down at her with wooden features. Only his eyes were alive, bright with determination. He grabbed her to him, his mouth coming down in a cruel kiss, his fingers biting into her arms. He bruised her lips, pressing her for an unspoken answer until at last he let her go. She staggered back, more than a little afraid of his violence.

"I'll never give up," he said in a voice she did not even recognize. "I will have you if I must cross through hell to reach you."

His words were like ice on her heart; he had truly become a stranger.

Grey stood quietly in the shadow of the pines, watching the rider gallop away, and his wife turn and go into the house. A slow ache spread through him, a weakness he would not have thought possible. He had seen his wife go to that other man, touch his

arm with tender pleading; their words had been muffled and distant, but the actions he had seen spoke
loudly. At the last, he had taken her into his arms,
savagely kissing her. There had been anger in
Glen's posture, followed by the sudden departure—
passion and anger blended together. And through it
all, Grey had been helpless, the blood coursing
through his veins with such force that his head
pounded; yet the bond between Kenna and himself
was too fragile for him to step forward and attack
Glen Kinross. She would look upon it as another intrusion, another demonstration he did not trust her.
How could he explain that it was by chance he had
seen them, that his horse had thrown its shoe and he
had walked the distance up the hill?

He had changed from the strong person he had
been, Grey realized suddenly, because he was weakened by his fear of losing her. Never again could he
face the pain of her going away, and Glen Kinross
was the one man who could take her away. He looked
toward the house; the yellow light from the curtained windows beckoned to him. Yet he could not
face the woman he ached for. Grey turned and
walked back down the steep hill, seeking the solitude of darkness.

August melted into September. The people in the
valley harvested their crops, for nearly every house
had a garden. With onions costing forty cents a
pound instead of six, and beans thirty-five, it was
very fashionable to grow vegetables.

Cattle grazed on hillsides, and a nearby dairy
farm delivered fresh milk every morning. The dairy
man arrived early, dipping his quart measure into

the large cans and filling the pitchers Ling Ti provided. Chablis, who liked no one but Kenna, condescended to be civil to one other person. He loved the dairyman.

Ling Ti would shoo him away in Chinese; she did not like the finicky animal. Kenna poured Chablis a small bowl of cream before turning to the serving girl. "Cedric is on a blanket in the parlor, and he should be fine until I get back from shopping."

"I will listen for him, Mrs. Fauvereau."

Kenna knew Ling Ti would rather hold the baby than do her chores. She left and drove the carriage to town. She stopped first at the Chinese laundry, but it was locked. This was most unusual, because it always opened early. She saw a large man carrying boxes to the back of the store; he was the man with the impressively huge chest and shoulders who did Mr. Weng's heavy work. Kenna thought about asking him where Mr. Weng was, but the sight of his sorrowful countenance discouraged her.

Instead she left her laundry in the back of the carriage. She went to the shoe shop and picked up Grey's boots, then to the mill to order a hundred-pound sack of flour to be delivered. And lastly, she picked up some items from the drugstore before heading home.

When she came in, she found Ling Ti sitting and rocking the baby. Cedric cooed at the girl, whose head was bent over him.

"Ling Ti!" Kenna cried. "What's wrong? Nothing happened to Cedric?"

"No, Mrs. Fauvereau. He is fine. I have taken very good care of him." She lifted up her face and Kenna saw the tears the girl could not stop.

"Then tell me what has happened?"

"It is Mai Lei," the girl said, weeping bitterly. "She is dead."

The day was cloudy, although there was no rain. The Chinese funeral procession traveled up the road to the cemetery, the shrill rhythm of the little band drowning out the song of forest birds. Kenna walked along beside the stone-faced Mr. Weng. The procession of marchers was long and dressed in Chinese finery, all except Kenna. She caught many sidelong glances, for it was rare indeed for a white woman to join in mourning the death of one of the true people.

Ling Ti was on her other side, dry-eyed. The large Chinese man Kenna had seen behind the laundry drove the little yellow cart in which lay the simple casket. His shoulders were slumped, and unhappiness was in his very posture.

Kenna remembered walking this road another time, but then her own misery had only been symbolized by the funeral. She still did not know how Mai Lei had died. The grandfather, who had found her, would not speak of it.

The mourners began to throw small square red papers in the air as they walked. They floated on the breeze, scattering colorfully along the road.

"The devil must pick up all these papers before he can catch up with Mai Lei and overtake her soul," Ling Ti said in a hushed voice.

Her words roused the grandfather. "Yes," he said, his voice sounding papery, old. "Mai Lei will be well on her way to the celestial heaven by then."

Kenna looked worriedly at the old man. He seemed frailer. She wished he would ride, but Ling

Ti said he insisted on walking the journey to show the misery he felt.

At last, they reached the gate of the Chinese cemetery and gathered around as the narrow casket was set into the earth; large clumps of dirt were shoveled onto the box until it was at last covered over. Then food was placed on the grave, for the Chinese believed that evil spirits would eat and appease their wrath.

Mr. Weng put his hand on Kenna's arm, and she could feel his surprising strength. "It was a good thing for you to come. I will not forget this."

She patted his hand and looked into his black, shiny eyes. "I am so sorry about Mai Lei."

They walked down the road as the sun set. There was no feasting celebration as accompanied many Chinese funerals, nothing seemed as sorrowful as the loss of such a gay young spirit.

That night, as she sat in the rocker in her bedroom, nursing the baby, Kenna felt a growing depression. She looked down at the small baby in her arms and was overwhelmed by how fragile he was; the more she studied him, the more she saw how delicate life itself was. Fear encircled her and unbidden tears came, burning her eyes.

"Kenna?" She heard Grey's voice as he walked into the room.

She looked up at him. "I don't understand death. It makes no sense. If it weren't a random shadow that falls across anyone, I could accept it better. But no matter how young someone is, how much energy or youth they have, death still can take them. I think about Braic who was so caught up in living until a small piece of metal went into his body and killed him." Kenna looked down at the baby. "He is so small. It almost makes me afraid to love him."

Grey leaned over her, taking out his handkerchief and drying her tears in a tender movement. He took Cedric from her and held him securely in his arms. "I think he is safe. He's protected by a great deal of love." Grey laid him in the cradle, then he came to her and pulled her to her feet. His hands were on her arms to pull her to him. She leaned her head against him, the tenseness easing from her. At that point she realized how much her husband had changed. Grey had been tempered into a stronger man. It was the strength from within him that she felt in his arms about her. His arms holding her, his fingers brushing her hair, his face against her forehead, verified that their love was no fragile thing, vulnerable to death. It was a powerful love, tempered and shaped until its substance was pure. Nothing could kill their love.

"I will love you forever," she whispered, making the tender confession.

He could not respond to her. Her words had sliced into him like sharp metal. He ached from the emotions he felt, from his need to hear those words. Yet the memory of her being held in another man's arms came to mind. Could he believe that his love for her was returned? With a soft groan, he closed his eyes, pulling her to him in such a tight embrace that it was as if he bound her to him with steel. In this one moment, she was his and no other's.

Chapter XVI

THE HILLS that sloped down into the valley were parched, pine needles dry and weeds yellowed. The long dry spell was an oddity, for every miner said the rains should have come by now. But no wind stirred the blades of grass, and there was a restless exhaustion that made things move slowly. Silver City seemed stark, lined by the dust-colored streets.

Kenna and Grey spent an afternoon by a mountain stream. Wu had packed a basket lunch, and the three lolled on a blanket most of the time, except when Cedric slept in the pram. Kenna took her shoes off and put her feet in the water, convincing Grey to do so. They sat on the bank and talked about the dragonflies, the clouds, the moss that lay like velvet on stones. Grey gave her some sour grass to chew on that had the tang of a lemon; they felt like children and the day seemed cooler. They kept Cedric's pram in the shade and ate cold ham and bread with applebutter; they picked watercress that grew wild and drank from the stream. When the idyllic day ended, they went home to a house that was hot. No breeze stirred to cool the air or billow the curtains.

After they finished eating dinner, they lingered at the table. "I have something to give you," Grey said.

Kenna looked at him in surprise. "A gift?"

"Yes. Do you like gifts?"

"You know I am really a child about getting things," she said.

"I didn't think you would ever admit that." He chuckled. "But you are. I've seen through you."

"Then I won't have to hide it from now on. Give me my gift, please," she said pleasantly.

"No, not so fast. You must guess what it is."

"A wind chime," she said after some thought.

He looked at her. "You want a wind chime?"

"No, but you said guess. A horse? A new bonnet?"

He shook his head, laughing at her playfulness. "Don't you want a clue?"

"I thought you wanted me just to guess for a few hours."

"No, so I'll tell you it is something you want."

Her countenance grew suddenly serious. "There is only one thing I want," she whispered.

The laughter of the moment faded. The room seemed very still as Kenna waited for his question.

"What do you want, m'lady?" he asked, almost trancelike.

"The one thing that I have wanted from the very beginning. The only thing I have ever truly asked for. I want . . . you . . . to love me."

Her words reached out to him, closing the distance between them. Grey could not move, or speak. Kenna sighed and leaned back in her chair, shutting her eyes against the heat of the day and the oppressive ache she felt. "Is it such a difficult thing I ask for?" she questioned unhappily.

"No, it is not such a difficult thing," he answered softly. "But there has been so much pain. When does trust begin?"

Kenna's eyes opened, and she stared at the rugged man who sat so intensely before her. She had never completely been sure of him in the past; she had always been afraid to trust him. Yet now, when she had come to love him, to believe in him, he carelessly tossed the word at her.

"Why do we speak of trust?"

He said nothing, the silence between them thickening. At last he spoke. "Tell me about Glen Kinross."

Her granite eyes widened in amazement. He leaned near, the muscles of his shoulders and arms tense. "I have never loved a woman—or given part of my soul to any woman—as I have you. Yet if I say out loud what I know, there will be no turning back! Tell me first if he has the power to take you away from me."

"Can you not let the past die!" she cried incredulously.

"Not until you let it die! Not until I know he has no claim on you!"

"What are you talking about?" she demanded, leaping to her feet.

"About the night he came here, wanting to take you away. The night he took you in his arms and kissed you," he said bitterly.

His words assaulted her very being. He was blind to the love she felt, to the bonds of trust she had forged! With a sob she turned and ran from the room, from the house. She fled down the steep road which led to the town, tears scalding her cheeks and blurring her path.

After a while, she slowed to a walk, her heart thudding dully within her breast. What hope was there for this marriage with a man who was so stubborn and blind? She loved him, and he could not see it! She remembered well the night that Glen had come to see her; how had Grey witnessed what happened? Had he been spying on her, or had it been an accident? Certainly he must have heard her tell Glen to forget about her, had seen her send him away? But . . . if he hadn't . . . if he had only seen them from afar, witnessing just their actions and the kiss? She groaned, realizing he would have interpreted it exactly as he had.

She loved Grey more than anything and desperately wanted their marriage to succeed. How could he not understand that she loved him? She was angry that he could be so stupid. The greatest truce between them was when they shared desire. Didn't he know that she could never respond the way she did without loving him? Couldn't he see that she didn't want any man but him?

Kenna reflected that the only time he had ever spoken of love at all was when they lay together. She remembered the first time, when he had told her that desire and love were the same. Perhaps, for him, it was truly so.

All I want is to be with you, to have you love me and forgive me, she said to herself as she walked through the town.

She thought of Glen, and the new problem he presented. She was discouraged and unhappy. How could she ever get the truth through to her thick-skulled husband?

Her thoughts were suddenly disrupted as she was startled by a foreign sight. Down the road was The Bank, its beautiful front scarred by streaks of flame. With a cry, she ran forward just as shouts went up and men poured from the building. The fire had taken on new strength with a gust of wind, lapping at the wood. She caught up her skirts, running forward to join the growing crowd of people who were gathering pails and hurrying to troughs and water pumps. She saw Ulrik stagger around the side of the building, blood matted in the back of his hair; Kenna ran to him.

"Ulrik!" she cried. "What happened?"

"Bad trouble. I saw that huge Chinese man behind The Bank. He was pouring kerosene on rags; when I try to stop him, we struggle and I hit my head. When I wake up, he is gone and there is fire and smoke coming from the back."

Kenna was amazed. There was only one huge Chinese man that fit Ulrik's description, and he worked for the Wengs' laundry. "Are you all right?" she asked as she watched him mount a horse.

"Ya! Where is Mr. Fauvereau?"

"Back at the house," she cried, watching him spur the horse forward.

She was sick. She took up a heavy bucket of sloshing water and went to stand at the head of the line that was forming.

She doused flames that were eating the beautiful double doors, every fiber of her being intent on saving her husband's livelihood.

* * *

Grey finally stood up and went out onto the porch, looking down into the valley where orange glowed like hot coals in the heart of the city. Foreboding swept over him like a wave of heat. The sky was the dusk-gray of early evening and the air was oppressive, smothering. A dark wind stirred, whipping up the leaves of trees, and a distant rumble echoed through the mountains. Dogs whined at the smell of the storm. Paralyzed, Grey stared down at the glowing nugget of orange red. The town was on fire.

The sound of galloping hoofbeats broke the spell. A breathless Ulrik hailed Grey as he threw himself from the horse.

"The Bank!" he managed. "It is on fire!" Grey could not move; Ulrik choked for breath. "I saw that big Chinese man; he lit the fire at the back of the saloon. I shout at him and we struggle. He knocked me out and then when I wake up, flames are all over the back."

"The big man that works at the Chinese laundry? The one with the long braid down his back?"

Ulrik nodded. "Ya! Same one, I think."

Galvanized into action, Grey threw himself on the back of Ulrik's horse. "Kenna!" he cried suddenly. "Did you see her?"

"Ya! She is with the brigade!"

Grey dug his heels into the horse and it bolted back down the road that slanted in front of him. The wind tangled his hair and the road was a blur beneath the animal's churning hooves. The dust choked him as the glowing ember in the heart of the city grew larger. Grey jerked the horse to a stop.

Fingers of fire licked at the wood, and sparks caught on the wind, taking a treacherous path.

371

Katherine Myers

Everyone had pitched in, passing water buckets from hand to hand, dousing the voracious flames, only to have them shoot to life again. Smoke choked the air and people ran with shovels, digging up the earth, trying to smother the flame. Sadie worked the pump continuously as buckets were thrust underneath and passed along. Jess was on the roof, laying down water-soaked blankets and quilts. Grey took over, shouting hoarse commands. He grabbed a cord thrown from an upper window and held it steady while men from a private poker game found the courage to slide down to safety.

He caught a glimpse of Kenna as she lifted overflowing buckets and passed them along. Hot ashes singed her hair and dress; smoke burned her eyes. Yet still she lifted the buckets until she thought her arms would break. One of the stained-glass windows exploded, sending splinters of colored glass in a molten wreath. She ran to help a man who was cut.

Kenna grabbed the man's kerchief and staunched the bleeding on his brow; the intense heat was everywhere. She heard her name shouted and saw Grey running toward her; he threw her to the ground, knocking the breath out of her. He beat the flames on her dress with his hands until they were extinguished. His palms were blistered but he paid no heed; grabbing her dress and petticoat, he ripped off the charred hem until there was no more chance of the muslin skirt catching fire. Kenna ignored her immodest state. She carried more buckets of water, throwing them on black, smoking wood.

Ulrik arrived on foot; he took over the pump just as Sadie was ready to collapse. Jess had climbed down from the roof and he, too, joined in carrying

372

buckets of water. The wind lifted more cinders and the air was choked with dust and smoke. The sky was now black overhead, dark and starless. A jagged knife of lightning split the sky as blades of flame cut upward from the building.

Kenna sagged against the rail near The Silver Empire, the heat driving her back. She stared at the insatiable fire, tears from smoke and frustration streaking her face. Grey still labored, beating at flames as sweat soaked his shirt. Hopelessness filled Kenna. The Bank was dying.

She was numb until a large hand grabbed her face, smothering her startled scream. In horror, she looked up at the huge Chinese man with the long braid. Kenna felt a surge of terror; she clawed at him, unable to breathe. His hands jerked her head and there was a sharp pain in her neck before blackness overtook her.

Spicy smoke invaded Kenna's consciousness and forced her mind to swim upward to awareness. She was disoriented and could not understand why a cool cloth wiped her face. Slowly her eyelids fluttered open. She felt bewildered, her ears buzzing. Someone wiped the dirt from her face. She tried to see, in the dim light, the man who bent over her. He rinsed his handkerchief out in a bowl of water and finished sponging the soot and tearstains from her face.

Her lips managed to say his name. "Glen."

He smiled down at her, the Scottish charm she knew so well shining in his features. "There, there, Kenna. Lie still. How did your face get so dirty?"

"The fire," she said, waiting for the dizziness she still felt to abate. "The town is on fire."

373

"Yes, I know." He looked at the remnants of her torn dress. "You should not be wearing these rags. I always said when I had enough money I would buy you beautiful gowns. Do you remember that, when we were children? I think I secretly loved you even when Braic and I only pretended to suffer your tagging along."

He stood and went to a chest, and opening it, retrieved a thin silk quilt. He brought it back and wrapped it around her legs. Kenna glanced around the room. It was dimly lit by hanging Oriental lanterns. She lay on a low, tapestried couch. A brass dragon sat atop a chest, incense smoke pouring from its nostrils. There was also another odor, a rich, sickly sweet smell that Kenna had never encountered. Across the room, on silk cushions, sat two young, beautiful Chinese women with straight black hair and dark eyes, wearing embroidered silk dresses. They watched Kenna.

"Glen," she said softly. "Where is this place?"

"Why, it is The Silver Empire, grandest entertainment palace in the territory!"

"I did not see this room when I toured your saloon," she said, still feeling weak.

"Ah, that is because no one sees this place but my best customers. I have made most of my money beneath my place of business."

"It looks Chinese," she said, bewildered by it all.

"Indeed! That is the genius of it. You see, my love, I have cornered the market on the dream powder of the Chinese. Perhaps you are aware of how the people in the city feel about the Chinese; no American man would be seen buying opium from one of the local merchants."

"Opium?" she asked. "I have never heard of it."

He held up a mahogany pipe with a long stem. "The Orientals sell this for about a quarter a teaspoon. Yet I charge a great deal more to my customers. The first time is free—a trial, you see. Then, afterward, my ladies assist them in using it." He nodded toward the girls. He took a long draw on the pipe.

"This dream powder can lull you into a world of wonder, and calm. I tried it once when I could not sleep for thinking of you. The more I took, the calmer I became, and I began to understand everything I must do."

She sat up, placing a palm to her head. "I have to go now. The fire was bad; the saloon was burned down."

The door opened and the large Chinese man entered. Kenna gasped. "Glen, he is the one who burned down The Bank. He brought me here!"

Glen pulled out a flat wallet and counted out some bills. "I know. Hong Wah works for me."

Hong Wah took the money and stood by the door. "But why?" Kenna cried. "If he burned down The Bank, it must have been on your orders. Why did you have him do it, Glen?"

"Because, although The Silver Empire was doing a good business, it did not ruin The Bank. That saloon has still managed to survive. I wanted to crush it, to see it fall. Already I have waited too long; my decision to have it burned down should have come months ago."

She looked at him. He was a stranger to her. "Do you hate me so?"

"No, Kenna. I did it because I love you so." He

Katherine Myers

came and sat down beside her, taking her hand. She pulled it away. "You were too blind to see that that man used you. He only wanted you to keep his saloon. I know all about him. I took SueAnn's money and hired the best American detective agency to find out everything they could about Fauvereau. I had to find the judge that married you by proxy to learn his name, then the Pinkertons did the rest. Now I have destroyed his saloon so he doesn't need a wife with a title anymore."

The shock of his words were like ice on her heart. "It's no coincidence you are here."

"Of course not."

"You found out where I was and came here."

"I couldn't just show up. I had to have a reason to come to this forsaken place, and The Silver Empire provided that. The detective agency only led me to San Francisco, where Fauvereau owns property. I had to find out where he had you. It was my greatest luck to happen on to a loudmouthed little man named Murphy Duke. He was the one who told me how Braic died. If I did not hate Fauvereau before, then I did after I learned what had happened. It was then that I began to understand how important his saloon was to him, and that through this I could be rid of the man. I sent Duke back to Silver City, and he set up the plans for building my place; unfortunately, the fool had to get himself killed in a house of ill-repute before I came."

Kenna looked at him. "Oh, Glen. All these plans have brought you nothing! You may have burned down my husband's saloon but it is not the most important thing in his life. If you wanted to hurt him

376

that was not the way. I have hurt him more than you have."

"Nor do I simply hate him for killing Braic," he continued coldly, as if she had not spoken. "I hate him for having you."

"Your hatred is in vain. I love Grey," she said, pity in her voice.

He grabbed her wrists. "Don't say that! Don't ever say that. You don't know what is right for you; loyalty holds you; you would say you loved me if I were your husband."

She did not know this man or understand the bizarre words he spoke. He scared her.

A scream broke the silence and they all looked at the Chinese girl, who spoke rapid, strange words. She pointed at a corner of the ceiling where smoke was beginning to curl.

Kenna looked at Glen. "Do you see what you have done! The wind has brought the fire to your own place!"

Glen grabbed her wrist, pulling her behind him, all of them filing out into the darkened corridor. Glen dragged her down a dark twisting passage that was filled with terror. He was leading her away from Grey. Panic rose in her throat, and it was all she could do to keep from crying out. Smoke filled the air and he stopped. Kenna jerked her hand away, bolting past the large Chinese man and down an unknown hallway. Glen's hoarse shout followed her, and she could hear them running after her. She pushed through a door that opened into a big room filled with crates.

Kenna ducked down, hiding behind a large box. Her heart was thudding loudly in her ears, and she held still, barely breathing. She could hear shouts as the door banged open and Glen came into the room, followed by Hong Wah. They searched for her fruitlessly, then Glen left, shouting to the Chinese man to find a torch.

She was shaking in panic as their footsteps ebbed. She had to get out of the place, but she had no idea where in the saloon she was, or which direction to go. Fear held her still.

A feeling of defeat washed over Grey as he stood watching his saloon being consumed by the fire. For the first time, he realized the hopelessness of his situation, seeing all that he had worked so hard for, destroyed.

Ulrik lumbered toward him, his face covered with soot and streaked with sweat. "Mr. Fauvereau!" he exclaimed. "Your wife!"

Grey was suddenly alert. "Where is she?"

"That big Chinese man, the one who started the fire! He has her! I saw him grab her and go down into The Silver Empire."

With renewed energy, Grey leaped toward the building across the street. He threw the door open and ran inside, and up the stairs, checking the rooms along the hall. No one stopped him or Ulrik, who canvassed the main floor. They met at the bottom of the staircase.

"Nothing!" Grey shouted. "Are you sure he brought her in here?"

"Ya! I am sure. There are stairs that go down behind the kitchen."

"Let's go," Grey said with cold determination as they ran back through the saloon. Dread filled him as they hurried down the stairs that led to a maze of narrow hallways. He had thought there was something not right about Glen Kinross, and as the thick smell of opium reached him his belief was confirmed. He slammed open doors, checking small, empty rooms, panic replacing his dread. What if Kenna was not here? What if they had taken her somewhere else?

His mind flew back to this afternoon, when she had asked for a simple avowal of love. He had been a stubborn, grudging fool! Yes, he loved her! Yes, he would tell her. Yes, he believed she loved him, too.

He smelled smoke and saw wisps of it seeping in from the ceiling. The thought of Kenna in danger, in the hands of Kinross and the Chinese man, filled him with an all-encompassing terror.

"Kenna!" he shouted in desperation. "Kenna!"

Kenna's heart froze as she heard the voice call her name, and she ran to the door, throwing it open. "Grey!" she sobbed, running into his arms.

"I've looked all over this place! There are tunnels under here," he said, holding her to him.

Kenna saw Ulrik behind him and she pulled them into the darkened room and shut the door. "Glen had that Chinese man burn down The Bank!" she whispered frantically. "Then he had him bring me down here."

"Ya!" Ulrik said. "I saw and then went to tell Mr. Fauvereau."

"He is selling something called opium," Kenna said, pulling back from Grey's embrace. "I don't know him at all anymore."

Ulrik let out a low whistle. "He is a bad one, that Kinross. We best get out of here."

Grey gave a curt nod, reaching for the door. Before

his hand could touch the knob, the door was thrown open, and Hong Wah and Glen Kinross stood blocking their way. Smoke wafted in behind them.

"So," Glen said slowly, his smile evil. "We meet at last on my territory."

Ulrik did not wait for words. He leaped forward, crashing his body into the Chinese man. They reeled out into the hall and then smashed back through the door. Grey swung his fist at Glen, striking his jaw. But the Scotsman, a wrestler, recovered and slammed into Grey, and the two fell on the floor.

A torch lay on the ground, charring the earth while fists struck faces and blood colored knuckles. Kenna cried out at the slashing of arms and bellows of rage; there was the sickening sound of breaking bone as Ulrick slumped to the floor, gritting his teeth, his arm at an odd angle. Grey buried his fist in his foe's stomach and Glen doubled over.

"Kill him!" Glen raged, staggering up. "Kill him now!"

Kenna screamed and threw herself in Hong Wah's path, but he shoved her aside as easily as if she were a child. She ran to Glen, who stood clutching his abdomen.

"No, Glen, no!"

Hong Wah headed toward Grey, his hands outstretched. Even the large Swede had been no match for him. Both men knew that it would only take one crushing embrace from the massive arms of Hong Wah to break Grey's back. Grey managed to dodge; he was quick, but it would only take one mistake.

Kenna turned to Glen. "Please!" she sobbed. "I'm begging you to stop him!" She fell to her knees, taking his hand. "Spare his life, Glen. I'll do anything you want!"

Angrily, he jerked her to her feet. "Don't beg for his life," he ground out. She turned in horror, watching Hong Wah grab Grey, circling him with a deathly embrace.

Kenna screamed.

"Hong Wah! Let Mr. Fauvereau go."

Astonished, everyone turned to the open door where Mr. Weng stood, his hands tucked in the long sleeves of his tunic.

"You must not kill Mr. Fauvereau," the old man said in a very calm voice; Hong Wah did not release him, but neither did he tighten the grip.

"Get out of here!" Glen snarled.

"But it is you I have come to see, Mr. Kinross." Smoke seeped through the ceiling and hot cinders lit the darkness. Still, his voice was calm. "You see, I have been planning to talk to you for many days now. But only today have I found the strength. My mourning has been long and deep."

Glen's features froze as he stared at the old man. Smoke drifted between them. "I have nothing to say to you!"

"Not even your sorrow at my loss? There should be much shame in you for what you did. But many of the white men do not regret their treachery. Mai Lei was my fragile flower. From the time she was a child, I loved her best. She knew no guile, for her heart was innocent. Mai Lei believed you when you said you would love her always. She thought you would marry her and accept her as you would a western woman."

The old man sighed as if he had all the hours in a

day to talk. "I tried to tell her that she was not one of you, that her beauty would only be used. But all she saw were the pretty clothes and playthings. I have come to ask you a question. Will you tell me what you said to Mai Lei when she came to you and told you she carried your child?"

Glen's face was pale. "I just explained the way it was in society. She understood she could not expect to marry me. There were no tears or other such feminine foolishness. I told her I was proud of the way she understood."

"Ah! I see. She did not tell you that she had disgraced her ancestry, that she bore a terrible shame? Mai Lei told me that the man who took her from her childhood, the man whose child she must bear, did not want her. She only told me your name, but not what words you had said to her, before the poison split her soul from her body. So you see, I have wondered what you said to her, and that is why I came."

Flames licked at the posts that held the ceiling; the heat intensified. Wood crackled and smoke seared their eyes. Mr. Weng turned to Hong Wah. "So you see, my old friend, Mr. Fauvereau is not the man who should die. Let him go."

Hong Wah needed no urging; his arms fell limply to his sides and Grey moved to the door, grabbing Kenna.

The large Chinese man looked at Glen, his eyes glazed with pain, his features hardening as he lunged at the man. He knocked into Glen Kinross, the two men staggering backward and smashing into a burning post. The charred wood broke and the blazing ceiling crashed down upon them in an explosion of heat.

Grey shoved Kenna through the door and helped Ulrik and Mr. Weng hurrying behind them. They ran down the twisting smoke-fogged corridors frantically, finally finding an opening through a cellar door. They broke through it, choking, into the night air. In another moment, The Silver Empire collapsed in on itself, a shower of cinders shooting out into the night.

Mr. Weng's hushed voice reached them. "Hong Wah loved Mai Lei. But she did not love him, and could never be his, so he loved her from afar. Yet in the end, he has shown the greater love. Oh," he sighed softly, "the foolishness of life."

Kenna turned and looked at The Bank. It still burned, its blackened timbers glowing red. Melted metal twisted grotesquely. Glass lay in blackened chunks on the earth; wood beams were broken, jagged where white ash burned like hot snow. Flames crackled and danced, the beauty of fire macabre in this setting.

The sky rumbled, a deep and mournful sound echoing through the valley. There was a flash of lightning across War Eagle Mountain, and smoke blurred the sky. Grey stood by Kenna while men still worked to kill the spreading flames. There was a hiss as a few drops of rain fell into the crackling ashes. The thunder clapped overhead again and the rain began spattering the ruins before them. Cold drops fell onto Kenna's face, mingling with her tears.

Grey pulled her into his arms, rocking her gently, lovingly, cradling her head against his chest.

"I thought I'd lost you! Oh, Kenna, I've never been so scared in my whole life!"

She looked up at him and he smiled at her ruefully, his black hair rumpled, his face smudged with soot. He had never looked more wonderful to her. Heedless of the rain, they clung to one another. Kenna's fingers grasped the muscles of his back and his strong arms held her tightly as they felt the intensity of the moment.

Grey bent his head and kissed her, a long, lingering, sweet kiss. When he finally pulled back, he stared into her eyes.

"Oh, Kenna. I love you so much!"

Epilogue

AFTERNOON SUNLIGHT fell through the hall windows
and spilled across the oak floor, turning the wood
from brown to dark gold. Beautiful furniture stood in
the entrance of Moldarn as if it had never been disturbed.

Kenna stood in the room caught up in the solitude
of the moment. It had been a thoughtful day for her,
and the mood had followed her through the afternoon.

After The Bank had burned down, Grey and Kenna sold their house on the hill to the Farwells. Then
they had gone to San Francisco where Grey sold all
of his properties there; with the accummulated
wealth, they set sail for Scotland. The gift which
Grey was going to give Kenna the night of the fire
was the deed to Moldarn House; he had purchased it
at the time they were wed by proxy.

In one last great gamble, Grey had decided to
refurnish the mansion. They had spent a year
searching out many of the items sold at auction; the
huge, carved master bed had been bought back at a
high price. The portraits of the M'ren thanes now

hung in the gallery again, and the crested china and silver had been bought from the jeweler who could not sell it. What items that could not be found were replaced by new pieces, so Moldarn was a mingling of the new and the old. It was an elegant mansion now.

The stables had been rebuilt and stocked with a good breed of horses, and the land about the house was freshly landscaped. A large staff was hired, with upstairs and downstairs maids, a cook and an assistant, and gardeners. Ulrik filled the position of stablemaster.

The Fauvereaus had opened the mansion as an inn. It had been a risk, but it was worth it to be back in her home, Kenna thought, and she had faith in Grey. They had sent out silver-printed announcements to all the people that Kenna's family had known. At first, only a few of her father's friends had come, but soon word spread. Since Auchinleck was between Galloway and Glasgow, and not far from the coast, its location was most desirable. Visitors could hunt in well-stocked forests, row on the lake behind the mansion, ride or fox hunt. The food and drink were excellent, as were the diversions.

In December, right before Christmas, they had the grandest ball in all of Ayr County. The trains arrived in Auchinleck and the travelers were met by sleighs festooned with bells and beribboned horses. The celebration lasted for a week, ending on New Year's Day. Almost all of Auchinleck turned out for the dancing.

The Fauvereaus were able to live comfortably. Kenna did not mind that strangers slept in her house, because it enabled her to raise her children in Scotland. Her American husband was well received by the people, for he had the talent and reputation for being a wonderful host, and that was the main reason their business was so successful.

There was the sound of running footsteps, and a little boy burst through the front doorway. He was breathless, his auburn hair—only a shade lighter than Kenna's—slightly rumpled. His blue eyes glanced about until they lit on his mother, and he marched forward.

"Mama!" he demanded. "Come see me race Jezebel. I can ride her all the way around the lake in ten minutes! Papa timed me. Where is Jess? He has to come see, too."

"Jess is busy in the library going over your father's records, so don't you be bothering him." Jess worked as secretary to Grey, setting up appointments, sending out the billing statements and keeping the financial records. He had been in Scotland only one year when he had married a young lass with green eyes and a brogue; Megan and Jess lived in a cottage on the estate.

"Then Sadie must come!"

Kenna looked at her handsome little son. "Sadie is arranging the menus with cook for when the guests arrive tomorrow. Ceddy," she said, kneeling down to look at him, "isn't it enough if Papa and I watch you race?"

He sighed. "Well, all right, then. Will you come now?"

"Yes. Go tell Jezebel she has to ride fast, and I'll get Brenna."

Cedric let out a whoop and ran out the door. There was a small hand tugging Kenna's skirt, a persistent beat. She looked down at the little girl who, only

minutes ago had been sitting in a square of sunlight
playing with a doll. A little face lifted up, one with
black baby curls framing it. Kenna stroked the silky
curls.

"Mama," the child said, still patting her mother.
"Mama."

"What, Brenna?"

" 'Side. 'Side, Mama." Brenna pointed to the door.

"Yes," Kenna said, lifting her up and placing the
child on her hip. "Let's go see Papa."

They went out the front door and down the path
that led around the house. It was bedecked on either
side by flowers. Trees shaded the path and birds
chorused together; Kenna and the child had passed
by the house when she looked up at the hills.

Sunlight glinted off white marble, where tombs
were marked like straight stone soldiers. The family
graveyard was encircled by white wrought-iron fencing, and flowers were planted by each stone. Gener-
ations of thanes lay in stately quiet. Only Lord Braic
Cedric M'ren lay far away, across an ocean. No one
cared for the stone or placed flowers around it;
whether it was heated one day by sun or buried by
snow on another, Kenna would never know. Yet she
had accepted the fact that she would not be able to
care for his gravestone and his final resting would be
an ocean away.

The two followed the trail that twisted toward the
lake, Brenna holding tight to her mother as they
skipped along. At last the mountain tarn came into
view, and she caught sight of Grey.

"Listen, Ceddy. Bend low, like this. It will make
the horse go faster because there will be less wind re-
sistance. That's right, now hold the reins tight."

"You say when to go, Papa!"

"Let me get my watch out," he said, smiling at Kenna and walking back to her. She looked as beautiful to him as she had the first day he saw her, standing on a dusty street, waiting to meet her husband.

Her hair hung freely down her back, and she wore a simple dress of dark green lawn. He thought she looked as young as a child. He kissed her.

"Papa!" a voice broke in. "Jezebel and I are waiting!"

Grey drew back, looking down into her eyes for a moment. Then he looked back at his son, whose pony stood at the edge of the path which went around the lake. He drew out his watch, waiting for the second hand to reach its zenith. "Go!" he shouted.

A little hand patted his arm. He smiled down at a face set with wide, gray-blue eyes. "Hello, bonnie Brenna!" He swept her up to sit on his arm. "Do you have a kiss for Papa?"

Brenna immediately offered her mouth, pressing it to his. He made a show of kissing the baby. "Lookit dat!" Brenna said, wrinkling up her nose and laughing. "Lookit dat!"

Cedric kicked his heels into Jezebel and slapped her hind quarters with his small crop. The pony only looked at him with woeful eyes. Grey laughed and went up, slapping the little horse so he would hurry off.

The parents watched their son guide his pony around the bend. The sun was a giant coin slipping behing the hills, spreading its glow across the mountain tarn. The water caught the golden light, reflecting it until the lake shone molten. It took on the brightness of a mirror, an intense silver. A thought came to Kenna. "You can take your treasure with you anywhere," she murmured, staring into the glistening water. "Just as long as the silver you have spent your life earning is love."

Grey slipped his arm about her, leaning his head against hers. They could glimpse their son riding toward them through the trees and they were silent; even little Brenna seemed caught up in the quiet of the moment.

The sun slipped lower, silhouetting the trees black against the sky. The silver in the water faded. But they knew the splendor would be back again tomorrow.